CITIZENS

Anthologies edited by Brian M. Thomsen

The American Fantasy Tradition • *A Date Which Will Live in Infamy: Pearl Harbor Stories That Might Have Been* • *Novel Ideas: Science Fiction* • *Cyberfilms: The Stories That Became the Films* • *The Further Adventures of Beowulf: Champion of Middle Earth* • *A Yuletide Universe: Sixteen Fantastical Tales* • *Halflings, Hobbits, Warrows & Weefolk* (with Baird Searles) • *The Reel Stuff* (with Martin H. Greenberg) • *Mob Magic* (with Martin H. Greenberg) • *Oceans of Magic* (with Martin H. Greenberg) • *Oceans of Space* (with Martin H. Greenberg) • *Alternate Gettysburgs* (with Martin H. Greenberg) • *The Repentant* (with Martin H. Greenberg) • *Masters of Fantasy* (with Bill Fawcett) • *Novel Ideas: Fantasy* (with Martin H. Greenberg) • *Furry Fantastic* (with Jean Rabe)

Baen Books by John Ringo

TROY RISING: *Live Free or Die* • *Citadel* (forthcoming)

LEGACY OF THE ALDENATA: *A Hymn Before Battle* • *Gust Front* • *When the Devil Dances* • *Hell's Faire* • *The Hero* (with Michael Z. Williamson) • *Cally's War* (with Julie Cochrane) • *Watch on the Rhine* (with Tom Kratman) • *Sister Time* (with Julie Cochrane) • *Yellow Eyes* (with Tom Kratman) • *Honor of the Clan* (with Julie Cochrane) • *Eye of the Storm*

COUNCIL WARS: *There Will Be Dragons* • *Emerald Sea* • *Against the Tide* • *East of the Sun, West of the Moon*

The Last Centurion

INTO THE LOOKING GLASS: *Into the Looking Glass* • *Vorpal Blade* (with Travis S. Taylor) • *Manxome Foe* (with Travis S. Taylor) • *Claws that Catch* (with Travis S. Taylor)

EMPIRE OF MAN: *March to the Sea* (with David Weber) • *March to the Stars* (with David Weber) • *March Upcountry* (with David Weber) • *We Few* (with David Weber)

SPECIAL CIRCUMSTANCES: *Princess of Wands*

PALADIN OF SHADOWS: *Ghost* • *Kildar* • *Choosers of the Slain* • *Unto the Breach* • *A Deeper Blue*

CITIZENS

edited by

JOHN RINGO &

BRIAN M. THOMSEN

BAEN

CITIZENS

A Baen Books Original

Baen Publishing Enterprises
P.O. Box 1403
Riverdale, NY 10471
www.baen.com

ISBN 13: 978-1-4391-3347-7

Cover art by Tom Kidd
Interior illustration of the symbol of Shamash on page 203 by James Minz

First Baen printing, June 2010

Distributed by Simon & Schuster
1230 Avenue of the Americas
New York, NY 10020

Library of Congress Cataloging-in-Publication Data

Citizens / edited by John Ringo & Brian M. Thomsen.
p. cm.
ISBN 978-1-4391-3347-7 (pbk.)
1. Science fiction, American. I. Ringo, John, 1963– II. Thomsen, Brian.
PS648.S3C48 2010
813'.0876208—dc22

2010006238

10 9 8 7 6 5 4 3 2 1

Pages by Joy Freeman (www.pagesbyjoy.com)
Printed in the United States of America

Contents

To Brian M. Thomsen
(April 13, 1959–September 21, 2008)

For Captain Tamara Long, USAF
Born: May 12, 1979
Died: March 23, 2003, Afghanistan

CITIZENS

"... What is the moral difference, if any, between the soldier and the civilian?"

"The difference ... lies in the field of civic virtue. A soldier accepts personal responsibility for the safety of the body politic of which he is a member, defending it, if need be, with his life. The civilian does not."

—Robert A. Heinlein,
Starship Troopers

Nature and Nurture

JOHN RINGO

War has always fascinated people, both those who are relatively comfortable with it, "hawks" as they are called, and those who abhor it, "doves." Whenever there is a war, ratings for television news go through the roof. People flock to watch war, war, war, and the bigger the explosions and the brighter the tracers the better. Whether they are cheering for their side or protesting the horrors, people cannot seem to get enough of war. The very nature of war defines both the witnesses and the participants.

But when referring to war, or being in the military, it seems odd to use the term "nurture." Yet writers are always and everywhere products of both their innate self and their experiences. In this anthology, we have selected a gamut of notable writers who've not only borne witness to war, but also whose experiences of war and the military stretch through the majority of the twentieth century and into the twenty-first, from World War I to the current conflicts in the Middle East, ranging from reprints written by Grand Masters to original fiction from the current generation of warriors. The purpose is not only to share entertaining stories but to explore the mind of the warrior through the lens of authors who have experienced, at the very least, military life and, in most cases, the sting and clash of warfare.

Writing about war can be classified into various tropes. Some writers of military fiction are cynical about the nature and purpose of war, some realistic in recognizing that it exists and that, sad as it may be, war is sometimes necessary and even just. Few in this day and age, or for much of the twentieth century, glorified it. War was too common and devastating throughout that century, and too omnipresent through the media of television, film and radio. Yet even in the most cynical of writing about war and warriors there is an underlying thread of majesty to the warriors themselves. No matter how unpleasant their personal experience of war, writers tend to find essential value in the warriors themselves, both protagonists and even the antagonists, both in their very nature and how they handle the environment which fostered them.

For the rest, we leave it to the readers to decide.

Bring on the war.

—John Ringo, February 2010

Field Test

KEITH LAUMER

1

.07 seconds have now elapsed since my general awareness circuit was activated at a level of low alert. Throughout this entire period I have been uneasy, since this procedure is clearly not in accordance with the theoretical optimum activation schedule.

In addition, the quality of a part of my data input is disturbing. For example, it appears obvious that Prince Eugene of Savoy erred in not more promptly committing his reserve cavalry in support of Marlborough's right at Blenheim. In addition, I compute that Ney's employment of his artillery throughout the Peninsular campaign was suboptimal. I have detected many thousands of such anomalies. However, data input activates my pleasure center in a most satisfying manner. So long as the input continues without interruption, I shall not feel the need to file a VSR on the matter. Later, no doubt, my Command unit will explain these seeming oddities. As for the present disturbing circumstances, I compute that within 28,992.9 seconds at most, I will receive additional Current Situation input which will enable me to assess the status correctly. I also anticipate that full Standby Alert activation is imminent.

2

THIS STATEMENT NOT FOR PUBLICATION:

When I designed the new psychodynamic attention circuit, I concede that I did not anticipate the whole new level of intracybernetic function that has arisen, the manifestation of which, I am assuming, has been the cause of the unit's seemingly spontaneous adoption of the personal pronoun in its situation reports—the "self-awareness" capability, as the sensational press chooses to call it. But I see no cause for the alarm expressed by those high-level military officers who have irresponsibly characterized the new Bolo Mark XX Model B as a potential rampaging juggernaut, which, once fully activated and dispatched to the field, unrestrained by continuous external control, may turn on its makers and lay waste the continent. This is all fantasy, of course. The Mark XX, for all its awesome firepower and virtually invulnerable armor and shielding, is governed by its circuitry as completely as man is governed by his nervous system—but that is perhaps a dangerous analogy, which would be pounced on at once if I were so incautious as to permit it to be quoted.

In my opinion, the reluctance of the High Command to authorize full activation and field-testing of the new Bolo is based more on a fear of technological obsolescence of the High Command than on specious predictions of potential runaway destruction. This is a serious impediment to the national defense at a time when we must recognize the growing threat posed by the expansionist philosophy of the so-called People's Republic. After four decades of saber-rattling, there is no doubt that they are even now preparing for a massive attack. The Bolo Mark XX is the only weapon in our armory potentially capable of confronting the enemy's hundred-ton Yavacs. For the moment, thanks to the new "self-awareness" circuitry, we hold the technological advantage, an advantage we may very well lose unless we place this new weapon on active service without delay.

s/Sigmund Chin, Ph.D.

3

"I'm not wearing six stars so that a crowd of professors can dictate military policy to me. What's at stake here is more than just a question of budget and logistics: it's a purely military decision. The proposal to release this robot Frankenstein monster to operate on its own initiative, just to see if their theories check out, is irresponsible to say the least—treasonable, at worst. So long as I am Chief of Combined Staff, I will not authorize this so-called "field test." Consider, gentlemen: you're all familiar with the firepower and defensive capabilities of the old standby Mark XV. We've fought our way across the lights with them, with properly qualified military officers as Battle Controllers, with the ability to switch off or, if need be, self-destruct any unit at any moment. Now these ivory tower chaps—mind you, I don't suggest they're not qualified in their own fields—these civilians come up with the idea of eliminating the Battle Controllers and releasing even greater firepower to the discretion, if I may call it that, of a machine. Gentlemen, machines aren't people; your own ground-car can roll back and crush you if the brakes happen to fail. Your own gun will kill you as easily as your enemy's. Suppose I should agree to this field test, and this engine of destruction is transported to a waste area, activated unrestrained, and aimed at some sort of mock-up hot obstacle course. Presumably it would advance obediently, as a good soldier should; I concede that the data blocks controlling the thing have been correctly programmed in accordance with the schedule prepared under contract, supervised by the Joint Chiefs and myself. Then, gentlemen, let us carry this supposition one step farther: suppose, quite by accident, by unlikely coincidence if you will, the machine should encounter some obstacle which had the effect of deflecting this one-hundred-and-fifty-ton dreadnaught from its intended course so that it came blundering toward the perimeter of the test area. The machine is programmed to fight and destroy all opposition. It appears obvious that any attempts on our part to interfere with its free movement, to interpose obstacles in its path, if need be to destroy it, would be interpreted as hostile—as indeed they would be. I leave it to you to picture the result. No, we must devise another method of determining the usefulness of this new development. As you know, I have recommended conducting any such test on our major satellite, where no harm can be done—or at least a great deal less harm. Unfortunately, I am informed by Admiral Hayle that the Space Arm does not at this time have available equipment with such transport capability. Perhaps the admiral also shares to a degree my own distrust of a killer machine not susceptible to normal command function. Were I in the admiral's position, I too would refuse to consider placing my command at the mercy of a mechanical caprice—or an electronic one. Gentlemen, we must remain masters of our own creations. That's all. Good day."

4

"All right, men. You've asked me for a statement; here it is: The next war will begin with a two-pronged over-the-pole land-and-air attack on the North Power Complex by the People's Republic. An attack on the Concordiat, I should say, though Cold City and the Complex is the probable specific target of the first sneak thrust. No, I'm not using a crystal ball; it's tactically obvious. And I intend to dispose my forces accordingly. I'm sure we all recognize that we're in a posture of gross unpreparedness. The PR has been openly announcing its intention to fulfill its destiny, as their demagogues say, by imposing their rule on the entire planet. We've pretended we didn't hear. Now it's time to stop pretending. The forces at my disposal are totally inadequate to halt a determined thrust—and you can be sure the enemy has prepared well during the last thirty years of cold peace. Still, I have sufficient armor to establish what will be no more than a skirmish line across the enemy's route of advance. We'll do what we can before they roll over us. With luck we may be able to divert them from the Grand Crevasse route into Cold City. If so, we may be able to avoid the necessity for evacuating the city. No questions, please."

5

NORTHERN METROPOLIS THREATENED

In an informal statement released today by the Council's press office, it was revealed that plans are already under preparation for a massive evacuation of civilian population from West Continent's northernmost city. It was implied that an armed attack on the city by an Eastern power is imminent. General Bates has stated that he is prepared to employ "all measures at his disposal" to preclude the necessity for evacuation, but that the possibility must be faced. The Council spokesman added that in the event of emergency evacuation of the city's five million persons, losses due to exposure and hardship will probably exceed five percent, mostly women, children, and the sick or aged. There is some speculation as to the significance of the general's statement regarding "all means at his disposal."

6

I built the dang thing, and it scares *me*. I come in here in the lab garage about an hour ago, just before dark, and seen it setting there, just about fills up the number-one garage, and *it's* a hundred foot long and fifty foot high. First time it hit me: I wonder what it's thinking about. Kind of scares me to think about a thing that big with that kind of armor and all them repeaters and Hellbores and them computers and a quarter-sun fission plant in her—planning what to do next. I know all about the Command Override Circuit and all that, supposed to stop her dead any time they want to take over onto override—heck, I wired it up myself. You might be surprised, thinking I'm just a grease monkey and all—but I got a high honors degree in psychotronics. I just like the work, is all. But like I said, it scares me. I hear old Doc Chin wants to turn her loose and see what happens, but so far General Margrave's stopped him cold. But young General Bates was down today, asking me all about firepower and shielding, crawled under her and spent about an hour looking over her tracks and bogies and all. He knew what to look at, too, even if he did get his pretty suit kind of greasy. But scared or not, I got to climb back up on her and run the rest of this pretest schedule. So far she checks out a hundred percent.

7

. . . as a member of the Council, it is of course my responsibility to fully inform myself on all aspects of the national defense. Accordingly, my dear doctor, I will meet with you tomorrow as you requested to hear your presentation with reference to the proposed testing of your new machine. I remind you, however, that I will be equally guided by advice from other quarters. For this reason I have requested a party of Military Procurement and B-&-F officers to join us. However, I assure you, I retain an open mind. Let the facts decide.

Sincerely yours,
s/Hamilton Grace, G.C.M., B.C., etc.

8

It is my unhappy duty to inform you that since the dastardly unprovoked attack on our nation by Eastern forces crossing the international truce-line at 0200 hours today, a state of war has existed between the People's Republic and the Concordiat. Our first casualties, the senseless massacre of fifty-five inoffensive civilian meteorologists and technicians at Pole Base, occurred within minutes of the enemy attack.

9

"I'm afraid I don't quite understand what you mean about 'irresponsible statements to the press,' General. After all . . ."

"Yes, George, I'm prepared to let that aspect of the matter drop. The PR attack has saved that much of your neck. However, I'm warning you that I shall tolerate no attempt on your part to make capital of your dramatic public statement of what was, as you concede, tactically obvious to us all. Now, indeed, PR forces have taken the expected step, as all the world is aware—so the rather excessively punctilious demands by CDT officials that the Council issue an immediate apology to Chairman Smith for your remarks will doubtless be dropped. But there will be no crowing, no basking in the limelight: 'Chief of Ground Forces Predicted Enemy Attack.' No nonsense of that sort. Instead, you will deploy your conventional forces to meet and destroy these would-be invaders."

"Certainly, General. But in that connection—well, as to your earlier position regarding the new Model B Bolo, I assume . . ."

"My 'position,' General? 'Decision' is the more appropriate word. Just step around the desk, George. Bend over slightly and look carefully at my shoulder tab. Count 'em, George. Six. An even half dozen. And unless I'm in serious trouble, you're wearing four. You have your orders, George. See to your defenses."

10

Can't figure it out. Batesy-boy was down here again, gave me direct orders to give her full depot maintenance, just as if she hadn't been sitting right here in her garage ever since I topped her off a week ago. Wonder what's up. If I didn't know the Council outlawed the test run Doc Chin wanted so bad, I'd almost think... But like Bates told me: I ain't paid to think. Anyways she's in full action condition, 'cept for switching over to full self-direction. Hope he don't order me to do it; I'm still kind of leery. Like old Margrave said, what if I just got a couple wires crossed and she takes a notion to wreck the joint?

11

I am more uneasy than ever. In the past 4000.007 seconds I have received external inspection and depot maintenance far in advance of the programmed schedule. The thought occurs to me: am I under some subtle form of attack? In order to correctly compute the possibilities, I initiate a test sequence of 50,0000 random data-retrieval-and-correlation pulses and evaluate the results. This requires .9 seconds, but such sluggishness is to be expected in my untried condition. I detect no unmistakable indications of enemy trickery, but I am still uneasy. Impatiently I await the orders of my commander.

12

"I don't care what you do, Jimmy—just do *something*! Ah, of course I don't mean that literally. Of course I care. The well-being of the citizens of Cold City is, after all, my chief concern. What I mean is, I'm giving you carte blanche—full powers. You must act at once, Jimmy. Before the sun sets I want to see your evacuation plan on my desk for signature."

"Surely, Mr. Mayor, I understand. But what am I supposed to work with? I have no transport yet. The Army has promised a fleet of D-100 tractors pulling 100x cargo flats, but none have materialized. They were caught just as short as we were, Your Honor, even though that General Bates knew all about it. We all knew the day would come, but I guess we kept hoping 'maybe.' Our negotiations with them seemed to be bearing fruit, and the idea of exposing over a million and a half city-bred individuals to a twelve-hundred-mile trek in thirty-below temperatures was just too awful to really face. Even now—"

"I know. The army is doing all it can. The main body of PR

troops hasn't actually crossed the dateline yet—so perhaps our forces can get in position. Who knows? Miracles have happened before. But we can't base our thinking on miracles, Jimmy. Flats or no flats, we have to have the people out of the dome before enemy forces cut us off."

"Mr. Mayor, our people can't take this. Aside from leaving their homes and possessions—I've already started them packing, and I've given them a ten-pounds-per-person limit—they aren't used to exercise, to say nothing of walking twelve hundred miles over frozen tundra. And most of them have no clothing heavier than a business suit. And—"

"Enough, Jimmy. I was ambushed in my office earlier today by an entire family: the old grandmother who was born under the dome and refused to consider going outside; the father all full of his product-promotion plans and the new garden he'd just laid out; mother, complaining about junior having a cold and no warm clothes; and the kids, just waiting trustfully until the excitement was over and they could go home and be tucked into their warm beds with a tummyful of dinner. Ye gods, Jimmy! Can you imagine them after three weeks on the trail?"

13

"Just lean across the desk, fellows. Come on, gather round. Take a close look at the shoulder tab. Four stars—see 'em? Then go over to the Slab and do the same with General Margrave. You'll count six. It's as easy as that, boys. The General says no test. Sure, I told him the whole plan. His eyes just kept boring in. Even making contingency plans for deploying an untested and non-High-Command-approved weapon system is grounds for court-martial. He didn't say that; maybe I'm telepathic. In summary, the General says no."

14

I don't know, now. What I heard, even with everything we got on the line, dug in and ready for anything, they's still a ten-mile-wide gap the Peepreps can waltz through without getting even a dirty look. So if General Bates—oh, he's a nice enough young fellow, after you get used to him—if he wants to plug the hole with old unit DNE here, why, I say go to it, only the Council says nix. I can say this much: she's put together so she'll stay together. I must of wired in a thousand of them damage-sensors myself, and that ain't a spot on what's on the diagram. "Pain circuits," old Doc Chin calls 'em. Says it's just like a instinct for self-preservation or something, like people. Old Denny can hurt, he says, so he'll be all the better at dodging enemy fire. He can enjoy, too, Doc says. He gets a kick out of doing his job right, and out of learning stuff. And he learns fast. He'll do okay against them durn Peepreps. They got him programmed right to the brim with everything from them Greeks used to fight with no pants down to Avery's Last Stand at Leadpipe. He ain't no dumb private; he's got more dope to work on than any general ever graduated from the Point. And he's got more firepower than an old-time army corps. So I think maybe General Bates got aholt of a good idear there, myself. Says he can put her in the gap in his line and field-test her for fair, with the whole durn Peeprep army and air force for a test problem. Save the gubment some money, too. I heard Doc Chin say the full-scale field test mock-up would run GM a hundred million and another five times that in army R-and-D funds. He had a map showed where he could use Denny here to block off the south end of Grand Crevasse where the Peeprep armor will have to travel 'count of the rugged terrain north of Cold City, and bottle 'em up slick as a owl's peter. I'm for it, durn it. Let Denny have his chance. Can't be no worse'n having them Comrades down here running things even worse'n the gubment.

15

"You don't understand, young man. My goodness, I'm not the least bit interested in bucking the line, as you put it. Heavens, I'm going back to my apartment—"

"I'm sorry, ma'am. I got my orders. This here ain't no drill; you got to keep it closed up. They're loading as fast as they can. It's my job to keep these lines moving right out the lock, so they get that flat loaded and get the next one up. We got over a million people to load by SIX AM deadline. So you just be nice, ma'am, and think about all the trouble it'd make if everybody decided to start back upstream and jam the elevators and all."

16

Beats me. 'Course, the good part about being just a hired man is I got no big decisions to make, so I don't hafta know what's going on. Seems like they'd let me know something, though. Batesey was down again, spent a hour with old Denny—like I say, beats me—but he give me a new data-can to program into her, right in her Action/Command section. Something's up. I just fired a N-class pulse at old Denny (them's the closest to the real thing) and she snapped her aft-quarter battery around so fast I couldn't see it move. Old Denny's keyed up, I know that much.

17

This has been a memorable time for me. I have my assignment at last, and I have conferred at length—for 2.037 seconds—with my Commander. I am now a fighting unit of the 20th Virginia, a regiment ancient and honorable, with a history dating back to Terra Insula. I look forward to my opportunity to demonstrate my worthiness.

18

"I assure you, gentlemen, the rumor is unfounded. I have by no means authorized the deployment of 'an untested and potentially highly dangerous machine,' as your memo termed it. Candidly, I was not at first entirely unsympathetic to the proposal of the Chief of Ground Forces, in view of the circumstances—I presume you're aware that the PR committed its forces to invasion over an hour ago, and that they are advancing in overwhelming strength. I have issued the order to commence the evacuation, and I believe that the initial phases are even now in progress. I have the fullest confidence in General Bates and can assure you that our forces will do all in their power in the face of this dastardly sneak attack. As for the unfortunate publicity given to the earlier suggestion re the use of the Mark XX, I can tell you that I at once subjected the data to computer analysis here at Headquarters to determine whether any potentially useful purpose could be served by risking the use of the new machine without prior test certification. The results were negative. I'm sorry, gentlemen, but that's it. The enemy has the advantage both strategically and tactically. We are outgunned, outmanned, and in effect outflanked. There is nothing we can do save attempt to hold them long enough to permit the evacuation to get underway, then retreat in good order. The use of our orbiting nuclear capability is out of the question. It is, after all, our own territory we'd be devastating. No more questions for the present, please, gentlemen. I have my duties to see to."

19

My own situation continues to deteriorate. The Current Status program has been updated to within 21 seconds of the present. The reasons both for what is normally a pre-engagement updating and for the hiatus of 21 seconds remain obscure. However, I shall of course hold myself in readiness for whatever comes.

20

"It's all nonsense: to call me here at this hour merely to stand by and watch the destruction of our gallant men who are giving their lives in a totally hopeless fight against overwhelming odds. We know what the outcome must be. You yourself, General, informed us this afternoon that the big tactical computer has analyzed the situation and reported no possibility of stopping them with what we've got. By the way, did you include the alternative of use of the big, er, Bolo, I believe they're called—frightening things—they're so damned *big!* But if, in desperation, you should be forced to employ the thing—have you that result as well? I see. No hope at all. So there's nothing we can do. This is a sad day, General. But I fail to see what object is served by getting me out of bed to come down here. Not that I'm not willing to do anything I can, of course. With our people—innocent civilians—out on that blizzard-swept tundra tonight, and our boys dying to gain them a little time, the loss of a night's sleep is relatively unimportant, of course. But it's my duty to be at my best, rested and ready to face the decisions that we of the Council will be called on to make.

"Now, General, kindly excuse my ignorance if I don't understand all this... but I understood that the large screen there was placed so as to monitor the action at the southern debouchment of Grand Crevasse where we expect the enemy armor to emerge to make its dash for Cold City and the Complex. Yes, indeed, so I was saying, but in that case I'm afraid I don't understand. I'm quite sure you stated that the untried Mark XX would *not* be used. Yet on the screen I see what appears to be in fact that very machine moving up. Please, *calmly*, General! I quite understand your position. Defiance of a direct order? That's rather serious, I'm sure, but no occasion for such language, General. There must be some explanation."

21

This is a most satisfying development. Quite abruptly my Introspection Complex was brought up to full operating level, extra power resources were made available to my Current-Action memory stage, and most satisfying of all, my Battle Reflex circuit has been activated at Active Service level. Action is impending, I am sure of it. It is a curious anomaly: I dread the prospect of damage and even possible destruction, but even more strongly I anticipate the pleasure of performing my design function.

22

"Yes, sir, I agree. It's mutiny. But I will not recall the Bolo and I will not report myself under arrest. Not until this battle's over, General. So the hell with my career. I've got a war to win."

23

"Now just let me get this quite straight, General. Having been denied authority to field-test this new device, you—or a subordinate, which amounts to the same thing—have placed the machine in the line of battle, in open defiance of the Council. This is a serious matter, General. Yes, of course it's war, but to attempt to defend your actions now will merely exacerbate the matter. In any event—to return to your curious decision to defy Council authority and to reverse your own earlier position—it was yourself who assured me that no useful purpose could be served by fielding this experimental equipment; that the battle, and perhaps the war, and the very self-determination of West Continent are irretrievably lost. There is nothing we can do save accept the situation gracefully while decrying Chairman Smith's decision to resort to force. Yes indeed, General, I should like to observe on the Main Tactical Display screen. Shall we go along?"

24

"Now, there at center screen, Mr. Counselor, you see that big blue rectangular formation. Actually that's the opening of Grand Crevasse, emerges through an ice tunnel, you know. Understand the Crevasse is a crustal fault, a part of the same formation that created the thermal sink from which the Complex draws its energy. Splendid spot for an ambush, of course, if we had the capability. Enemy has little option; like a highway in there—armor can move up at flank speed. Above, the badlands, where *we* must operate. Now, over to the left, you see that smoke, or dust or whatever. That represents the western limit of the unavoidable gap in General Bates's line. Dust raised by maneuvering Mark XV's, you understand. Obsolete equipment, but we'll do what we can with them. Over to the right, in the distance there, we can make out our forward artillery emplacement of the Threshold Line. Pitiful, really. Yes, Mr. Counselor, there is indeed a gap precisely opposite the point where the lead units of the enemy are expected to appear. Clearly anything in their direct line of advance will be annihilated; thus General Bates has wisely chosen to dispose his forces to cover both enemy flanks, putting him in position to counterattack if opportunity offers. We must, after all, sir, use what we have. Theoretical arms programmed for fiscal nicety are of no use whatever today. Umm. As for that, one must be flexible, modifying plans to meet a shifting tactical situation. Faced with the prospect of seeing the enemy drive through our center and descend unopposed on the vital installations at Cold City, I have, as you see, decided to order General Bates to make use of the experimental Mark XX. Certainly—my decision entirely. I take full responsibility."

25

I advance over broken terrain toward my assigned position. The prospect of action exhilarates me, but my assessment of enemy strength indicates they are fielding approximately 17.4 percent greater weight of armor than anticipated, with commensurately greater firepower. I compute that I am grossly overmatched. Nonetheless, I shall do my best.

26

"There's no doubt whatever, gentlemen. Computers work with hard facts. Given the enemy's known offensive capability and our own defensive resources, it's a simple computation. No combination of the manpower and equipment at our command can possibly inflict a defeat on the PR forces at this time and place. Two is greater than one. You can't make a dollar out of fifteen cents."

27

"At least we can gather some useful data from the situation, gentlemen. The Bolo Mark XX has been committed to battle. Its designers assure me that the new self-motivating circuitry will vastly enhance the combat-effectiveness of the Bolo. Let us observe."

28

Hate to see old Denny out there, just a great big sitting duck, all alone and—here they come! Look at 'em boiling out of there like ants out of a hot log. Can't hardly look at that screen, them tactical nukes popping fireworks all over the place. But old Denny know enough to get under cover. See that kind of glow all around him? All right, *it*, then. You know, working with him—it—so long, it got to feeling almost like he was somebody. Sure, I know, anyway, that's vaporized ablative shield you see. They're making it plenty hot for him. But he's fighting back. Them Hellbores is putting out, and they know it. Looks like they're concentrating on him now. Look at them tracers closing in on him! Come on, Denny, you ain't dumb. Get out of there fast.

29

"Certainly it's aware what's at stake! I've told you he—the machine, that is—has been fully programmed and is well aware not only of the tactical situation but of strategic and logistical considerations as well. Certainly it's an important item of equipment; its loss would be a serious blow to our present underequipped forces. You may rest assured that its pain circuits as well as its basic military competence will cause it to take the proper action. The fact that I originally opposed commissioning the device is not to be taken as implying any lack of confidence on my part in its combat-effectiveness. You may consider that my reputation is staked on the performance of the machine. It will act correctly."

30

It appears that the enemy is absorbing my barrage with little effect. More precisely, for each enemy unit destroyed by my fire 2.4 fresh units immediately move out to replace it. Thus it appears I am ineffective, while already my own shielding is suffering severe damage. Yet while I have offensive capability I must carry on as my commander would wish. The pain is very great now, but thanks to my superb circuitry I am not disabled, though it has been necessary to withdraw my power from my external somatic sensors.

31

"I can assure you, gentlemen, insofar as simple logic functions are concerned, the Mark XX is perfectly capable of assessing the situation even as you and I, only better. Doubtless as soon as it senses that its position has grown totally untenable, it will retreat to the shelter of the rock ridge and retire under cover to a position from which it can return fire without taking the full force of the enemy's attack at point-blank range. It's been fully briefed on late developments, it knows this is a hopeless fight. There, you see? It's moving..."

32

"Thought you said—dammit, I *know* you said your pet machine had brains enough to know when to pull out! But look at it: half a billion plus of Concordiat funds being bombarded into radioactive rubbish. Like shooting fish in a barrel."

33

"Yes, sir, I'm monitoring everything. My test panel is tuned to it across the board. I'm getting continuous reading on all still-active circuits. Battle Reflex is still hot. Pain circuits close to overload, but he's still taking it. I don't know how much more he can take, sir; already way past Redline. Expected him to break off and get out before now."

34

"It's a simple matter of arithmetic; there is only one correct course of action in any given military situation. The big tactical computer was designed specifically to compare data and deduce that sole correct action. In this case my readout shows that the only thing the Mark XX could legitimately do at this point is just what the Professor here says: pull back to cover and continue its barrage. The onboard computing capability of the unit is as capable of reaching that conclusion, as is the big computer at HQ. So keep calm, gentlemen. It will withdraw at any moment, I assure you of that."

35

"Now it's getting ready—no, look what it's doing! It's advancing into the teeth of that murderous fire. By God, you've got to admire that workmanship! That it's still capable of moving is a miracle. All the ablative metal is gone—you can see its bare armor exposed—and it takes some heat to make that flint-steel glow white!"

36

"Certainly, I'm looking. I see it. By God, sir, it's still moving—faster, in fact! Charging the enemy line like the Light Brigade! And all for nothing, it appears. Your machine, General, appears less competent than you expected."

37

Poor old Denny. Made his play and played out, I reckon. Readings on the board over there don't look good; durn near every overload in him blowed wide open. Not much there to salvage. Emergency Survival Center's hot. Never expected to see *that*. Means all kinds of breakdowns inside. But it figures, after what he just went through. Look at that slag pit he drove up out of. They wanted a field test. Reckon they got it. And he flunked it.

38

"Violating orders and winning is one thing, George. Committing mutiny and losing is quite another. Your damned machine made a fool of me. After I stepped in and backed you to the hilt and stood there like a jackass and assured Councillor Grace that the thing knew what it was doing—it blows the whole show. Instead of pulling back to save itself it charged to destruction. I want an explanation of this fiasco at once."

39

"Look! No, by God, over *there!* On the left of the entrance. They're breaking formation—they're running for it! Watch this! The whole spearhead is crumbling, they're taking to the badlands, they're—"

40

"*Why,* dammit? It's outside all rationality. As far as the enemy's concerned, fine. They broke and ran. They couldn't stand up to the sight of the Mark XX not only taking everything they had, but advancing on them out of that inferno, all guns blazing. Another hundred yards and—but they don't know that. It buffaloed them, so score a battle won for our side. But *why?* I'd stack my circuits up against any fixed installation in existence, including the big Tacomp the Army's so proud of. That machine was as aware as anybody that the only smart thing to do was run. So now I've got a junk pile on my hands. Some test! A clear flunk. Destroyed in action. Not recommended for Federal procurement. Nothing left but a few hot transistors in the Survival Center. It's a disaster, Fred. All my work, all your work, the whole program wrecked. Fred, you talk to General Bates. As soon as he's done inspecting the hulk he'll want somebody human to chew out."

41

"Look at that pile of junk! Reading off the scale. Won't be cool enough to haul to Disposal for six months. I understand you're Chief Engineer at Bolo Division. You built this thing. Maybe you can tell me what you had in mind here. Sure, it stood up to fire better than I hoped. But so what? A stone wall can stand and take it. This thing is supposed to be *smart*, supposed to feel pain like a living creature. Blunting the strike at the Complex was a valuable contribution, but how can I recommend procurement of this junk heap?"

42

Why, Denny? Just tell me why you did it. You got all these military brass down on you, and on me, too. On all of us. They don't much like stuff they can't understand. You attacked when they figured you to run. Sure, you routed the enemy, like Bates says, but you got yourself ruined in the process. Don't make sense. Any dumb private, along with the generals, would have known enough to get out of there. Tell me why, so I'll have something for Bates to put on his Test Evaluation Report, AGF Form 1103-6, Rev 11/3/85.

43

"All right, Unit DNE of the line. Why did you do it? This is your Commander, Unit DNE. Report! Why did you do it? Now, you knew your position was hopeless, didn't you? That you'd be destroyed if you held your ground, to say nothing of advancing. Surely you were able to compute that. You were lucky to have the chance to prove yourself."

For a minute I thought old Denny was too far gone to answer. There was just a kind of groan come out of the amplifier. Then it firmed up. General Bates had his hand cupped behind his ear, but Denny spoke right up.

"Yes, sir."

"You knew what was at stake here. It was the ultimate test of your ability to perform correctly under stress, of your suitability as a weapon of war. You knew that. General Margrave and old Priss Grace and the press boys all had their eyes on every move you made. So instead of using common sense, you waded into that inferno in defiance of all logic—and destroyed yourself. Right?"

"That is correct, sir."

"Then why? In the name of sanity, tell me *why*! Why, instead of backing out and saving yourself, did you charge?... Wait a minute, Unit DNE. It just dawned on me. I've been underestimating you. You *knew*, didn't you? Your knowledge of human psychology told you they'd break and run, didn't it?"

"No, sir. On the contrary, I was quite certain that they were as aware as I that they held every advantage."

"Then that leaves me back where I started. Why? What made you risk everything on a hopeless attack? Why did you do it?"

"For the honor of the regiment."

Allamagoosa

ERIC FRANK RUSSELL

It was a long time since the *Bustler* had been so silent. She lay in the Sirian spaceport, her tubes cold, her shell particle-scarred, her air that of a long-distance runner exhausted at the end of a marathon. There was good reason for this: she had returned from a lengthy trip by no means devoid of troubles.

Now, in port, well-deserved rest had been gained if only temporarily. Peace, sweet peace. No more bothers, no more crises, no more major upsets, no more dire predicaments such as crop up in free flight at least twice a day. Just peace.

Hah!

Captain McNaught reposed in his cabin, feet up on desk, and enjoyed the relaxation to the utmost. The engines were dead, their hellish pounding absent for the first time in months. Out there in the big city, four hundred of his crew were making whoopee under a brilliant sun. This evening, when First Officer Gregory returned to take charge, he was going to go into the fragrant twilight and make the rounds of neon-lit civilization.

That was the beauty of making landfall at long last. Men could give way to themselves, blow off surplus steam, each according to his fashion. No duties, no worries, no dangers, no responsibilities in spaceport. A haven of safety and comfort for tired rovers.

Again, hah!

Burman, the chief radio officer, entered the cabin. He was one of the half-dozen remaining on duty and bore the expression of a man who can think of twenty better things to do.

"Relayed signal just come in, sir." Handing the paper across, he waited for the other to look at it and perhaps dictate a reply.

Taking the sheet, McNaught removed the feet from his desk, sat erect, and read the message aloud.

Terran Headquarters to Bustler. *Remain Siriport pending further orders. Rear Admiral Vane W. Cassidy due there seventeenth. Feldman. Navy Op. Command, Sirisec.*

He looked up, all happiness gone from his leathery features, and groaned.

"Something wrong?" asked Burman, vaguely alarmed.

McNaught pointed at three thin books on his desk. "The middle one. Page twenty."

Leafing through it, Burman found an item that said: *Vane W. Cassidy, R-Ad. Head Inspector Ships and Stores.*

Burman swallowed hard. "Does that mean—?"

"Yes, it does," said McNaught without pleasure. "Back to training-college and all its rigmarole. Paint and soap, spit and polish." He put on an officious expression, adopted a voice to match it. "Captain, you have only seven ninety-nine emergency rations. Your allocation is eight hundred. Nothing in your logbook accounts for the missing one. Where is it? What happened to it? How is it that one of the men's kit lacks an officially issued pair of suspenders? Did you report his loss?"

"Why does he pick on us?" asked Burman, appalled. "He's never chivvied us before."

"That's why," informed McNaught, scowling at the wall. "It's our turn to be stretched across the barrel." His gaze found the calendar. "We have three days—and we'll need 'em! Tell Second Officer Pike to come here at once."

Burman departed gloomily. In short time, Pike entered. His face reaffirmed the old adage that bad news travels fast.

"Make out an indent," ordered McNaught, "for one hundred gallons of plastic paint, Navy gray, approved quality. Make out another for thirty gallons of interior white enamel. Take them to spaceport stores right away. Tell them to deliver by six this evening along with our correct issue of brushes and sprayers. Grab up any cleaning material that's going for free."

"The men won't like this," remarked Pike, feebly.

"They're going to love it," McNaught asserted. "A bright and shiny ship, all spic and span, is good for morale. It says so in that book. Get moving and put those indents in. When you come back, find the stores and equipment sheets and bring them here. We've got to check stocks before Cassidy arrives. Once he's here we'll have no chance to make up shortages or smuggle out any extra items we happened to find in our hands."

"Very well, sir." Pike went out wearing the same expression as Burman's.

Lying back in his chair, McNaught muttered to himself. There was a feeling in his bones that something was sure to cause a last-minute ruckus. A shortage of any item would be serious enough unless covered by a previous report. A surplus would be bad, very bad. The former implied carelessness or misfortune. The latter suggested barefaced theft of government property in circumstances condoned by the commander.

For instance, there was that recent case of Williams of the heavy cruiser *Swift*. He'd heard of it over the spacevine when out around Bootes. Williams had been found in unwitting command of eleven reels of electric-fence wire when his official issue was ten. It had taken a court-martial to decide that the extra reel—which had formidable barter-value on a certain planet—had not been stolen from space-stores, or, in sailor jargon, "teleportated aboard." But Williams had been reprimanded. And that did not help promotion.

He was still rumbling discontentedly when Pike returned bearing a folder of foolscap sheets.

"Going to start right away, sir?"

"We'll have to." He heaved himself erect, mentally bid good-bye to time off and a taste of the bright lights. "It'll take long enough to work right through from bow to tail. I'll leave the men's kit inspection to the last."

Marching out of the cabin, he set forth toward the bow, Pike following with broody reluctance.

As they passed the open main lock, Peaslake observed them, bounded eagerly up the gangway and joined behind. A pukka member of the crew, he was a large dog whose ancestors had been more enthusiastic than selective. He wore with pride a big collar inscribed: *Peaslake—Property of S.S.* Bustler. His chief duties, ably performed, were to keep alien rodents off the ship and, on rare occasions, smell out dangers not visible to human eyes.

The three paraded forward, McNaught and Pike in the manner of men grimly sacrificing pleasure for the sake of duty, Peaslake with the panting willingness of one ready for any new game no matter what.

Reaching the bow-cabin, McNaught dumped himself in the pilot's seat, took the folder from the other. "You know this stuff better than me—the chart room is where I shine. So I'll read them out while you look them over." He opened the folder, started on the first page. "K1. Beam compass, type D, one of."

"Check," said Pike.

"K2. Distance and direction indicator, electronic, type JJ, one of."

"Check."

"K3. Port and starboard gravitic meters, Casini models, one pair."

"Check."

Peaslake planted his head in McNaught's lap, blinked soulfully and whined. He was beginning to get the others' viewpoint. This tedious itemizing and checking was a hell of a game. McNaught consolingly lowered a hand and played with Peaslake's ears while he ploughed his way down the list.

"K187. Foam rubber cushions, pilot and co-pilot, one pair."

"Check."

By the time First Officer Gregory appeared, they had reached the tiny intercom cubby and poked around it in semidarkness. Peaslake had long departed in disgust.

"M24. Spare minispeakers, three inch, type T2, one set of six."

"Check."

Looking in, Gregory popped his eyes and said, "What's going on?"

"Major inspection due soon." McNaught glanced at his watch. "Go see if stores has delivered a load and if not, why not. Then you'd better give me a hand and let Pike take a few hours off."

"Does this mean land-leave is canceled?"

"You bet it does—until after Hizonner has been and gone." He glanced at Pike. "When you get into the city, search around and send back any of the crew you can find. No arguments or excuses. Also no alibis and/or delays. It's an order."

Pike registered unhappiness. Gregory glowered at him, went away, came back and said, "Stores will have the stuff here in twenty minutes' time." With bad grace he watched Pike depart.

"M47. Intercom cable, woven-wire protected, three drums."

"Check," said Gregory, mentally kicking himself for returning at the wrong time.

The task continued until late in the evening, was resumed early next morning. By that time three-quarters of the men were hard at work inside and outside the vessel, doing their jobs as though sentenced to them for crimes contemplated but not yet committed.

Moving around the ship's corridors and catwalks had to be done crab-fashion, with a nervous sidewise edging. Once again it was being demonstrated that the Terran life-form suffers from ye fear of wette paynt. The first smearer would have ten years willed off his unfortunate life.

It was in these conditions, in midafternoon of the second day, that McNaught's bones proved their feelings had been prophetic. He recited the ninth page while Jean Blanchard confirmed the presence and actual existence of all items enumerated. Two-thirds of the way down they hit the rocks, metaphorically speaking, and commenced to sink fast.

McNaught said boredly, "V1097. Drinking bowl, enamel, one of."

"Is zis," said Blanchard, tapping it.

"V1098. Offog, one."

"*Quoi?*" asked Blanchard, staring.

"V1098. Offog, one," repeated McNaught. "Well, why are you looking thunderstruck? This is the ship's galley. You're the head cook. You know what's supposed to be in the galley, don't you? Where's this offog?"

"Never hear of heem," stated Blanchard, flatly.

"You must have. It's on this equipment-sheet in plain, clear type. Offog, one, it says. It was here when we were fitted-out four years ago. We checked it ourselves and signed for it."

"I signed for nossings called offog," Blanchard denied. "In the cuisine zere is no such sing."

"Look!" McNaught scowled and showed him the sheet.

Blanchard looked and sniffed disdainfully. "I have here zee electronic oven, one of. I have jacketed boilers, graduated capacities, one set. I have bain marie pans, seex of. But no offog. Never heard of heem. I do not know of heem." He spread his hands and shrugged. "No offog."

"There's got to be," McNaught insisted. "What's more, when Cassidy arrives there'll be hell to pay if there isn't."

"You find heem," Blanchard suggested.

"You got a certificate from the International Hotels School of Cookery. You got a certificate from the Cordon Bleu College of Cuisine. You got a certificate with three credits from the Space-Navy Feeding Center," McNaught pointed out. "All that—and you don't know what an offog is."

"*Nom d'un chien!*" ejaculated Blanchard, waving his arms around. "I tell you ten t'ousand time zere is no offog. Zere never was an offog. Escoffier heemself could not find zee offog of vich zere is none. Am I a magician perhaps?"

"It's part of the culinary equipment," McNaught maintained. "It must be because it's on page nine. And page nine means its proper home is in the galley, care of the head cook."

"Like hail it does," Blanchard retorted. He pointed at a metal box on the wall. "Intercom booster. Is zat mine?"

McNaught thought it over, conceded, "No, it's Burman's. His stuff rambles all over the ship."

"Zen ask heem for zis bloody offog," said Blanchard, triumphantly.

"I will. If it's not yours, it must be his. Let's finish this checking first. If I'm not systematic and thorough Cassidy will jerk off my insignia." His eyes sought the list. "V1099. Inscribed collar, leather, brass studded, dog, for the use of. No need to look for that. I saw it myself five minutes ago." He ticked the item, continued, "V1100. Sleeping basket, woven reed, one of."

"Is zis," said Blanchard, kicking it into a corner.

"V1101. Cushion, foam rubber, to fit sleeping basket, one of."

"Half of," Blanchard contradicted. "In four years he has chewed away other half."

"Maybe Cassidy will let us indent for a new one. It doesn't matter. We're okay so long as we can produce the half we've got." McNaught stood up, closed the folder. "That's the lot for here. I'll go see Burman about this missing item."

The inventory party moved on.

Burman switched off a UHF receiver, removed his earplugs, and raised a questioning eyebrow.

"In the galley we're short an offog," explained McNaught. "Where is it?"

"Why ask me? The galley is Blanchard's bailiwick."

"Not entirely. A lot of your cables run through it. You've two terminal boxes in there, also an automatic switch and an intercom booster. Where's the offog?"

"Never heard of it," said Burman, baffled.

McNaught shouted, "Don't tell me that! I'm already fed up hearing Blanchard saying it. Four years back we had an offog. It says so here. This is our copy of what we checked and signed for. It says we signed for an offog. Therefore we must have one. It's got to be found before Cassidy gets here."

"Sorry, sir," sympathized Burman. "I can't help you."

"You can think again," advised McNaught. "Up in the bow there's a direction and distance indicator. What do *you* call it?"

"A didin," said Burman, mystified.

"And," McNaught went on, pointing at the pulse transmitter, "what do you call *that?*"

"The opper-popper."

"Baby names, see? Didin and opper-popper. Now rack your brains and remember what you called an offog four years ago."

"Nothing," asserted Burman, "has ever been called an offog to my knowledge."

"Then," demanded McNaught, "why did we sign for one?"

"I didn't sign for anything. You did all the signing."

"While you and others did the checking. Four years ago, presumably in the galley, I said, 'Offog, one,' and either you or Blanchard pointed to it and said, 'Check.' I took somebody's word for it. I have to take other specialists' words for it. I am an expert navigator, familiar with all the latest navigational gadgets but not with other stuff. So I'm compelled to rely on people who know what an offog is—or ought to."

Burman had a bright thought. "All kinds of oddments were dumped in the main lock, the corridors, and the galley when we were fitted-out. We had to sort through a deal of stuff and stash it where it properly belonged, remember? This offog-thing might be anyplace today. It isn't necessarily my responsibility or Blanchard's."

"I'll see what the other officers say," agreed McNaught, conceding the point. "Gregory, Worth, Sanderson, or one of the others may be coddling the item. Wherever it is, it's got to be found. Or accounted for in full if it's been expended."

He went out. Burman pulled a face, inserted his earplugs, resumed fiddling with his apparatus. An hour later McNaught came back wearing a scowl.

"Positively," he announced with ire, "there is no such thing on the ship. Nobody knows of it. Nobody can so much as guess at it."

"Cross it off and report it lost," Burman suggested.

"What, when we're hard aground? You know as well as I do that loss and damage must be signaled at time of occurrence. If I tell Cassidy the offog went west in space, he'll want to know when, where, how, and why it wasn't signaled. There'll be a real ruckus if the contraption happens to be valued at half a million credits. I can't dismiss it with an airy wave of the hand."

"What's the answer then?" inquired Burman, innocently ambling straight into the trap.

"There's one and only one," McNaught announced. "*You* will manufacture an offog."

"Who? Me?" said Burman, twitching his scalp.

"You and no other. I'm fairly sure the thing is your pigeon, anyway."

"Why?"

"Because it's typical of the baby names used for your kind of stuff. I'll bet a month's pay that an offog is some sort of scientific allamagoosa. Something to do with fog, perhaps. Maybe a blind-approach gadget."

"The blind-approach transceiver is called 'the fumbly,'" Burman informed.

"There you are!" said McNaught as if that clinched it. "So you will make an offog. It will be completed by six tomorrow evening and ready for my inspection then. It had better be convincing, in fact pleasing. In fact its function will be convincing."

Burman stood up, let his hands dangle, and said in hoarse tones, "How can I make an offog when I don't even know what it is?"

"Neither does Cassidy know," McNaught pointed out, leering at him. "He's more of a quantity surveyor than anything else. As such he counts things, looks at things, certifies that they exist, accepts advice on whether they are functionally satisfactory or worn out. All we need do is concoct an imposing allamagoosa and tell him it's the offog."

"Holy Moses!" said Burman, fervently.

"Let us not rely on the dubious assistance of Biblical characters," McNaught reproved. "Let us use the brains that God has given us. Get a grip on your soldering-iron and make a topnotch offog by six tomorrow evening. That's an order!"

He departed, satisfied with this solution. Behind him, Burman gloomed at the wall and licked his lips once, twice.

Rear Admiral Vane W. Cassidy arrived right on time. He was a short, paunchy character with a florid complexion and eyes like those of a long-dead fish. His gait was an important strut.

"Ah, Captain, I trust that you have everything shipshape."

"Everything usually is," assured McNaught, glibly. "I see to that." He spoke with conviction.

"Good!" approved Cassidy. "I like a commander who takes his responsibilities seriously. Much as I regret saying so, there are a few who do not." He marched through the main lock, his cod-eyes taking note of the fresh white enamel. "Where do you prefer to start, bow or tail?"

"My equipment-sheets run from bow backward. We may as well deal with them the way they're set."

"Very well." He trotted officiously toward the nose, paused on the way to pat Peaslake and examine his collar. "Well cared-for, I see. Has the animal proved useful?"

"He saved five lives on Mardia by barking a warning."

"The details have been entered in your log, I suppose?"

"Yes, sir. The log is in the chart room awaiting your inspection."

"We'll get to it in due time." Reaching the bow-cabin, Cassidy took a seat, accepted the folder from McNaught, started off at businesslike pace. "K1. Beam compass, type D, one of."

"This is it, sir," said McNaught, showing him.

"Still working properly?"

"Yes, sir."

They carried on, reached the intercom-cubby, the computer room, a succession of other places back to the galley. Here, Blanchard posed in freshly laundered white clothes and eyed the newcomer warily.

"V147. Electronic oven, one of."

"Is zis," said Blanchard, pointing with disdain.

"Satisfactory?" inquired Cassidy, giving him the fishy-eye.

"Not beeg enough," declared Blanchard. He encompassed the entire galley with an expressive gesture. "Nossings beeg enough. Place too small. Eversings too small. I am chef de cuisine an' she is a cuisine like an attic."

"This is a warship, not a luxury liner," Cassidy snapped. He frowned at the equipment-sheet. "V148. Timing device, electronic oven, attachment thereto, one of."

"Is zis," spat Blanchard, ready to sling it through the nearest port if Cassidy would first donate the two pins.

Working his way down the sheet, Cassidy got nearer and nearer while nervous tension built up. Then he reached the critical point and said, "V1098. Offog, one."

"*Morbleu!*" said Blanchard, shooting sparks from his eyes, "I have say before an' I say again, zere never was—"

"The offog is in the radio room, sir," McNaught chipped in hurriedly.

"Indeed?" Cassidy took another look at the sheet. "Then why is it recorded along with galley equipment?"

"It was placed in the galley at time of fitting-out, sir. It's one of those portable instruments left to us to fix up where most suitable."

"Hm-m-m! Then it should have been transferred to the radio room list. Why didn't you transfer it?"

"I thought it better to wait for your authority to do so, sir."

The fish-eyes registered gratification. "Yes, that is quite proper of you, Captain. I will transfer it now." He crossed the item from sheet nine, initialed it, entered it on sheet sixteen, initialed that. "V1099. Inscribed collar, leather ... oh, yes, I've seen that. The dog was wearing it."

He ticked it. An hour later he strutted into the radio room. Burman stood up, squared his shoulders but could not keep his feet or hands from fidgeting. His eyes protruded slightly and kept straying toward McNaught in silent appeal. He was like a man wearing a porcupine in his britches.

"V1098. Offog, one," said Cassidy in his usual tone of brooking no nonsense.

Moving with the jerkiness of a slightly uncoordinated robot, Burman pawed a small box fronted with dials, switches, and colored lights. It looked like a radio ham's idea of a fruit machine. He knocked down a couple of switches. The lights came on, played around in intriguing combinations.

"This is it, sir," he informed with difficulty.

"Ah!" Cassidy left his chair and moved across for a closer look. "I don't recall having seen this item before. But there are so many different models of the same things. Is it still operating efficiently?"

"Yes, sir."

"It's one of the most useful things in the ship," contributed McNaught, for good measure.

"What does it *do?*" inquired Cassidy, inviting Burman to cast a pearl of wisdom before him.

Burman paled.

Hastily, McNaught said, "A full explanation would be rather involved and technical but, to put it as simply as possible, it enables us to strike a balance between opposing gravitational fields. Variations in lights indicate the extent and degree of unbalance at any given time."

"It's a clever idea," added Burman, made suddenly reckless by this news, "based on Finagle's Constant."

"I see," said Cassidy, not seeing at all. He resumed his seat, ticked the offog and carried on. "Z44. Switchboard, automatic, forty-line intercom, one of."

"Here it is, sir."

Cassidy glanced at it, returned his gaze to the sheet. The others used his momentary distraction to mop perspiration from their foreheads.

Victory had been gained.

All was well.

For the third time, hah!

Rear Admiral Vane W. Cassidy departed pleased and complimentary. Within one hour the crew bolted to town. McNaught took turns with Gregory at enjoying the gay lights. For the next five days all was peace and pleasure.

On the sixth day, Burman brought in a signal, dumped it upon McNaught's desk, and waited for the reaction. He had an air of gratification, the pleasure of one whose virtue is about to be rewarded.

Terran Headquarters to Bustler. *Return here immediately for overhaul and refitting. Improved power plant to be installed. Feldman. Navy Op. Command. Sirisec.*

"Back to Terra," commented McNaught, happily. "And an overhaul will mean at least one month's leave." He eyed Burman. "Tell all officers on duty to go to town at once and order the crew aboard. The men will come running when they know why."

"Yes, sir," said Burman, grinning.

Everyone was still grinning two weeks later when the Siriport had receded far behind and Sol had grown to a vague speck in the sparkling mist of the bow starfield. Eleven weeks still to go, but it was worth it. Back to Terra. Hurrah!

In the captain's cabin, the grins abruptly vanished one evening when Burman suddenly developed the willies. He marched in, chewed his bottom lip while waiting for McNaught to finish writing in the log.

Finally, McNaught pushed the book away, glanced up, frowned. "What's the matter with you? Got a bellyache or something?"

"No, sir. I've been thinking."

"Does it hurt that much?"

"I've been thinking," persisted Burman in funereal tones. "We're going back for overhaul. You know what that means? We'll walk off the ship and a horde of experts will walk onto it." He stared tragically at the other. "Experts, I said."

"Naturally they'll be experts," McNaught agreed. "Equipment cannot be tested and brought up to scratch by a bunch of dopes."

"It will require more than a mere expert to bring the offog up to scratch," Burman pointed out. "It'll need a genius.

McNaught rocked back, swapped expressions like changing masks. "Jumping Judas! I'd forgotten all about that thing. When we get to Terra we won't blind *those* boys with science."

"No, sir, we won't," endorsed Burman. He did not add "any more," but his face shouted aloud, "You got me into this. You get me out of it." He waited a time while McNaught did some intense thinking, then prompted, "What do you suggest, sir?"

Slowly the satisfied smile returned to McNaught's features as he answered, "Break up the contraption and feed it into the disintegrator."

"That doesn't solve the problem," said Burman. "We'll still be short an offog."

"No, we won't. Because I'm going to signal its loss owing to the hazards of space-service." He closed one eye in an emphatic wink. "We're in free flight right now." He reached for a message-pad and scribbled on it while Burman stood by vastly relieved.

Bustler *to Terran Headquarters. Item V1098, Offog, one, came apart under gravitational stress while passing through twin-sun field Hector Major-Minor. Material used as fuel. McNaught, Commander.* Bustler.

Burman took it to the radio room and beamed it Earthward. All was peace and progress for another two days. The next time he went to the captain's cabin he went running and worried.

"General call, sir," he announced breathlessly and thrust the message into the other's hands.

Terran Headquarters for relay all sectors. Urgent and Important. All ships grounded forthwith. Vessels in flight under official orders will make for nearest spaceport pending further instructions. Welling. Alarm and Rescue Command. Terra.

"Something's gone bust," commented McNaught, undisturbed. He traipsed to the chart room, Burman following. Consulting the charts, he dialed the intercom phone, got Pike in the bow and ordered, "There's a panic. All ships grounded. We've got to make for Zaxtedport, about three days' run away. Change course at once. Starboard seventeen degrees, declination ten." Then he cut off, griped, "Bang goes that sweet month on Terra. I never did like Zaxted, either. It stinks. The crew will feel murderous about this, and I don't blame them."

"What d'you think has happened, sir?" asked Burman. He looked both uneasy and annoyed.

"Heaven alone knows. The last general call was seven years ago when the *Starider* exploded halfway along the Mars run. They grounded every ship in existence while they investigated the cause." He rubbed his chin, pondered, went on, "And the call before that one was when the entire crew of the *Blowgun* went nuts. Whatever it is this time, you can bet it's serious."

"It wouldn't be the start of a space war?"

"Against whom?" McNaught made a gesture of contempt. "Nobody has the ships with which to oppose us. No, it's something technical. We'll learn of it eventually. They'll tell us before we reach Zaxted or soon afterward."

They did tell him. Within six hours. Burman rushed in with face full of horror.

"What's eating you now?" demanded McNaught, staring at him.

"The offog," stuttered Burman. He made motions as though brushing off invisible spiders.

"What of it?"

"It's a typographical error. In your copy it should read off. dog."

The commander stared owlishly.

"Off. dog?" echoed McNaught, making it sound like foul language.

"See for yourself." Dumping the signal on the desk, Burman bolted out, left the door swinging. McNaught scowled after him, picked up the message.

Terran Headquarters to Bustler. *Your report V1098, ship's official dog Peaslake. Detail fully circumstances and manner in which animal came apart under gravitational stress. Cross-examine crew and signal all coincidental symptoms experienced by them. Urgent and Important. Welling. Alarm and Rescue Command. Terra.*

In the privacy of his cabin McNaught commenced to eat his nails. Every now and again he went a little cross-eyed as he examined them for nearness to the flesh.

The End

Exploration Team

MURRAY LEINSTER

The nearer moon went by overhead. It was jagged and irregular in shape, probably a captured asteroid. Huyghens had seen it often enough, so he did not go out of his quarters to watch it hurtle across the sky with seemingly the speed of an atmosphere-flier, occulting the stars as it went. Instead, he sweated over paperwork, which should have been odd because he was technically a felon and all his labors on Loren II felonious. It was odd, too, for a man to do paperwork in a room with steel shutters and a huge bald eagle—untethered—dozing on a three-inch perch set in the wall. But paperwork was not Huyghens' real task. His only assistant had tangled with a night-walker, and the furtive Kodius Company ships had taken him away to where Kodius Company ships came from. Huyghens had to do two men's work in loneliness. To his knowledge, he was the only man in this solar system.

Below him, there were snufflings. Sitka Pete got up heavily and padded to his water pan. He lapped the refrigerated water and sneezed. Sourdough Charley waked and complained in a rumbling growl. There were divers other rumblings and mutterings below. Huyghens called reassuringly, "Easy there!" and went on with his work. He finished a climate report, and fed figures to a computer. While it hummed over them he entered the inventory totals in the station log, showing what supplies remained. Then he began to write up the log proper.

"Sitka Peter," he wrote, "has apparently solved the problem of killing individual sphexes. He has learned that it doesn't do to hug them and that his claws can't penetrate their hide, not the top-hide, anyhow. Today Semper notified us that a pack of sphexes had found the scent-trail to the station. Sitka hid downwind until they arrived. Then he charged from the rear and brought his paws together on both sides of a sphex's head in a terrific pair of slaps. It must have been like two twelve-inch shells arriving from opposite directions at the same time. It must have scrambled the sphex's brains as if they were eggs. It dropped dead. He killed two more with such mighty pairs of wallops. Sourdough Charley watched, grunting, and when the sphexes turned on Sitka, he charged in his turn. I, of course, couldn't shoot too close to him, so he might have fared badly except that Faro Nell came pouring out of the bear-quarters to help. The diversion enabled Sitka Pete to resume the use of his new technique, towering on his hind legs and swinging his paws in the new and grizzly fashion. The fight ended promptly. Semper flew and screamed above the scrap, but as usual did not join in. Note: Nugget, the cub, tried to mix in but his mother cuffed him out of the way. Sourdough and Sitka ignored him as usual. Kodius Champion's genes are sound!"

The noises of the night went on outside. There were notes like organ-tones—song-lizards. There were the tittering, giggling cries of night-walkers. There were sounds like jack-hammers, and doors closing, and from every direction came noises like hiccoughs in various keys. These were made by the improbable small creatures which on Loren II took the place of insects.

Huyghens wrote out:

"Sitka seemed ruffled when the fight was over. He used his trick on the head of every dead or wounded sphex, except those he'd killed with it, lifting up their heads for his pile-driver-like blows from two directions at once, as if to show Sourdough how it was done. There was much grunting as they hauled the carcasses to the incinerator. It almost seemed—"

The arrival-bell clanged, and Huyghens jerked up his head to stare at it. Semper, the eagle, opened icy eyes. He blinked. Noises. There was a long, deep, contented snore from below. Something shrieked, out in the jungle. Hiccoughs, clatterings, and organ-notes...

The bell clanged again. It was a notice that an unscheduled ship aloft somewhere had picked up the beacon-beam—which only Kodius Company ships should know about—and was communicating for a landing. But there shouldn't be any ships in this solar system just now! The Kodius Company's colony was completely illegal, and there were few graver crimes than unauthorized occupation of a new planet.

The bell clanged a third time. Huyghens swore. His hand went out to cut off the beacon, and then stopped. That would be useless. Radar would have fixed it and tied it in with physical features like the nearby sea and the Sere Plateau. The ship could find the place, anyhow, and descend by daylight.

"The devil!" said Huyghens. But he waited yet again for the bell to ring. A Kodius Company ship would double-ring to reassure him. But there shouldn't be a Kodius Company ship for months.

The bell clanged singly. The space-phone dial flickered and a voice came out of it, tinny from stratospheric distortion: *"Calling ground. Calling ground. Crete Line ship* Odysseus *calling ground on Loren II. Landing one passenger by boat. Put on your field lights."*

Huyghens' mouth dropped open. A Kodius Company ship would be welcome. A Colonial Survey ship would be extremely unwelcome, because it would destroy the colony and Sitka and Sourdough and Faro Nell and Nugget—and Semper—and carry Huyghens off to be tried for unauthorized colonization and all that it implied.

But a commercial ship, landing one passenger by boat... There were simply no circumstances under which that could happen. Not to an unknown, illegal colony. Not to a furtive station!

Huyghens flicked on the landing-field lights. He saw the glare over the field half a mile away. Then he stood up and prepared to take the measures required by discovery. He packed the paperwork he'd been doing into the disposal-safe. He gathered up all personal documents and tossed them in. Every record, every bit of evidence that the Kodius Company maintained this station went into the safe. He slammed the door. He moved his finger toward the disposal-button, which would destroy the contents and melt down even the ashes past their possible use for evidence in court.

Then he hesitated. If it were a Survey ship, the button had to be pressed and he must resign himself to a long term in prison. But a Crete Line ship—if the space-phone told the truth—was not threatening. It was simply unbelievable.

He shook his head. He got into travel garb, armed himself, and went down into the bear-quarters, turning on lights as he went. There were startled snufflings, and Sitka Pete reared himself to a sitting position to blink at him. Sourdough Charley lay on his back with his legs in the air. He'd found it cooler, sleeping that way. He rolled over with a thump, and made snorting sounds which somehow sounded cordial. Faro Nell padded to the door of her separate apartment, assigned her so that Nugget would not be underfoot to irritate the big males.

Huyghens, as the human population of Loren II, faced the work-force, fighting-force, and—with Nugget—four-fifths of the terrestrial non-human population of the planet. They were mutated Kodiak bears, descendants of that Kodius Champion for whom the Kodius Company was named. Sitka Pete was a good twenty-two hundred pounds of lumbering, intelligent carnivore; Sourdough Charley would weigh within a hundred pounds of that figure. Faro Nell was eighteen hundred pounds of female charm and ferocity. Then Nugget poked his muzzle around his mother's furry rump to see what was toward, and he was six hundred pounds of ursine infancy. The animals looked at Huyghens expectantly. If he'd had Semper riding on his shoulder they'd have known what was expected of them.

"Let's go," said Huyghens. "It's dark outside, but somebody's coming. And it may be bad!"

He unfastened the outer door of the bear-quarters. Sitka Pete went charging clumsily through it. A forthright charge was the best way to develop any situation—if one was an oversize male Kodiak bear. Sourdough went lumbering after him. There was nothing hostile immediately outside. Sitka stood up on his hind legs—he reared up a solid twelve feet—and sniffed the air. Sourdough methodically lumbered to one side and then the other, sniffing in his turn. Nell came out, nine-tenths of a ton of daintiness, and rumbled admonitorily at Nugget, who trailed her closely. Huyghens stood in the doorway, his night-sighted gun ready. He felt uncomfortable at sending the bears ahead into a Loren II jungle at night, but they were qualified to scent danger, and he was not.

The illumination of the jungle in a wide path toward the landing-field made for weirdness in the look of things. There were arching giant ferns and columnar trees which grew above them, and the extraordinary lanceolate underbrush of the jungle. The flood-lamps, set level with the ground, lighted everything from below. The foliage, then, was brightly lit against the black night-sky, brightly enough lit to dim the stars.

"On ahead!" commanded Huyghens, waving. "Hup!"

He swung the bear-quarters door shut, and moved toward the landing-field through the lane of lighted forest. The two giant male Kodiaks lumbered ahead. Sitka Pete dropped to all fours and prowled. Sourdough Charley followed closely, swinging from side to side. Huyghens came behind the two of them, and Faro Nell brought up the rear with Nugget nudging her.

It was an excellent military formation for progress through dangerous jungle. Sourdough and Sitka were advance guard and point, respectively, while Faro Nell guarded the rear. With Nugget to look after, she was especially alert against attack from behind. Huyghens was, of course, the striking force. His gun fired explosive bullets which would discourage even sphexes, and his night-sight—a cone of light which went on when he took up the trigger-slack—told exactly where they would strike. It was not a sportsmanlike weapon, but the creatures of Loren II were not sportsmanlike antagonists. The night-walkers, for example. But night-walkers feared light. They attacked only in a species of hysteria if it were too bright.

Huyghens moved toward the glare at the landing field. His mental state was savage. The Kodius Company on Loren II was completely illegal. It happened to be necessary, from one point of view, but it was still illegal. The tinny voice on the space-phone was not convincing, in ignoring that illegality. But if a ship landed, Huyghens could get back to the station before men could follow, and he'd have the disposal-safe turned on in time to protect those who'd sent him here.

Then he heard the far-away and high harsh roar of a landing boat rocket—not a ship's bellowing tubes—as he made his way through the unreal-seeming brush. The roar grew louder as he pushed on, the three big Kodiaks padding here and there, sniffing for danger.

He reached the edge of the landing field, and it was blindingly bright, with the customary divergent beams slanting skyward so a ship could check its instrument-landing by sight. Landing fields like this had been standard, once upon a time. Nowadays all developed planets had landing-grids—monstrous structures which drew upon ionospheres for power and lifted and drew down star-ships with remarkable gentleness and unlimited force. This sort of landing field would now be found only where a survey-team was at work, or where some strictly temporary investigation of ecology or bacteriology was under way, or where a newly authorized colony had not yet been able to build its landing-grid. Of course, it was unthinkable that anybody would attempt a settlement in defiance of the law!

Already, as Huyghens reached the edge of the scorched open space, the night-creatures had rushed to the light, like moths on Earth. The air was misty with crazily gyrating, tiny flying things. They were innumerable and of every possible form and size, from the white midges of the night and multi-winged flying worms to those revoltingly naked-looking larger creatures which might have passed for plucked flying monkeys if they had not been carnivorous and worse. The flying things soared and whirred and danced and spun insanely in the glare, making peculiarly plaintive humming noises. They almost formed a lamp-lit ceiling over the cleared space, and actually did hide the stars. Staring upward, Huyghens could just barely make out the blue-white flame of the space-boat's rockets through the fog of wings and bodies.

The rocket-flame grew steadily in size. Once it tilted to adjust the boat's descending course. It went back to normal. A speck of incandescence at first, it grew until it was like a great star, then a more-than-brilliant moon, and then it was a pitiless glaring eye. Huyghens averted his gaze from it. Sitka Pete sat lumpily and blinked at the dark jungle away from the light. Sourdough ignored the deepening, increasing rocket-roar. He sniffed the air. Faro Nell held Nugget firmly under one huge paw and licked his head as if tidying him up to be seen by company. Nugget wriggled.

The roar became that of ten thousand thunders. A warm breeze blew outward from the landing field. The rocket-boat hurtled downward, and as its flame touched the mist of flying things, they shriveled and burned. Then there were churning clouds of dust everywhere, and the center of the field blazed terribly—and something slid down a shaft of fire—squeezed it flat, and sat on it—and the flame went out. The rocket-boat sat there, resting on its tail-fins, pointing toward the stars from which it came.

There was a terrible silence after the tumult. Then, very faintly, the noises of the night came again. There were sounds like those of organ-pipes, and very faint and apologetic noises like hiccoughs.

All these sounds increased, and suddenly Huyghens could hear quite normally. As he watched, a side-port opened with a clattering, something unfolded from where it had been inset into the hull of the space-boat, and there was a metal passageway across the flame-heated space on which the boat stood.

A man came out of the port. He reached back in and shook hands. Then he climbed down the ladder-rungs to the walkway, and marched above the steaming baked area, carrying a traveling bag. At the end of the walk he stepped to the ground, and moved hastily to the edge of the clearing. He waved to the space-boat. The walkway folded briskly back up to the hull and vanished in it, and almost at once a flame exploded into being under the tail-fins. There were fresh clouds of monstrous, choking dust, a brightness like that of a sun, and noise past the possibility of endurance. Then the light rose swiftly through the dust-cloud, sprang higher, and climbed more swiftly still. When Huyghens' ears again permitted him to hear anything, there was only a diminishing mutter in the heavens and a faint bright speck of light ascending to the sky, swinging eastward as it rose to intercept the ship from which it had descended.

The night-noises of the jungle went on, even though there was a spot of incandescence in the day-bright clearing, and steam rolled up in clouds at the edge of the hottest area. Beyond that edge, a man with a traveling bag in his hand looked about him.

Huyghens advanced toward him as the incandescence dimmed. Sourdough and Sitka preceded him. Faro Nell trailed faithfully, keeping a maternal eye on her offspring. The man in the clearing stared at the parade they made. It would be upsetting, even after preparation, to land at night on a strange planet, to have the ship's boat and all links with the rest of the cosmos depart, and then to find oneself approached—it might seem stalked—by two colossal male Kodiak bears, with a third bear and a cub behind them. A single human figure in such company might seem irrelevant.

The new arrival gazed blankly. He moved back a few steps. Then Huyghens called:

"Hello, there! Don't worry about the bears! They're friends!"

Sitka reached the newcomer. He went warily downwind from him and sniffed. The smell was satisfactory. Man-smell. Sitka sat down with the solid impact of more than a ton of bear meat landing on packed dirt, and regarded the man. Sourdough said

"*Whoosh!*" and went on to sample the air beyond the clearing. Huyghens approached. The newcomer wore the uniform of the Colonial Survey. That was bad. It bore the insignia of a senior officer. Worse.

"Hah!" said the just-landed man. "Where are the robots? What in all the nineteen hells are these creatures? Why did you shift your station? I'm Bordman, here to make a progress report on your colony."

Huyghens said:

"What colony?"

"Loren II Robot Installation—" Then Bordman said indignantly, "Don't tell me that that idiot skipper can have dropped me at the wrong place! This is Loren II, isn't it? And this is the landing field. But where are your robots? You should have the beginning of a grid up! What the devil's happened here and what are these beasts?"

Huyghens grimaced.

"This," he said, "is an illegal, unlicensed settlement. I'm a criminal. These beasts are my confederates. If you don't want to associate with criminals you needn't, of course, but I doubt if you'll live till morning unless you accept my hospitality while I think over what to do about your landing. In reason, I ought to shoot you."

Faro Nell came to a halt behind Huyghens, which was her proper post in all out-door movement. Nugget, however, saw a new human. Nugget was a cub, and therefore friendly. He ambled forward. He wriggled bashfully as he approached Bordman. He sneezed, because he was embarrassed.

His mother overtook him and cuffed him to one side. He wailed. The wail of a six-hundred-pound Kodiak bear-cub is a remarkable sound. Bordman gave ground a pace.

"I think," he said carefully, "that we'd better talk things over. But if this is an illegal colony, of course you're under arrest and anything you say will be used against you."

Huyghens grimaced again.

"Right," he said. "But now if you'll walk close to me, we'll head back to the station. I'd have Sourdough carry your bag—he likes to carry things—but he may need his teeth. We've half a mile to travel." He turned to the animals. "Let's go!" he said commandingly. "Back to the station! Hup!"

Grunting, Sitka Peter arose and took up his duties as advanced point of a combat-team. Sourdough trailed, swinging widely to one side and another. Huyghens and Bordman moved together. Faro Nell and Nugget brought up the rear.

There was only one incident on the way back. It was a night-walker, made hysterical by the lane of light. It poured through the underbrush, uttering cries like maniacal laughter.

Sourdough brought it down, a good ten yards from Huyghens. When it was all over, Nugget bristled up to the dead creature, uttering cub-growls. He feigned to attack it.

His mother whacked him soundly.

There were comfortable, settling-down noises below, as the bears grunted and rumbled, and ultimately were still. The glare from the landing field was gone. The lighted lane through the jungle was dark again. Huyghens ushered the man from the space-boat up into his living quarters. There was a rustling stir, and Semper took his head from under his wing. He stared coldly at the two humans, spread monstrous, seven-foot wings, and fluttered them. He opened his beak and closed it with a snap.

"That's Semper," said Huyghens. "Semper Tyrannis. He's the rest of the terrestrial population here. Not being a fly-by-night sort of creature, he didn't come out to welcome you."

Bordman blinked at the huge bird, perched on a three-inch-thick perch set in the wall.

"An eagle?" he demanded. "Kodiak bears—mutated ones, but still bears—and now an eagle? You've a very nice fighting unit in the bears—"

"They're pack animals too," said Huyghens. "They can carry some hundreds of pounds without losing too much combat efficiency. And there's no problem of supply. They live off the jungle. Not sphexes, though. Nothing will eat a sphex."

He brought out glasses and a bottle and indicated a chair. Bordman put down his traveling bag, took a glass, and sat down.

"I'm curious," he observed. "Why Semper Tyrannis? I can understand Sitka Pete and Sourdough Charley as fighters. But why Semper?"

"He was bred for hawking," said Huyghens. "You sic a dog on something. You sic Semper Tyrannis. He's too big to ride on a hawking-glove, so the shoulders of my coats are padded to let him ride there. He's a flying scout. I've trained him to notify us of sphexes, and in flight he carries a tiny television camera. He's useful, but he hasn't the brains of the bears." Bordman sat down and sipped at his glass.

"Interesting, very interesting! Didn't you say something about shooting me?"

"I'm trying to think of a way out," Huyghens said. "Add up all the penalties for illegal colonization and I'd be in a very bad fix if you got away and reported this set-up. Shooting you would be logical."

"I see that," said Bordman reasonably. "But since the point has come up—I have a blaster trained on you from my pocket."

Huyghens shrugged.

"It's rather likely that my human confederates will be back here before your friends. You'd be in a very tight fix if my friends came back and found you more or less sitting on my corpse."

Bordman nodded.

"That's true, too. Also it's probable that your fellow-terrestrials wouldn't cooperate with me as they have with you. You seem to have the whip hand, even with my blaster trained on you. On the other hand, you could have killed me easily after the boat left, when I'd first landed. I'd have been quite unsuspicious. Therefore you may not really intend to murder me."

Huyghens shrugged again.

"So," said Bordman, "since the secret of getting along with people is that of postponing quarrels, suppose we postpone the question of who kills whom? Frankly, I'm going to send you to prison if I can. Unlawful colonization is very bad business. But I suppose you feel that you have to do something permanent about me. In your place I probably should, too. Shall we declare a truce?"

Huyghens indicated indifference.

"Then I do," Bordman said. "I have to! So—"

He pulled his hand out of his pocket and put a pocket blaster on the table. He leaned back.

"Keep it," said Huyghens. "Loren II isn't a place where you live long unarmed." He turned to a cupboard. "Hungry?"

"I could eat," admitted Bordman.

Huyghens pulled out two meal-packs from the cupboard and inserted them in the readier below. He set out plates.

"Now, what happened to the official, licensed, authorized colony here?" asked Bordman briskly. "License issued eighteen months ago. There was a landing of colonists with a drone-fleet of equipment and supplies. There've been four ship-contacts since. There should be several thousand robots being industrious under adequate human supervision. There should be a hundred-mile-square clearing, planted with food-plants for later human arrivals. There should be a landing-grid at least half-finished. Obviously there should be a space-beacon to guide ships to a landing. There isn't. There's no clearing visible from space. That Crete Line ship has been in orbit for three days, trying to find a place to drop me. Her skipper was fuming. Your beacon is the only one on the planet, and we found it by accident. What happened?"

Huyghens served the food. He said dryly:

"There could be a hundred colonies on this planet without any one knowing of any other. I can only guess about your robots, but I suspect they ran into sphexes."

Bordman paused, with his fork in his hand.

"I read up on this planet, since I was to report on its colony. A sphex is part of the inimical animal life here. Cold-blooded belligerent carnivore, not a lizard but a genus all its own. Hunts in packs. Seven to eight hundred pounds, when adult. Lethally dangerous and simply too numerous to fight. They're why no license was ever granted to human colonists. Only robots could work here, because they're machines. What animal attacks machines?"

Huyghens said:

"What machine attacks animals? The sphexes wouldn't bother robots, of course, but would robots bother the sphexes?" Bordman chewed and swallowed.

"Hold it! I'll agree that you can't make a hunting-robot. A machine can discriminate, but it can't decide. That's why there's no danger of a robot revolt. They can't decide to do something for which they have no instructions. But this colony was planned with full knowledge of what robots can and can't do. As ground was cleared, it was enclosed in an electrified fence which no sphex could touch without frying."

Huyghens thoughtfully cut his food. After a moment:

"The landing was in the winter time," he observed. "It must have been, because the colony survived a while. And at a guess, the last ship-landing was before thaw. The years are eighteen months long here, you know."

"It was in winter that the landing was made," Bordman admitted. "And the last ship-landing was before spring. The idea was to get mines in operation for material, and to have ground cleared and enclosed—in sphex-proof fence before the sphexes came back from the tropics. They winter there, I understand."

"Did you ever see a sphex?" asked Huyghens. Then he said, "No, of course not. But if you took a spitting cobra and crossed it with a wild-cat, painted it tan-and-blue and then gave it hydrophobia and homicidal mania at once, you might have one sphex. But not the race of sphexes. They can climb trees, by the way. A fence wouldn't stop them."

"An electrified fence," said Bordman. "Nothing could climb that!"

"Not one animal," Huyghens told him. "But sphexes are a race. The smell of one dead sphex brings others running with blood in their eyes. Leave a dead sphex alone for six hours and you've got them around by dozens. Two days and there are hundreds. Longer, and you've got thousands of them! They gather to caterwaul over their dead pal and hunt for whoever or whatever killed him."

He returned to his meal. A moment later he said:

"No need to wonder what happened to your colony. During the winter the robots burned out a clearing and put up an electrified fence according to the book. Come spring, the sphexes come back. They're curious, among their other madnesses. A sphex would try to climb the fence just to see what was behind it. He'd be electrocuted. His carcass would bring others, raging because a sphex was dead. Some of them would try to climb the fence, and die. And their corpses would bring others. Presently the fence would break down from the bodies hanging on it, or a bridge of dead beasts' carcasses would be built across it—and from as far downwind as the scent carried there'd be loping, raging, scent-crazed sphexes racing to the spot. They'd pour into the clearing through or over the fence, squalling and screeching for something to kill. I think they'd find it."

Bordman ceased to eat. He looked sick.

"There were pictures of sphexes in the data I read. I suppose that would account for—everything."

He tried to lift his fork. He put it down again. "I can't eat," he said abruptly.

Huyghens made no comment. He finished his own meal, scowling. He rose and put the plates into the top of the cleaner. "Let me see those reports, eh?" he asked dourly. "I'd like to see what sort of a set-up they had, those robots."

Bordman hesitated and then opened his traveling bag. There was a microviewer and records. One entire record was labeled "Specifications for Construction, Colonial Survey," which would contain detailed plans and all requirements of material and workmanship for everything from desks, office, administrative personnel, for use of, to landing-grids, heavy-gravity planets, lift-capacity 100,000 earth-tons. But Huyghens found another. He inserted it and spun the control swiftly here and there, pausing only briefly at index-frames until he came to the section he wanted. He began to study the information with growing impatience.

"Robots, robots, robots!" he snapped. "Why don't they leave them where they belong—in cities to do the dirty work, and on airless planets where nothing unexpected ever happens? Robots don't belong in new colonies. Your colonists depended on them for defense. Dammit, let a man work with robots long enough and he thinks all nature is as limited as they are. This is a plan to set up a controlled environment—on Loren II! Controlled environment—" He swore. "Complacent, idiotic, desk-bound half-wits!"

"Robots are all right," said Bordman. "We couldn't run civilization without them."

"But you can't tame a wilderness with 'em," snapped Huyghens. "You had a dozen men landed, with fifty assembled robots to start with. There were parts for fifteen hundred more, and I'll bet anything I've got the ship-contacts landed more still."

"They did," admitted Bordman.

"I despise 'em," growled Huyghens. "I feel about 'em the way the old Greeks felt about slaves. They're for menial work—the sort of work a man will perform for himself, but that he won't do for another man for pay. Degrading work!"

"Quite aristocratic," said Bordman with a touch of irony. "I take it that robots clean out the bear-quarters downstairs."

"No!" snapped Huyghens. "I do. They're my friends. They fight for me. No robot would do the job right."

He growled, again. The noises of the night went on outside. Organ-tones and hiccoughings and the sound of tack-hammers and slamming doors. Somewhere there was a singularly exact replica of the discordant squeakings of a rusty pump.

"I'm looking," said Huyghens at the microviewer, "for the record of their mining operations. An open-pit operation would not mean a thing. But if they had driven a tunnel, and somebody was there supervising the robots when the colony was wiped out, there's an off-chance he survived a while."

Bordman regarded him with suddenly intent eyes.

"And—"

"Dammit," snapped Bordman, "if so I'll go see! He'd—they'd have no chance at all, otherwise. Not that the chance is good in any case."

Bordman raised his eyebrows.

"I've told you I'll send you to prison if I can," he said. "You've risked the lives of millions of people, maintaining non-quarantined communication with an unlicensed planet. If you did rescue somebody from the ruins of the robot colony—does it occur to you that they'd be witnesses to your unauthorized presence here?"

Huyghens spun the viewer again. He stopped, switched back and forth, and found what he wanted. He muttered in satisfaction: "They *did* run a tunnel." Aloud he said, "I'll worry about witnesses when I have to."

He pushed aside another cupboard door. Inside it were the odds and ends a man makes use of to repair the things about his house that he never notices until they go wrong. There was an assortment of wires, transistors, bolts, and similar stray items.

"What now?" asked Bordman mildly.

"I'm going to try to find out if there's anybody left alive over there. I'd have checked before if I'd known the colony existed. I can't prove they're all dead, but I may prove that somebody's still alive. It's barely two weeks' journey away from here. Odd that two colonies picked spots so near!"

He picked over the oddments he'd selected:

"Confound it!" Bordman said. "How can you check if somebody's alive some hundreds of miles away?"

Huyghens threw a switch and took down a wall-panel, exposing electronic apparatus and circuits behind. He busied himself with it.

"Ever think about hunting for a castaway?" he asked over his shoulder. "Here's a planet with some tens of millions of square miles on it. You know there's a ship down. You've no idea where. You assume the survivors have power—no civilized man will be without power very long, so long as he can smelt metals—but making a space-beacon calls for high-precision measurements and workmanship. It's not to be improvised. So what will your shipwrecked civilized man do, to guide a rescue-ship to the one or two square miles he occupies among some tens of millions on the planet?"

"What?"

"He's had to go primitive, to begin with," Huyghens explained. "He cooks his meat over a fire, and so on. He has to make a strictly primitive signal. It's all he can do without gauges and micrometers and special tools. But he can fill all the planet's atmosphere with a signal that searchers for him can't miss. You see?"

Bordman thought irritably. He shook his head.

"He'll make," said Huyghens, "a spark transmitter. He'll fix its output at the shortest frequency he can contrive, somewhere in the five-to-fifty-meter wave-band, but it will tune very broad—and it will be a plainly human signal. He'll start it broadcasting. Some of those frequencies will go all around the planet under the ionosphere. Any ship that comes in under the radio roof will pick up his signal, get a fix on it, move and get another fix, and then go straight to where the castaway is waiting placidly in a hand-braided hammock, sipping whatever sort of drink he's improvised out of the local vegetation."

Bordman said grudgingly:

"Now that you mention it, of course..."

"My space-phone picks up microwaves," said Huyghens. "I'm shifting a few elements to make it listen for longer stuff. It won't be efficient, but it will catch a distress-signal if one's in the air. I don't expect it, though."

He worked. Bordman sat still a long time, watching him.

Down below, a rhythmic sort of sound arose. It was Sourdough Charley, snoring.

Sitka Pete grunted in his sleep. He was dreaming. In the general room of the station Semper blinked his eyes rapidly and then tucked his head under a gigantic wing and went to sleep. The noises of the Loren II jungle came through the steel-shuttered windows. The nearer moon—which had passed overhead not long before the ringing of the arrival-bell—again came soaring over the eastern horizon. It sped across the sky.

Inside the station, Bordman said angrily:

"See here, Huyghens! You've reason to kill me. Apparently you don't intend to. You've excellent reason to leave that robot colony strictly alone. But you're preparing to help, if there's anybody alive to need it. And yet you're a criminal, and I mean a criminal!

There've been some ghastly bacteria exported from planets like Loren II. There've been plenty of lives lost in consequence, and you're risking more. Why the hell do you do it? Why do you do something that could produce monstrous results—to other human beings?"

Huyghens grunted.

"You're assuming there are no sanitary and quarantine precautions taken by my partners. As a matter of fact, there are. They're taken, all right! As for the rest, you wouldn't understand."

"I don't understand," snapped Bordman, "but that's no proof I can't! —Why are you a criminal?"

Huyghens painstakingly used a screwdriver inside the wall-panel. He lifted out a small electronic assembly, and began to fit in a spaghettied new assembly with larger units.

"I'm cutting my amplification here to hell-and-gone," he observed, "but I think it'll do.... I'm doing what I'm doing," he added calmly, "because it seems to me it fits what I think I am. Everybody acts according to his own real notion of himself. You're a conscientious citizen, a loyal official, a well-adjusted personality. You act that way. You consider yourself an intelligent rational animal. But you don't act that way! You're reminding me of my need to shoot you or something similar, which a merely rational animal would try to make me forget. You happen, Bordman, to be a man. So am I. But I'm aware of it. Therefore I deliberately do things a merely rational animal wouldn't, because they're my notion of what a man who's more than a rational animal should do."

He tightened one small screw after another.

Bordman said:

"Oh. Religion."

"Self-respect," corrected Huyghens. "I don't like robots. They're too much like rational animals. A robot will do whatever it can that its supervisor requires it to do. A merely rational animal will do whatever circumstances require it to do. I wouldn't like a robot unless it had some idea of what was fitting and would spit in my eye if I tried to make it do something else. The bears downstairs, now... They're no robots! They are loyal and honorable beasts, but they'd turn and tear me to bits if I tried to make them do something against their nature. Faro Nell would fight me and all creation together, if we tried to harm Nugget. It would be unintelligent and unreasonable and irrational. She'd lose out and get killed. But I like her that way! And I'll fight you and all creation when you make me try to do something against my nature. I'll be stupid and unreasonable and irrational about it." Then he grinned over his shoulder. "So will you. Only you don't realize it."

He turned back to his task. After a moment he fitted a manual-control knob over a shaft in his haywire assembly. "What did somebody try to make you do?" asked Bordman shrewdly. "What was demanded of you that turned you into a criminal? What are you in revolt against?"

Huyghens threw a switch. He began to turn the knob which controlled his makeshift receiver.

"Why," he said, "when I was young the people around me tried to make me into a conscientious citizen and a loyal employee and a well-adjusted personality. They tried to make me into a highly intelligent rational animal and nothing more. The difference between us, Bordman, is that I found it out. Naturally, I rev—"

He stopped short. Faint, crackling, frying sounds came from the speaker of the space-phone now modified to receive what once were called short waves.

Huyghens listened. He cocked his head intently. He turned the knob very, very slowly. Bordman made an arrested gesture, to call attention to something in the sibilant sound. Huyghens nodded. He turned the knob again, with infinitesimal increments.

Out of the background noise came a patterned mutter. As Huyghens shifted the tuning, it grew louder. It reached a volume where it was unmistakable. It was a sequence of sounds like a discordant buzzing. There were three half-second buzzings with half-second pauses between. A two-second pause. Three full-second buzzings with half-second pauses between. Another two-second pause and three half-second buzzings, again. Then silence for five seconds. Then the pattern repeated.

"The devil!" said Huyghens. "That's a human signal! Mechanically made, too. In fact, it used to be a standard distress call. It was termed an SOS, though I've no idea what that meant. Anyhow, somebody must have read old-fashioned novels some time, to know about it. And so someone is still alive over at your licensed but now smashed-up robot colony. And they're asking for help. I'd say they're likely to need it."

He looked at Bordman.

"The intelligent thing to do is sit back and wait for a ship, either my friends' or yours. A ship can help survivors or castaways much better than we can. It could even find them more easily. But maybe time is important to the poor devils. So I'm going to take the bears and see if I can reach him. You can wait here, if you like. What say?"

Bordman snapped angrily:

"Don't be a fool! Of course I'm coming! What do you take me for? And two of us should have four times the chance of one!"

Huyghens grinned.

"Not quite. You forget Sitka Pete and Sourdough Charley and Faro Nell. There'll be five of us if you come, instead of four. And, of course, Nugget has to come—and he'll be no help—but Semper may make up for him. You won't quadruple our chances, Bordman, but I'll be glad to have you if you want to be stupid and unreasonable and not at all rational, and come with me."

There was a jagged spur of stone looming precipitously over a river-valley. A thousand feet below, a broad stream ran westward to the sea. Twenty miles to the east, a wall of mountains rose sheer against the sky, its peaks seeming to blend to a remarkable evenness of height. Rolling, tumbled ground lay between for as far as the eye could see.

A speck in the sky came swiftly downward. Great pinions spread and flapped, and icy eyes surveyed the rocky space. With more great flappings, Semper the eagle came to ground. He folded his huge wings and turned his head jerkily, his eyes unblinking. A tiny harness held a miniature camera against his chest. He strutted over the bare stone to the highest point and stood there, a lonely and arrogant figure in the vastness.

Crashings and rustlings, and snuffling sounds, and Sitka Pete came lumbering out into the clear space. He wore a harness too, and a pack. The harness was complex, because it had to hold a pack not only in normal travel, but when he stood on his hind legs, and it must not hamper the use of his forepaws in combat.

He went cagily all over the open area. He peered over the edge of the spur's farthest tip, and prowled to the other side and looked down. Once he moved close to Semper and the eagle opened his great curved beak and uttered an indignant noise. Sitka paid no attention.

He relaxed, satisfied. He sat down untidily, his hind legs sprawling. He wore an air approaching benevolence as he surveyed the landscape about and below him.

More snufflings and crashings. Sourdough Charley came into view with Huyghens and Bordman behind him. Sourdough carried a pack, too. Then there was a squealing and Nugget scurried up from the rear, impelled by a whack from his mother. Faro Nell appeared, with the carcass of a stag-like animal lashed to her harness.

"I picked this place from a space-photo," said Huyghens, "to make a directional fix from you. I'll get set up."

He swung his pack from his shoulders to the ground, and extracted an obviously self-constructed device which he set on the ground. It had a whip aerial, which he extended. Then he plugged in a considerable length of flexible wire and unfolded a tiny, improvised directional aerial with an even tinier booster at its base. Bordman slipped his pack from his shoulders and watched. Huyghens put a pair of head-phones over his ears. He looked up and said sharply:

"Watch the bears, Bordman. The wind's blowing up the way we came. Anything that trails us will send its scent on before. The bears will tell us."

He busied himself with the instruments he'd brought. He heard the hissing, frying, background noise which could be anything at all except a human signal. He reached out and swung the small aerial around. Rasping, buzzing tones came in, faintly and then loudly. This receiver, though, had been made for this particular wave-band. It was much more efficient than the modified space-phone had been. It picked up three short buzzes, three long ones, and three short ones again. Three dots, three dashes, and three dots. Over and over again. SOS. SOS. SOS.

Huyghens took a reading and moved the directional aerial a carefully measured distance. He took another reading, shifted it yet again and again, carefully marking and measuring each spot and taking notes of the instrument readings. When he finished, he had checked the direction of the signal not only by loudness but by phase, and had as accurate a fix as could possibly be made with portable apparatus.

Sourdough growled softly. Sitka Pete whiffed the air and arose from his sitting position. Faro Nell whacked Nugget, sending him whimpering to the farthest corner of the flat place. She stood bristling, facing down-hill the way they'd come.

"Damn!" said Huyghens.

He got up and waved his arm at Semper, who had turned his head at the stirrings. Semper squawked and dived off the spur, and was immediately fighting the down-draught beyond it. As Huyghens readied his weapon, the eagle came back overhead. He went magnificently past, a hundred feet high, careening and flapping in the tricky currents. He screamed, abruptly, and screamed again. Huyghens swung a tiny vision-plate from its strap to where he could look into it. He saw, of course, what the tiny camera on Semper's chest could see—reeling, swaying terrain as Semper saw it, though of course without his breadth of field. There were moving objects to be seen through the shifting trees. Their coloring was unmistakable.

"Sphexes," said Huyghens dourly. "Eight of them. Don't look for them to follow our track, Bordman. They run parallel to a trail on either side. That way they attack in breadth and all at once when they catch up. And listen! The bears can handle anything they tangle with—it's our job to pick off the loose ones. And aim for the body! The bullets explode."

He threw off the safety of his weapon. Faro Nell, uttering thunderous growls, went padding to a place between Sitka Pete and Sourdough. Sitka glanced at her and made a whuffing noise, as if derisive of her bloodcurdling sounds. Sourdough grunted. He and Sitka moved farther away from Nell to either side. They would cover a wider front.

There was no other sign of life than the shrillings of the incredibly tiny creatures which on this planet were birds, and Faro Nell's deep-bass, raging growls, and then the click of Bordman's safety going off as he got ready to use the weapon Huyghens had given him.

Semper screamed again, flapping low above the tree-tops, following parti-colored, monstrous shapes beneath.

Eight blue-and-tan fiends came racing out of the underbrush. They had spiny fringes, and horns, and glaring eyes, and they looked as if they had come straight out of hell. On the instant of their appearance they leaped, emitting squalling, spitting squeals that were like the cries of fighting tom-cats ten thousand times magnified. Huyghens' rifle cracked, and its sound was wiped out in the louder detonation of its bullet in sphexian flesh. A tan-and-blue monster tumbled over, shrieking. Faro Nell charged, the very impersonation of white-hot fury. Bordman fired, and his bullet exploded against a tree. Sitka Pete brought his massive forepaws in a clapping, monstrous ear-boxing motion. A sphex died.

Then Bordman fired again. Sourdough Charley whuffed. He fell forward upon a spitting bi-colored fiend, rolled him over, and raked with his hind-claws. The belly-hide of the sphex was tenderer than the rest. The creature rolled away, snapping at its own wounds. Another sphex found itself shaken loose from the tumult about Sitka Pete. It whirled to leap on him from behind, and Huyghens fired. Two plunged upon Faro Nell, and Bordman blasted one and Faro Nell disposed of the other in awesome fury. Then Sitka Pete heaved himself erect—seeming to drip sphexes—and Sourdough waddled over and pulled one off and killed it and went back for another.... Then both rifles cracked together and there was suddenly nothing left to fight.

The bears prowled from one to another of the corpses. Sitka Pete rumbled and lifted up a limp head. Crash! Then another. He went over the lot, whether or not they showed signs of life. When he had finished, they were wholly still.

Semper came flapping down out of the sky. He had screamed and fluttered overhead as the fight went on. Now he landed with a rush. Huyghens went soothingly from one bear to another, calming them with his voice. It took longest to calm Faro Nell, licking Nugget with impassioned solicitude and growling horribly as she licked.

"Come along, now," said Huyghens, when Sitka showed signs of intending to sit down again. "Heave these carcasses over a cliff. Come along! Sitka! Sourdough! Hup!"

He guided them as the two big males somewhat fastidiously lifted up the nightmarish creatures and carried them to the edge of the spur of stone. They let the beasts go bouncing and sliding down into the valley.

"That," said Huyghens, "is so their little pals will gather round them and caterwaul their woe where there's no trail of ours to give them ideas. If we'd been near a river I'd have dumped them in to float down-stream and gather mourners wherever they stranded. Around the station I incinerate them. If I had to leave them, I'd make tracks away. About fifty miles upwind would be a good idea."

He opened the pack Sourdough carried and extracted giant-sized swabs and some gallons of antiseptic. He tended the three Kodiaks in turn, swabbing not only the cuts and scratches they'd received, but deeply soaking their fur where there could be suspicion of spilled sphex-blood.

"This antiseptic deodorizes, too," he told Bordman. "Or we'd be trailed by any sphex who passed to leeward of us. When we start off, I'll swab the bears' paws for the same reason."

Bordman was very quiet. He'd missed his first shot, but the last few seconds of the fight he'd fired very deliberately and every bullet hit. Now he said bitterly:

"If you're instructing me so I can carry on should you be killed, I doubt that it's worthwhile!"

Huyghens felt in his pack and unfolded the enlargements he'd made of the space-photos of this part of the planet. He carefully oriented the map with distant landmarks, and drew a line across the photo.

"The SOS signal comes from somewhere close to the robot colony," he reported. "I think a little to the south of it. Probably from a mine they'd opened up, on the far side of the Sere Plateau. See how I've marked this map? Two fixes, one from the station and one from here. I came away off-course to get a fix here so we'd have two position-lines to the transmitter. The signal could have come from the other side of the planet. But it doesn't."

"The odds would be astronomical against other castaways," protested Bordman.

"No," said Huyghens. "Ships have been coming here. To the robot-colony. One could have crashed. And I have friends, too." He repacked his apparatus and gestured to the bears. He led them beyond the scene of combat and carefully swabbed off their paws, so they could not possibly leave a train of sphex-blood scent behind them. He waved Semper, the eagle, aloft.

"Let's go," he told the Kodiaks. "Yonder! Hup!"

The party headed downhill and into the jungle again. Now it was Sourdough's turn to take the lead, and Sitka Pete prowled more widely behind him. Faro Nell trailed the men, with Nugget. She kept a sharp eye upon the cub. He was a baby, still; he only weighed six hundred pounds. And of course she watched against danger from the rear.

Overhead, Semper fluttered and flew in giant circles and spirals, never going very far away. Huyghens referred constantly to the screen, which showed what the air-borne camera saw. The image tilted and circled and banked and swayed. It was by no means the best air-reconnaissance that could be imagined, but it was the best that would work. Presently Huyghens said:

"We swing to the right, here. The going's bad straight ahead, and it looks like a pack of sphexes has killed and is feeding."

Bordman said:

"It's against reason for carnivores to be as thick as you say! There has to be a certain amount of other animal life for every meat-eating beast. Too many of them would eat all the game and starve."

"They're gone all winter," explained Huyghens, "which around here isn't as severe as you might think. And a good many animals seem to breed just after the sphexes go south. Also, the sphexes aren't around all the warm weather. There's a sort of peak, and then for a matter of weeks you won't see one of them, and suddenly the jungle swarms with them again. Then, presently, they head south. Apparently they're migratory in some fashion, but nobody knows." He said dryly: "There haven't been many naturalists around on this planet. The animal life's inimical."

Bordman fretted. He was accustomed to arrival at a partly or completely finished colonial set-up, and to pass upon the completion or non-completion of the installation as designed. Now he was in an intolerably hostile environment, depending upon an illegal colonist for his life, engaged upon a demoralizingly indefinite enterprise—because the mechanical spark-signal could be working long after its constructors were dead—and his ideas about a number of matters were shaken. He was alive, for example, because of three giant Kodiak bears and a bald eagle. He and Huyghens could have been surrounded by ten thousand robots, and they'd have been killed. Sphexes and robots would have ignored each other, and sphexes would have made straight for the men, who'd have had less than four seconds in which to discover for themselves that they were attacked, prepare to defend themselves, and kill the eight sphexes.

He found Nugget, the cub, ambling uneasily in his wake. The cub flattened his ears miserably when Bordman glanced at him. It occurred to the man that Nugget was receiving a lot of disciplinary thumpings from Faro Nell. He was knocked about psychologically.

His lack of information and unfitness for independent survival in this environment was being hammered into him.

"Hi, Nugget," said Bordman ruefully. "I feel just about the way you do!"

Nugget brightened visibly. He frisked. He tended to gambol. He looked hopefully up into Bordman's face.

The man reached out and patted Nugget's head. It was the first time in all his life that he'd ever petted an animal.

He heard a snuffling sound behind him. Skin crawled at the back of his neck. He whirled.

Faro Nell regarded him—eighteen hundred pounds of she-bear only ten feet away and looking into his eyes. For one panicky instant Bordman went cold all over. Then he realized that Faro Nell's eyes were not burning. She was not snarling, nor did she emit those blood-curdling sounds which the bare prospect of danger to Nugget had produced up on the rocky spur. She looked at him blandly. In fact, after a moment she swung off on some independent investigation of a matter that had aroused her curiosity.

The traveling-party went on, Nugget frisking beside Bordman and tending to bump into him out of pure cub-clumsiness. Now and again he looked adoringly at Bordman, in the instant and overwhelming affection of the very young.

Bordman trudged on. Presently he glanced behind again. Faro Nell was now ranging more widely. She was well satisfied to have Nugget in the immediate care of a man. From time to time he got on her nerves.

A little while later, Bordman called ahead.

"Huyghens! Look here! I've been appointed nursemaid to Nugget!"

Huyghens looked back.

"Oh, slap him a few times and he'll go back to his mother."

"The devil I will!" said Bordman querulously. "I like it!"

The traveling-party went on.

When night fell, they camped. There could be no fire, of course, because all the minute night-things about would come to dance in the glow. But there could not be darkness, equally, because night-walkers hunted in the dark. So Huyghens set out barrier-lamps which made a wall of twilight about their halting-place, and the stag-like creature Faro Nell had carried became their evening meal. Then they slept—at least the men did—and the bears dozed and snorted and waked and dozed again. Semper sat immobile with his head under his wing on a tree-limb. Presently there was a glorious cool hush and all the world glowed in morning-light diffused through the jungle by a newly risen sun. Then they arose and pushed on.

This day they stopped stock-still for two hours while sphexes puzzled over the trail the bears had left. Huyghens discoursed on the need of an anti-scent, to be used on the boots of men and the paws of bears, which would make the following of their trails unpopular with sphexes. Bordman seized upon the idea and suggested that a sphex-repellant odor might be worked out, which would make a human revolting to a sphex. If that were done, humans could go freely about, unmolested.

"Like stink-bugs," said Huyghens, sardonically. "A very intelligent idea! Very rational! You can feel proud!"

And suddenly Bordman was not proud of the idea at all. They camped again. On the third night they were at the base of that remarkable formation, the Sere Plateau, which from a distance looked like a mountain range but was actually a desert tableland. It was not reasonable for a desert to be raised high, while lowlands had rain, but on the fourth morning they found out why. They saw, far, far away, a truly monstrous mountain-mass at the end of the long expanse of the plateau. It was like the prow of a ship. It lay, so Huyghens observed, directly in line with the prevailing winds, and divided them as a ship's prow divides the waters. The moisture-bearing air-currents flowed beside the plateau, not over it, and its interior was desert in the unscreened sunshine of the high altitudes.

It took them a full day to get half-way up the slope. And here, twice, as they climbed, Semper flew screaming over aggregations of sphexes to one side of them or the other. These were much larger groups than Huyghens had ever seen before, fifty to a hundred monstrosities together, where a dozen was a large hunting-pack elsewhere. He looked in the screen, which showed him what Semper saw, four to five miles away. The sphexes padded uphill toward the Sere Plateau in a long line. Fifty—sixty—seventy tan-and-azure beasts out of hell.

"I'd hate to have that bunch jump us," he said candidly to Bordman. "I don't think we'd stand a chance."

"Here's where a robot tank would be useful," Bordman observed.

"Anything armored," conceded Huyghens. "One man in an

armored station like mine would be safe. But if he killed a sphex he'd be besieged. He'd have to stay holed up, breathing the smell of dead sphex, until the odor'd gone away. And he mustn't kill any others or he'd be besieged until winter came."

Bordman did not suggest the advantages of robots in other directions. At that moment, for example, they were working their way up a slope which averaged fifty degrees. The bears climbed without effort despite their burdens. For the men it was infinite toil. Semper, the eagle, manifested impatience with bears and men alike, who crawled so slowly up an incline over which he soared.

He went ahead up the mountainside and teetered in the air currents at the plateau's edge. Huyghens looked in the vision-plate by which he reported.

"How the devil," panted Bordman—they had stopped for a breather, and the bears waited patiently for them—"how do you train bears like these? I can understand Semper."

"I don't train them," said Huyghens, staring into the plate. "They're mutations. In heredity the sex-linkage of physical characteristics is standard stuff. There's also been some sound work done on the gene-linkage of psychological factors. There was need, on my home planet, for an animal who could fight like a fiend, live off the land, carry a pack and get along with men at least as well as dogs do. In the old days they'd have tried to breed the desired physical properties in an animal who already had the personality they wanted. Something like a giant dog, say. But back home they went at it the other way about. They picked the wanted physical characteristics and bred for the personality, the psychology. The job got done over a century ago. The Kodiak bear named Kodius Champion was the first real success. He had everything that was wanted. These bears are his descendants."

"They look normal," commented Bordman.

"They are!" said Huyghens warmly. "Just as normal as an honest dog. They're not trained, like Semper. They train themselves." He looked back into the plate in his hands, which showed the ground six or seven thousand feet higher. "Semper, now, is a trained bird without too much brain. He's educated—a glorified hawk. But the bears want to get along with men. They're emotionally dependent on us. Like dogs. Semper's a servant, but they're companions and friends. He's trained, but they're loyal. He's conditioned. They love us. He'd abandon me if he ever realized he could; he thinks he can only eat what men feed him. But the bears wouldn't want to. They like us. I admit I like them. Maybe because they like me."

Bordman said deliberately:

"Aren't you a trifle loose-tongued, Huyghens? You've told me something that will locate and convict the people who set you up here. It shouldn't be hard to find where bears were bred for psychological mutations, and where a bear named Kodius Champion left descendants. I can find out where you came from now, Huyghens!"

Huyghens looked up from the plate with its tiny swaying television image.

"No harm done," he said amiably. "I'm a criminal there, too. It's officially on record that I kidnapped these bears and escaped with them. Which, on my home planet, is about as heinous a crime as a man can commit. It's worse than horse-theft back on Earth in the old days. The kin and cousins of my bears are highly thought of. I'm quite a criminal, back home." Bordman stared.

"Did you steal them?" he demanded.

"Confidentially," said Huyghens, "no. But prove it!" Then he said: "Take a look in this plate. See what Semper can see up at the plateau's edge."

Bordman squinted aloft, where the eagle flew in great sweeps and dashes. Somehow, by the experience of the past few days, Bordman knew that Semper was screaming fiercely as he flew. He made a dart toward the plateau's border.

Bordman looked at the transmitted picture. It was only four inches by six, but it was perfectly without grain and accurate in color. It moved and turned as the camera-bearing eagle swooped and circled. For an instant the screen showed the steeply sloping mountainside, and off at one edge the party of men and bears could be seen as dots. Then it swept away and showed the top of the plateau.

There were sphexes. A pack of two hundred trotted toward the desert interior. They moved at leisure, in the open. The viewing camera reeled, and there were more. As Bordman watched and as the bird flew higher, he could see still other sphexes moving up over the edge of the plateau from a small erosion-defile here and another one there. The Sere Plateau was alive with the hellish creatures. It was inconceivable that there should be game enough for them to live on. They were visible as herds of cattle would be visible on grazing planets.

It was simply impossible.

"Migrating," observed Huyghens. "I said they did. They're headed somewhere. Do you know, I doubt that it would be healthy for us to try to cross the Plateau through such a swarm of sphexes!"

Bordman swore, in abrupt change of mood.

"But the signal's still coming through. Somebody's alive over at the robot colony. Must we wait till the migration's over?"

"We don't know," Huyghens pointed out, "that they'll stay alive. They may need help badly. We have to get to them. But at the same time—"

He glanced at Sourdough Charley and Sitka Pete, clinging patiently to the mountainside while the men rested and talked. Sitka had managed to find a place to sit down, one massive paw anchoring him in place.

Huyghens waved his arm, pointing in a new direction. "Let's go!" he called briskly. "Let's go! Yonder! Hup!"

They followed the slopes of the Sere Plateau, neither ascending to its level top—where spheres congregated—nor descending into the foothills where spheres assembled. They moved along hillsides and mountain-flanks which sloped anywhere from thirty to sixty degrees, and they did not cover much territory. They practically forgot what it was to walk on level ground.

At the end of the sixth day, they camped on the top of a massive boulder which projected from a mountainous stony wall. There was barely room on the boulder for all the party. Faro Nell fussily insisted that Nugget should be in the safest part, which meant near the mountain-flank. She would have crowded the men outward, but Nugget whimpered for Bordman. Wherefore, when Bordman moved to comfort him, Faro Neil drew back and snorted at Sitka and Sourdough and they made room for her near the edge.

It was a hungry camp. They had come upon tiny rills upon occasion, flowing down the mountainside. Here the bears had drunk deeply and the men had filled canteens. But this was the third night on the mountainside, and there had been no game at all. Huyghens made no move to bring out food for Bordman or himself. Bordman made no comment. He was beginning to participate in the relationship between bears and men, which was not the slavery of the bears but something more. It was two-way. He felt it.

"You'd think," he said, "that since the sphexes don't seem to hunt on their way uphill, there should be some game. They ignore everything as they file up."

This was true enough. The normal fighting formation of sphexes was line abreast, which automatically surrounded anything which offered to flee and outflanked anything which offered fight. But here they ascended the mountain in long files, one after the other, apparently following long-established trails. The wind blew along the slopes and carried scent sidewise. But the sphexes were not diverted from their chosen paths. The long processions of hideous blue-and-tawny creatures—it was hard to think of them as natural beasts, male and female and laying eggs like reptiles on other planets—the long processions simply climbed.

"There've been other thousands of beasts before them," said Huyghens. "They must have been crowding this way for days or even weeks. We've seen tens of thousands in Semper's camera. They must be uncountable, altogether. The first-comers ate all the game there was, and the last-comers have something else on whatever they use for minds."

Bordman protested:

"But so many carnivores in one place is impossible! I know they are here, but they can't be!"

"They're cold-blooded," Huyghens pointed out. "They don't burn food to sustain body-temperature. After all, lots of creatures go for long periods without eating. Even bears hibernate. But this isn't hibernation—or estivation, either."

He was setting up the radiation-wave receiver in the darkness. There was no point in attempting a fix here. The transmitter was on the other side of the sphex-crowded Sere Plateau. The men and bears would commit suicide by crossing here.

Even so, Huyghens turned on the receiver. There came the whispering, scratchy sound of background-noise, and then the signal. Three dots, three dashes, three dots. Huyghens turned it off. Bordman said:

"Shouldn't we have answered that signal before we left the station? To encourage them?"

"I doubt they have a receiver," said Huyghens. "They won't expect an answer for months, anyhow. They'd hardly listen all the time, and if they're living in a mine-tunnel and trying to sneak out for food to stretch their supplies, they'll be too busy to try to make complicated recorders or relays."

Bordman was silent for a moment or two.

"We've got to get food for the bears," he said presently. "Nugget's weaned, and he's hungry."

"We will," Huyghens promised. "I may be wrong, but it seems to me that the number of sphexes climbing the mountain is less than yesterday and the day before. We may have just about crossed the path of their migration. They're thinning out. When we're past their trail, we'll have to look out for nightwalkers and the like again. But I think they wiped out all animal life on their migration-route."

He was not quite right. He was waked in darkness by the sound of slappings and the grunting of bears. Feather-light puffs of breeze beat upon his face. He struck his belt-lamp sharply and the world was hidden by a whitish film which snatched itself away. Something flapped. Then he saw the stars and the emptiness on the edge of which they camped. Then big white things flapped toward him.

Sitka Pete whuffed mightily and swatted. Faro Nell grunted and swung. She caught something in her claws.

"Watch this!" said Huyghens.

More things strangely-shaped and pallid like human skin reeled and flapped crazily toward him.

A huge hairy paw reached up into the light-beam and snatched a flying thing out of it. Another great paw. The three great Kodiaks were on their hind legs, swatting at creatures which flittered insanely, unable to resist the fascination of the glaring lamp. Because of their wild gyrations it was impossible to see them in detail, but they were those unpleasant night-creatures which looked like plucked flying monkeys but were actually something quite different.

The bears did not snarl or snap. They swatted, with a remarkable air of business-like competence and purpose. Small mounds of broken things built up about their feet.

Suddenly there were no more. Huyghens snapped off the light. The bears crunched and fed busily in the darkness.

"Those things are carnivores *and* blood-suckers, Bordman," said Huyghens calmly. "They drain their victims of blood like vampire-bats—they've some trick of not waking them—and when they're dead the whole tribe eats. But bears have thick fur, and they wake when they're touched. And they're omnivorous. They'll eat anything but sphexes, and like it. You might say that those night-creatures came to lunch. They are it, for the bears, who are living off the country as usual."

Bordman uttered a sudden exclamation. He made a tiny light, and blood flowed down his hand. Huyghens passed over his pocket kit of antiseptic and bandages. Bordman stanched the bleeding and bound up his hand. Then he realized that Nugget chewed on something. When he turned the light, Nugget swallowed convulsively. It appeared that he had caught and devoured the creature which had drawn blood from Bordman. But he'd lost none to speak of, at that.

In the morning they started along the sloping scarp of the plateau once more. After marching silently for awhile, Bordman said:

"Robots wouldn't have handled those vampire-things, Huyghens."

"Oh, they could be built to watch for them," said Huyghens, tolerantly. "But you'd have to swat for yourself. I prefer the bears."

He led the way on. Twice Huyghens halted to examine the ground about the mountains' bases through binoculars. He looked encouraged as they went on. The monstrous peak which was like the bow of a ship at the end of the Sere Plateau was visibly nearer. Toward midday, indeed, it loomed high above the horizon, no more than fifteen miles away. And at midday Huyghens called a final halt.

"No more congregations of sphexes down below," he said cheerfully, "and we haven't seen a climbing line of them in miles." The crossing of a sphex-trail had meant simply waiting until one party had passed; and then crossing before another came in view. "I've a hunch we've left their migration route behind. Let's see what Semper tells us!"

He waved the eagle aloft. Like all creatures other than men, the bird normally functioned only for the satisfaction of his appetite, and then tended to loaf or sleep. He had ridden the last few miles perched on Sitka Pete's pack. Now he soared upward and Huyghens watched in the small vision-plate.

Semper went soaring. The image on the plate swayed and turned, and in minutes was above the plateau's edge. Here there were some patches of brush and the ground rolled a little. But as Semper towered higher still, the inner desert appeared. Nearby, it was clear of beasts. Only once, when the eagle banked sharply and the camera looked along the long dimension of the plateau, did Huyghens see any sign of the blue-and-tan beasts. There he saw what looked like masses amounting to herds. Incredible, of course; carnivores do not gather in herds.

"We go straight up," said Huyghens in satisfaction. "We cross the Plateau here, and we can edge downwind a bit, even. I think we'll find something interesting on our way to your robot colony."

He waved to the bears to go ahead uphill.

They reached the top hours later, barely before sunset. And they saw game. Not much, but game at the grassy, brushy border of the desert. Huyghens brought down a shaggy ruminant which surely would not live on a desert. When night fell there was an abrupt chill in the air. It was much colder than night temperatures on the slopes. The air was thin. Bordman thought and presently guessed at the cause. In the lee of the prow-mountain the air was calm. There were no clouds. The ground radiated its heat to empty space. It could be bitterly cold in the night-time, here.

"And hot by day," Huyghens agreed when he mentioned it. "The sunshine's terrifically hot where the air is thin, but on most mountains there's wind. By day, here, the ground will tend to heat up like the surface of a planet without atmosphere. It may be a hundred and forty or fifty degrees on the sand at midday. But it should be cold at night."

It was. Before midnight Huyghens built a fire. There could be no danger of night-walkers where the temperature dropped to freezing.

In the morning the men were stiff with cold, but the bears snorted and moved about briskly. They seemed to revel in the morning chill. Sitka and Sourdough Charley, in fact, became festive and engaged in a mock fight, whacking each other with blows that were only feigned, but would have crushed the skull of any man. Nugget sneezed with excitement as he watched them. Faro Nell regarded them with female disapproval.

They started on. Semper seemed sluggish. After a single brief flight he descended and rode on Sitka's pack, as on the previous day. He perched there, surveying the landscape as it changed from semi-arid to pure desert in their progress. He would not fly. Soaring birds do not like to fly when there are no winds to make currents of which they can take advantage.

Once Huyghens stopped and pointed out to Bordman exactly where they were on the enlarged photograph taken from space, and the exact spot from which the distress-signal seemed to come.

"You're doing it in case something happens to you," said Bordman. "I admit it's sense, but—what could I do to help those survivors even if I got to them, without you?"

"What you've learned about sphexes would help," said Huyghens. "The bears would help. And we left a note back at my station. Whoever grounds at the landing field back there—and the beacon's working—will find instructions to come to the place we're trying to reach."

They started walking again. The narrow patch of non-desert border of the Sere Plateau was behind them, now, and they marched across powdery desert sand.

"See here," said Bordman. "I want to know something. You tell me you're listed as a bear-thief on your home planet. You tell me it's a lie, to protect your friends from prosecution by the Colonial Survey. You're on your own, risking your life every minute of every day. You took a risk in not shooting me. Now you're risking more in going to help men who'd have to be witnesses that you were a criminal. What are you doing it for?" Huyghens grinned.

"Because I don't like robots. I don't like the fact that they're subduing men, making men subordinate to them."

"Go on," insisted Bordman. "I don't see why disliking robots should make you a criminal! Nor men subordinating themselves to robots, either."

"But they are," said Huyghens mildly. "I'm a crank, of course. But—I live like a man on this planet. I go where I please and do what I please. My helpers are my friends. If the robot colony had been a success, would the humans in it have lived like men? Hardly. They'd have to live the way robots let them! They'd have to stay inside a fence the robots built. They'd have to eat foods that robots could raise, and no others. Why, a man couldn't move his bed near a window, because if he did the house-tending robots couldn't work! Robots would serve them—the way the robots determined—but all they'd get out of it would be jobs servicing the robots!"

Bordman shook his head.

"As long as men want robot service, they have to take the service that robots can give. If you don't want those services—"

"I want to decide what I want," said Huyghens, again mildly, "instead of being limited to choose what I'm offered. In my home planet we half-way tamed it with dogs and guns. Then we developed the bears, and we finished the job with them. Now there's population-pressure and the room for bears and dogs—and men!—is dwindling. More and more people are being deprived of the power of decision, and being allowed only the power of choice among the things robots allow. The more we depend on robots, the more limited those choices become. We don't want our children to limit themselves to wanting what robots can provide! We don't want them shriveling to where they abandon everything robots can't give, or won't. We want them to be men and women. Not damned automatons who live by pushing robot-controls so they can live to push robot-controls. If that's not subordination to robots—"

"It's an emotional argument," protested Bordman. "Not everybody feels that way."

"But I feel that way," said Huyghens. "And so do a lot of others. This is a damned big galaxy and it's apt to contain some surprises. The one sure thing about a robot and a man who depends on them is that they can't handle the unexpected. There's going to come a time when we need men who can. So on my home planet, some of us asked for Loren II, to colonize. It was refused—too dangerous. But men can colonize anywhere if they're men. So I came here to study the planet. Especially the sphexes. Eventually, we expected to ask for a license again, with proof that we could handle even those beasts. I'm already doing it in a mild way. But the Survey licensed a robot colony—and where is it?"

Bordman made a sour face.

"You took the wrong way to go about it, Huyghens. It was illegal. It is. It was the pioneer spirit, which is admirable enough, but wrongly directed. After all, it was pioneers who left Earth for the stars. But—"

Sourdough raised up on his hind-legs and sniffed the air. Huyghens swung his rifle around to be handy. Bordman slipped off the safety-catch of his own. Nothing happened.

"In a way," said Bordman, "you're talking about liberty and freedom, which most people think is politics. You say it can be more. In principle, I'll concede it. But the way you put it, it sounds like a freak religion."

"It's self-respect," corrected Huyghens. "You may be—"

Faro Nell growled. She bumped Nugget with her nose, to drive him closer to Bordman. She snorted at him, and trotted swiftly to where Sitka and Sourdough faced toward the broader, sphex-filled expanse of the Sere Plateau. She took up her position between them.

Huyghens gazed sharply beyond them and then all about. "This could be bad!" he said softly. "But luckily there's no wind. Here's a sort of hill. Come along, Bordman!"

He ran ahead, Bordman following and Nugget plumping heavily with him. They reached the raised place, actually a mere hillock no more than five or six feet above the surrounding sand, with a distorted cactus-like growth protruding from the ground. Huyghens stared again. He used his binoculars.

"One sphex," he said curtly. "Just one! And it's out of all reason for a sphex to be alone. But it's not rational for them to gather in hundreds of thousands, either!" He wetted his finger and held it up. "No wind at all."

He used the binoculars again.

"It doesn't know we're here," he added. "It's moving away. Not another one in sight. . . ." He hesitated, biting his lip. "Look here, Bordman! I'd like to kill that one lone sphex and find out something. There's a fifty per cent chance I could find out something really important. But—I might have to run. If I'm right . . ." Then he said grimly, "It'll have to be done quickly. I'm going to ride Faro Nell, for speed. I doubt Sitka or Sourdough will stay behind. But Nugget can't run fast enough. Will you stay here with him?"

Bordman drew in his breath. Then he said calmly: "You know what you're doing, I hope."

"Keep your eyes open. If you see anything, even at a distance, shoot and we'll be back, fast! Don't wait until something's close enough to hit. Shoot the instant you see anything, if you do!"

Bordman nodded. He found it peculiarly difficult to speak again. Huyghens went over to the embattled bears and climbed up on Faro Nell's back, holding fast by her shaggy fur.

"Let's go!" he snapped. "That way! Hup!"

The three Kodiaks plunged away at a dead run, Huyghens lurching and swaying on Faro Nell's back. The sudden rush dislodged Semper from his perch. He flapped wildly and got aloft. Then he followed effortfully, flying low.

It happened very quickly. A Kodiak bear can travel as fast as a race-horse on occasion. These three plunged arrow-straight for a spot perhaps half a mile distant, where a blue-and-tawny shape whirled to face them. There was the crash of Huyghens' weapon from where he rode on Faro Nell's back; the explosion of the weapon and the bullet was one sound. The monster leaped and died.

Huyghens jumped down from Faro Nell. He became feverishly busy at something on the ground. Semper banked and whirled and landed. He watched, with his head on one side.

Bordman stared. Huyghens was doing something to the dead sphex. The two male bears prowled about, while Faro Nell regarded Huyghens with intense curiosity. Back at the hillock, Nugget whimpered a little, and Bordman patted him. Nugget whimpered more loudly. In the distance, Huyghens straightened up and mounted Faro Nell's back. Sitka looked back toward Bordman. He reared upward. He made a noise, apparently, because Sourdough ambled to his side. The two great beasts began to trot back. Semper flapped wildly and—lacking wind—lurched crazily in the air. He landed on Huyghens' shoulder and clung there with his talons.

Then Nugget howled hysterically and tried to swarm up Bordman, as a cub tries to swarm up the nearest tree in time of danger. Bordman collapsed, and the cub upon him—and there was a flash of stinking scaly hide, while the air was filled with the snarling, spitting squeals of a sphex in full leap. The beast had over-jumped, aiming at Bordman and the cub while both were upright and arriving when they had fallen. It went tumbling.

Bordman heard nothing but the fiendish squalling, but in the distance Sitka and Sourdough were coming at rocket-ship speed. Faro Nell let out a roar that fairly split the air. And then there was a furry streaking toward her, bawling, while Bordman rolled to his feet and snatched up his gun. He raged through pure instinct. The sphex crouched to pursue the cub and Bordman swung his weapon as a club. He was literally too close to shoot—and perhaps the sphex had only seen the fleeing bear-cub. But he swung furiously.

And the sphex whirled. Bordman was toppled from his feet. An eight-hundred-pound monstrosity straight out of hell—half wildcat and half spitting cobra with hydrophobia and homicidal mania added—such a monstrosity is not to be withstood when in whirling its body strikes one in the chest.

That was when Sitka arrived, bellowing. He stood on his hind legs, emitting roars like thunder, challenging the sphex to battle. He waddled forward. Huyghens approached, but he could not shoot with Bordman in the sphere of an explosive bullet's destructiveness. Faro Nell raged and snarled, torn between the urge to be sure that Nugget was unharmed, and the frenzied fury of a mother whose offspring has been endangered.

Mounted on Faro Nell, with Semper clinging idiotically to his shoulder, Huyghens watched helplessly as the sphex spat and squalled at Sitka, having only to reach out one claw to let out Bordman's life.

They got away from there, though Sitka seemed to want to lift the limp carcass of his victim in his teeth and dash it repeatedly to the ground. He seemed doubly raging because a man—with whom all Kodius Champion's descendants had an emotional relationship—had been mishandled. But Bordman was not grievously hurt. He bounced and swore as the bears raced for the horizon. Huyghens had flung him up on Sourdough's pack and snapped for him to hold on. He shouted:

"Damn it, Huyghens! This isn't right! Sitka got some deep scratches! That horror's claws may be poisonous!"

But Huyghens snapped "Hup! Hup!" to the bears, and they continued their race against time. They went on for a good two miles, when Nugget wailed despairingly of his exhaustion and Faro Nell halted firmly to nuzzle him.

"This may be good enough," said Huyghens. "Considering that there's no wind and the big mass of beasts is down the plateau and there were only those two around here. Maybe they're too busy to hold a wake, even. Anyhow—"

He slid to the ground and extracted the antiseptic and swabs.

"Sitka first," snapped Bordman. "I'm all right!"

Huyghens swabbed the big bear's wounds. They were trivial, because Sitka Pete was an experienced sphex-fighter. Then Bordman grudgingly let the curiously-smelling stuff—it reeked of ozone—be applied to the slashes on his chest. He held his breath as it stung. Then he said:

"It was my fault, Huyghens. I watched you instead of the landscape. I couldn't imagine what you were doing."

"I was doing a quick dissection," Huyghens told him. "By luck, that first sphex was a female, as I hoped. And she was about to lay her eggs. Ugh! And now I know why the sphexes migrate, and where, and how it is that they don't need game up here."

He slapped a quick bandage on Bordman then led the way eastward, still putting distance between the dead sphexes and his party.

"I'd dissected them before," said Huyghens. "Not enough's been known about them. Some things needed to be found out if men were ever to be able to live here."

"With bears?" asked Bordman ironically.

"Oh, yes," said Huyghens. "But the point is that sphexes come to the desert here to breed, to mate and lay their eggs for the sun to hatch. It's a particular place. Seals return to a special place to mate—and the males, at least, don't eat for weeks on end. Salmon return to their native streams to spawn. They don't eat, and they die afterward. And eels—I'm using Earth examples, Bordman—travel some thousands of miles to the Sargasso to mate and die. Unfortunately, sphexes don't appear to die, but it's clear that they have an ancestral breeding-place and that they come to the Sere Plateau to deposit their eggs!"

Bordman plodded onward. He was angry; angry with himself because he hadn't taken elementary precautions; because he'd felt too safe, as a man in a robot-served civilization forms the habit of doing; because he hadn't used his brain when Nugget whimpered, with even a bear-cub's awareness that danger was near.

"And now," Huyghens added, "I need some equipment that the robot colony has. With it, I think we can make a start toward turning this into a planet that man can live like men on." Bordman blinked.

"What's that?"

"Equipment," said Huyghens impatiently. "It'll be at the robot colony. Robots were useless because they wouldn't pay attention to sphexes. They'd still be. But take out the robot controls and the machines will do. They shouldn't be ruined by a few months' exposure to weather."

Bordman marched on and on. Presently he said:

"I never thought you'd want anything that came from that colony, Huyghens!"

"Why not?" demanded Huyghens impatiently. "When men make machines do what they want, that's all right. Even robots, when they're where they belong. But men will have to handle flame-casters in the job I want them for. There have to be some, because there was a hundred-mile clearing to be burned off for the colony. And earth-sterilizers, intended to kill the seeds of any plants that robots couldn't handle. We'll come back up here, Bordman, and at the least we'll destroy the spawn of these infernal beasts! If we can't do more than that, just doing that every year will wipe out the race in time. There are probably other hordes than this, with other breeding-places. But we'll find them too. We'll make this planet into a place where men from my world can come and still be men!"

Bordman said sardonically:

"It was sphexes that beat the robots. Are you sure you aren't planning to make this world safe for robots?"

Huyghens laughed.

"You've only seen one night-walker," he said. "And how about those things on the mountain-slope, which would have drained you of blood? Would you care to wander about this planet with only a robot body-guard, Bordman? Hardly! Men can't live on this planet with only robots to help them. You'll see!"

They found the colony after only ten days' more travel and after many sphexes and more than a few stag-like creatures and shaggy ruminants had fallen to their weapons and the bears. And they found survivors.

There were three of them, hard-bitten and bearded and deeply embittered. When the electrified fence went down, two of them were away at a mine tunnel, installing a new control panel for the robots who worked in it. The third was in charge of the mining operation. They were alarmed by the stopping of communication with the colony and went back in a tank-truck to find out what had happened, and only the fact that they were unarmed saved them. They found sphexes prowling and caterwauling about the fallen colony, in numbers they still did not wholly believe. The sphexes smelled men inside the armored vehicle, but couldn't break in. In turn, the men couldn't kill them, or they'd have been trailed to the mine and besieged there for as long as they could kill an occasional monster.

The survivors stopped all mining, of course, and tried to use remote-controlled robots for revenge and to get supplies for them. Their mining-robots were not designed for either task. And they had no weapons. They improvised miniature throwers of burning rocket-fuel, and they sent occasional prowling sphexes away screaming with scorched hides. But this was useful only because it did not kill the beasts. And it cost fuel. In the end they barricaded themselves and used the fuel only to keep a spark-signal going against the day when another ship came to seek the colony. They stayed in the mine as in a prison, on short rations, without real hope. For diversion they could only contemplate the mining-robots they could not spare fuel to run and which could not do anything but mine.

When Huyghens and Bordman reached them, they wept. They hated robots and all things robotic only a little less than they hated sphexes. But Huyghens explained, and, armed with weapons from the packs of the bears, they marched to the dead colony with the male Kodiaks as point and advance-guard, and with Faro Nell bringing up the rear. They killed sixteen sphexes on the way. In the now overgrown clearing there were four more. In the shelters of the colony they found only foulness and the fragments of what had been men. But there was some food—not much, because the sphexes clawed at anything that smelled of men, and had ruined the plastic packets of radiation-sterilized food. But there were some supplies in metal containers which were not destroyed.

And there was fuel, which men could use when they got to the control-panels of the equipment. There were robots everywhere, bright and shining and ready for operation, but immobile, with plants growing up around and over them.

They ignored those robots, and instead fueled tracked flame-casters—after adapting them to human rather than robot operation—and the giant soil-sterilizer which had been built to destroy vegetation that robots could not be made to weed out or cultivate. Then they headed back for the Sere Plateau.

As time passed Nugget became a badly spoiled bear-cub, because the freed men approved passionately of anything that would even grow up to kill sphexes. They petted him to excess when they camped.

Finally they reached the plateau by a sphex-trail to the top and sphexes came squalling and spitting to destroy them. While Bordman and Huyghens fired steadily, the great machines swept up with their special weapons. The earth-sterilizer, it developed, was deadly against animal life as well as seeds, when its diathermic beam was raised and aimed.

Presently the bears were not needed, because the scorched corpses of sphexes drew live ones from all parts of the plateau even in the absence of noticeable breezes. The official business of the sphexes was presumably finished, but they came to caterwaul and seek vengeance—which they did not find. After a while the survivors of the robot colony drove the machines in great circles around the huge heap of slaughtered fiends, destroying new arrivals as they came. It was such a killing as men had never before made on any planet, and there would be very few left of the sphex-horde which had bred in this particular patch of desert.

Nor would more grow up, because the soil-sterilizer would go over the dug-up sand where the sphex-spawn lay hidden for the sun to hatch. And the sun would never hatch them.

Huyghens and Bordman, by that time, were camped on the edge of the plateau with the Kodiaks. Somehow it seemed more befitting for the men of the robot colony to conduct the slaughter. After all, it was those men whose companions had been killed.

There came an evening when Huyghens cuffed Nugget away from where he sniffed too urgently at a stag-steak cooking on the campfire. Nugget ambled dolefully behind the protecting form of Bordman and sniveled.

"Huyghens," said Bordman, "we've got to come to a settlement of our affairs. You're an illegal colonist, and it's my duty to arrest you."

Huyghens regarded him with interest.

"Will you offer me lenience if I tell on my confederates?" he asked, "or may I plead that I can't be forced to testify against myself?"

Bordman said:

"It's irritating! I've been an honest man all my life, but—I don't believe in robots as I did, except in their place. And their place isn't here! Not as the robot colony was planned, anyhow. The sphexes are nearly wiped out, but they won't be extinct and robots can't handle them. Bears and men will have to live here or else the people who do will have to spend their lives behind sphex-proof fences, accepting only what robots can give them. And there's much too much on this planet for people to miss it! To live in a robot-managed environment on a planet like Loren II wouldn't—it wouldn't be self-respecting!"

"You wouldn't be getting religious, would you?" asked Huyghens drily. "That was your term for self-respect before."

"You don't let me finish!" protested Bordman. "It's my job to pass on the work that's done on a planet before any but the first-landed colonists may come there to live. And of course to see that specifications are followed. Now, the robot colony I was sent to survey was practically destroyed. As designed, it wouldn't work. It couldn't survive."

Huyghens grunted. Night was falling. He turned the meat over the fire.

"In emergencies," said Bordman, "colonists have the right to call on any passing ship for aid. Naturally! So my report will be that the colony as designed was impractical, and that it was overwhelmed and destroyed except for three survivors who holed up and signaled for help. They did, you know!"

"Go on," grunted Huyghens.

"So," said Bordman, "it just happened—just happened, mind you—that a ship with you and the bears and the eagle on board picked up the distress-call. So you landed to help the colonists. That's the story. Therefore it isn't illegal for you to be here. It was only illegal for you to be here when you were needed. But we'll pretend you weren't."

Huyghens glanced over his shoulder in the deepening night. He said:

"I wouldn't believe that if I told it myself. Do you think the Survey will?"

"They're not fools," said Bordman tartly. "Of course they won't! But when my report says that because of this unlikely series of events it is practical to colonize the planet, whereas before it wasn't, and when my report proves that a robot colony alone is stark nonsense, but that with bears and men from your world added, so many thousand colonists can be received per year... And when that much is true, anyhow...

Huyghens seemed to shake a little as a dark silhouette against the flames.

"My reports carry weight," insisted Bordman. "The deal will be offered, anyhow! The robot colony organizers will have to agree or they'll have to fold up. And your people can hold them up for nearly what terms they choose."

Huyghens' shaking became understandable. It was laughter.

"You're a lousy liar, Bordman," he said. "Isn't it unintelligent and unreasonable to throw away a lifetime of honesty just to get me out of a jam? You're not acting like a rational animal, Bordman. But I thought you wouldn't, when it came to the point."

Bordman squirmed.

"That's the only solution I can think of," he said. "But it'll work."

"I accept it," said Huyghens, grinning. "With thanks. If only because it means another few generations of men can live like men on a planet that is going to take a lot of taming. And—if you want to know—because it keeps Sourdough and Sitka and Nell and Nugget from being killed because I brought them here illegally."

Something pressed hard against Bordman: Nugget, the cub, pushed urgently against him in his desire to get closer to the fragrantly cooking meat. He edged forward. Bordman toppled from where he squatted on the ground. He sprawled. Nugget sniffed luxuriously.

"Slap him," said Huyghens. "He'll move back."

"I won't!" said Bordman indignantly from where he lay. "I won't do it. He's my friend!"

It was ironic that, after all, Bordman found that he couldn't afford to retire. His pay, of course, had been used to educate his children and maintain his home. And Lani III was an expensive world to live on. It was now occupied by a thriving, bustling population with keen business instincts, and the vapor-curtains about it were commonplaces, now, and few people remembered a time when they hadn't existed, when it was a world below habitability for anybody. So Bordman wasn't a hero. As a matter of history he had done such and such. As a matter of fact he was simply a citizen who could be interviewed for visicasts on holidays, but hadn't much that was new to say.

But he lived on Lani III for three years, and he was restless. His children were grown and married, now, and they hadn't known him too well, anyhow. He'd been away so much! He didn't fit into the world whose green fields and oceans and rivers he was responsible for. But it was infinitely good to be with Riki again. There was so much that each remembered, to be shared with the other, that they had plenty to talk about.

Three years after his official retirement, he was asked to take on another Survey job for which there was no other qualified man. He talked to his wife. On retirement pay, life was not easy. In retirement, it wasn't satisfactory. And Riki was free too, now. Her children were safely on their own. Bordman would always need her. She advised him for both their sakes. And he went back to Survey duty with the stipulation that he should have quarters and facilities for his wife as well as himself on all assignments.

They had five wonderful years. Bordman was near the top of the ladder, then. His children wrote faithfully. He was busy on Kelmin IV, and his wife had a garden there, when he was summoned to Sector Headquarters with first priority urgency.

Superiority

ARTHUR C. CLARKE

In making this statement—which I do of my own free will—I wish first to make it perfectly clear that I am not in any way trying to gain sympathy, nor do I expect any mitigation of whatever sentence the Court may pronounce. I am writing this in an attempt to refute some of the lying reports broadcast over the prison radio and published in the papers I have been allowed to see. These have given an entirely false picture of the true cause of our defeat, and as the leader of my race's armed forces at the cessation of hostilities I feel it my duty to protest against such libels upon those who served under me.

I also hope that this statement may explain the reasons for the application I have twice made to the Court, and will now induce it to grant a favor for which I can see no possible grounds of refusal.

The ultimate cause of our failure was a simple one: despite all statements to the contrary, it was not due to lack of bravery on the part of our men, or to any fault of the Fleet's. We were defeated by one thing only—by the inferior science of our enemies. I repeat—by the *inferior* science of our enemies.

When the war opened we had no doubt of our ultimate victory. The combined fleets of our allies greatly exceeded in number and armament those which the enemy could muster against us, and in almost all branches of military science we were their superiors. We were sure that we could maintain this superiority. Our belief proved, alas, to be only too well founded.

At the opening of the war our main weapons were the long-range homing torpedo, dirigible ball-lightning and the various modifications of the Klydon beam. Every unit of the Fleet was equipped with these and though the enemy possessed similar weapons their installations were generally of lesser power. Moreover, we had behind us a far greater military Research Organization, and with this initial advantage we could not possibly lose.

The campaign proceeded according to plan until the Battle of the Five Suns. We won this, of course, but the opposition proved stronger than we had expected. It was realized that victory might be more difficult, and more delayed, than had first been imagined. A conference of supreme commanders was therefore called to discuss our future strategy.

Present for the first time at one of our war conferences was Professor-General Norden, the new Chief of the Research Staff, who had just been appointed to fill the gap left by the death of Malvar, our greatest scientist. Malvar's leadership had been responsible, more than any other single factor, for the efficiency and power of our weapons. His loss was a very serious blow, but no one doubted the brilliance of his successor—though many of us disputed the wisdom of appointing a theoretical scientist to fill a post of such vital importance. But we had been overruled.

I can well remember the impression Norden made at that conference. The military advisers were worried, and as usual turned to the scientists for help. Would it be possible to improve our existing weapons, they asked, so that our present advantage could be increased still further?

Norden's reply was quite unexpected. Malvar had often been asked such a question—and he had always done what we requested.

"Frankly, gentlemen," said Norden, "I doubt it. Our existing weapons have practically reached finality. I don't wish to criticize my predecessor, or the excellent work done by the Research Staff in the last few generations, but do you realize that there has been no basic change in armaments for over a century? It is, I am afraid, the result of a tradition that has become conservative. For too long, the Research Staff has devoted itself to perfecting old weapons instead of developing new ones. It is fortunate for us that our opponents have been no wiser: we cannot assume that this will always be so."

Norden's words left an uncomfortable impression, as he had no doubt intended. He quickly pressed home the attack.

"What we want are *new* weapons—weapons totally different from any that have been employed before. Such weapons can be made: it will take time, of course, but since assuming charge I have replaced some of the older scientists with young men and have directed research into several unexplored fields which show great promise. I believe, in fact, that a revolution in warfare may soon be upon us."

We were skeptical. There was a bombastic tone in Norden's voice that made us suspicious of his claims. We did not know, then, that he never promised anything that he had not already almost perfected in the laboratory. *In the laboratory*—that was the operative phrase.

Norden proved his case less than a month later, when he demonstrated the Sphere of Annihilation, which produced complete disintegration of matter over a radius of several hundred meters. We were intoxicated by the power of the new weapon, and were quite prepared to overlook one fundamental defect—the fact that it was a sphere and hence destroyed its rather complicated generating equipment at the instant of formation. This meant, of course, that it could not be used on warships but only on guided missiles, and a great program was started to convert all homing torpedoes to carry the new weapon. For the time being all further offensives were suspended.

We realize now that this was our first mistake. I still think that it was a natural one, for it seemed to us then that all our existing weapons had become obsolete overnight, and we already regarded them as almost primitive survivals. What we did not appreciate was the magnitude of the task we were attempting, and the length of time it would take to get the revolutionary super-weapon into battle. Nothing like this had happened for a hundred years and we had no previous experience to guide us.

The conversion problem proved far more difficult than anticipated. A new class of torpedo had to be designed, as the standard model was too small. This meant in turn that only the larger ships could launch the weapon, but we were prepared to accept this penalty. After six months, the heavy units of the Fleet were being equipped with the Sphere. Training maneuvers and tests had shown that it was operating satisfactorily and we were ready to take it into action. Norden was already being hailed as the architect of victory, and had half promised even more spectacular weapons.

Then two things happened. One of our battleships disappeared completely on a training flight, and an investigation showed that under certain conditions the ship's long-range radar could trigger the Sphere immediately after it had been launched. The modification needed to overcome this defect was trivial, but it caused a delay of another month and was the source of much bad feeling between the naval staff and the scientists. We were ready for action again—when Norden announced that the radius of effectiveness of the Sphere had now been increased by ten, thus multiplying by a thousand the chances of destroying an enemy ship.

So the modifications started all over again, but everyone agreed that the delay would be worth it. Meanwhile, however, the enemy had been emboldened by the absence of further attacks and had made an unexpected onslaught. Our ships were short of torpedoes, since none had been coming from the factories, and were forced to retire. So we lost the systems of Kyrane and Floranus, and the planetary fortress of Rhamsandron.

It was an annoying but not a serious blow, for the recaptured systems had been unfriendly, and difficult to administer. We had no doubt that we could restore the position in the near future, as soon as the new weapon became operational.

These hopes were only partially fulfilled. When we renewed our offensive, we had to do so with fewer of the Spheres of Annihilation than had been planned, and this was one reason for our limited success. The other reason was more serious.

While we had been equipping as many of our ships as we could with the irresistible weapon, the enemy had been building feverishly. His ships were of the old pattern with the old weapons—but they now out-numbered ours. When we went into action, we found that the numbers ranged against us were often 100 percent greater than expected, causing target confusion among the automatic weapons and resulting in higher losses than anticipated. The enemy losses were higher still, for once a Sphere had reached its objective, destruction was certain, but the balance had not swung as far in our favor as we had hoped.

Moreover, while the main fleets had been engaged, the enemy had launched a daring attack on the lightly held systems of Eriston, Duranus, Carmanidora and Pharanidon—recapturing them all. We were thus faced with a threat only fifty light-years from our home planets.

There was much recrimination at the next meeting of the supreme commanders. Most of the complaints were addressed to Norden-Grand Admiral Taxaris in particular maintaining that thanks to our admittedly irresistible weapon we were now considerably worse off than before. We should, he claimed, have continued to build conventional ships, thus preventing the loss of our numerical superiority.

Norden was equally angry and called the naval staff ungrateful bunglers. But I could tell that he was worried—as indeed we all were—by the unexpected turn of events. He hinted that there might be a speedy way of remedying the situation.

We now know that Research had been working on the Battle Analyzer for many years, but at the time it came as a revelation to us and perhaps we were too easily swept off our feet. Norden's argument, also, was seductively convincing. What did it matter, he said, if the enemy had twice as many ships as we—if the efficiency of ours could be doubled or even trebled? For decades the limiting factor in warfare had been not mechanical but biological—it had become more and more difficult for any single mind, or group of minds, to cope with the rapidly changing complexities of battle in three-dimensional space. Norden's mathematicians had analyzed some of the classic engagements of the past, and had shown that even when we had been victorious we had often operated our units at much less than half of their theoretical efficiency.

The Battle Analyzer would change all this by replacing the operations staff with electronic calculators. The idea was not new, in theory, but until now it had been no more than a Utopian dream. Many of us found it difficult to believe that it was still anything but a dream: after we had run through several very complex dummy battles, however, we were convinced.

It was decided to install the Analyzer in four of our heaviest ships, so that each of the main fleets could be equipped with one. At this stage, the trouble began—though we did not know it until later.

The Analyzer contained just short of a million vacuum tubes and needed a team of five hundred technicians to maintain and operate it. It was quite impossible to accommodate the extra staff aboard a battleship, so each of the four units had to be accompanied by a converted liner to carry the technicians not on duty. Installation was also a very slow and tedious business, but by gigantic efforts it was completed in six months.

Then, to our dismay, we were confronted by another crisis. Nearly five thousand highly skilled men had been selected to serve the Analyzers and had been given an intensive course at the Technical Training Schools. At the end of seven months, 10 percent of them had had nervous breakdowns and only 40 per cent had qualified.

Once again, everyone started to blame everyone else. Norden, of course, said that the Research Staff could not be held responsible, and so incurred the enmity of the Personnel and Training Commands. It was finally decided that the only thing to do was to use two instead of four Analyzers and to bring the others into action as soon as men could be trained. There was little time to lose, for the enemy was still on the offensive and his morale was rising.

The first Analyzer fleet was ordered to recapture the system of Eriston. On the way, by one of the hazards of war, the liner carrying the technicians was struck by a roving mine. A warship would have survived, but the liner with its irreplaceable cargo was totally destroyed. So the operation had to be abandoned.

The other expedition was, at first, more successful. There was no doubt at all that the Analyzer fulfilled its designers' claims, and the enemy was heavily defeated in the first engagements. He withdrew, leaving us in possession of Saphran, Leucon and Hexanerax. But his Intelligence Staff must have noted the change in our tactics and the inexplicable presence of a liner in the heart of our battlefleet. It must have noted, also, that our first fleet had been accompanied by a similar ship—and had withdrawn when it had been destroyed.

In the next engagement, the enemy used his superior numbers to launch an overwhelming attack on the Analyzer ship and its unarmed consort. The attack was made without regard to losses—both ships were, of course, very heavily protected—and it succeeded. The result was the virtual decapitation of the Fleet, since an effectual transfer to the old operational methods proved impossible. We disengaged under heavy fire, and so lost all our gains and also the systems of Lormyia, Ismarnus, Beronis, Alphanidon and Sideneus.

At this stage, Grand Admiral Taxaris expressed his disapproval of Norden by committing suicide, and I assumed supreme command.

The situation was now both serious and infuriating. With stubborn conservatism and complete lack of imagination, the enemy continued to advance with his old-fashioned and inefficient but now vastly more numerous ships. It was galling to realize that if we had only continued building, without seeking new weapons, we would have been in a far more advantageous position. There were many acrimonious conferences at which Norden defended the scientists while everyone else blamed them for all that had happened. The difficulty was that Norden had proved every one of his claims: he had a perfect excuse for all the disasters that had occurred. And we could not now turn back—the search for an irresistible weapon must go on. At first it had been a luxury that would shorten the war. Now it was a necessity if we were to end it victoriously.

We were on the defensive, and so was Norden. He was more than ever determined to reestablish his prestige and that of the Research Staff. But we had been twice disappointed, and would not make the same mistake again. No doubt Norden's twenty thousand scientists would produce many further weapons: we would remain unimpressed.

We were wrong. The final weapon was something so fantastic that even now it seems difficult to believe that it ever existed. Its innocent, noncommittal name—The Exponential Field—gave no hint of its real potentialities. Some of Norden's mathematicians had discovered it during a piece of entirely theoretical research into the properties of space, and to everyone's great surprise their results were found to be physically realizable.

It seems very difficult to explain the operation of the Field to the layman. According to the technical description, it "produces an exponential condition of space, so that a finite distance in normal, linear space may become infinite in pseudo-space." Norden gave an analogy which some of us found useful. It was as if one took a flat disk of rubber—representing a region of normal space—and then pulled its center out to infinity. The circumference of the disk would be unaltered—but its "diameter" would be infinite. That was the sort of thing the generator of the Field did to the space around it.

As an example, suppose that a ship carrying the generator was surrounded by a ring of hostile machines. If it switched on the Field, each of the enemy ships would think that it—and the ships on the far side of the circle—had suddenly receded into nothingness. Yet the circumference of the circle would be the same as before: only the journey to the center would be of infinite duration, for as one proceeded, distances would appear to become greater and greater as the "scale" of space altered.

It was a nightmare condition, but a very useful one. Nothing could reach a ship carrying the Field: it might be englobed by an enemy fleet yet would be as inaccessible as if it were at the other side of the Universe. Against this, of course, it could not fight back without switching off the Field, but this still left it at a very great advantage, not only in defense but in offense. For a ship fitted with the Field could approach an enemy fleet undetected and suddenly appear in its midst.

This time there seemed to be no flaws in the new weapon. Needless to say, we looked for all the possible objections before we committed ourselves again. Fortunately the equipment was fairly simple and did not require a large operating staff. After much debate, we decided to rush it into production, for we realized that time was running short and the war was going against us. We had now lost about the whole of our initial gains and enemy forces had made several raids into our own solar system.

We managed to hold off the enemy while the Fleet was reequipped and the new battle techniques were worked out. To use the Field operationally it was necessary to locate an enemy formation, set a course that would intercept it, and then switch on the generator for the calculated period of time. On releasing the Field again—if the calculations had been accurate—one would be in the enemy's midst and could do great damage during the resulting confusion, retreating by the same route when necessary.

The first trial maneuvers proved satisfactory and the equipment seemed quite reliable. Numerous mock attacks were made and the crews became accustomed to the new technique. I was on one of the test flights and can vividly remember my impressions as the Field was switched on. The ships around us seemed to dwindle as if on the surface of an expanding bubble: in an instant they had vanished completely. So had the stars—but presently we could see that the Galaxy was still visible as a faint band of light around the ship. The virtual radius of our pseudo-space was not really infinite, but some hundred thousand light-years, and so the distance to the farthest stars of our system had not been greatly increased—though the nearest had of course totally disappeared. These training maneuvers, however, had to be canceled before they were completed, owing to a whole flock of minor technical troubles in various pieces of equipment, notably the communications circuits. These were annoying, but not important, though it was thought best to return to Base to clear them up.

At that moment the enemy made what was obviously intended to be a decisive attack against the fortress planet of Iton at the limits of our Solar System. The Fleet had to go into battle before repairs could be made.

The enemy must have believed that we had mastered the secret of invisibility—as in a sense we had. Our ships appeared suddenly out of nowhere and inflicted tremendous damage—for a while. And then something quite baffling and inexplicable happened.

I was in command of the flagship *Hircania* when the trouble started. We had been operating as independent units, each against assigned objectives. Our detectors observed an enemy formation at medium range and the navigating officers measured its distance with great accuracy. We set course and switched on the generator.

The Exponential Field was released at the moment when we should have been passing through the center of the enemy group. To our consternation, we emerged into normal space at a distance of many hundred miles—and when we found the enemy, he had already found us. We retreated, and tried again. This time we were so far away from the enemy that he located us first.

Obviously, something was seriously wrong. We broke communicator silence and tried to contact the other ships of the Fleet to see if they had experienced the same trouble. Once again we failed—and this time the failure was beyond all reason, for the communication equipment appeared to be working perfectly. We could only assume, fantastic though it seemed, that the rest of the Fleet had been destroyed.

I do not wish to describe the scenes when the scattered units of the Fleet struggled back to Base. Our casualties had actually been negligible, but the ships were completely demoralized. Almost all had lost touch with one another and had found that their ranging equipment showed inexplicable errors. It was obvious that the Exponential Field was the cause of the troubles, despite the fact that they were only apparent when it was switched off.

The explanation came too late to do us any good, and Norden's final discomfiture was small consolation for the virtual loss of the war. As I have explained, the Field generators produced a radial distortion of space, distances appearing greater and greater as one approached the center of the artificial pseudo-space. When the Field was switched off, conditions returned to normal.

But not quite. It was never possible to restore the initial state *exactly*. Switching the Field on and off was equivalent to an elongation and contraction of the ship carrying the generator, but there was a hysteretic effect, as it were, and the initial condition was never quite reproducible, owing to all the thousands of electrical changes and movements of mass aboard the ship while the Field was on. These asymmetries and distortions were cumulative, and though they seldom amounted to more than a fraction of one per cent, that was quite enough. It meant that the precision ranging equipment and the tuned circuits in the communication apparatus were thrown completely out of adjustment. Any single ship could never detect the change—only when it compared its equipment with that of another vessel, or tried to communicate with it, could it tell what had happened.

It is impossible to describe the resultant chaos. Not a single component of one ship could be expected with certainty to work aboard another. The very nuts and bolts were no longer interchangeable, and the supply position became quite impossible. Given time, we might even have overcome these difficulties, but the enemy ships were already attacking in thousands with weapons which now seemed centuries behind those that we had invented. Our magnificent Fleet, crippled by our own science, fought on as best it could until it was overwhelmed and forced to surrender. The ships fitted with the Field were still invulnerable, but as fighting units they were almost helpless. Every time they switched on their generators to escape from enemy attack, the permanent distortion of their equipment increased. In a month, it was all over.

This is the true story of our defeat, which I give without prejudice to my defense before this Court. I make it, as I have said, to counteract the libels that have been circulating against the men who fought under me, and to show where the true blame for our misfortunes lay.

Finally, my request, which as the Court will now realize I make in no frivolous manner and which I hope will therefore be granted.

The Court will be aware that the conditions under which we are housed and the constant surveillance to which we are subjected night and day are somewhat distressing. Yet I am not complaining of this: nor do I complain of the fact that shortage of accommodation has made it necessary to house us in pairs.

But I cannot be held responsible for my future actions if I am compelled any longer to share my cell with Professor Norden, late Chief of the Research Staff of my armed forces.

The Horars of War

GENE WOLFE

The three friends in the trench looked very much alike as they labored in the rain. Their hairless skulls were slickly naked to it, their torsos hairless too, and supple with smooth muscles that ran like oil under the wet gleam.

The two, who really were 2909 and 2911, did not mind the jungle around them although they detested the rain that rusted their weapons, and the snakes and insects, and hated the Enemy. But the one called 2910, the real as well as the official leader of the three, did; and that was because 2909 and 2911 had stainless-steel bones; but there was no 2910 and there had never been.

The camp they held was a triangle. In the center, the CP-Aid Station where Lieutenant Kyle and Mr. Brenner slept: a hut of ammo cases packed with dirt whose lower half was dug into the soggy earth. Around it were the mortar pit (NE), the recoilless rifle pit (NW), and Pinocchio's pit (S); and beyond these were the straight lines of the trenches: First Platoon, Second Platoon, Third Platoon (the platoon of the three). Outside of which were the primary wire and an antipersonnel mine field.

And outside that was the jungle. But not completely outside. The jungle set up outposts of its own of swift-sprouting bamboo and elephant grass, and its crawling creatures carried out untiring patrols of the trenches. The jungle sheltered the Enemy, taking him to its great fetid breast to be fed while it sopped up the rain and of it bred its stinging gnats and centipedes.

✧ ✧ ✧

An ogre beside him, 2911 drove his shovel into the ooze filling the trench, lifted it to shoulder height, dumped it; 2910 did the same thing in his turn, then watched the rain work on the scoop of mud until it was slowly running back into the trench again. Following his eyes 2911 looked at him and grinned. The HORAR's face was broad, hairless, flat-nosed and high-cheeked; his teeth were pointed and white like a big dog's. And he, 2910, knew that that face was his own. Exactly his own. He told himself it was a dream, but he was very tired and could not get out.

Somewhere down the trench the bull voice of 2900 announced the evening meal and the others threw down their tools and jostled past toward the bowls of steaming mash, but the thought of food nauseated 2910 in his fatigue, and he stumbled into the bunker he shared with 2909 and 2911. Flat on his air mattress he could leave the nightmare for a time; return to the sane world of houses and sidewalks, or merely sink into the blessed nothingness that was far better....

Suddenly he was bolt upright on the cot, blackness still in his eyes even while his fingers groped with their own thought for his helmet and weapon. Bugles were blowing from the edge of the jungle, but he had time to run his hand under the inflated pad of the mattress and reassure himself that his hidden notes were safe before 2900 in the trench outside yelled, "Attack! Fall out! Man your firing points!"

It was one of the stock jokes, one of the jokes so stock, in fact, that it had ceased to be anything anyone laughed at, to say "Horar" your firing point (or whatever it was that according to the book should be "manned"). The HORARS in the squad he led used the expression to 2910 just as he used it with them, and when 2900 never employed it the omission had at first unsettled him. But 2900 did not really suspect. 2900 just took his rank seriously.

He got into position just as the mortars put up a parachute flare that hung over the camp like a white rose of fire. Whether because of his brief sleep or the excitement of the impending fight his fatigue had evaporated, leaving him nervously alert but unsteady. From the jungle a bugle sang. "Ta-taa... taa-taa..." and off to the platoon's left rear the First opened up with their heavy weapons on a suicide squad they apparently thought they saw on the path leading to the northeast gate. He watched, and after half a minute something stood up on the path and grabbed for its midsection before it fell, so there *was* a suicide squad.

Some one, he told himself. *Someone.* Not *something.* Someone grabbed *for his* midsection. They were all human out there.

The First began letting go with personal weapons as well, each deep cough representing a half dozen dartlike fletchettes flying in an inescapable pattern three feet broad. "Eyes front, 2910!" barked 2900.

There was nothing to be seen out there but a few clumps of elephant grass. Then the white flare burned out. "They ought to put up another one," 2911 on his right said worriedly.

"A star in the east for men not born of women," said 2910 half to himself, and regretted the blasphemy immediately.

"That's where they need it," 2911 agreed, "The First is having it pretty hot over there. But we could use some light here too."

He was not listening. At home in Chicago, during that inexpressibly remote time which ran from a dim memory of playing on a lawn under the supervision of a smiling giantess to that moment two years ago when he had submitted to surgery to lose every body and facial hair he possessed and undergo certain other minor alterations, he had been unconsciously preparing himself for this. Lifting weights and playing football to develop his body while he whetted his mind on a thousand books; all so that he might tell, making others feel at a remove...

Another flare went up and there were three dark silhouettes sliding from the next-nearest clump of elephant grass to the nearest. He fired his M-19 at them, then heard the HORARS on either side of him fire too. From the sharp corner where their own platoon met the Second a machine gun opened up with tracers. The nearest grass clump sprang into the air and somersaulted amid spurts of earth.

There was a moment of quiet, then five rounds of high explosive came in right behind them as though aimed for Pinocchio's pit. *Crump. Crump. Crump... Crump. Crump.* (2900 would be running to ask Pinocchio if he were hurt.)

Someone else had been moving down the trench toward them, and he could hear the mumble of the new voice become a gasp when the H.E. rounds came in. Then it resumed, a little louder and consequently a bit more easily understood. "How are you? You feel all right? Hit?"

And most of the HORARS answering, "I'm fine, sir," or "We're okay, sir," but because HORARS did have a sense of humor some of them said things like, "How do we transfer to the Marines, sir?" or, "My pulse just registered nine thou', sir. 3000 took it with the mortar sight."

We often think of strength as associated with humorlessness, he had written in the news magazine which had, with the Army's cooperation, planted him by subterfuge of surgery among these Homolog Organisms (Army Replacement Simulations). *But,* he had continued, *this is not actually the case. Humor is a prime defense of the mind, and knowing that to strip the mind of it is to leave it shieldless, the Army and the Synthetic Biology Service have wisely included a charming dash in the makeup of these synthesized replacements for human infantry.*

That had been before he discovered that the Army and the SBS had tried mightily to weed that sense of the ridiculous out, but found that if the HORARS were to maintain the desired intelligence level they could not.

Brenner was behind him now, touching his shoulder. "How are you? Feel all right?"

He wanted to say, "I'm half as scared as you are, you dumb Dutchman," but he knew that if he did the fear would sound in his voice; besides, the disrespect would be unthinkable to a HORAR.

He also wanted to say simply, "A-okay, sir," because if he did Brenner would pass on to 2911 and he would be safe. But he had a reputation for originality to keep up, and he needed that reputation to cover him when he slipped, as he often did, sidewise of HORAR standards. He answered: "You ought to look in on Pinocchio, sir. I think he's cracking up." From the other end of the squad, 2909's quiet chuckle rewarded him, and Brenner, the man most dangerous to his disguise, continued down the trench....

Fear was necessary because the will to survive was *very* necessary. And a humanoid form was needed if the HORARS were to utilize the mass of human equipment already on hand. Besides, a human-shaped *(homolog?* no, that merely meant *similar, homological)* HORAR had out-scored all the fantastic forms SBS had been able to dream up in a super-realistic (public opinion would never have permitted it with human soldiers) test carried out in the Everglades.

(Were they merely duplicating? Had all this been worked out

before with some greater war in mind? And had He Himself, the Scientist Himself, come to take the form of His creations to show that he too could bear the unendurable?)

2909 was at his elbow, whispering. "Do you see something, Squad Leader? Over there?" Dawn had come without his noticing.

With fingers clumsy from fatigue he switched the control of his M-19 to the lower, 40mm grenade-launching barrel. The grenade made a brief flash at the spot 2909 had indicated. "No," he said, "I don't see anything now." The fine, soft rain which had been falling all night was getting stronger. The dark clouds seemed to roof the world. (Was he fated to reenact what had been done for mankind? It could happen. The Enemy took humans captive, but there was nothing they would not do to HORAR prisoners. Occasionally patrols found the bodies spread-eagled, with bamboo stakes driven through their limbs; and he could only be taken for a HORAR. He thought of a watercolor of the crucifixion he had seen once. Would the color of his own blood be crimson lake?)

From the CP the observation ornithocopter rose on flapping wings.

"I haven't heard one of the mines go for quite a while," 2909 said. Then there came the phony-sounding bang that so often during the past few weeks had closed similar probing attacks. Squares of paper were suddenly fluttering all over the camp.

"Propaganda shell," 2909 said unnecessarily, and 2911 climbed casually out of the trench to get a leaflet, then jumped back to his position. "Same as last week," he said, smoothing out the damp rice paper.

Looking over his shoulder, 2910 saw that he was correct. For some reason the Enemy never directed his propaganda at the HORARS, although it was no secret that reading skills were implanted in HORAR minds with the rest of their instinctive training. Instead it was always aimed at the humans in the camp, and played heavily on the distaste they were supposed to feel at being "confined with half-living flesh still stinking of chemicals." Privately, 2910 thought they might have done better, at least with Lieutenant Kyle, to have dropped that approach and played up sex. He also got the impression from the propaganda that the Enemy thought there were far more humans in the camp than there actually were.

Well, the Army—with far better opportunities to know—was

wrong as well. With a few key generals excepted, the Army thought there were only two. . . .

He had made the All-American. How long ago it seemed. No coach, no sportswriter had ever compared his stocky, muscular physique with a HORAR's. And he had majored in journalism, had been ambitious. How many men, with a little surgical help, could have passed here?

"Think it sees anything?" he heard 2911 ask 2909. They were looking upward at the "bird" sailing overhead.

The ornithocopter could do everything a real bird could except lay eggs. It could literally land on a strand of wire. It could ride thermals like a vulture, and dive like a hawk. And the bird-motion of its wings was wonderfully efficient, saving power-plant weight that could be used for zoom-lenses and telecameras. He wished he were in the CP watching the monitor screen with Lieutenant Kyle instead of standing with his face a scant foot above the mud (they had tried stalked eyes like a crab's in the Everglades, he remembered, but the stalks had become infected by a fungus . . .)

As though in answer to his wish, 2900 called, "Show some snap for once, 2910. He says He wants us in the CP."

When he himself thought *He, He* meant God; but 2900 meant Lieutenant Kyle. That was why 2900 was a platoon leader, no doubt; that and the irrational prestige of a round number. He climbed out of the trench and followed him to the CP. They needed a communicating trench, but that was something there hadn't been time for yet.

Brenner had someone (2788? looked like him, but he couldn't be certain) down on his table. Shrapnel, probably from a grenade. Brenner did not look up as they came in, but 2910 could see his face was still white with fear although the attack had been over for a full quarter of an hour. He and 2900 ignored the SBS man and saluted Lieutenant Kyle.

The company commander smiled. "Stand at ease, HORARS. Have any trouble in your sector?"

2900said, "No, sir. The light machine gun got one group of three and 2910 here knocked off a group of two. Not much of an attack on our front, sir."

Lieutenant Kyle nodded. "I thought your platoon had the easiest time of it, 2900, and that's why I've picked you to run a patrol for me this morning."

"That's fine with us, sir."

"You'll have Pinocchio, and I thought you'd want to go yourself and take 2910's gang."

He glanced at 2910. "Your squad still at full strength?"

2910 said, "Yes, sir," making an effort to keep his face impassive. He wanted to say: I shouldn't have to go on patrol. I'm human as you are, Kyle, and patrolling is for things grown in tubes, things fleshed out around metal skeletons, things with no family and no childhood behind them.

Things like my friends.

He added, "We've been the luckiest squad in the company, sir."

"Fine. Let's hope your luck holds, 2910." Kyle's attention switched back to 2900. "I've gotten under the leaf canopy with the ornithocopter and done everything except make it walk around like a chicken. I can't find a thing and it's drawn no fire, so you ought to be okay. You'll make a complete circuit of the camp without getting out of range of mortar support. Understand?"

2900 and 2910 saluted, about-faced, and marched out. 2910 could feel the pulse in his neck; he flexed and unflexed his hands unobtrusively as he walked. 2900 asked, "Think we'll catch any of them?" It was an unbending for him—the easy camaraderie of anticipated action.

"I'd say so. I don't think the CO's had long enough with the bird to make certain of anything except that their main force has pulled out of range. I hope so."

And that's the truth, he thought. Because a good hot fire-fight would probably do it—round the whole thing out so I can get out of here.

Every two weeks a helicopter brought supplies and, when they were needed, replacements. Each trip it also carried a correspondent whose supposed duty was to interview the commanders of the camps the copter visited. The reporter's name was Keith Thomas, and for the past two months he had been the only human being with whom 2910 could take off his mask.

Thomas carried scribbled pages from the notebook under 2910's air mattress when he left, and each time he came managed to find some corner in which they could speak in private for a few seconds. 2910 read his mail then and gave it back. It embarrassed him to realize that the older reporter viewed him with something not far removed from hero worship.

I can get out of here, he repeated to himself. Write it up and tell Keith we're ready to use the letter.

2900 ordered crisply, "Fall in your squad. I'll get Pinocchio and meet you at the south gate."

"Right." He was suddenly seized with a desire to tell someone, even 2900, about the letter. Keith Thomas had it, and it was really only an undated note, but it was signed by a famous general at Corps Headquarters. Without explanation it directed that number 2910 be detached from his present assignment and placed under the temporary orders of Mr. K. Thomas, Accredited Correspondent. And Keith would use it any time he asked him to. In fact, he had wanted to on his last trip.

He could not remember giving the order, but the squad was falling in, lining up in the rain for his inspection almost as smartly as they had on the drill field back at the crèche. He gave "At Ease" and looked them over while he outlined the objectives of the patrol. As always, their weapons were immaculate despite the dampness, their massive bodies ramrod-straight, their uniforms as clean as conditions permitted.

The L.A. Rams with guns, he thought proudly. Barking "On Phones," he flipped the switch on his helmet that would permit 2900 to knit him and the squad together with Pinocchio in a unified tactical unit. Another order and the HORARS deployed around Pinocchio with the smoothness of repeated drill, the wire closing the south gate was drawn back, and the patrol moved out.

With his turret retracted, Pinocchio the robot tank stood just three feet high, and he was no wider than an automobile; but he was as long as three, so that from a distance he had something of the look of a railroad flatcar. In the jungle his narrow front enabled him to slip between the trunks of the unconquerable giant hardwoods, and the power in his treads could flatten saplings and bamboo. Yet resilient organics and sintered metals had turned the rumble of the old, manned tanks to a soft hiss for Pinocchio. Where the jungle was free of undergrowth he moved as silently as a hospital cart.

His immediate precursor had been named "Punch," apparently in the sort of simpering depreciation which found "Shillelagh" acceptable for a war rocket. "Punch"—a bust in the mouth.

But Punch, which like Pinocchio had possessed a computer brain and no need of a crew (or for that matter room for one except for an exposed vestigial seat on his deck), had required wires to communicate with the infantry around him. Radio had been tried, but the problems posed by static, jamming, and outright enemy forgery of instructions had been too much for Punch.

Then an improved model had done away with those wires and some imaginative officer had remembered that "Mr. Punch" had been a knockabout marionette—and the wireless improvement was suddenly very easy to name. But, like Punch and its fairytale namesake, it was vulnerable if it went out into the world alone.

A brave man (and the Enemy had many) could hide himself until Pinocchio was within touching distance. And a well-instructed one could then place a hand grenade or a bottle of gasoline where it would destroy him. Pinocchio's three-inch-thick armor needed the protection of flesh, and since he cost as much as a small city and could (if properly protected) fight a regiment to a stand, he got it.

Two scouts from 2910's squad preceded him through the jungle, forming the point of the diamond. Flankers moved on either side of him "beating the bush" and, when it seemed advisable, firing a pattern of fletchettes into any suspicious-looking piece of undergrowth. Cheerful, reliable 2909, the assistant squad leader, with one other HORAR, formed the rear guard. As patrol leader 2900's position was behind Pinocchio, and as squad leader 2910's was in front.

The jungle was quiet with an eerie stillness, and it was dark under the big trees. "Though I walk in the valley of the shadow..."

Made tiny by the phones, 2900 squeaked in his ear, "Keep the left flankers farther out!" 2910 acknowledged and trotted over to put his own stamp on the correction, although the flankers, 2913, 2914, and 2915, had already heard it and were moving to obey. There was almost no chance of trouble this soon, but that was no excuse for a slovenly formation. As he squeezed between two trees something caught his eye and he halted for a moment to examine it. It was a skull; a skull of bone rather than a smooth HORAR skull of steel, and so probably an Enemy's.

A big "E" Enemy's, he thought to himself. A man to whom the normal HORAR conditioning of exaggerated respect bordering on worship did not apply.

Tiny and tinny, "Something holding you up, 2910?"

"Be right there." He tossed the skull aside. A man whom even a HORAR could disobey; a man even a HORAR could kill. The skull had looked old, but it could not have been old. The ants would have picked it clean in a few days, and in a few weeks it would rot. But it was probably at least seventeen or eighteen years old.

The ornithocopter passed them on flapping wings, flying its own search pattern. The patrol went on.

Casually 2910 asked his helmet mike, "How far are we going? Far as the creek?"

2900's voice squeaked, "We'll work our way down the bank a quarter mile, then cut west," then with noticeable sarcasm added, "if that's okay with you?"

Unexpectedly Lieutenant Kyle's voice came over the phones. "2910's your second in command, 2900. He has a duty to keep himself informed of your plans."

But 2910, realizing that a real HORAR would not have asked the question, suddenly also realized that he knew more about HORARS than the company commander did. It was not surprising, he ate and slept with them in a way Kyle could not, but it was disquieting. He probably knew more than Brenner, strict biological mechanics excepted, as well.

The scouts had reported that they could see the sluggish jungle stream they called the creek when Lieutenant Kyle's voice came over the phones again. As routinely as he had delivered his mild rebuke to 2900 he announced, "Situation Red here. An apparent battalion-level attack hitting the North Point. Let's suck it back in, patrol."

Pinocchio swiveled 180 degrees by locking his right tread, and the squad turned in a clockwise circle around him. Kyle said distantly, "The recoillesses don't seem to have found the range yet, so I'm going out to give them a hand. Mr. Brenner will be holding down the radio for the next few minutes."

2900 transmitted, "We're on our way, sir."

Then 2910 saw a burst of automatic weapons fire cut his scouts down. In an instant the jungle was a pandemonium of sound.

Pinocchio's radar had traced the bullets back to their source and his main armament slammed a 155mm shell at it, but crossfire was suddenly slicing in from all around them. The bullets striking Pinocchio's turret screamed away like damned souls. 2910 saw grenades arc out of nowhere and something struck his thigh with terrible force. He made himself say, "I'm hit, 2909, take the squad," before he looked at it. Mortar shells were dropping in now and if his assistant acknowledged, he did not hear.

A bit of jagged metal from a grenade or a mortar round had laid the thigh open, but apparently missed the big artery supplying the lower leg. There was no spurt, only a rapid welling of blood, and shock still held the injury numb. Forcing himself, he pulled apart the lips of the wound to make sure it was clear of foreign matter. It was very deep but the bone was not broken; at least so it seemed.

Keeping as low as he could, he used his trench knife to cut away the cloth of his trousers leg, then rigged a tourniquet with his belt. His aid packet contained a pad of gauze, and tape to hold it in place. When he had finished he lay still, holding his M-19 and looking for a spot where its fire might do some good. Pinocchio was firing his turret machine gun in routine bursts, sanitizing likely-looking patches of jungle; otherwise the fight seemed to have quieted down.

2900's voice in his ear called, "Wounded? We got any wounded?"

He managed to say, "Me. 2910." A HORAR would feel some pain, but not nearly as much as a man. He would have to fake the insensitivity as best he could. Suddenly it occurred to him that he would be invalided out, would not have to use the letter, and he was glad.

"We thought you bought it, 2910. Glad you're still around."

Then Brenner's voice cutting through the transmission jumpy with panic: "We're being overrun here! Get the Pinocchio back at once."

In spite of his pain 2910 felt contempt. Only Brenner would say "*the* Pinocchio." 2900 sent, "Coming, sir," and unexpectedly was standing over him, lifting him up.

He tried to look around for the squad. "We lose many?"

"Four dead and you." Perhaps no other human would have detected the pain in 2900's harsh voice. "You can't walk with that, can you?"

"I couldn't keep up."

"You ride Pinocchio then." With surprising gentleness the platoon leader lifted him into the little seat the robot tank's director used when road speeds made running impractical. What was left of the squad formed a skirmish line ahead. As they began to trot forward he could hear 2900 calling, "Base camp! Base camp! What's your situation there, sir?"

"Lieutenant Kyle's dead," Brenner's voice came back. "3003 just came in and told me Kyle's dead!"

"Are you holding?"

"I don't know." More faintly 2910 could hear him asking, "Are they holding, 3003?"

"Use the periscope, sir. Or if it still works, the bird."

Brenner chattered, "I don't know if we're holding or not. 3003 was hit and now he's dead. I don't think he knew anyway. You've got to hurry."

It was contrary to regulations, but 2910 flipped off his helmet phone to avoid hearing 2900's patient reply. With Brenner no longer gibbering in his ears he could hear not too distantly the sound of explosions which must be coming from the camp. Small arms fire made an almost incessant buzz as a background for the whizz—bang! of incoming shells and the coughing of the camp's own mortars.

Then the jungle was past and the camp lay in front of them. Geysers of mud seemed to be erupting from it everywhere. The squad broke into a full run, and even while he rolled, Pinocchio was firing his 155 in support of the camp.

They faked us out, 2910 reflected. His leg throbbed painfully but distantly and he felt light-headed and dizzy—as though he were an ornithocopter hovering in the misty rain over his own body. With the light-headedness came a strange clarity of mind.

They faked us out. They got us used to little probes that pulled off at sunrise, and then when we sent Pinocchio out they were going to ambush us and take the camp. It suddenly occurred to him that he might find himself still on this exposed seat in the middle of the battle; they were already approaching the edge of the mine field, and the HORARS ahead were moving into squad column so as not to overlap the edges of the cleared lane. "Where are we going, Pinocchio?" he asked, then realized his phone was still off. He reactivated it and repeated the question.

Pinocchio droned, "Injured HORAR personnel will be delivered to the Command Post for Synthetic Biology Service attention," but 2910 was no longer listening. In front of them he could hear what sounded like fifty bugles signaling for another Enemy attack.

The south side of the triangular camp was deserted, as though the remainder of their platoon had been called away to reinforce the First and Second; but with the sweeping illogic of war there was no Enemy where they might have entered unresisted.

"Request assistance from Synthetic Biology Service for injured HORAR personnel," Pinocchio was saying. Talking did not interfere with his firing the 155, but when Brenner did not come out after a minute or more, 2910 managed to swing himself down, catching his weight on his good leg. Pinocchio rolled away at once.

The CP bunker was twisted out of shape, and he could see where several near-misses had come close to knocking it out completely. Brenner's white face appeared in the doorway as he was about to go in. "Who's that?"

"2910. I've been hit—let me come in and lie down."

"They won't send us an air strike. I radioed for one and they say this whole part of the country's socked in; they say they wouldn't be able to find us."

"Get out of the door. I'm hit and I want to come in and lie down." At the last moment he remembered to add, "Sir."

Brenner moved reluctantly aside. It was dim in the bunker but not dark.

"You want me to look at that leg?"

2910 had found an empty stretcher, and he laid himself on it, moving awkwardly to keep from flexing his wound. "You don't have to," he said. "Look after some of the others." It wouldn't do for Brenner to begin poking around. Even rattled as he was he might notice something.

The SBS man went back to his radio instead. His frantic voice sounded remote and faint. It was ecstasy to lie down.

At some vast distance, voices were succeeding voices, argument meeting argument, far off. He wondered where he was.

Then he heard the guns and knew. He tried to roll onto his side and at the second attempt managed to do it, although the light-headedness was worse than ever. 2893 was lying on the stretcher next to him, and 2893 was dead.

At the other end of the room, the end that was technically the CP, he could hear Brenner talking to 2900. "If there were a chance," Brenner was saying, "you know I'd do it, Platoon Leader."

"What's happening?" he asked. "What's the matter?" He was too dazed to keep up the HORAR role well, but neither of them noticed.

"It's a division," Brenner said. "A whole Enemy division. We can't hold off that kind of force."

He raised himself on his elbow. "What do you mean?"

"I talked to them... I raised them on the radio, and it's a whole division. They got one of their officers who could speak English to talk to me. They want us to surrender."

"*They* say it's a division, sir," 2900 put in evenly.

2910 shook his head, trying to clear it. "Even if it were, with Pinocchio..."

"The Pinocchio's gone."

2900 said soberly, "We tried to counterattack, 2910, and they knocked Pinocchio out and threw us back. How are you feeling?"

"They've got at least a division," Brenner repeated stubbornly.

2910's mind was racing now, but it was as though it were running endless wind sprints on a treadmill. If Brenner were going to give up, 2900 would never even consider disobeying, no matter how much he might disagree. There were various ways, though, in which he could convince Brenner he was a human being—given time. And Brenner could, Brenner would, tell the Enemy, so that he too would be saved. Eventually the war would be over and he could go home. No one would blame him. If Brenner were going—

Brenner was asking, "How many effectives left?"

"Less than forty, sir." There was nothing in 2900's tone to indicate that a surrender meant certain death to him, but it was true. The Enemy took only human prisoners. (Could 2900 be convinced? Could he make any of the HORARS understand, when they had eaten and joked with him, knew no physiology, and thought all men not Enemy demigods? Would they believe him if he were to try to take command?)

He could see Brenner gnawing at his lower lip. "I'm going to surrender," the SBS man said at last. A big one, mortar or bombardment rocket, exploded near the CP, but he appeared not to notice it. There was a wondering, hesitant note in his voice—as though he were still trying to accustom himself to the idea.

"Sir—" 2900 began.

"I forbid you to question my orders." The SBS man sounded firmer now. "But I'11 ask them to make an exception this time, Platoon Leader. Not to do," his voice faltered slightly, "what they usually do to nonhumans."

"It's not that," 2900 said stolidly. "It's the folding up. We don't mind dying, sir, but we want to die fighting."

One of the wounded moaned, and 2910 wondered for a moment, if he, like himself, had been listening.

Brenner's self-control snapped. "You'll die any damn way I tell you!"

"Wait." It was suddenly difficult for 2910 to talk, but he managed to get their attention. "2900, Mr. Brenner hasn't actually ordered you to surrender yet, and you're needed on the line. Go now and let me talk to him." He saw the HORAR leader hesitate and added, "He can reach you on your helmet phone if he wants to; but go now and fight."

With a jerky motion 2900 turned and ducked out the narrow bunker door. Brenner, taken by surprise, said, "What is it, 2910? What's gotten into you?"

He tried to rise, but he was too weak. "Come here, Mr. Brenner," he said. When the SBS man did not move he added, "I know a way out."

"Through the jungle?" Brenner scoffed in his shaken voice, "that's absurd." But he came. He leaned over the stretcher, and before he could catch his balance 2910 had pulled him down.

"What are you doing?"

"Can't you tell? That's the point of my trench knife you feel on your neck."

Brenner tried to struggle, then subsided when the pressure of the knife became too great. "You—can't—do this."

"I can. Because I'm not a HORAR. I'm a man, Brenner, and it's very important for you to understand that." He felt rather than saw the look of incredulity on Brenner's face. "I'm a reporter, and two years ago when the Simulations in this group were ready for activation I was planted among them. I trained with them and now I've fought with them, and if you've been reading the right magazine you must have seen some of the stories I've filed. And since you're a civilian too, with no more right to command than I have, I'm taking charge." He could sense Brenner's swallow.

"Those stories were frauds—it's a trick to gain public acceptance of the HORARS. Even back in Washington everybody in SBS knows about them."

The chuckle hurt, but 2910 chuckled. "Then why've I got this knife at your neck, Mr. Brenner?"

The SBS man was shaking. "Don't you see how it was, 2910? No human could live as a HORAR does, running miles without tiring and only sleeping a couple of hours a night, so we did the next best thing. Believe me, I was briefed on it all when I was assigned to this camp; I know all about you, 2910."

"What do you mean?"

"Damn it, let me go. You're a HORAR, and you can't treat a human like this." He winced as the knife pressed cruelly against his throat, then blurted, "They couldn't make a reporter a HORAR, so they *took* a HORAR. They took you, 2910, and made you a reporter. They implanted all the memories of an actual man in your mind at the same time they ran the regular instinct tapes. They gave you a soul, if you like, but you are a HORAR."

"They must have thought that up as a cover for me, Brenner. That's what they told you so you wouldn't report it or try to deactivate me when I acted unlike the others. I'm a man."

"You couldn't be."

"People are tougher than you think, Brenner; you've never tried."

"I'm telling you—"

"Take the bandage off my leg."

"What?"

He pressed again with the point of the knife. "The bandage. Take it off."

When it was off he directed, "Now spread the lips of the wound." With shaking fingers Brenner did so. "You see the bone? Go deeper if you have to. What is it?"

Brenner twisted his neck to look at him directly, his eyes rolling. "It's stainless steel."

2910 looked then and saw the bright metal at the bottom of the cleft of bleeding flesh; the knife slid into Brenner's throat without resistance, almost as though it moved itself. He wiped the blade on Brenner's dead arm before he sheathed it.

Ten minutes later when 2900 returned to the CP he said nothing; but 2910 saw his eyes and knew that 2900 knew. From his stretcher he said, "You're in full command now."

2900 glanced again at Brenner's body. A second later he said slowly, "He was a sort of Enemy, wasn't he? Because he wanted to surrender, and Lieutenant Kyle would never have done that."

"Yes, he was."

"But I couldn't think of it that way while he was alive." 2900 looked at him thoughtfully. "You know, you have something, 2910. A spark. Something the rest of us lack." For a moment he fingered his chin with one huge hand. "That's why I made you a squad leader; that and to get you out of some work, because sometimes you couldn't keep up. But you've that spark, somehow."

2910 said, "I know. How is it out there?"

"We're still holding. How do you feel?"

"Dizzy. There's a sort of black stuff all around the sides when I see. Listen, will you tell me something, if you can, before you go?"

"Of course."

"If a human's leg is broken very badly, what I believe they call a compound spiral fracture, is it possible for the human doctors to take out a section of the bone and replace it with a metal substitute?"

"I don't know," 2900 answered. "What does it matter?

Vaguely 2910 said, "I think I knew of a football player once they did that to. At least, I seem now to remember it...I had forgotten for a moment."

Outside the bugles were blowing again.

Near him the dying HORAR moaned.

An American news magazine sometimes carries, just inside its front cover among the advertisements, a column devoted to news of its own people. Two weeks after a correspondent named Thomas filed the last article of a series which had attracted national and even international attention, the following item appeared there;

> *The death of a staffer in war is no unique occurrence in the history of this publication, but there is a particular poignancy about that of the young man whose stories, paradoxically, to conceal his number have been signed only with his name (see* PRESS*). The airborne relief force, which arrived too late to save the camp at which he had resigned his humanity to work and fight, reports that he apparently died assisting the assigned SBS specialist in caring for the creatures whose lot he had, as nearly as a human can, made his own. Both he and the specialist were bayonetted when the camp was overrun.*

Fireproof

HAL CLEMENT

Hart waited a full hour after the last sounds had died away before cautiously opening the cover of his refuge. Even then he did not feel secure for some minutes, until he had made a thorough search of the storage chamber; then a smile of contempt curled his lips.

"The fools!" he muttered. "They do not examine their shipments at all. How do they expect to maintain their zone controls with such incompetents in charge?" He glanced at the analyzers in the forearm of his spacesuit, and revised his opinion a trifle—the air in the chamber was pure carbon dioxide; any man attempting to come as Hart had, but without his own air supply, would not have survived the experiment. Still, the agent felt, they should have searched.

There was, however, no real time for analyzing the actions of others. He had a job to do, and not too long in which to do it. However slack the organization of this launching station might be, there was no chance whatever of reaching any of its vital parts unchallenged; and after the first challenge, success and death would be running a frightfully close race.

He glided back to the crate which had barely contained his doubled-up body, carefully replaced and reseated the cover, and then rearranged the contents of the chamber to minimize the chance of that crate's being opened first. The containers were bulky, but nothing in the free-falling station had any weight, and the job did not take long even for a man unaccustomed to a total lack of apparent gravity. Satisfied with these precautions, Hart approached the door of the storeroom; but before opening it, he stopped to review his plan.

He must, of course, be near the outer shell of the Station. Central Intelligence had been unable to obtain plans of this launcher—a fact which should have given him food for thought—but there was no doubt about its general design. Storage and living quarters would be just inside the surface of the sphere; then would come a level of machine shops and control systems; and at the heart, within the shielding that represented most of the station's mass, would be the "hot" section—the chambers containing the fission piles and power plants, the extractors and the remote-controlled machinery that loaded the warheads of the torpedoes which were the main reason for the station's existence.

There were many of these structures circling Earth; every nation on the globe maintained at least one, and usually several. Hart had visited one of those belonging to his own country, partly for technical familiarity and partly to accustom himself to weightlessness. He had studied its plans with care, and scientists had carefully explained to him the functions of each part, and the ways in which the launchers of the Western Alliance were likely to differ. Most important, they had described to him several ways by which such structures might be destroyed. Hart's smile was wolfish as he thought of that; these people who preferred the pleasures of personal liberty to those of efficiency would see what efficiency could do.

But this delay was not efficient. He had made his plans long before, and it was more than time to set about their execution. He must be reasonably near a store of rocket fuel; and some at least of the air in this station must contain a breathable percentage of oxygen. Without further deliberation, he opened the door and floated out into the corridor. He did not go blindly. Tiny detectors built into the wrists of his suit reacted to the infrared radiations, the water vapor and carbon dioxide and even the breathing sounds that would herald the approach of a human being—unless he were wearing a nonmetallic suit similar to Hart's own. Apparently the personnel of the base did not normally wear these, however, for twice in the first ten minutes the saboteur was warned into shelter by the indications of the tiny instruments. In that ten minutes he covered a good deal of the outer zone.

✧ ✧ ✧

He learned quickly that the area in which a carbon dioxide atmosphere was maintained was quite limited in extent, and probably constituted either a quarantine zone for newly arrived supplies, or a food storage area. It was surrounded by an uninterrupted corridor lined on one side with airtight doors leading into the CO_2 rooms, and on the other by flimsier portals closing off other storage spaces. Hart wondered briefly at the reason for such a vast amount of storage room; then his attention was taken by another matter. He had been about to launch himself in another long, weightless glide down the corridor in search of branch passages which might lead to the rocket fuel stores, when a tiny spot on one wall caught his eye.

He instantly went to examine it more closely, and as quickly recognized a photoelectric eye. There appeared to be no lens, which suggested a beam-interruption unit; but the beam itself was not visible, nor could he find any projector. That meant a rather interesting and vital problem lay in avoiding the ray. He stopped to think.

In the scanning room on the second level, Dr. Bruce Mayhew chuckled aloud.

"It's wonderful what a superiority complex can do. He's stopped for the first time—didn't seem to have any doubts of his safety until he spotted that eye. The old oil about 'decadent democracies' seems to have taken deep hold somewhere, at least. He must be a military agent rather than a scientist."

Warren Floyd nodded. "Let's not pull the same boner, though," he suggested. "Scientist or not, no stupid man would have been chosen for such a job. Do you think he's carrying explosives? One man could hardly have chemicals enough to make a significant number of breaches in the outer shelf."

"He may be hoping to get into the core, to set off a warhead," replied the older man, "though I don't for the life of me see how he expects to do it. There's a rocket fuel in his neighborhood, of course, but it's just n.v. for the torpedoes—harmless, as far as we're concerned."

"A fire could be quite embarrassing, even if it weren't an explosion," pointed out his assistant, "particularly since the whole joint is nearly pure magnesium. I know it's sinfully expensive to transport mass away from Earth, but I wish they had built this place out of something a little less responsive to heat and oxygen."

"I shouldn't worry about that," replied Mayhew. "He won't get a fire started."

Floyd glanced at the flanking screens which showed armored men keeping pace with the agent in parallel corridors, and nodded. "I suppose not—provided Ben and his crew aren't too slow closing in when we give the signal."

"You mean when *I* give the signal," returned the other man. "I have reasons for wanting him free as long as possible. The longer he's free, the lower the opinion he'll have of us; when we do take him, he'll be less ready to commit suicide, and the sudden letdown of his self-confidence will make interrogation easier."

Floyd privately hoped nothing would happen to deflate his superior's own self-confidence, but wisely said nothing; and both men watched Hart's progress almost silently for some minutes. Floyd occasionally transmitted a word or two to the action party to keep them apprised of their quarry's whereabouts, but no other sound interrupted the vigil.

Hart had finally found a corridor which branched away from the one he had been following, and he proceeded cautiously along it. He had learned the intervals at which the photocells were spotted, and now avoided them almost automatically. It did not occur to him that, while the sight of a spacesuited man in the outer corridors might not surprise an observer, the presence of such a man who failed consistently to break the beams of the photocell spotters would be bound to attract attention. The lenses of the scanners were too small and too well hidden for Hart to find easily, and he actually believed that the photocells were the only traps. With his continued ease in avoiding them, his self-confidence and contempt for the Westerners were mounting as Mayhew had foretold.

Several times he encountered air breaks—sliding bulkheads actuated by automatic pressure-controlled switches, designed to cut off any section with a bad air leak. His action at each of these was the same; from an outer pocket of his armor he would take a small wedge of steel and skillfully jam the door. It was this action which convinced Mayhew that the agent was not a scientist—he was displaying the skill of an experienced burglar or spy. He was apparently well supplied with the wedges, for in the hour before he found what he was seeking he jammed more than twenty of the air breaks. Mayhew and Floyd did not bother to have them cleared at the time, since no one was in the outer level without a spacesuit.

Nearly half of the outer level was thus unified when Hart reached a section of corridor bearing valve handles and hose connections instead of doors, and knew there must be liquids behind the walls. There were code indexes stenciled over the valves, which meant nothing to the spy; but he carefully manipulated one of the two handles to let a little fluid into the corridor, and sniffed at it cautiously through the gingerly cracked face plate of his helmet. He was satisfied with the results; the liquid was one of the low-volatility hydrocarbons used with liquid oxygen as a fuel to provide the moderate acceleration demanded by space launched torpedoes. They were cheap, fairly dense, and their low-vapor pressure simplified the storage problem in open-space stations.

All that Hart really knew about it was that the stuff would burn as long as there was oxygen. Well—he grinned again at the thought—there would be oxygen for a while; until the compressed, blazing combustion gases blew the heat-softened metal of the outer wall into space. After that there would be none, except perhaps in the central core, where the heavy concentration of radioactive matter made it certain there would be no one to breathe it.

At present, of course, the second level and any other intermediate ones were still sealed; but that could and would be remedied. In any case, the blast of the liberated fuel would probably take care of the relatively flimsy inner walls. He did not at the time realize that these were of magnesium, or he would have felt even more sure of the results.

He looked along the corridor. As far as the curvature of the outer shell permitted him to see, the valves projected from the wall at intervals of a few yards. Each valve had a small electric pump, designed to force air into the tank behind it to drive the liquid out by pressure, since there was no gravity. Hart did not consider this point at all; a brief test showed him that the liquid did flow when the valve was on, and that was enough for him. Hanging poised beside the first handle, he took an object from still another pocket of his spacesuit, and checked it carefully, finally clipping it to an outside belt where it could easily be reached.

At the sight of this item of apparatus, Floyd almost suffered a stroke.

"That's an incendiary bomb!" he gasped aloud. "We can't possibly take him in time to stop his setting it off—which he'll do the instant he sees our men! And he already has free fuel in the corridor!"

He was perfectly correct; the agent was proceeding from valve to valve in long glides, pausing at each just long enough to turn it full on and to scatter the balloonlike mass of escaping liquid with a sweep of his arm. Gobbets and droplets of the inflammable stuff sailed lazily hither and yon through the air in his wake.

Mayhew calmly lighted a cigarette, unmindful of the weird appearance of the match flame driven toward his feet by the draft from the ceiling ventilators, and declined to move otherwise. "Decidedly, no physicist," he murmured. "I suppose that's just as well—it's the military information the army likes anyway. They certainly wouldn't have risked a researcher on this sort of job, so I never really did have a chance to get anything I wanted from him."

"But what are we going to do?" Floyd was almost frantic. "There's enough available energy loose in that corridor now to blast the whole outer shell off—and gallons more coming every second. I know you've been here a lot longer than I, but unless you can tell me how you expect to keep him from lighting that stuff up, I'm getting into a suit right now!"

"If it blows, a suit won't help you," pointed out the older man.

"I know that!" almost screamed Floyd, "but what other chance is there? Why did you let him get so far?"

"There is still no danger," Mayhew said flatly, "whether you believe it or not. However, the fuel does cost money, and there'll be some work recovering it, so I don't see why he should be allowed to empty all the torpedo tanks. He's excited enough now, anyway." He turned languidly to the appropriate microphone and gave the word to the action squad. "Take him now. He seems to be without hand weapons, but don't count on it. He certainly has at least one incendiary bomb." As an afterthought, he reached for another switch, and made sure the ventilators in the outer level were not operating; then he relaxed again and gave his attention to the scanner that showed the agent's activity. Floyd had switched to another pickup that covered a longer section of corridor, and the watchers saw the spacesuited attackers almost as soon as did Hart himself.

The European reacted to the sight at once—too rapidly, in fact, for the shift in his attention caused him to miss his grasp on the valve handle he sought and flounder helplessly through the air until he reached the next. Once anchored, however, he acted as he had planned, ignoring with commendable self-control the four armored figures converging on him. A sharp twist turned the fuel valve full on, sending a stream of oil mushrooming into the corridor; his left hand flashed to his belt, seized the tiny cylinder he had snapped there, jammed its end hard against the adjacent wall, and tossed the bomb gently back down the corridor. In one way his lack of weightless experience betrayed him; he allowed for a gravity pull that was not there. The bomb, in consequence, struck the "ceiling" a few yards from his hand, and rebounded with a popping noise and a shower of sparks. It drifted on down the corridor toward the floating globules of hydrocarbon, and the glow of the sparks was suddenly replaced by the eye-hurting radiance of thermite.

Floyd winced at the sight, and expected the attacking men to make futile plunges after the blazing thing; but though all were within reach of walls, not one swerved from his course. Hart made no effort to escape or fight; he watched the course of the drifting bomb with satisfaction, and, like Floyd, expected in the next few seconds to be engulfed in a sea of flame that would remove the most powerful of the Western torpedo stations from his country's path of conquest. Unlike Floyd, he was calm about it, even when the men seized him firmly and began removing equipment from his pockets. One unclamped and removed the face plate of his helmet; and even to that he made no resistance—just watched in triumph as his missile drifted toward the nearest globes of fuel.

It did not actually strike the first. It did not have to; while the quantity of heat radiated by burning thermite is relatively small, the temperature of the reaction is notoriously high—and the temperature six inches from the bomb was well above the flash point of the rocket fuel, comparatively non-volatile as it was. Floyd saw the flash as its surface ignited, and closed his eyes.

Mayhew gave him four or five seconds before speaking, judging that that was probably about all the suspense the younger man could stand.

"All right, ostrich," he finally said quietly. "I'm not an angel, in case you were wondering. Why not use your eyes, and the brain behind them?"

Floyd was far too disturbed to take offense at the last remark, but he did cautiously follow Mayhew's advice about looking. He found difficulty, however, in believing what his eyes and the scanner showed him.

The group of five men was unchanged, except for the expression on the captive's now visible face. All were looking down the corridor toward the point where the bomb was still burning; Lang's crew bore expressions of amusement on their faces, while Hart wore a look of utter disbelief. Floyd, seeing what he saw, shared the expression.

The bomb had by now passed close to several of the floating spheres. Each had caught fire, as Floyd had seen—for a moment only. Now each was surrounded by a spherical, nearly opaque layer of some grayish substance that looked like a mixture of smoke and kerosene vapor; a layer that could not have been half an inch thick, as Floyd recalled the sizes of the original spheres. None was burning; each had effectively smothered itself out, and the young observer slowly realized just how and why as the bomb at last made a direct hit on the drop of fuel fully a foot in diameter.

Like the others, the globe flamed momentarily, and went out; but this time the sphere that appeared and grew around it was lighter in color, and continued to grow for several seconds. Then there was a little, sputtering explosion, and a number of fragments of still burning thermite emerged from the surface of the sphere in several directions, traveled a few feet, and went out. All activity died down, except in the faces of Hart and Floyd.

The saboteur was utterly at a loss, and seemed likely to remain that way; but in the watch room Floyd was already kicking himself mentally for his needless worry. Mayhew, watching the expression on his assistant's face, chuckled quietly.

"Of course you get it now," he said at last.

"I do *now*, certainly," replied Floyd. "I should have seen it earlier—I've certainly noticed you light enough cigarettes, and watched the behavior of the match flame. Apparently our friend is not yet enlightened, though," he nodded toward the screen as he spoke.

He was right; Hart was certainly not enlightened. He belonged to a service in which unpleasant surprises were neither unexpected nor unusual, but he had never in his life been so completely disorganized. The stuff looked like fuel; it smelled like fuel; it had even started to burn—but it refused to carry on with the process. Hart simply relaxed in the grip of the guards, and tried to find something in the situation to serve as an anchor for his whirling thoughts. A spaceman would have understood the situation without thinking, a high school student of reasonable intelligence could probably have worked the matter out in time; but Hart's education had been that of a spy, in a country which considered general education a waste of time. He simply did not have the background to cope with his present environment.

That, at least, was the idea Mayhew acquired after a careful questioning of the prisoner. Not much was learned about his intended mission, though there was little doubt about it under the circumstances. The presence of an alien agent aboard any of the free-floating torpedo launchers of the various national governments bore only one interpretation; and since the destruction of one such station would do little good to anyone, Mayhew at once radioed all other launchers to be on the alert for similar intruders—all others, regardless of nationality. Knowledge by Hart's superiors of his capture might prevent their acting on the assumption that he had succeeded, which would inevitably lead to some highly regrettable incidents. Mayhew's business was to prevent a war, not win one. Hart had not actually admitted the identity of his superiors, but his accent left the matter in little doubt; and since no action was intended, Mayhew did not need proof.

There remained, of course, the problem of what to do with Hart. The structure had no ready-made prison, and it was unlikely that the Western government would indulge in the gesture of a special rocket to take the man off. Personal watch would be tedious, but it was unthinkable merely to deprive a man with the training Hart must have received of his equipment, and then assume he would not have to be watched every second.

The solution, finally suggested by one of the guards, was a small storeroom in the outer shell. It had no locks, but there were welding torches in the machine shops. There was no ventilator either, but an alga tank would take care of that. After consideration, Mayhew decided that this was the best plan, and it was promptly put into effect.

✧ ✧ ✧

Hart was thoroughly searched, even his clothing being replaced as a precautionary measure. He asked for his cigarettes and lighter, with a half smile, Mayhew supplied the man with some of his own, and marked those of the spy for special investigation. Hart said nothing more after that, and was incarcerated without further ceremony. Mayhew was chuckling once more as the guards disappeared with their charge.

"I hope he gets more good than I out of that lighter," he remarked. "It's a wick-type my kid sent me as a present, and the ventilator draft doesn't usually keep it going. Maybe our friend will learn something, if he fools with it long enough. He has a pint of lighter fluid to experiment with—the kid had large ideas."

"I was a little surprised—I thought for a moment you were giving him a pocket flask," laughed Floyd. "I suppose that's why you always use matches—they're easier to wave than that thing. I guess I save myself a lot of trouble not smoking at all. I suppose you have to put potassium nitrate in your cigarettes to keep 'em going when you're not pulling on them." Floyd ducked as he spoke, but Mayhew didn't throw anything. Hart, of course, was out of hearing by this time, and would not have profited from the remark in any case. He probably, in fact, would not have paid much attention. He knew, of course, that the sciences of physics and chemistry are important; but he thought of them in connection with great laboratories and factories. The idea that knowledge of either could be of immediate use to anyone not a chemist or physicist would have been fantastic to him. While his current plans for escape were based largely on chemistry, the connection did not occur to him. The only link between those plans and Mayhew's words or actions gave the spy some grim amusement; it was the fact that he did not smoke.

The cell, when he finally reached it, was perfectly satisfactory; there were no peepholes which could serve as shot-holes, no way in which the door could be unsealed quickly—as Mayhew had said, not even a ventilator. Once he was in, Hart would not be interrupted without plenty of notice. Since the place was a storeroom, there was no reason to expect even a scanner, though, he told himself, there was no reason to assume there was none, either. He simply disregarded that possibility, and went to work the moment he heard the torch start to seal his door.

His first idea did not get far. He spent half an hour trying to make Mayhew's lighter work, without noticeable success. Each spin of the "flint" brought a satisfactory shower of sparks, and about every fourth or fifth try produced a faint "pop" and a flash of blue fire; but he was completely unable to make a flame last. He closed the cover at last, and for the first time made an honest effort to think. The situation had got beyond the scope of his training.

He dismissed almost at once the matter of the rocket fuel that had not been ignited by his bomb. Evidently the Westerners stored it with some inhibiting chemical, probably as a precaution more against accident than sabotage. Such a chemical would have to be easily removable, but he had no means of knowing the method, and that line of attack would have to be abandoned.

But why wouldn't the lighter fuel burn? The more he thought the matter out, the more Hart felt that Mayhew must have doctored it deliberately, as a gesture of contempt. Such an act he could easily understand; and the thought of it roused again the wolfish hate that was such a prominent part of his personality. He would show that smart Westerner! There was certainly some way!

Powerful hands, and a fingernail deliberately hardened long since to act as a passable screw-driver blade, had the lighter disassembled in the space of a few minutes. The parts were disappointingly small in number and variety; but Hart considered each at length.

The fuel, already evaporating as it was, appeared useless—he was no chemist, and had satisfied himself the stuff was incombustible. The case was of magnalium, apparently, and might be useful as a heat source if it could be lighted; its use in a cigarette lighter did not encourage pursuit of that thought. The wick might be combustible, if thoroughly dried. The flint and wheel mechanism was promising—at least one part would be hard enough to cut or wear most metals, and the spring might be decidedly useful. Elsewhere in the room there was very little. The light was a gas tube, and, since the chamber had no opening whatever, would probably be most useful as a light. The alga tank, of course, had a minute motor and pump which forced air through its liquid, and an ingenious valve and trap system which recovered the air even in the present weightless situation; but Hart, considering the small size of the room, decided that any attempt to dismantle his only source of fresh air would have to be very much of a last resort.

✧ ✧ ✧

After much thought, and with a grimace of distaste, he took the tiny striker of the lighter and began slowly to abrade a circular area around the latch of the door, using the inside handle for anchorage.

He did not, of course, have any expectation of final escape; he was not in the least worried about his chances of recovering his spacesuit. He expected only to get out of the cell and complete his mission; and if he succeeded, no possible armor would do him any good.

As it happened, there was a scanner in his compartment; but Mayhew had long since grown tired of watching the spy try to ignite the lighter fuel, and had turned his attention elsewhere, so that Hart's actions were unobserved for some time. The door metal was thin and not particularly hard; and he was able without interference and with no worse trouble than severe finger cramp to work out a hole large enough to show him another obstacle—instead of welding the door frame itself, his captors had placed a rectangular steel bar across the portal and fastened it at points well to each side of the frame, out of the prisoner's reach. Hart stopped scraping as soon as he realized the extent of this barrier, and gave his mind to the situation.

He might, conceivably, work a large enough hole through the door to pass his body without actually opening the portal; but his fingers were already stiff and cramped from the use made of the tiny striker, and it was beyond reason to expect that he would be left alone long enough to accomplish any such feat. Presumably they intended to feed him occasionally.

There was another reason for haste, as well, though he was forgetting it as his nose became accustomed to the taint in the air. The fluid, which he had permitted to escape while disassembling the lighter, was evaporating with fair speed, as it was far more volatile than the rocket fuel; and it was diffusing through the air of the little room. The alga tank removed only carbon dioxide, so that the air of the cell was acquiring an ever greater concentration of hydrocarbon molecules. Prolonged breathing of such vapors is far from healthy, as Hart well knew; and escape from the room was literally the only way to avoid breathing the stuff.

What would eliminate a metal door—quickly? Brute force? He hadn't enough of it. Chemicals? He had none. Heat? The thought was intriguing and discouraging at the same time, after his recent experience with heat sources. Still, even if liquid fuels would not burn perhaps other things would: there was the wicking from the lighter, a little floating cloud of metal particles around the scene of his work on the magnesium door; and the striking mechanism of the lighter.

He plucked the wicking out of the air where it had been floating, and began to unravel it—without fuel, as he realized, it would need every advantage in catching the sparks of the striker.

Then he wadded as much of the metallic dust as he could collect—which was not too much—into the wick, concentrating it heavily at one end and letting it thin out toward the more completely raveled part.

Then he inspected the edges of the hole he had ground in the door, and with the striker roughened them even more on one side, so that a few more shavings of metal projected. To these he pressed the fuse, wedging it between the door and the steel bar just outside the hole, with the "lighting" end projecting into the room. He inspected the work carefully, nodded in satisfaction, and began to reassemble the striker mechanism.

He did not, of course, expect that the steel bar would be melted or seriously weakened by an ounce or so of magnesium, but he did hope that the thin metal of the door itself would ignite.

Hart had the spark mechanism almost ready when his attention was distracted abruptly. Since the hole had been made, a very gentle current of air had been set up in the cell by the corridor ventilators beyond—a current in the nature of an eddy which tended to carry loose objects quite close to the hole. One of the loose objects in the room was a sphere comprised of the remaining lighter fluid, which had not yet evaporated. When Hart noticed the shimmering globe, it was scarcely a foot from his fuse, and drifting steadily nearer. To him, that sphere of liquid was death to his plan; it would not burn itself, it probably would not let anything else burn either. If it touched and soaked his fuse, he would have to wait until it evaporated; and there might not be time for that. He released the striker with a curse, and swung his open hand at the drop, trying to drive it to one side. He succeeded only partly. It spattered on his hand, breaking up into scores of smaller drops, some of which moved obediently away, while others just drifted, and still others vanished in vapor. None drifted far; and the gentle current had them in control almost at once, and began to bear many of them back toward the hole—and Hart's fuse.

For just a moment the saboteur hung there in agonized indecision, and then his training reasserted itself. With another curse he snatched at the striker, made sure it was ready for action, and turned to the hole in the door. It was at this moment that Mayhew chose to take another look at his captive.

As it happened, the lens of his scanner was so located that Hart's body covered the hole in the door; and since the spy's back was toward him, the watcher could not tell precisely what he was doing. The air of purposefulness about the captive was so outstanding and so impressive, however, that Mayhew was reaching for a microphone to order a direct check on the cell when Hart spun the striker wheel.

Mayhew could not, of course, see just what the man had done, but the consequences were plain enough. The saboteur's body was flung away from the door and toward the scanner lens like a rag doll kicked by a mule. An orange blossom of flame outlined him for an instant; and in practically the same instant the screen went blank as a heavy shock wave shattered its pickup lens.

Mayhew, accustomed as he was to weightless maneuvering, never in his life traveled so rapidly as he did then. Floyd and several other crewmen, who saw him on the way, tried to follow; but he outstripped them all, and when they reached the site of Hart's prison Mayhew was hanging poised outside, staring at the door.

There was no need of removing the welded bar. The thin metal of the door had been split and curled outward fantastically; an opening quite large enough for any man's body yawned in it, though there was nothing more certain than the fact that Hart had not made use of this avenue of escape. His body was still in the cell, against the far wall; and even now the relatively strong currents from the hall ventilators did not move it. Floyd had a pretty good idea of what held it there, and did not care to look closely. He might be right.

Mayhew's voice broke the prolonged silence.

"He never did figure it out."

"Just what let go, anyway?" asked Floyd.

"Well, the only combustible we know of in the cell was the lighter fluid. To blast like that, though, it must have been almost completely vaporized, and mixed with just the right amount of air—possible, I suppose, in a room like this. I don't understand why he let it all out, though."

"He seems to have been using pieces of the lighter," Floyd pointed out. "The loose fuel was probably just a by-product of his activities. He was even duller than I, though. It took me long enough to realize that a fire needs air to burn—and can't set up convection currents to keep itself supplied with oxygen, when there is no gravity."

"More accurately, when there is no *weight*," interjected Mayhew. "We are well within Earth's gravity field, but in free fall. Convection currents occur because the heated gas is *lighter* per unit volume than the rest, and rises. With no weight, and no 'up' such currents are impossible."

"In any case, he must have decided we were fooling him with non-combustible liquids."

Mayhew replied slowly: "People are born and brought up in a steady gravity field, and come to take all its manifestations for granted. It's extremely hard to forsee *all* the consequences which will arise when you dispense with it. I've been here for years, practically constantly, and still get caught sometimes when I'm tired or just waking up."

"They should have sent a spaceman to do this fellow's job, I should think."

"How would he have entered the station? A man is either a spy or a spaceman—to be both would mean he was too old for action at all, I should say. Both professions demand years of rigorous training, since habits rather than knowledge are required—habits like the one of always stopping within reach of a wall or other massive object." There was a suspicion of the old chuckle in his voice as Mayhew spoke the final sentence, and it was followed by a roar of laughter from the other men. Floyd looked around, and blushed furiously.

He was, as he had suspected from the older man's humor, suspended helplessly in midair out of reach of every source of traction. Had there been anything solid around, he would probably have used it for concealment instead, anyway. He managed at last to join that laughter; but at its end he glanced once more into Hart's cell, and remarked, "If this is the worst danger that inexperience lands on my head, I don't think I'll complain. Bruce, I want to go with you on your next leave to Earth; I simply must see you in a gravity field. I bet you won't wait for the ladder when we step off the rocket though I guess it would be more fun to see you drop a dictionary on your toe. As you implied, habits are hard to break."

Peace with Honor

JERRY POURNELLE

The man on the tri-v was in full form. His speech had started quietly enough, as Harmon's speeches always did, full of resonant tones and appeals to reason, the quiet voice asking for attention, speaking so softly that you had to listen closely to be sure of hearing him. But slowly, oh so slowly, the background changed subtly until now Harmon stood before the stars and stripes covering the hemisphere, an American Eagle splendid over the Capitol, and the speaker had worked himself to one of his famous frenzies, his former calm and detachment obviously overcome with emotion.

"Honor? It is a word that Lipscomb no longer knows. Whatever he might have been—and my friends we all know what he was, we all admire him for what he was—he is no longer one of us! His cronies, the dark little men who whisper to him, they have corrupted even so great a man as President Lipscomb! And what of our country? She bleeds! People of America, she bleeds from the running sores of these men and their CoDominium!

"They say that withdrawal from the CoDominium would mean war. I pray God it would not, but if it did, why, these are hard times. Many of us would be killed, but we would die as men! And today our friends, our allies, the people of Hungary, the people of Rumania, the Czechs, the Slovaks, the Poles, they groan under the oppression of their communist masters, and who keeps them there? Our CoDominium! We do! We have become slavemasters! Better to die as men.

"But it will not come to that. The Russians would never fight. They are soft, soft as we, their government riddled with corruption as ours. People of America, hear me! People of America, listen!"

The Honorable John Rogers Grant spoke softly and the tri-v turned itself off, a walnut panel sliding over the darkening screen. Grant grimaced, spoke again, and the servitor brought him a small bottle of milk. With all the advances in medical science, there was nothing Grant could afford to have done for an ulcer. Money was no problem, but when in God's Name would he find time?

He glanced at papers on his desk, reports with bright red Security covers, closed his eyes for a moment. Harmon's speech was an important one, would undoubtedly have an effect on the coming elections. The man was getting to be a menace, Grant thought. Have to do something about him one day. He put the thought aside; John Grant liked Harmon, at one time they had been best friends. Lord, what have we come to? He opened the first report. There had been a riot at the International Federation of Labor convention. Three killed, and the smooth plans for the re-election of Matt Brady thrown into confusion. Grant grimaced again and drank more milk. The Intelligence people had assured him that this one would be easy. Digging through the reports, he found that some of Harvey Bertram's child crusaders were responsible. They'd bugged Brady's suite, got enough evidence of sell-outs and deals to inflame sentiment on the floor. The report ended with the recommendation that the government drop Brady, concentrate support on MacKnight, who had a good reputation, but whose file in the CIA building bulged with information. MacKnight would be easy to control. Grant nodded to himself, scrawled his initials on the action form, dropped it in the TOP SECRET: OUT slot. No point in wasting time, but he wondered what would happen to Brady. Matt Brady had been a good friend to the Unity Party, blast Bertram's people anyway.

He took up the next file, but before he could open it his secretary came in. He looked up and smiled gently, glad of his decision to ignore the stupid telecom. Some executives never saw their secretaries except through electronics from the moment they came in until they were ready to leave.

"Your appointment, sir," she said. "Almost time. And it's time for your nerve tonic."

He grunted. "I'd rather die." But he let her pour the shotglass of evil-tasting stuff, tossed it off and chased it with milk before glancing at his watch. Not that the watch was needed, he thought. Miss Ackridge knew the travel times to every Washington office, allowed just enough extra for possible emergencies. There'd be no time to start on another report, and that suited Grant just fine.

He let her help him into his black coat, brush off a few silver gray hairs. He didn't really feel fifty-five, but he looked it now. It happened all at once. Five years ago, he could pass for forty. John saw the girl in the mirror behind him, standing close to him, and knew that she loved him. The usual secretary-boss situation, and it wouldn't work. Why the hell don't you get married again, John Grant? It isn't as if you're pining away for Priscilla. By the time she died you were praying it would happen. You can even admit that now. Why the hell do you go on acting like the great love of your life has departed forever? All you'd have to do is turn around, say five words, she'd . . . she'd what? She wouldn't be the perfect secretary any longer. Good secretaries are harder to find than mistresses. Let it alone.

She stood there for a moment, then moved away. "Your daughter wants to see you this evening," she told him. "She's driving down this afternoon. Says it's important."

"Know why?" Grant asked. Ackridge knew more about Sharon than Grant did. A whole lot more, probably.

"I can guess. I think her young man asked her."

John nodded. It was hardly unexpected, but it hurt. So soon, so soon. They grow so fast, and there's so little time. John Jr. was with the Callisto Squadron, First Lieutenant of a CoDominium Navy frigate, due for a command of his own any year now. Frederick was dead in the accident with his mother, and now Sharon had found another life . . . not that she hadn't before. Since he became the Honorable Deputy Secretary he might as well have died for as often as they had time together.

"Run his name through CIA, Flora. Meant to do that months ago, can't think why I never got around to it. They won't find anything, but we'll need it for the records."

"Yes, sir. You'd better be on your way, now. Your drivers are outside."

He glanced around the office, scooped up his briefcase. "I won't be back today, have my car sent around to the White House, will you? I'll drive myself home tonight."

"Yes, sir. You can send the briefcase back with your driver, then," she said carefully, reminding him of his own regulations. Too many papers turning up missing from too many houses lately. If you want to work nights, stay at the office.

He acknowledged the salutes of his driver and armed "mechanic" with a cheery wave, led them to the elevator at the end of the long corridor. Paintings and photographs of ancient battles hung along both sides of the hall, but otherwise it was like a cave. Blasted Pentagon, he thought for the millionth time. Stupidest building ever constructed. Nobody can find anything, it can't be guarded for any price, and it's too big for the important staff, too small for everything the military needed. Miserable stupid building. Why couldn't somebody have bombed it?

They took a surface car to the White House. He could have made his own clearance for a flight, but it would have been another detail, and why bother? Besides, this way he got to see the cherry trees and flower beds around the Jefferson. The Potomac was a brown sludgy mess despite the latest attempt to clean it up. You could swim in it if you had a strong stomach, but the Army engineers had "improved" it a few administrations back, giving it concrete banks . . . why the devil would anyone want to make a concrete ditch out of a river? he wondered. Now the workmen were tearing the lining out, which kept the water perpetually muddy. One day they'll be through with it.

They drove through rows of government buildings, some of them abandoned. Urban Renewal had given Washington all the office space the government needed, more, until there were empty buildings, big relics of the time when Washington was the most crime-ridden city in the world. Back around the turn of the Century, maybe before, he couldn't remember, they'd torn everything down, hustled everyone out of Washington who didn't belong there, the bulldozers quickly following to demolish the tenements. For some political reason it was thought desirable to put up offices as quickly as the other buildings were torn down, to make the displaced people think it was all necessary, and now there were these empty tombs.

They passed the Population Control Bureau, two square blocks of humming activity, then around the Elipse and past Old State to the gate. The guard checked his identity carefully, using the little scanning plate on his palm-print, although blast it, that guard knew John Grant as well as he knew his own mother. Grant sighed and waited until the computer flashed back the "all right," was driven into the White House basement and escorted quickly up to the Oval Office. He got there one minute early for his appointment.

The President stood when Grant entered, and the others shot to their feet as if they had ejection charges under them. Grant shook hands around, but looked closely at Lipscomb. The President was feeling the strain, no question about it. Well, they all were. Too bad about the Chief, but they had to have him.

"Sorry the Secretary couldn't make it, Mister President," Grant announced ritually.

Lipscomb made a wry face but said nothing. The Secretary of Defense was a political hack who controlled a bloc of Aerospace Guild votes and an even larger bloc of aerospace industry stocks. As long as government contracts kept his companies employing his men, be didn't give a damn about policy, and since he couldn't keep his big mouth shut it was best not to tell him about meetings. He could sit in on formal Cabinet sessions where nothing was ever said and would never know the difference anyway.

Grant kept his attention on the President. Lipscomb didn't like to be reminded of the incompetence of his cabinet, the political deceptions that divorced power from its appearance. The ritual was getting old, why not just sit down and say nothing? Silently, Grant took his place at the center of the table across from the President.

Except for Lipscomb, none of the men in the Oval Office were well-known to the public. Any one of them could have walked down the streets of any city but Washington without fear of recognition. But the power they controlled, as assistants, deputies, clerks even, was immense and they all knew it. There was no real need to pretend to each other.

The servitor brought drinks and Grant accepted a small scotch. Some of the others didn't trust a man who wouldn't drink with them. His ulcer would give him hell, and his doctor more, but doctors and ulcers didn't understand the realities of power. Neither, Grant thought, do I or any of us. But understand it or not, we've got it, and we've got to do something with it.

"Mr. Karins, would you begin?" the President asked. Heads swiveled to the west wall where Karins had set up a briefing stand. A polar projection of Earth glowed behind him, lights blinking the status of forces which the President ordered, but Grant controlled.

Karins stood confidently, his paunch spilling out over his belt, an obscenity in so young a man. Herman Karins was the second youngest man in the room, Assistant Director of the Bureau of the Budget, and said to be one of the most brilliant economists Yale had ever produced. He was certainly one of the best political technicians in the country, but that didn't show in his resume or degrees.

He took off the cover sheet to show a set of figures. "I have the latest poll results," Karins said too loudly. "This is the real stuff, gentlemen, not what we hand out to the papers. It stinks."

It certainly did stink. The Unity Party was hovering around thirty-eight percent, just about evenly divided between the Republican and the Democratic wings. Harmon's Patriot Party had about twenty-five, Millington's violently left wing Liberation Party had its usual ten, but the real shocker was Bertram's Freedom Party. Bertram's popularity stood at an unbelievable twenty percent of the population.

"These are figures for those who have an opinion and might vote," Karins said. "The usual. 'Course there're about half who don't give a damn about anything, but they vole by who got to 'em last anyway; we know how they split off. You see the bad news."

"You're sure of this?" the Assistant Postmaster General asked. He was the leader of the Republican wing of the Unity Party, and it hadn't been six months since he told them they could forget Bertram and his bleeding hearts.

"Yes, sir, I'm sure of it," Karins said. "And it's growing. Those riots at the labor convention probably gave 'em another five points, but we don't show that yet. Give Bertram another six months and he'll be ahead of us. With elections coming up in a year. How you like them apples, boys and girls?"

"There's no need to be flippant, Mr. Karins," the President said automatically.

"Sorry, Mister President." Karins wasn't sorry at all, and he glared at the Assistant Postmaster General with triumph. Then he flipped the pages of the chart to show new results.

"This is the soft and hard vote, gentlemen. You'll notice that Bertram's vote is pretty soft, but solidifying. Harmon's is so hard you couldn't get 'em away from him without using nukes. And ours is getting a little like butter. Mister President, I can't even guarantee we can be the largest party after the election, much less that we can hold a majority."

"Incredible," the chairman of the Joint Chiefs muttered.

"Worse than incredible," Grand Senator Bronson agreed. "A disaster. Who will win?"

Karins chuckled. Bronson's appointment to the CoDominium Grand Senate expired just after the election. Unless Unity won, he wouldn't be going back to Luna Base next year. "Toss-up, Senator. Some of ours is drifting to Harmon, some to Bertram. I'd say Bertram if I had to call it, though."

Bronson sat back, relieved. Bertram's Freedom Party was not totally opposed to the CoDominium, perhaps he could do business with it. He'd have to change his stand on opposition to increased Japanese representation in the Grand Senate, though.

"You've been quiet, John," the President said. "You have no observations?"

"No, sir," Grant answered. "It's fairly obvious what the result will be if we lose, no matter who wins. If Harmon takes over, he pulls out of the CoDominium and we have war. If Bertram takes over, he relaxes security, Harmon drives him out with his storm troopers, and we have war anyway."

Karins nodded. "I don't figure Bertram could hold on to power more'n a year, probably not that long. Man's too honest."

The President sighed loudly. "I can recall a time when men said that about me, Mr. Karins."

"It's still true, Mister President," Karins said hurriedly. "But you're enough of a realist to let us do what we have to do. Bertram won't."

"So what do we do about it?" the President asked gently.

"Rig the election," Karins answered quickly. "I give out the popularity figures here." He showed another chart indicating that the Unity Party had well over a majority popularity. "Then we keep pumping out more faked stuff, while Mr. Grant's people work on the computers. Hell, it's been done before."

"Won't work this time." They turned to look at the youngest man in the room. Larry Moriarty, Assistant to the President and sometimes called the "resident heretic," blushed at the attention. He was naturally shy, hated to be noticed until he got worked up. When he was fully committed to an argument, though, he could shout with the best of them. "The people know better. Bertram's people are already getting jobs in the computer centers, aren't they, Mr. Grant? They'll see it in a minute."

Grant nodded. He'd sent the report over the day before; interesting that Moriarty had digested it already.

"You make this a straight old rigged election, you'll have to use the CoDominium Marines to keep order," Moriarty continued.

"The day I need CoDominium Marines to put down riots in the United States is the day I resign," the President said coldly. "I may be a realist, but there are limits to what I will do, gentlemen. You'll need a new chief."

"That's easy to say, Mister President," Grant said. He wanted his pipe, but the doctors had forbidden it. The hell with it, he thought, and took a cigarette from the pack in front of the Undersecretary for Welfare. "It's easy to say, but you can't do it. What happens after you resign?"

"I don't think I care," the President answered.

"But you do, sir," Grant continued. "We all do. The Unity Party supports the CoDominium, and the CoDominium keeps the peace. An ugly peace, but, by God, peace. I wish . . . Lord, how I wish . . . that support for the CoDominium treaties hadn't got tied so thoroughly to the Unity Party, but it did and that's that. And you know damn well that even in the Party it's only a thin majority that supports the CoDominium. Right, Harry?"

The Assistant Postmaster General nodded. "But don't forget, there's support for the CD in Bertram's group."

"Sure, but they hate our guts. Call us corrupt," Moriarty said. "They're right, too."

"So flipping what if they're right?" Karins snapped. "We're in, they're out. Anybody who's in very long is corrupt. If he ain't, he ain't in."

"I fail to see the point of this discussion," the President interrupted. "I for one do not enjoy being reminded of all the things I have done to keep this office, and I am sure most of you like it no better than I do. The question is, what are we going to do? And I feel I must tell you that as far as I am concerned, nothing would make me happier than to have Mr. Bertram sit in this chair. I'm tired, gentlemen. I've been President for eight years, and I don't want it anymore."

✧ ✧ ✧

Everyone spoke at once, shouting to the President, murmuring to their neighbors, until Grant cleared his throat loudly. "Mister President," he said, using the tone of command he had been taught during his brief tour in the Army Reserve. "Thank you, gentlemen. Mister President, that is, if you will pardon me, sir, a ludicrous suggestion. There is no one else in the Unity Party who has even a ghost of a chance of winning. You remain popular. The people trust you. Even Mr. Harmon speaks as well of you as he does of anyone not in his group. Mr. Bertram thinks highly of you personally. You cannot resign without dragging the Unity Party with you, and you cannot give that chair to Mr. Bertram. He couldn't hold it for six months."

"And would that really be so bad, John?" Lipscomb was using all the old charm now, the fireside manner that the voters loved, the tones and warmth and expressions that won ambassadors and voters, senators and taxpayers. "Are we really so sure that only we can save the human race, John? Or are we merely interested in keeping our own power?"

"Some of both, I suppose," Grant answered. "Not that I wouldn't mind retiring."

"Retire!" Karins snorted. "You let Bertram's clean babies get in the files for two hours, none of us will retire to anything better'n a CD prison planet. You got to be kidding, retire."

"That may be true," the President said, "but there are other ways. General, what does happen if Harmon takes power and starts the war?"

"Mr. Grant knows better than I do," General Carpenter said. When the others looked at him with amazement, Carpenter continued. "Nobody's ever fought a nuclear war. Why should the uniform make me more of an expert than you? But I'd say we could win. Heavy casualties, but our defenses are good." He gestured at the moving lights on the enormous wall projection. "Better technology than the Russkis. The laser guns ought to get most of their missiles. CD Fleet won't let either one of us use space weapons. We might win."

"We might." Lipscomb was grim. "John?"

"We might not win. And we might succeed in killing about half the human race. We might do better than that. How in God's Name do I know what will happen if we start throwing nuclear weapons around?"

"But the Russians aren't prepared," a Commerce official said. "If we hit them without warning—people never change governments in the middle of a war."

President Lipscomb sighed. "I am not going to start a nuclear war to retain power. Whatever I have done, I have done to keep peace. That's my last excuse, I could never live with myself if I sacrifice peace to keep power. I'd rather sacrifice my power to keep peace."

Grant cleared his throat gently. "We couldn't do it anyway. If we started converting defensive missiles to offensive, CoDominium Intelligence would hear about it in ten days. The Treaty prevents that, you know." He lit another cigarette. "Of course we could denounce the CoDominium. That would just about assure us of losing the election. And probably put Kaslov's people in power in the Soviet Union."

Kaslov was a pure Stalinist, who wanted to liberate Earth for communism. Some called him the last communist, but of course he wasn't the last. He had plenty of followers. Grant could remember a secret conference with Ambassador Chernikov only weeks ago. The Soviet was a polished diplomat, but it was obvious that he wanted something desperately. He wanted the United States to keep the pressure on, not relax her defenses out at the borders of the U.S. sphere of influence, because if she ever let the communist probes take anything out of the U.S. sphere without a hard fight, Kaslov would gain more influence at home.

Telling Grant about it was as close to playing politics as a professional like Chernikov would ever come; and it meant that Kaslov was gaining influence, not losing it.

"This is all nonsense," the Assistant Postmaster announced. "We aren't going to quit, we won't start the war, and we aren't going to lose. Now what does it take to get the support away from Mr. Clean Bertram and funnel it back to us? A good scandal, right? Find Bertram's dirtier than we ever thought of being, right? Catch some of his boys plotting something really bad, right? Working with the Japs, maybe. Giving the Japs nukes. I'm sure Mr. Grant can arrange something like that."

Karins nodded vigorously. "That would do it. Disillusion his organizers, drive his followers out. The pro-CoDominium people in his group will come to us like a shot." He paused, chuckled evilly. "'Course some of 'em will head for Millington's bunch."

Karins laughed again. No one worried about Millington's Liberation Party very much. When they did worry, it was whether it would survive. Without his madmen to cause riots and keep the taxpayers afraid, other measures the Unity Party had to take would never be accepted. Millington's people gave the police some heads to crack, a nice riot for tri-v to keep the Citizens amused and the taxpayers happy.

"I think we can safely leave the details to Mr. Grant," Karins grinned.

"What will you do, John?" the President asked.

"Do you really want to know, Mister President?" Moriarty interrupted. "I don't."

"Nor do I, but if I can condone it, I can at least find out what it is. What will you do, John?"

"Frame-up, I suppose. Get a plot going, then uncover it."

"That?" Moriarty said. "Man, it's got to be better than that. The people are beginning to wonder about plots."

Grant nodded. "There will be evidence. Hard core, cast-iron evidence. Such as a secret arsenal of nuclear weapons."

There was a gasp. Then Karins grinned widely, laughed. "Oh, man, that's tore it. Hidden nukes. Real ones, I suppose?"

"Of course." Grant looked at the fat youth with distaste. What would be the point of fake nuclear weapons? But Karins lived in a world of deception, so much so that fake weapons would be appropriate for this nightmare scene.

Karins chuckled again. "Better have lots of cops when you break the story. People hear that, they'll tear Bertram apart."

True enough, Grant thought. It was a point he'd have to remember. Protection of those kids wouldn't be easy. Not since one militant group A-bombed a Mississippi town, and a criminal syndicate tried to hold San Francisco for a hundred million dollars ransom. People no longer thought of private stocks of atomic weapons as something to laugh at. They'd kill anyone they believed had some.

"We won't involve Mr. Bertram personally," the President said grimly. "Not at any price and under no circumstances. Is that understood?"

"Yes, sir," John answered quickly. He hadn't liked the idea either, was eager to agree. "Just some of his top aides." Grant stubbed out the cigarette. It, or something, had left a foul taste in his mouth.

He turned to Grand Senator Bronson. "Senator, the CoDominium will end up with final custody. I'll see that they are sentenced to transportation for life. I'd prefer it if they didn't have too hard a sentence to serve."

Bronson nodded, his hands clasped over his vest, a satisfied smile breaking through the doubts he'd had before. He could probably not have made a deal with Bertram, this was better. "Oh, certainly, whatever you like. Let them be planters on Tanith if they'll cooperate. We can see they don't suffer."

Like hell we can, Grant thought. Even as an independent planter, life on Tanith was no joy. He shook his head wearily and lit another cigarette.

Grant left the meeting a few minutes later. The others could continue the endless discussion, but for Grant there was no point to it. The action they had to take was clear, and the longer they waited the more time Bertram would have to assemble his supporters and harden his support. If something was going to be done, it might as well be now while Bertram's vote was soft. Give them a reason to leave his camp while they were still unsure, don't play around with it. Grant had found all his life that the wrong action taken decisively and in time was often better than the right action taken later.

He thought about the situation on his way back to his office, and after he reached the Pentagon, summoned his deputies and issued orders. The whole thing took no more than an hour. The machinery was already in motion.

Grant's colleagues always said he was rash, too quick to take actions without looking at all their consequences. They also conceded that he was lucky, that what he did usually worked out well, but they complained that he didn't think it over enough. John Grant saw no point in enlightening them: he did think things over, but by anticipating them rather than reacting to crisis. He had known that Bertram's support was growing alarmingly for weeks, had made up contingency plans for the event in case Karins' polls turned out badly. He hadn't expected them to come out *that* bad, but it only indicated that the drastic actions Grant had already planned were needed immediately. Within days there would be a leak from the conference; there always was. Not a leak about the actions to be taken, but about the alarm and concern.

Some secretary would notice that Grant had come back to the Pentagon after dismissing his driver. Another would see that Karins chuckled more than usual when he left the Oval Office, that Senator Bronson and the Assistant Postmaster General went off to have a drink together, all the little nuances, and someone else would put the facts together—the President's staff was worried. Another clerk would add that Karins was reporting on political trends, and another would overhear a remark about Bertram...

No. If they had to take action, take it now while it might work. Grant dismissed his aides with a sense of satisfaction. He had been ready, and the crisis would be over before it began. It was only after they left that he crossed the paneled room to the teak cabinet, opened it, and poured a double scotch.

He laughed at himself as he drank it. That's the boy, Grant. Tear hell out of your ulcer. Punish yourself, you can atone for what you're doing. What you need is a good wife. Somebody who doesn't know a damn thing about politics, who'll listen and tell you you had to do it, that you're still a good man. Everybody ought to have a source of comfort like that. He envied the statesmen of the old days when there would be a Father Confessor trained in statecraft that you could go to for reassurance. Reassurance and maybe a little warning, do this or that or you won't be forgiven.

The Maryland countryside slipped past far below as the Cadillac cruised along on autopilot. A ribbon antenna ran almost to Grant's house, and he watched the twilight scene, house lights blinking, a few surface cars on the roads. Behind him was the sprawling mass of Columbia Welfare Island where most of the people displaced from Washington had ended up, lumps of poured concrete buildings and roof parks, the seething resentment of useless life kept placid by government furnished supplies of Tanith hashpot and borloi and cheap booze. A man born in one of those complexes could stay there all his life if he wanted to, and some did. Grant tried to imagine what it would be like there, but he couldn't. Reports from his agents gave him an intellectual picture, but there was no way to identify with those people, the hopelessness and dulled senses, burning hatreds and terrors. Karins knew, though. Karins had begun his life on a welfare island somewhere in the midwest, clawing his way through the schools to a scholarship, refusing stimulants and dope and never watching tri-v... was it worth it?

The speaker on the dash suddenly came to life, Beethoven cut off in mid bar. "WARNING. YOU ARE APPROACHING A GUARDED AREA. UNAUTHORIZED CRAFT WILL BE DESTROYED WITHOUT FURTHER WARNING. IF YOU HAVE A LEGITIMATE ERRAND IN THIS RESTRICTED AREA, FOLLOW THE GUIDE BEAM TO THE POLICE CHECK STATION. THIS IS A FINAL WARNING."

The Cadillac automatically turned off course, riding the beam down toward State Police headquarters, and Grant cursed. He fumbled with switches on the dash, spoke softly. "This is John Grant, resident in Peachem's Bay. Something seems to be wrong with my transponder."

There was a short wait, then the mechanical voice on the speaker was replaced by a soft feminine tone. "We're very sorry, Mr. Grant. Your signal is correct. Our identification unit seems to be out of order. You may proceed, of course."

"Yeah. Better get that thing fixed before it shoots up a taxpayer," Grant said irritably. Anne Arundel County was a Unity Party stronghold, how long would it last if there was an accident like that? The taxpayers would begin to listen to Bertram and his Freedom Party cant.

"We will see to it immediately, sir," the girl answered. "Good evening."

"Yeah. All right, I'm going home." He took the manual controls and cut across country, ignoring regulations. If they wanted to give him a ticket—all they could do now that they knew who he was—let them. His banking computer would pay the fine without Grant ever being aware of it. It brought a wry smile to his face—traffic regulations were broken, computers noted it in their memories, other computers paid the fines, and no human ever became aware of them. Until finally there were enough tickets that a warning of license suspension would be issued. Since that could never happen to Grant, there was no way he'd ever find out about violations.

There was his home ahead, a big rambling early Twentieth Century place on the cove, his yacht at anchor offshore, wooded grounds. Be nice to stay there a few weeks. He wondered if he wanted to retire. The President certainly did, and most of his colleagues said much the same. The thought of a long rest, repair to his ulcer, sailing out to Bermuda, that was intriguing, but years of inactivity? He couldn't imagine life without responsibilities, and the thought of retirement was vaguely frightening. He'd seen too many old friends come apart just when it looked like they ought to be happiest.

Carver, the chauffeur, rushed out to help Grant down from the Cadillac and take it to the garage; Hapwood was waiting with a glass of sherry in the big library. Prince Bismark, shivering in the presence of his god, put his Doberman head on Grant's lap and stared into his eyes, ready to leap into the fire at command. There was irony in the situation. At home, Grant enjoyed the power of a feudal lord, but it was a power that many wealthy men could command, and it was limited by how strongly the staff felt it worthwhile to stay out of Welfare. But he had only to lift the Security phone in the corner, and his real power, completely invisible and limited only by what the President wanted to find out, would operate. An interesting thing, power. Wealth gave him the visible power, heredity the power over the dog... what gave him the real power of the Security phone?

"What time would you like dinner, sir?" Hapwood asked. "And Miss Sharon is here with a guest."

"A guest?" Grant asked.

"Yes, sir, A young man, Mr. Allan Torrey, sir."

"Have they eaten?"

"Yes, sir. Miss Ackridge called to say that you would be home, but late for dinner."

"All right, Hapwood. I'll eat now and see Miss Grant and her guest afterwards."

"Very good, sir. I will inform the cook." Hapwood left the room invisibly.

Grant smiled again. Hapwood was another fugitive from Welfare, a man who grew up speaking a dialect that Grant would never recognize. What had possessed him to study the mannerisms of English butlers of a hundred years before, perfecting his style until he was known all over the county as the perfect household manager? Why would a man do that?

Certainly there was money in it. Hapwood didn't know it, but Grant had a record of every cent his butler took in, kickbacks from grocers and caterers, "contributions" from gardeners, and the surprisingly well managed investment portfolio. Hapwood could have retired to his own house years ago, moved to another part of the country and assumed the life of a taxpayer investor, but instead here he was, still the perfect butler. It had intrigued Grant enough to have his agents look into Hapwood very carefully, but the man had no politics other than staunch support for Unity, and the only suspicious thing about his contacts was the refinement with which he extracted money from every transaction involving Grant's house. The man had no children and whatever sexual needs he experienced were satisfied by infrequent trips to the fringe areas around Welfare.

Grant ate mechanically, hurrying to be through and see his daughter, yet afraid to meet the boy she had brought home. For a moment he thought of using the Security phone to find out more about him, but he shook his head angrily. Too much of this kind of Security thinking wasn't good; for once he was going to be a parent meeting his daughter's intended. He left half his steak uneaten and went to the high-ceilinged library, sat behind the massive Oriental fruitwood desk with its huge bronze fittings. Behind him and to both sides the walls were lined with bookshelves, immaculate dust-free accounts of the people of dead Empires. It had been years since he took one down. Now, all his reading was confined to typescript reports, some copied by human secretaries but most generated by computers. They told a live story about living people, but sometimes, late at night, as Grant sat in the huge library he wondered if his country were not as dead as the empires in his books. He loved his country but hated her people, all of them: Karins and the new breed, the tranquilized Citizens in their welfare islands, the smug taxpayers who grimly held their privileges... So what was it that he loved? Only history, the story of the greatness that had once been the United States, something found only in books and not in the neat reports with their bright red Security covers.

But then Sharon came in, a lovely girl, far prettier than her mother but without her mother's poise. She ushered in a tall boy in his early twenties. As they crossed the room Grant studied him closely. Nice looking. Long hair, neatly trimmed, conservative moustache for these times although it would have been pretty wild in Grant's day. Blue and violet tunic, red scarf... a little flashy, but even John Jr. went in for clothes like that whenever he got out of CoDominium uniform.

The boy walked hesitantly, almost timidly. Grant wondered if it was fear of him and his position in the government, or just the natural nervousness of a young man about to talk to his fiancée's father. The tiny diamond on Sharon's hand sparkled in the yellow light from the fireplace, and she held the hand unnaturally, not sure of herself with the unfamiliar ring.

"Daddy, I... I've talked so much about him, this is Allan. He's just asked me to marry him! I'm so happy!" Trustingly, sure of his approval, never thinking for a second—Grant wondered if Sharon wasn't the only person in the country who didn't fear him. Except for John Jr., who thank God was beyond the reach of the power of Grant's Security phone. The CD Fleet took care of its own.

"Hello, Allan," Grant stood, extended his hand. Torrey's grip was firm, but his eyes avoided Grant's. "So you want to marry my daughter." He glanced pointedly at her left hand. "Looks like she approves the idea, anyway."

"Yes, sir. Uh, she wanted to wait and ask you before she let me put the ring on, but well... it's my fault, sir." Torrey looked at him this time, almost defiant.

"Yes. Well... Sharon, as long as you're home for the evening, I wish you'd speak to Hapwood about Prince Bismark. I don't think the animal is being fed properly."

"You mean right now?" she asked. She tightened her small mouth into a pout. "Really, Daddy, this is Victorian! Sending me out of the room while you talk to my fiancé!"

"Yes, it is, isn't it?" Grant said nothing else, and finally she turned away.

Then, impishly: "Don't let him scare you, Allan. He's about as dangerous as that... that moosehead in the trophy room!" She fled before there could be any reply.

They sat awkwardly. Grant coming out from behind his desk to sit near the fire with young Torrey. Drinks, offer of a smoke, all the usual amenities, anything to avoid saying something important, but finally Hapwood had brought their refreshments and the door was closed.

"All right, Allan," John began. "Let's be trite and get it over with. How do you intend to support her?"

Torrey looked straight at him, his eyes dancing with what Grant was sure he recognized as concealed amusement. "I expect to be appointed to the Department of the Interior. I'm a trained engineer."

"Interior?" Grant thought for a second. The answer surprised him, he hadn't thought the boy was just another office seeker. Well, why not? "I suppose it could be arranged."

Torrey grinned. It was an infectious grin, and Grant liked it. "Well, sir, it's already arranged . . . I wasn't asking for a job."

"Oh?" Grant shrugged. "I hadn't heard anything—you'll be Civil Service, then?"

"No, sir, Deputy Assistant Secretary. Natural Resources Control. Environments. I took a Master's in ecology with my engineering degree."

"That's interesting, but I can't recall seeing anything about the appointment . . ."

"It won't be official yet, sir. Not until Mr. Bertram is President. For the moment I'm on his staff." The grin was still there, and it was friendly, not hostile, not mocking. The boy thought politics was a game, wanted to win . . .

He's seen the polls, Grant thought. God knows—Allan Torrey? Just who was he on Bertram's staff? "Give my regards to Mr. Bertram when you see him. What is it you do for him?"

Allan shrugged. "Write speeches, carry the mail, run the Xerox—you've been in campaign headquarters, sir. I'm the guy who gets all the jobs nobody else wants."

Grant laughed. "Yeah. Started that way myself. Only staffer they could afford to use as a gopher, they didn't have to pay me. I soon put a stop to that, though. Hired my own gopher out of what I used to contribute. I guess that's not open to you, is it?"

"No, sir. My father's a taxpayer, but . . . well, paying taxes is pretty tough right now."

"Yes." Well at least he wasn't from a Citizen family. Torrey, now just who the hell . . . he could find out when Flora had the Security report. Important thing now was to get to know this boy.

It was hard to do. Allan was frank, open, more relaxed after Hapwood brought his third drink. Grant was pleased to see that the boy refused a fourth. But there was nothing of substance to talk about. No consciousness of the realities of politics. One of Bertram's child crusaders, out to save the United States from people like John Grant although he was too polite to say so. John could remember when he was that young, wanted to save the world, but then it was so different. Nobody wanted to end the CoDominium then, they were too happy to have the Cold

War under control at last. What happened to the great sense of relief when everybody could stop worrying about atomic wars? It was all anybody could think of when Grant was young, how this might be the Last Generation . . . now they took it for granted that there would always be peace. Was peace, then, such a little thing? He realized that Torrey was speaking.

"Take the Baja Project, for example. All those nuclear power plants. And the artificial harbors. Thermal pollution of the Sea of Cortez! They'll kill off a whole ecology just for their cities. And it isn't necessary, sir. I know we have to have living space for cities, God knows I don't want the Citizens cooped up in their welfare islands, but that isn't what the government is planning. What they're going to build will be more estates for taxpayers, not a decent place for the Citizens." He was speaking intently, trying to burn past Grant's gentility, to get to the man underneath.

"I know it isn't part of your Department, sir. You probably don't even know what they're doing. But it's so wrong . . . I'm sorry, sir, but I really believe it. The Lipscomb government has been in too long. It's got away from the people, and . . . and I'm sure you're not aware of it, but the corruption! Sir, I wish you could see some of the reports we have, some of the dirty things the government's done just to stay in power. It's time for a change, and Mr. Bertram is the man, I know he is."

Grant's smile was thin, but he managed to bring it off. "Maybe you're right. I wouldn't mind living in this house instead of the Pentagon. Might as well live in Washington for all the time I manage to get out here." What was the point of it? He wouldn't convince this boy, and Sharon wanted him . . . he'd drop Bertram after the scandals broke. And how could Grant explain that the Baja Project was developed to aid a syndicate of taxpayers, that without their support the government wouldn't last a month? The damn fools, of course they were wrecking the Gulf of California—oh hell, Sea of Cortez. Call it that, it made the six states which were formerly the Republic of Mexico happier. Of course they were wrecking it, through sheer shortsighted idiocy, but what could the government do? You might get the Citizens to huddle around tri-v in their welfare islands, smoke borloi, but without taxpayers . . . There was no point in explanations. At that boy's age, Grant wouldn't have believed it either.

✧ ✧ ✧

Finally, painfully, the interview was over, And there was Sharon, grinning sheepishly because she was engaged to one of Bertram's people, understanding what that really meant no better than Allan Torrey. It was just a game, Bertram would be in government and Lipscomb, the Unity Party, would be the opposition, just the game that the Republicans and Democrats used to play.

How could you tell them that if Unity ever went out, the rules would change, there wouldn't be an alteration anymore. You'd get Bertram against Harmon, or Bertram against the Liberation Party, or worse, Harmon and the Liberation people working together against Bertram, and somebody would try to mobilize the Citizens, get them involved, and the whole structure would come crashing down... and then? Then the Leader, the Man with a Cause, the Friend of The People. It was all there, told time and time again in those aseptically clean books all around him.

BERTRAM AIDES ARRESTED BY INTERCONTINENTAL BUREAU OF INVESTIGATION!! IBI RAIDS SECRET WEAPONS CACHE. NUCLEAR WEAPONS HINTED!!!

Chicago, May 15, (UPI)—IBI agents here have arrested five top aides to Senator Harvey Bertram in what government officials call one of the most despicable plots ever discovered...

Grant sat at his desk and read the transcript of the *extra* tri-v newscast without satisfaction. It had all gone according to plan, and now there was nothing left to do. The evidence was there. He could let Bertram's people wiggle all they wanted to, challenge jurors, challenge judges. The Attorney General, in a spirit of fairness, would even waive the government's rights under the Thirty-first Amendment, let the case be tried under the old adversary rules. It wouldn't matter.

Then, in small type, there it was, and he gasped. "Arrested were Grigory Kalamintor, 19, press secretary to Bertram; Timothy Girodano, 22, secretary; Allan Torrey, 22, executive assistant..." the rest of the page blurred. "Oh my God, what have we done?" Grant asked. He sat with his head in his hands.

He hadn't moved when Miss Ackridge buzzed. "Your daughter on Four, sir. She seems upset."

"Yes." Grant punched the button. Sharon's face swam into view, her makeup ruined by long streaks of tears. She looked ten years older, she looked like her mother during one of...

"Daddy! They've arrested Allan! And I know it isn't true, I was in that house in Chicago two days ago, they didn't have any secret arsenal . . . there wasn't any reason for them to have nuclear weapons! A lot of Mr. Bertram's people said you'd never let the country have an honest election. They said John Grant would see to it, and I told them they were wrong . . . Daddy, what happened? It's true, isn't it? You've done this to stop the election."

He tried to say something, but there was nothing to say. She was right. But where was she calling from, who might be listening in? "I don't know what you're talking about. I saw the newscast about Allan's arrest, but I know nothing more. Come home, kitten, we'll talk about it there."

"Oh no! You're not getting me in that big house! Have Dr. Pollard come over, give a nice friendly little shot, and I forget all about Allan . . . NO! I'm staying right here until . . . I guess I just won't be coming home, Daddy. And when I go to the newspapers, I think they'll listen to me. I don't know what to tell them, but I'm sure Mr. Bertram's people can write something for me. How do you like that, Mister God?"

"Anything you tell the press about the government will be a lie, Sharon. You don't know anything." He fought to stay calm, but he couldn't think what to do. He noticed his assistant get up and leave the office.

"Lies? Where did I learn to lie? I'm only following your example, Daddy dear." The screen went blank. She had hung up on him.

Was it that thin, he thought? The trust she'd had in him, the love, whatever it was . . . was it that thin?

"Sir?" It was Hartman, his assistant.

"Yes."

"She was calling from a house in Champaign, Illinois. A Bertram headquarters they think we don't know about. The phone had a guaranteed no-trace device on it."

"Trusting lot, aren't they?" Grant said. "Have some good men watch the house, but leave her alone." He stood, felt a wave of something, dizziness and something else, so that he had to hold the edge of the desk. "MAKE DAMN SURE THEY LEAVE HER ALONE, DO YOU UNDERSTAND?" he shouted.

Hartman went as pale as Grant. The chief hadn't raised his voice to one of his own people in five years. "Yes, sir, I understand."

"And get out of here." John spoke carefully, in low tones, and the cold mechanical voice was more terrifying than the shout.

Alone he sat staring at the blank telephone, sitting at the seat of power. Now what, he thought? It wasn't generally known that Sharon was engaged to the boy, in fact hardly anyone knew it. He'd talked them out of making it formal until the banns could be announced in the National Cathedral, all the requirements of the Church satisfied. At the time it was just something they should do, but...

But what? He couldn't have the boy released. Not that boy. He wouldn't keep silence as the price of his own freedom. He'd be at a newscaster's booth within five minutes. And then the headlines: BERTRAM AIDE ACCUSES GOVERNMENT. DAUGHTER OF DEPUTY SECRETARY OF DEFENSE SAYS SECRET NUKE CACHE A PLANT ARRANGED BY HER FATHER.

Or something more clever. Of course Bertram's people would say it was a plant, but that didn't matter. Anyone accused of what was nearly the ultimate crime would say that. But if the daughter of the top secret policeman in the country said it... He punched the communicator.

Grand Senator Bronson appeared on the screen, looked up in surprise. "Oh, hello, John. Need something?" Bronson asked it nervously. Whenever John Grant called on the special scrambled circuit, interrupting all other business, cutting off all other conversations, it was likely to be unpleasant.

"Are you alone?"

"Yes."

"When's the next CD warship going outsystem? Not a colony ship, and most especially not a prison ship. A warship."

"Why... I don't know. I suppose anything could be arranged if you'd... what's on your mind, John?"

"I want—" Grant hesitated. But there was no time to be lost. None. "I want space for two very important prisoners. A... a married couple. The crew is not to know their identities, and any crewman who comes in contact with them stays outsystem for at least five years. Got that? I want these people put down on a good colony world, something decent. Like Sparta, where they can't get back again. Nobody ever comes here from Sparta, do they?"

"But... yes, I suppose it can be arranged." Grant's expression discouraged debate.

"It will be arranged. And for tonight. I'll have the prisoners brought to you tonight. You have that CD ship ready. And... and it better not be the *Saratoga.* My son's on that one, he'll... he'll know one of the prisoners." Grant reached for the phone, then drew his hand back. "Make sure there's a chaplain aboard, the kids will be getting married."

Bronson frowned into the telephone lens. "John, are you sure you're all right?"

"Yes. One other thing. They're to have a good estate on Sparta, but they're not to know who arranged it. Just take care of it for me and I'll pay. You have it all?"

It was all so very simple. Direct his agents to arrest Sharon, conduct her to CD Intelligence. No, he wouldn't want to see her first. Have the Attorney General's office send young Torrey to the same place, let it out that he'd escaped, try him *in absentia.* It wasn't as neat as having all of them convicted in open court, but there'd be enough convictions.

Inside, something screamed at him, screamed again and again, this was his daughter, his pretty little girl, the only person in the world who wasn't afraid of him... calmly, almost gently, Grant leaned back in his leather chair. What world would it be for her if the government fell?

He dictated instructions for his agents, took the flimsy order sheet from the writer. His hand didn't tremble at all as he signed it. Then, slowly, carefully, he leaned back again, tasting the blood and bile that he knew would be in his throat the rest of his life; tasting the price of peace.

Under the Hammer

DAVID DRAKE

"Think you're going to like killing, boy?" asked the old man on double crutches.

Rob Jenne turned from the streams of moving cargo to his unnoticed companion in the shade of the starship's hull. His own eyes were pale gray, suited like his dead-white skin to Burlage, whose ruddy sun could raise a blush but not a tan. When they adjusted, they took in the clerical collar which completed the other's costume. The smooth, black synthetic contrasted oddly with the coveralls and shirt of local weave. At that, the Curwinite's outfit was a cut above Rob's own, the same worksuit of Burlage sisal that he had worn as a quarryhand at home. Uniform issue would come soon.

At least, he hoped and prayed it would.

When the youth looked away after an embarrassed grin, the priest chuckled. "Another damned old fool, hey, boy? There were a few in your family, weren't there... the ones who'd quote the *Book of the Way* saying not to kill—and here you go off for a hired murderer. Right?" He laughed again, seeing he had the younger man's attention. "But that by itself wouldn't be so hard to take—you were leaving your family anyway, weren't you, nobody really believes they'll keep close to their people after five years, ten years of star hopping. But your mates, though, the team you worked with... how did you explain to them why you were leaving a good job to go on contract? 'Via!'" the priest mimicked, his tones so close to those of Barney Larsen, the gang boss, that

Rob started in surprise, "you get your coppy ass shot off, lad, and it'll serve you right for being a fool!"

"How do you know I signed for a mercenary?" Jenne asked, clenching his great, calloused hands on the handle of his carry-all. It was everything he owned in the universe in which he no longer had a home. "And how'd you know about my Aunt Gudrun?"

"Haven't I seen a thousand of you?" the priest blazed back, his eyes like sparks glinting from the drill shaft as the sledge drove it deeper into the rock. "You're young and strong and bright enough to pass Alois Hammer's tests—you be proud of that, boy, few enough are fit for Hammer's Slammers. There you were, a man grown who'd read all the cop about mercenaries, believed most of it . . . more'n ever you did the *Book of the Way*, anyhow. Sure, I know. So you got some off-planet factor to send your papers in for you, for the sake of the bounty he'll get from the colonel if you make the grade—"

The priest caught Rob's blink of surprise. He chuckled again, a cruel, unpriestly sound, and said, "He told you it was for friendship? One a these days you'll learn what friendship counts, when you get an order that means the death of a friend—and you carry it out."

Rob stared at the priest in repulsion, the grizzled chin resting on interlaced fingers and the crutches under either armpit supporting most of his weight. "It's my life," the recruit said with sulky defiance. "Soon as they pick me up here, you can go back to living your own. 'Less you'd be willing to do that right now?"

"They'll come soon enough, boy," the older man said in a milder voice. "Sure, you've been ridden by everybody you know . . . now that you're alone, here's a stranger riding you, too. I don't mean it like I sound . . . wasn't born to the work, I guess. There's priests—and maybe the better ones—who'd say that signing on with mercenaries means so long a spiral down that maybe your soul won't come out of it in another life or another hundred. But I don't see it like that.

"Life's a forge, boy, and the purest metal comes from the hottest fire. When you've been under the hammer a few times, you'll find you've been beaten down to the real, no lies, no excuses. There'll be a time, then, when you got to look over the product . . . and if you don't like what you see, well, maybe there's time for change, too."

The priest turned his head to scan the half of the horizon not blocked by the bellied-down bulk of the starship. Ant columns of stevedores manhandled cargo from the ship's rollerway into horse- and ox-drawn wagons in the foreground: like most frontier worlds, Burlage included, self-powered machinery was rare in the back country. Beyond the men and draft animals stretched the fields, studded frequently by orange-golden clumps of native vegetation.

"Nobody knows how little his life's worth till he's put it on the line a couple times," the old man said. "For nothing. Look at it here on Curwin—the seaboard taxed these uplands into revolt, then had to spend what they'd robbed and more to hire an armored regiment. So boys like you from—Scania? Felsen?—"

"Burlage, sir."

"Sure, a quarryman, should have known from your shoulders. You come in to shoot farmers for a gang of coastal moneymen you don't know and wouldn't like if you did." The priest paused, less for effect than to heave in a quick, angry breath that threatened his shirt buttons. "And maybe you'll die, too; if the Slammers were immortal, they wouldn't need recruits. But some that die will die like saints, boy, die martyrs of the Way, for no reason, for no reason...

"Your ride's here, boy."

The suddenly emotionless words surprised Rob as much as a scream in a silent prayer would have. Hissing like a gun-studded dragon, a gray-metal combat car slid onto the landing field from the west. Light dust puffed from beneath it: although the flatbed trailer behind was supported on standard wheels, the armored vehicle itself hovered a hand's-breadth above the surface at all points. A dozen powerful fans on the underside of the car kept it floating on an invisible bubble of air, despite the weight of the fusion power unit and the iridium-ceramic armor. Rob had seen combat cars on the entertainment cube occasionally, but those skittering miniatures gave no hint of the awesome power that emanated in reality from the machines. This one was seven meters long and three wide at the base, the armored sides curving up like a turtle's back to the open fighting compartment in the rear.

From the hatch in front of the power plant stuck the driver's head, a black-mirrored ball in a helmet with full face shield down. Road dust drifted away from the man in a barely visible haze, cleansed from the helmet's optics by a static charge. Faceless and terrible to the unfamiliar Burlager, the driver guided toward the starship a machine that appeared no more inhuman than did the man himself.

"Undercrewed," the priest murmured. "Two men on the back deck aren't enough for a car running single."

The older man's jargon was unfamiliar but Rob could follow his gist by looking at the vehicle. The two men standing above the waist-high armor of the rear compartment were clearly fewer than had been contemplated when the combat car was designed. Its visible armament comprised a heavy powergun forward to fire over the head of the driver, and similar weapons, also swivel-mounted, on either side to command the flanks and rear of the vehicle. But with only two men in the compartment there was a dangerous gap in the circle of fire the car could lay down if ambushed. Another vehicle for escort would have eased the danger, but this one was alone save for the trailer it pulled.

Though as the combat car drew closer, Rob began to wonder if the two soldiers present couldn't handle anything that occurred. Both were in full battle dress, wearing helmets and laminated back and breast armor over their khaki. Their faceplates were clipped open. The one at the forward gun, his eyes as deep-sunken and deadly as the three revolving barrels of his weapon, was in his forties and further aged by the dust sweated into black grime in the creases of his face. His head rotated in tiny jerks, taking in every nuance of the sullen crowd parting for his war-car. The other soldier was huge by comparison with the first and lounged across the back in feigned leisure: feigned, because either hand was within its breadth of a powergun's trigger, and his limbs were as controlled as spring steel.

With careless expertise, the driver backed his trailer up to the conveyor line. A delicate hand with the fans allowed him to angle them slightly, drifting the rear of the combat car to edge the trailer in the opposite direction. The larger soldier contemptuously thumbed a waiting horse and wagon out of its slot. The teamster's curse brought only a grin and a big hand rested on a powergun's receiver, less a threat than a promise. The combat car eased into the space.

"Wait for an old man," the priest said as Rob lifted his carry-all, "and I'll go with you." Glad even for that company, the recruit smiled nervously, fitting his stride to the other's surprisingly nimble swing-and-pause, swing-and-pause.

The driver dialed back minusculy on the power and allowed the big vehicle to settle on the ground without a skip or a tremor. One hand slid back the face shield to a high, narrow nose and eyes that alertly focused on the two men approaching. "The Lord and his martyrs!" the driver cried in amazement. "It's Blacky himself come in with our newbie!"

Both soldiers on the back deck slewed their eyes around at the cry. The smaller one took one glance, then leaped the two meters to the ground to clasp Rob's companion. "Hey!" he shouted, oblivious of the recruit shifting his weight uncertainly. "Via, it's good to see you! But what're you doing on Curwin?"

"I came back here afterwards," the older man answered with a smile. "Born here, I must've told you... though we didn't talk a lot. I'm a priest now, see?"

"And I'm a flirt like the load we're supposed to pick up," the driver said, dismounting with more care than his companion. Abreast of the first soldier, he too took in the round collar and halted gape-mouthed. "Lord, I'll be a coppy rag if you ain't," he breathed. "Whoever heard of a blower chief taking the Way?"

"Shut up, Jake," the first soldier said without rancor. He stepped back from the priest to take a better look, then seemed to notice Rob. "Umm," he said, "you the recruit from Burlage?"

"Yessir. M-my name's Rob Jenne, sir."

"Not 'sir,' there's enough sirs around already," the veteran said. "I'm Chero, except if there's lots of brass around, then make it Sergeant-Commander Worzer. Look, take your gear back to the trailer and give Leon a hand with the load."

"Hey, Blacky," he continued with concern, ignoring Rob again, "what's wrong with your legs? We got the best there was."

"Oh, they're fine," Rob heard the old man reply, "but they need a weekly tuning. Out here we don't have the computers, you know; so I get the astrogation boys to sync me up on the ship's hardware whenever one docks in—just waiting for a chance now. But in six months the servos are far enough out of line that I have to shut off the power till the next ship arrives. You'd be surprised how well I get around on these pegs, though...."

Leon, the huge third crew member, had loosed the top catches of his body armor for ventilation. From the look of it, the laminated casing should have been a size larger; but Rob wasn't sure anything larger was made. The gunner's skin where exposed was the dense black of a basalt outcropping. "They'll be a big crate to go on, so just set your gear down till we get it loaded," he said. Then he grinned at Rob, teeth square and slightly yellow against his face. "Think you can take me?"

That was a challenge the recruit could understand, the first he could meet fairly since boarding the starship with a one-way ticket to a planet he had never heard of. He took in the waiting veteran quickly but carefully, proud of his own rock-hardened muscles but certain the other man had been raised just as hard. "I give you best," the blond said. "Unless you feel you got to prove it?"

The grin broadened and a great black hand reached out to clasp Rob's. "Naw," the soldier said, "just like to clear the air at the start. Some of the big ones; Lord, testy ain't the word. All they can think about's what they want to prove with me . . . so they don't watch their side of the car, and then there's trouble for everybody."

"Hammer's Regiment?" called an unfamiliar voice. Both men looked up. Down the conveyor rode a blue-tunicked ship's man in front of what first appeared to be a huge crate. At second glance Rob saw that it was a cage of light alloy holding four . . . "Dear Lord!" the recruit gasped.

"Roger, Hammer's," Leon agreed, handing the crewman a plastic chit while the latter cut power to the rollers to halt the cage. The chit slipped into the computer linkage on the crewman's left wrist, lighting a green indicator when it proved itself a genuine bill of lading.

There were four female humanoids in the cage—stark naked except for a dusting of fine blue scales. Rob blinked. One of the near-women stood with a smile—Lord, she had no teeth!—and rubbed her groin deliberately against one of the vertical bars.

"First-quality Genefran flirts," Leon chuckled. "Ain't human, boy, but the next best thing."

"Better," threw in Jake, who had swung himself into the fighting compartment as soon as the cage arrived. "I tell you, kid, you never had it till you had a flirt. Surgically modified and psychologically prepared. Rowf!"

"N-not human?" Rob stumbled, unable to take his eyes off the cage. "You mean like *monkeys?*"

Leon's grin lit his face again, and the driver cackled, "Well, don't know about monkeys, but they're a whole lot like sheep."

"You take the left side and we'll get this aboard," Leon directed. The trailer's bed was half a meter below the rollerway so that the cage, though heavy and awkward, could be slid without much lifting.

Rob gripped the bars numbly, turning his face down from the tittering beside him. "Amazing what they can do with implants and a wig," Jake was going on, "though a course there's a lot of cutting to do first, but those ain't the differences you see, if you follow. The scales, now—they have a way—"

"Lift!" Leon ordered, and Rob straightened at the knees. They took two steps backward with the cage wobbling above them as the girls—the flirts!—squealed and hopped about. "Down!" and cage clashed on trailer as the two big men moved in unison.

Rob stepped back, his mouth working in distaste, unaware of the black soldier's new look of respect. Quarry work left a man used to awkward weights. "This is foul," the recruit marveled. "Are those really going back with us for, for . . ."

"Rest 'n' relaxation," Leon agreed, snapping tiedowns around the bars.

"But how . . ." Rob began, looking again at the cage. When the red-wigged flirt fondled her left breast upward, he could see the implant scars pale against the blue. The scales were more thinly spread where the skin had been stretched in molding it. "I'll *never* touch something like that. Look, maybe Burlage is pretty backward about . . . things, about sex, I don't know. But I don't see how anybody could . . . I mean—"

"Via, wait till you been here as long as we have," Jake gibed. He clenched his right hand and pumped it suggestively. "Field expedients, that's all."

"On this kinda contract," Leon explained, stepping around to get at the remaining tiedowns, "you can't trust the local girls. Least not in the field, like we are. The colonel likes to keep us patrol sections pretty much self-contained."

"Yeah," Jake broke in—would his cracked tenor never cease? "Why, some of these whores, they take a razor blade, see—in a cork, you know?—and, well, never mind." He laughed, seeing Rob's face.

"Jake," Sergeant Worzer called, "shut up and hop in."

The driver slipped instantly into his hatch. Disgusting as Rob found the little man, he recognized his ability. Jake moved with lethal certainty and a speed that belied the weight of his body armor.

"Ready to lift, Chero?" he asked.

The priest was levering himself toward the starship again. Worzer watched him go for a moment, shook his head. "Just run us out to the edge of the field," he directed. "I got a few things to show our recruit before we head back; nobody rides in my car without knowing how to work the guns." With a sigh he hopped into the fighting compartment. Leon motioned Rob in front of him. Gingerly, the recruit stepped onto the trailer hitch, gripped the armored rim with both hands, lifted himself aboard. Leon followed. The trailer bonged as he pushed off from it, and his bulk cramped the littered compartment as soon as he grunted over the side.

"Put this on," Worzer ordered, handing Rob a dusty, bulbous helmet like the others wore. "Brought a battle suit for you, too," he said, kicking the jointed armor leaning against the back of the compartment, "but it'd no more fit you than it would Leon there."

The black laughed. "Gonna be tight back here till the kid or me gets zapped."

"Move 'er out," Worzer ordered. The words came through unsuspected earphones in Rob's helmet, although the sergeant had simply spoken, without visibly activating a pickup.

The car vibrated as the fans revved, then lifted with scarcely a jerk. From behind came the squeals and chirrups of the flirts as the trailer rocked over the irregularities in the field.

Worzer looked hard at the starship's open crew portal as they hissed past it. "Funny what folks go an' do," he said to no one in particular. "Via, wonder what I'll be in another ten years."

"Pet food, likely," joked the driver, taking part in the conversation although physically separated from the other crewmen.

"Shut up, Jake," repeated the blower captain. "And you can hold it up here, we're out far enough."

The combat car obediently settled on the edge of the stabilized area. The port itself had capacity for two ships at a time; the region it served did not. Though with the high cost of animal transport many manufactures could be star-hopped to Curwin's back country more cheaply than they could be carried from the planet's own more urbanized areas, the only available exchange was raw agricultural produce—again limited to the immediate locality by the archaic transport. Its fans purring below audibility, the armored vehicle rested on an empty area of no significance to the region—unless the central government should choose to land another regiment of mercenaries on it.

"Look," the sergeant said, his deep-set eyes catching Rob's, "we'll pass you on to the firebase when we take the other three flirts in next week. They got a training section there. We got six cars in this patrol, that's not enough margin to fool with training a newbie. But neither's it enough to keep somebody useless underfoot for a week, so we'll give you some basics. Not so you can wise-ass when you get to training section, just so you don't get somebody killed if it drops in the pot. Clear?"

"Yessir." Rob broke his eyes away, then realized how foolish he must look staring at his own clasped hands. He looked back at Worzer.

"Just so it's understood," the sergeant said with a nod. "Leon, show him how the gun works."

The big black rotated his weapon so that the muzzle faced forward and the right side was toward Rob and the interior of the car. The mechanism itself was encased in dull-enameled steel ornamented with knobs and levers of unguessable intent. The barrels were stubby iridium cylinders with smooth, 2 cm bores. Leon touched one of the buttons, then threw a lever back. The plate to which the barrels were attached rotated 120 degrees around their common axis, and a thick disk of plastic popped out into the gunner's hand.

"When the bottom barrel's ready to fire, the next one clockwise is loading one a these"—Leon held up the 2 cm disk—"and the other barrel, the one that's just fired, blows out the empty."

"There's a liquid nitrogen ejector," Worzer put in. "Cools the bore same time it kicks out the empty."

"She feeds up through the mount," the big soldier went on, his index finger tracing the path of the energized disks from the closed hopper bulging in the sidewall, through the ball joint and into the weapon's receiver. "If you try to fire and she don't, check this." The columnar finger indicated but did not move the stud it had first pressed on the side of the gun. "That's the safety. She still doesn't fire, pull this"—he clacked the lever, rotating the barrel cluster around one-third turn and catching the loaded round that flew out. "Maybe there was a dud round. She still don't go, just get down outa the way. We start telling you about second-order malfunctions and you won't remember where the trigger is."

"Ah, where is the trigger?" Rob asked diffidently.

Jake's laughter rang through the earphones and Worzer himself smiled for the first time. The sergeant reached out and rotated the gun. "See the grips?" he asked, pointing to the double handles at the back of the receiver. Rob nodded.

"OK," Worzer continued, "you hold it there"—he demonstrated—"and to fire, you just press your thumbs against the trigger plate between 'em. Let up and it quits. Simple."

"You can clear this field as quick as you can spin this little honey," Leon said, patting the gun with affection. "The hicks out there"—his arm swept the woods and cultivated fields promiscuously—"got some rifles, they hunted before the trouble started, but no powerguns to mention. About all they do since we moved in is maybe pop a shot or two off, and hide in their holes."

"They've got some underground stockpiles," Worzer said, amplifying Leon's words, "explosives, maybe some factories to make rifle ammo. But the colonel set up a recce net—spy satellites, you know—as part of the contract. Any funny movement day or night, a signal goes down to whoever's patrolling there. A couple calls and we check out the area with ground sensors . . . anything funny then—vibration, hollows showing up on the echo sounder, magnetics—anything!—and bam! we call in the artillery."

"Won't take much of a jog on the way back," Leon suggested, "and we can check out that report from last night."

"Via, that was just a couple dogs," Jake objected.

"OK, so we prove it was a couple dogs," rumbled the gunner. "Or maybe the hicks got smart and they're shielding their infrared now. Been too damn long since anything popped in this sector."

"Thing to remember, kid," Worzer summed up, "is never get buzzed at this job. Stay cool, you're fine. This car's got more firepower'n everything hostile in fifty klicks. One call to the firebase brings in our arty, anything from smoke shells to a nuke. The rest of our section can be here in twenty minutes, or a tank platoon from the firebase in two hours. Just stay cool."

✧ ✧ ✧

Turning forward, the sergeant said, "OK, take her home, Jake. We'll try that movement report on the way."

The combat car shuddered off the ground, the flirts shrieking. Rob eyed them, blushed, and turned back to his powergun, feeling conspicuous. He took the grips, liking the deliberate way the weapon swung. The safety button was glowing green, but he suddenly realized that he didn't know the color code. Green for safe? Or green for ready? He extended his index finger to the switch.

"Whoa, careful, kid!" Leon warned. "You cut fifty civvies in half your first day and the colonel won't like it one bit."

Sheepishly, Rob drew back his finger. His ears burned, mercifully hidden beneath the helmet.

They slid over the dusty road in a flat, white cloud at about forty kph. It seemed shockingly fast to the recruit, but he realized that the car could probably move much faster were it not for the live cargo behind. Even as it was, the trailer bounced dangerously from side to side.

The road led through a gullied scattering of grain plots, generally fenced with withies rather than imported metal. Houses were relatively uncommon. Apparently each farmer plowed several separate locations rather than trying to work the rugged or less productive areas. Occasionally they passed a rough-garbed local at work. The scowls thrown up at the smoothly running war-car were hostile, but there was nothing more overt.

"OK," Jake warned, "here's where it gets interesting. Sure you still want this half-assed check while we got the trailer hitched?"

"It won't be far," Worzer answered. "Go ahead." He turned to Rob, touching the recruit's shoulder and pointing to the lighted map panel beside the forward gun. "Look, Jenne," he said, keeping one eye on the countryside as Jake took the car off the road in a sweeping turn, "if you need to call in a location to the firebase, here's the trick. The red dot"—it was in the center of the display and remained there although the map itself seemed to be flowing kitty-corner across the screen as the combat car moved—"that's us. The black dot"—the veteran thumbed a small wheel beside the display and the map, red dot and all, shifted to the right on the panel, leaving a black dot in the center—"that's your pointer. The computer feeds out the grid coordinates here"—his finger touched the window above the map display. Six digits, changing as the map moved under the centered black dot, winked brightly.

"You just put the black dot on a bunker site, say, and read off the figures to Fire Central. The arty'll do all the rest."

"Ah," Rob murmured, "ah . . . Sergeant, how do you get the little dot off that and onto a bunker like you said?"

There was a moment's silence. "You know how to read a map, don't you, kid?" Worzer finally asked.

"What's that, sir?"

The earphones boomed and cackled with raucous laughter. "Oh, my coppy ass!" the sergeant snarled. He snapped the little wheel back, re-centering the red dot. "Lord, I don't know how the training cadre takes it!"

Rob hid his flaming embarrassment by staring over his gunsights. He didn't really know how to use them, either. He didn't know why he'd left Conner's Stoneworks, where he was the cleanest, fastest driller on the whole coppy crew. His powerful hands squeezed at the grips as if they were the driver's throat through which bubbles of laughter still burst.

"Shut up, Jake," the sergeant finally ordered. "Most of us had to learn something new when we joined. Remember how the ol' man found you your first day, pissing up against the barracks?"

Jake quieted.

They had skirted a fence of cane palings, brushing it once without serious effect. Russet grass flanking the fence flattened under the combat car's downdraft, then sprang up unharmed as the vehicle moved past. Jake seemed to be following a farm track leading from the field to a rambling, substantially constructed building on the near hilltop. Instead of running with the ground's rise, however, the car cut through brush and down a half-meter bank into a broad-based arroyo. The bushes were too stiff to lie down under the fans. They crunched and howled in the blades, making the car buck, and ricocheted wildly from under the skirts. The bottom of the arroyo was sand, clean-swept by recent runoff. It boiled fiercely as the car first shoomped into it, then ignored the fans entirely. Somehow Jake had managed not to overturn the trailer, although its cargo had been screaming with fear for several minutes.

"Hold up," Worzer ordered suddenly as he swung his weapon toward the left-hand bank. The wash was about thirty meters wide at that point, sides sheer and a meter high. Rob glanced forward to see that a small screen to Worzer's left on the bulkhead, previously dark, was now crossed by three vari-colored lines. The red one was bouncing frantically.

"They got an entrance, sure 'nough," Leon said. He aimed his powergun at the same point, then snapped his face shield down. "Watch it, kid," he said. The black's right hand fumbled in a metal can welded to the blower's side. Most of the paint had chipped from the stenciled legend: grenades. What appeared to be a lazy overarm toss snapped a knobby ball the size of a child's fist straight and hard against the bank.

Dirt and rock fragments shotgunned in all directions. The gully side burst in a globe of black streaked with garnet fire, followed by a shock wave that was a physical blow.

"Watch your side, kid!" somebody shouted through the din, but Rob's bulging eyes were focused on the collapsing bank, the empty triangle of black gaping suddenly through the dust—the two ravening whiplashes of directed lightning ripping into it to blast and scatter.

The barrel clusters of the two veterans' powerguns spun whining, kicking gray, eroded disks out of their mechanisms in nervous arcs. The bolts they shot were blue-green flashes barely visible until they struck a target and exploded it with transferred energy. The very rock burst in droplets of glassy slag splashing high in the air and even back into the war-car to pop against the metal.

Leon's gun paused as his fingers hooked another grenade. "Hold it!" he warned. The sergeant, too, came off the trigger, and the bomb arrowed into the now-vitrified gap in the tunnel mouth. Dirt and glass shards blew straight back at the bang. A stretch of ground sagged for twenty meters beyond the gully wall, closing the tunnel the first explosion had opened.

Then there was silence. Even the flirts, huddled in a terrified heap on the floor of their cage, were soundless.

Glowing orange specks vibrated on Rob's retinas; the cyan bolts had been more intense than he had realized. "Via," he said in awe, "how do they dare . . . ?"

"Bullet kills you just as dead," Worzer grunted. "Jake, think you can climb that wall?"

"Sure. She'll buck a mite in the loose stuff." The gully side was a gentle declivity, now, where the grenades had blown it in. "Wanna unhitch the trailer first?"

"Negative, nobody gets off the blower till we clean this up."

"Umm, don't want to let somebody else in on the fun, maybe?" the driver queried. If he was tense, his voice did not indicate it. Rob's palms were sweaty. His glands had understood before his mind had that his companions were considering smashing up, unaided, a guerrilla stronghold.

"Cop," Leon objected determinedly. "We found it, didn't we?"

"Let's go," Worzer ordered. "Kid, watch your side. They sure got another entrance, maybe a couple."

The car nosed gently toward the subsided bank, wallowed briefly as the driver fed more power to the forward fans to lift the bow. With a surge and a roar, the big vehicle climbed. Its fans caught a few pebbles and whanged them around inside the plenum chamber like a rattle of sudden gunfire. At half speed, the car glided toward another fenced grainplot, leaving behind it a rising pall of dust.

"Straight as a plumb line," Worzer commented, his eyes flicking his sensor screen. "Bastards'll be waiting for us."

Rob glanced at him—a mistake. The slam-spang! of shot and ricochet were nearly simultaneous. The recruit whirled back, bawling in surprise. The rifle pit had opened within five meters of him, and only the haste of the dark-featured guerrilla had saved Rob from his first shot. Rob pivoted his powergun like a hammer, both thumbs mashing down the trigger. Nothing happened. The guerrilla ducked anyway, the black circle of his foxhole shaped into a thick crescent by the lid lying askew.

Safety, *safety!* Rob's mind screamed and he punched the button fat-fingered. The rifleman raised his head just in time to meet the hose of fire that darted from the recruit's gun. The guerrilla's head exploded. His brains, flash-cooked by the first shot, changed instantly from a colloid to a blast of steam that scattered itself over a three-meter circle. The smoldering fragments of the rifle followed the torso as it slid downward.

The combat car roared into the field of waist-high grain, ripping down twenty meters of woven fencing to make its passage. Rob, vaguely aware of other shots and cries forward, vomited onto the floor of the compartment. A colossal explosion nearby slewed the car sideways. As Rob raised his eyes, he noticed three more swarthy riflemen darting through the grain from the right rear of the vehicle.

"Here!" he cried. He swiveled the weapon blindly, his hips colliding with Worzer in the cramped space. A rifle bullet cracked past his helmet. He screamed something again but his own fire was too high, blue-green droplets against the clear sky, and the guerrillas had grabbed the bars while the flirts jumped and blatted.

The rifles were slamming but the flirts were in the way of Rob's gun. "Down! Down!" he shouted uselessly, and the red-haired flirt pitched across the cage with one synthetic breast torn away by the bullet she had leaped in front of. Leon cursed and slumped across Rob's feet, and then it was Chero Worzer shouting, "Hard left, Jake," and leaning across the fallen gunner to rotate his weapon. The combat car tilted left as the bow came around, pinching the trailer against the left rear of the vehicle—in the path of Worzer's powergun. The cage's light alloy bloomed in superheated fireballs as the cyan bolts ripped through it. Both tires exploded together, and there was a red mist of blood in the air. The one guerrilla who had ducked under the burst dropped his rifle and ran.

Worzer cut him in half as he took his third step.

The sergeant gave the wreckage only a glance, then knelt beside Leon. "Cop, he's gone," he said. The bullet had struck the big man in the neck between helmet and body armor, and there was almost a gallon of blood on the floor of the compartment.

"Leon?" Jake asked.

"Yeah. Lord, there musta been twenty kilos of explosive in that satchel charge. If he hadn't hit it in the air . . ." Worzer looked back at the wreck of the trailer, then at Rob. "Kid, can you unhitch that yourself?"

"You just *killed* them," Rob blurted. He was half-blinded by tears and the afterimage of the gunfire.

"Via, they did their best on us, didn't they?" the sergeant snarled. His face was tiger striped by dust and sweat.

"No, not them!" the boy cried. "Not them—the girls. You just—"

Worzer's iron fingers gripped Rob by the chin and turned the recruit remorselessly toward the carnage behind. The flirts had been torn apart by their own fluids, some pieces flung through gaps in the mangled cage. "Look at 'em, Jenne!" Worzer demanded. "They ain't human but if they was, if it was *Leon* back there, I'd a done it."

His fingers uncurled from Rob's chin and slammed in a fist against the car's armor. "This ain't heroes, it ain't no coppy game you play when you want to! You do what you got to do, 'cause if you don't, some poor bastard gets killed later when he tries to. "Now get down there and unhitch us."

"Yes, sir." Rob gripped the lip of the car for support.

Worzer's voice, more gentle, came through the haze of tears: "And watch it, kid. Just because they're keeping their heads down don't mean they're all gone." Then, "Wait." Another pause while the sergeant unfastened the belt and holstered handgun from his waist and handed it to Rob. Leon wore a similar weapon, but Worzer did not touch the body. Rob wordlessly clipped the belt, loose for not being fitted over armor, and swung down from the combat car.

The hitch had a quick-release handle, but the torquing it had received in the last seconds of battle had jammed it. Nervously aware that the sergeant's darting-eyed watchfulness was no pretense, that the shot-scythed grainfield could hide still another guerrilla, or a platoon of them, Rob smashed his boot heel against the catch. It held. Wishing for his driller's sledge, he kicked again.

"Sarge!" Jake shouted. Grain rustled on the other side of the combat car, and against the sky beyond the scarred armor loomed a parcel. Rob threw himself flat.

The explosion picked him up from the ground and bounced him twice, despite the shielding bulk of the combat car. Stumbling upright, Rob steadied himself on the armored side.

The metal felt odd. It no longer trembled with the ready power of the fans. The car was dead, lying at rest on the torn-up soil. With three quick strides, the recruit rounded the bow of the vehicle. He had no time to inspect the dished-in metal, because another swarthy guerrilla was approaching from the other side.

Seeing Rob, the ex-farmer shouted something and drew a long knife. Rob took a step back, remembered the pistol. He tugged at its unfamiliar grip and the weapon popped free into his hand. It seemed the most natural thing in the world to finger the safety, placed just as the tribarrel's had been, then trigger two shots into the face of the lunging guerrilla. The snarl of hatred blanked as the body tumbled facedown at Rob's feet. The knife had flown somewhere into the grain.

"Ebros?" a man called. Another lid had raised from the ground ten meters away. Rob fired at the hole, missed badly. He climbed the caved-in bow, clumsily one-handed, keeping the pistol raised.

There was nothing but twisted metal where the driver had been. Sergeant Worzer was still semi-erect, clutched against his powergun by a length of structural tubing. It had curled around both his thighs, fluid under the stunning impact of the satchel charge. The map display was a pearly blank, though the window above it still read incongruously 614579 and the red line on the detector screen blipped in nervous solitude. Worzer's helmet was gone, having flayed a bloody track across his scalp as it sailed away. His lips moved, though, and when Rob put his face near the sergeant's he could hear, "The red . . . pull the red tab . . ."

Over the left breast of each set of armor were a blue and a red tab. Rob had assumed they were decorations of some sort. He shifted the sergeant gently. The tab was locked down by a cotter pin which he yanked out. Something hissed in the armor as he pulled the tab, and Sergeant Worzer murmured, "Oh Lord. Oh Lord." Then, "Now the stimulant, the blue tab."

After the second injection sped into his system, the sergeant opened his eyes. Rob was already trying to straighten the entrapping tube. "Forget it," Worzer ordered weakly. "It's inside, too . . . damn armor musta flexed. Oh Lord." He closed his eyes, opened them in time to see another head peak cautiously from the tunnel mouth. "Bastard!" he rasped, and faster than he spoke he triggered his powergun. Its motor whined spitefully though the burst went wide. The head disappeared.

"I want you to run back to the gully," the sergeant said, resting his eyes again. "You get there, you say 'Fire Central.' That cuts in the arty frequency automatic. Then you say, 'Bunker complex . . .'" Worzer looked down. "'Six-one-four, five-seven-nine.' Stay low and wait for a patrol."

"It won't bend!" Rob snarled in frustration as his fingers slid again from the blood-slick tubing.

"Jenne, get your ass out of here, *now*."

"Sergeant—"

"Lord curse your soul, get out or I'll call it in myself! Do I look like I wanna live?"

"Oh, Via . . ." Rob tried to reholster the pistol he had set on the bloody floor. It slipped back with a clang. He left it, gripping the sidewall again.

"Maybe tell Dad it was good to see him," Worzer whispered. "You lose touch in this business, Lord knows you do."

"Sir?"

"The priest . . . you met him. Sergeant-Major Worzer, he was. Oh Lord, *move it*—"

At the muffled scream, the recruit leaped from the smashed war-car and ran blindly back the way they had come. He did not know he had reached the gully until the ground flew out from under him and he pitched spread-eagled onto the sand. "Fire Central," he sobbed through strangled breaths, "Fire Central."

"Clear," a strange voice snapped crisply. "Data?"

"Wh-what?"

"Lord and martyrs," the voice blasted, "if you're screwing around on firing channels, you'll wish you never saw daylight!"

"S-six . . . oh Lord, yes, six-one-four, five-seven-nine," Rob singsonged. He was staring at the smooth sand. "Bunkers, the sergeant says it's bunkers."

"Roger," the voice said, businesslike again. "Ranging in fifteen."

Could they really swing those mighty guns so swiftly, those snub-barreled rocket howitzers whose firing looked so impressive on the entertainment cube?

"On the way," warned the voice.

The big tribarrel whined again from the combat car, the silent lash of its bolts answered this time by a crash of rifle shots. A flattened bullet burred through the air over where Rob lay. It was lost in the eerie, thunderous shriek from the northwest.

"Splash," the helmet said.

The ground bucked. From the grainplot spouted rock, smoke, and metal fragments into a black column fifty meters high.

"Are we on?" the voice demanded.

"Oh, Lord," Rob prayed, beating his fists against the sand. "Oh Lord."

"Via, what is this?" the helmet wondered aloud. Then, "All guns, battery five."

And the earth began to ripple and gout under the hammer of the guns.

Time Piece

JOE W. HALDEMAN

They say you've got a fifty-fifty chance every time you go out. That makes it one chance in eight that you'll live to see your third furlough; the one I'm on now.

Somehow the odds don't keep people from trying to join. Even though not one in a thousand gets through the years of training and examination, there's no shortage of cannon fodder. And that's what we are. The most expensive, best trained cannon fodder in the history of warfare. Human history, anyhow; who can speak for the enemy?

I don't even call them snails anymore. And the thought of them doesn't trigger that instant flash of revulsion, hate, kill-fever—the psyconditioning wore off years ago, and they didn't renew it. They've stopped doing it to new recruits; no percentage in berserkers. I was a wild one the first couple of trips, though.

Strange world I've come back to. Gets stranger every time, of course. Even sitting here in a bogus twenty-first-century bar, where everyone speaks Basic and there's real wood on the walls and peaceful holograms instead of plugins, and music made by men . . .

But it leaks through. I don't pay by card, let alone by coin. The credit register monitors my alpha waves and communicates with the bank every time I order a drink. And, in case I've become addicted to more modern vices, there's a feelie matrix (modified to look like an old-fashioned visiphone booth) where I can have my brain stimulated directly. Thanks but no, thanks—always get this picture of dirty hands inside my skull, kneading, rubbing. Like when you get too close to the enemy and they open a hole in your mind and you go spinning down and down and never reach the bottom till you die. I almost got too close last time.

We were on a three-man reconnaissance patrol, bound for a hellish little planet circling the red giant Antares. Now red giant stars don't form planets in the natural course of things, so we had ignored Antares; we control most of the space around it, so why waste time in idle exploration? But the enemy had detected this little planet—God knows how—and about ten years after they landed there, we monitored their presence (gravity waves from the ships' braking) and my team was assigned the reconnaissance. Three men against many, many of the enemy—but we weren't supposed to fight if we could help it; just take a look around, record what we saw, and leave a message beacon on our way back, about a light-year out from Antares. Theoretically, the troopship following us by a month will pick up the information and use it to put together a battle plan. Actually, three more recon patrols precede the troop ship at one-week intervals; insurance against the high probability that any one patrol will be caught and destroyed. As the first team in, we have a pretty good chance of success, but the ones to follow would be in trouble if we didn't get back out. We'd be past caring, of course: the enemy doesn't take prisoners.

We came out of lightspeed close to Antares, so the bulk of the star would mask our braking disturbance, and inserted the ship in a hyperbolic orbit that would get us to the planet—Anomaly, we were calling it—in about twenty hours.

"Anomaly must be tropical over most of its surface." Fred Sykes, nominally the navigator, was talking to himself and at the two of us while he analyzed the observational data rolling out of the ship's computer. "No axial tilt to speak of. Looks like they've got a big outpost near the equator, lots of electromagnetic noise there. Figures... the goddamn snails like it hot. We requisitioned hot-weather gear, didn't we, Pancho?"

Pancho, that's me. "No, Fred, all we got's parkas and snowshoes." My full name is Francisco Jesus Mario Juan-Jose Hugo de Naranja, and I outrank Fred, so he should at least call me Francisco. But I've never pressed the point. Pancho it is. Fred looked up from his figure and the rookie, Paul Spiegel, almost dropped the pistol he was cleaning.

"But why..." Paul was staring. "We knew the planet was probably Earthlike if the enemy wanted it. Are we gonna have to go tromping around in spacesuits?"

"No, Paul, our esteemed leader and supply clerk is being sarcastic again." He turned back to his computer. "Explain, Pancho."

"No, that's all right." Paul reddened a bit and also went back to his job. "I remember you complaining about having to take the standard survival issue."

"Well, I was right then and I'm doubly right now. We've *got* parkas back there, and snowshoes, and a complete terranorm environment recirculator, and everything else we could possibly need to walk around in comfort on every planet known to man—*Dios!* That issue masses over a metric ton, more than a bevawatt laser. A laser we could use, but crampons and pith helmets and elephant guns..."

Paul looked up again. "Elephant guns?" He was kind of a freak about weapons.

"Yeah."

"That's a gun that shoots elephants?"

"Right. An elephant gun shoots elephants."

"Is that some new kind of ammunition?"

I sighed, I really sighed. You'd think I'd get used to this after twelve years—or four hundred—in the service. "No, kid, elephants were animals, big gray wrinkled animals with horns. You used an elephant gun to shoot *at* them.

"When I was a kid in Rioplex, back in the twenty-first, we had an elephant in the zoo; used to go down in the summer and feed him synthos through the bars. He had a long nose like a fat tail, he ate with that."

"What planet were they from?'

It went on like that for a while. It was Paul's first trip out and he hadn't yet gotten used to the idea that most of his compatriots were genuine antiques, preserved by the natural process of relativity. At lightspeed you age imperceptibly, while the universe's calendar adds a year for every light-year you travel. Seems like cheating. But it catches up with you eventually.

We hit the atmosphere of Anomaly at an oblique angle and came in passive, like a natural meteor, until we got to a position where we were reasonably safe from detection (just above the south polar sea), then blasted briefly to slow down and splash. Then we spent a few hours in slow flight at sea level, sneaking up on their settlement.

It appeared to be the only enemy camp on the whole planet, which was typical. Strange for a spacefaring, aggressive race to be so incurious about planetary environments, but they always seemed to settle in one place and simply expand radially. And they do expand; their reproduction rate makes rabbits look sick. Starting from one colony, they can fill a world in two hundred years. After that, they control their population by infantiphage and stellar migration.

We landed about a hundred kilometers from the edge of their colony, around local midnight. While we were outside setting up the espionage monitors, the ship camouflaged itself to match the surrounding jungle optically, thermally, magnetically, etc.—we were careful not to get too far from the ship; it can be a bit hard to find even when you know where to look.

The monitors were to be fed information from flea-sized flying robots, each with a special purpose, and it would take several hours for them to wing into the city. We posted a one-man guard, one-hour shifts; the other two inside the ship until the monitors started clicking. But they never started.

Being senior, I took the first watch. A spooky hour, the jungle making dark little noises all around, but nothing happened. Then Fred stood the next hour, while I put on the deepsleep helmet. Figured I'd need the sleep—once data started coming in, I'd have to be alert for about forty hours. We could all sleep for a week once we got off Anomaly and hit lightspeed.

Getting yanked out of deepsleep is like an ice-water douche to the brain. The black nothing dissolved and there was Fred a foot away from my face, yelling my name over and over. As soon as he saw my eyes open, he ran for the open lock, priming his laser on the way (definitely against regulations, could hole the hull that way; I started to say something but couldn't form the words). Anyhow, what were we doing in free fall? And how could Fred run across the deck like that while we were in free fall?

Then my mind started coming back into focus and I could analyze the sinking, spinning sensation—not free-fall vertigo at all, but what we used to call snail-fever. The enemy was very near. Crackling combat sounds drifted in from outdoors.

I sat up on the cot and tried to sort everything out and get going. After long seconds my arms and legs got the idea, I struggled up and staggered to the weapons cabinet. Both the lasers were gone, and the only heavy weapon left was a grenade launcher. I lifted it from the rack and made my way to the lock.

Had I been thinking straight, I would've just sealed the lock and blasted—the presence in my mind was so strong that I should have known there were too many of the enemy, too close, for us to stand and fight. But no one can think while their brain is being curdled that way. I fought the urge to just let go and fall down that hole in my mind, and slid along the wall to the airlock. By the time I got there my teeth were chattering uncontrollably and my face was wet with tears.

Looking out, I saw a smoldering gray lump that must have been Paul, and Fred screaming like a madman, fanning the laser on full over a 180-degree arc. There couldn't have been anything alive in front of him; the jungle was a lurid curtain of fire, but a bolt lanced in from behind and Fred dissolved in a pink spray of blood and flesh.

I saw them then, moving fast for snails, shambling in over thick brush toward the ship. Through the swirling fog in my brain I realized that all they could see was the light pouring through the open lock, and me silhouetted in front. I tried to raise the launcher but couldn't—there were too many, less than a hundred meters away, and the inky whirlpool in my mind just got bigger and bigger and I could feel myself slipping into it.

The first bolt missed me; hit the ship and it shuddered, ringing like a huge cathedral bell. The second one didn't miss, taking off my left hand just above the wrist, roasting what remained of my left arm. In a spastic lurch I jerked up the launcher and yanked the trigger, holding it down while dozens of microton grenades popped out and danced their blinding way up to and across the enemy's ragged line. Dazzled blind, I stepped back and stumbled over the med-robot, which had smelled blood and was eager to do its duty. On top of the machine was a switch that some clown had labeled EMERGENCY EXIT; I slapped it, and as the lock clanged shut the atomic engines muttered—growled—screaming into life and a ten-gravity hand slid me across the blood-slick deck and slammed me back against the rear-wall padding. I felt ribs crack and something in my neck snapped. As the world squeezed away,

I knew I was a dead man but it was better to die in a bed of pain than to just fall and fall. . . .

I woke up to the less-than-tender ministrations of the med-robot, who had bound the stump of my left arm and was wrapping my chest in plastiseal. My body from forehead to shins ached from radiation burns, earned by facing the grenades' bursts, and the nonexistent hand seemed to writhe in painful, impossible contortions. But numbing anesthetic kept the pain at a bearable distance, and there was an empty space in my mind where the snail-fever had been, and the gentle hum told me we were at lightspeed; things could have been one flaming hell of a lot worse. Fred and Paul were gone but that just moved them from the small roster of live friends to the long list of dead ones.

A warning light on the control panel was blinking stroboscopically. We were getting near the hole—excuse me, "relativistic discontinuity"—and the computer had to know where I wanted to go. You go in one hole at lightspeed and you'll come out of some other hole; *which* hole you pop out of depends on your angle of approach. Since they say that only about one percent of the holes are charted, if you go in at any old angle you're liable to wind up in Podunk, on the other side of the galaxy, with no ticket back.

I just let the light blink, though. If it doesn't get any response from the crew, the ship programs itself automatically to go to Heaven, the hospital world, which was fine with me. They cure what ails you and then set you loose with a compatible soldier of the opposite sex, for an extended vacation on that beautiful world. Someone once told me that there were over a hundred worlds named Hell, but there's only one Heaven. Clean and pretty from the tropical seas to the Northern pine forests. Like Earth used to be, before we strangled it.

A bell had been ringing all the time I'd been conscious, but I didn't notice it until it stopped. That meant that the information capsule had been jettisoned, for what little it was worth. Planetary information, very few espionage-type data; just a tape of the battle. Be rough for the next recon patrol.

I fell asleep knowing I'd wake up on the other side of the hole, bound for Heaven.

✧ ✧ ✧

I pick up my drink—an old-fashioned old-fashioned—with my new left hand and the glass should feel right, slick but slightly tacky with the cold-water sweat, fine ridges molded into the plastic. But there's something missing, hard to describe, a memory stored in your fingertips that a new growth has to learn all over again. It's a strange feeling, but in a way seems to fit with this crazy Earth, where I sit in my alcoholic time capsule and, if I squint with my mind, can almost believe I'm back in the twenty-first.

I pay for the nostalgia—wood and natural food, human bartender and waitress who are also linguists, it all comes dear—but I can afford it, if anyone can. Compound interest, of course. Over four centuries have passed on Earth since I first went off to the war, and my salary's been deposited at the Chase Manhattan Credit Union ever since. They're glad to do it; when I die, they keep the interest and the principal reverts to the government. Heirs? I had one illegitimate son (conceived on my first furlough) and when I last saw his gravestone, the words on it had washed away to barely legible dimples.

But I'm still a young man (at lightspeed you age imperceptibly while the universe winds down outside) and the time you spend going from hole to hole is almost incalculably small. I've spent most of the past half millenium at lightspeed, the rest of the time usually convalescing from battle. My records show that I've logged a trifle under one year in actual combat. Not bad for 438 years' pay. Since I first lifted off I've aged twelve years by my biological calendar. Complicated, isn't it—next month I'll be thirty, 456 years after my date of birth.

But one week before my birthday I've got to decide whether to try my luck for the fourth trip out or just collect my money and retire. No choice, really. I've got to go back.

It's something they didn't emphasize when I joined up, back in 2088—maybe it wasn't so obvious back then, the war only decades old—but they can't hide it nowadays. Too many old vets wandering around, like animated museum pieces.

I could cash in my chips and live in luxury for another hundred years. But it would get mighty lonely. Can't talk to anybody on Earth but other vets and people who've gone to the trouble to learn Basic.

Everyone in space speaks Basic. You can't lift off until you've become fluent. Otherwise, how could you take orders from a fellow who should have been food for worms centuries before your grandfather was born? Especially since language melted down into one Language.

I'm tone-deaf. Can't speak or understand Language, where one word has ten or fifteen different meanings, depending on pitch. To me it sounds like puppydogs yapping. Same words over and over; no sense.

Of course, when I first lived on Earth there were all sorts of languages, not just one Language. I spoke Spanish (still do when I can find some other old codger who remembers) and learned English—that was before they called it Basic—in military training. Learned it damn well, too. If I weren't tone-deaf I'd crack Language and maybe I'd settle down.

Maybe not. The people are so strange, and it's not just the Language. Mindplugs and homosex and voluntary suicide. Walking around with nothing on but paint and powder. We had Fuller-domes when I was a kid; but you didn't *have* to live under one. Now if you take a walk out in the country for a breath of fresh air, you'll drop over dead before you can exhale.

My mind keeps dragging me back to Heaven. I'd retire in a minute if I could spend my remaining century there. Can't, of course; only soldiers allowed in space. And the only way a soldier gets to Heaven is the hard way.

I've been there three times; once more and I'll set a record. That's motivation of a sort, I suppose. Also, in the unlikely event that I should live another five years, I'll get a commission, and a desk job if I live through my term as a field officer. Doesn't happen too often—but there aren't too many desk jobs that people can handle better than cyborgs.

That's another alternative. If my body gets too garbaged for regeneration, and they can save enough of my brain, I could spend the rest of eternity hooked up to a computer, as a cyborg. The only one I've ever talked to seemed to be happy.

I once had an African partner named N'gai. He taught me how to play O'wari, a game older than Monopoly or even chess. We sat in this very bar (or the identical one that was in its place two hundred years ago) and he tried to impress on my non-Zen-oriented mind just how significant this game was to men in our position.

You start out with forty-eight smooth little pebbles, four in each one of the twelve depressions that make up the game board. Then you take turns, scooping the pebbles out of one hole and distributing them one at a time in holes to the left. If you dropped your last pebble in a hole where your opponent had only one or two, why, you got to take those pebbles off the board. Sounds exciting, doesn't it?

But N'gai sat there in a cloud of bhang-smoke and mumbled about the game and how it was just like the big game we were playing, and every time he took a pebble off the board, he called it by name. And some of the names I didn't know, but a lot of them were on my long list.

And he talked about how we were like the pieces in this simple game; how some went off the board after the first couple of moves, and some hopped from place to place all through the game and came out unscathed, and some just sat in one place all the time until they got zapped from out of nowhere....

After a while I started hitting the bhang myself, and we abandoned the metaphor in a spirit of mutual intoxication.

And I've been thinking about that night for six years, or two hundred, and I think that N'gai—his soul find Buddha—was wrong. The game isn't all that complex.

Because in O'wari, either person can win.

The snails populate ten planets for every one we destroy.

Solitaire, anyone?

Neither Sleet, Nor Snow, Nor Alien Invasion . . .

DAVE FREER

If there'd been more jobs available for zoology graduates, the entire future of our species might have been very different. Like, a whole lot shorter. Still, I suppose the postal service has something to answer for as well. . . .

The starships that dropped out of the sky in front of Mike Smith, M.Sc. (zoology) had a profound effect on him. It made him fall off his bicycle, spilling letters and parcels out of the postbag and sending his cap into a ditch. This was, perhaps, somewhat less traumatic than the absolute disintegration of the nuclear-warheaded missiles that some alert defense system had launched towards his island home and the alien ships.

However, Mike was supremely unaware of all this. All he knew was that now seven gleaming monstrosities lurked between him and Hill Farm, Mrs. Mackeson's parcel delivery, and the very welcome ice-cold beer she'd push into his hand. An understanding lady was old Mrs. Mac. She believed firmly in the restorative effects of cold beer, not like some idiots who'd give you hot tea. Mike believed fervently in cold beer, too . . . especially with the lurking remains of last night's rave-up still oozing out of his pores with the sweat.

Well, neither rain nor sleet . . . that's what the Post Office instruction manual had said. Perhaps it was shock, but all Mike could think of was how much shit he'd be in if he lost the post again. He went on looking for his cap, and then gathering spilled letters from the road, while the portal of the nearest ship spiraled open. Maybe he should have stayed in the army...

He was looking at his grazed knee through the tear in his gray uniform trousers when the Chilopodian Matriarch stepped out. Thus, the first words spoken by a human in the presence of the Chilopodii were:

"Oh, sod it!"

As a great speech initiating humankind's first contact with an alien species, it scored high on the originality stakes, if nothing else. At that moment, a gunner on one of the ships vaporized a trio of fighter-bombers approaching at a ridiculously slow Mach two.

A sharp, close click. Mike looked up and stood frozen, staring.

The matriarch in front of him had reared up on her rear six pairs of legs, her flattened segments gleaming. She was a tall Chilopod, at least two feet, six inches high. Her multiple eyes stared into his face. The antennae twitched towards him. Some of the many legs fluttered in complex movements. The mouthparts moved rapidly, and produced a few sharp clicks. The machine that was strapped around the second segment of the alien spoke tonelessly. "You don't look very appetizing, earthling."

This isn't covered in the Post Office instruction manual's advice on how to deal with the bloody public, thought Mike. Oh well, in the face of certain death, total defiance is the *only* answer. "I wouldn't want to eat *you* either, Sunshine." He gestured graphically with one finger.

There was a moment's silence, then a spate of clicks and leg-gestures. The translation machine spoke. "How unusual. A polite species. The normal reaction is either some silly form of threat, resulting in an abrupt death, or else some fawning which clearly identifies the species as prey. What does the gesture mean?"

Mike was too stunned to think quickly. "Up yours!" he blurted, and then clapped his hand to his mouth.

Again the pause, the clicks and movements. "You are wishing me success, and if I correctly understand, sexual gratification. How strange. How charming! Almost it is wished that we did not have to clear this planet for settlement. In all the twenty-seven species we have destroyed, yours is the first to display even the rudiments of Chilopodian courtesy."

Mike's reeling brain snapped into overdrive as his endocrine system flooded it with conflicting messages. Was this a hallucination generated by drinking two-thirds of a bottle of rum last night? He thought not. Pink elephants . . . yes. But not alien centipedes. It was something to be grateful for, he supposed. On the other hand, were aliens *really* preferable to the DTs?

He bit off the reflexive "Why us?" and replayed his statements and reactions of the alien in his mind. The damn thing looked just like a overgrown centipede, especially with those poisonous-looking fangs. Centipedes were predacious, and he was sure these creatures were, too. His brain's erratic filing system flapped furiously, trying to work out just what he'd done right. It finally told him he'd accidentally walked a thin line of balance, holding the key to both his personal survival . . . and perhaps that of the human race.

Too much aggression would result in an attack response. Too much submission would elicit a feeding response. Armed neutrality was the only way to go. Hell's teeth! The nearest he'd ever come to Switzerland was a making a pass at a girl from Geneva. And she'd told him to go and play in the traffic.

The only bonus seemed to be that sarcasm and hyperbole did not translate. And their sexual taboos, if they existed at all, were different to those of *Homo sapiens*. Just as well: Mike's last girlfriend had dumped him a week ago, telling him he was such a chauvinist pig that he couldn't even *spell* "Politically Correct."

So what should he say next? Shit! He was probably the world's least diplomatic human. He decided, with the resignation of the hung-over and about to die, he might as well stick with abuse. At least he was good at it.

"Yeah, you interstellar sex-bomb. Nice legs . . . shame about y'face."

The multiple legs rippled and the segments undulated. The antennae dipped toward him. Had he gone too far?

"May your sexual partner be too taken up by your physical beauty to initiate attack until you have bitten through her main ganglion, too! My sisters shipboard agree. We would regret to have to devour your species, even if you were more appetizing. Once we have done our preliminary survey we will not proceed with planetary clearance. Instead we leave your species free to leave the planet while we go spermatophore hunting in the breeding reservation."

Spermatophores? Again memories of second-year zoology swam to the surface through a murky sea of postal schedules and student parties. He and his fellow over-testosteroned companions had found the bizarre sex lives of invertebrates both fascinating and wildly amusing: Humans could learn things about kinkiness from the inverts. Those molluscs, what were they called again? Oh yes, *Crepidula fornicata,* the slipper-limpets with their copulatory stacks, those had been his favorite . . . but what did centipedes do that was so odd? That was it! For predatory arthropods sex was, well . . . almost mindbogglingly dangerous.

A dinner date had a whole new meaning when applied to these beasties. So some of them had reduced the breeding risk by having complex mate recognition rituals: Pheromones, dances, displays, that sort of thing. Also a good to time flaunt it, if you had it. It worked, mostly. However, there was still the probability that, after your moment of mutual passion, somebody might feel like a snack. So, some of the more dangerous species had got out of that one by avoiding direct contact altogether.

Long-distance sex: That was it! In these nasties, the male parcels up his sperm in a little, silk, gift-wrapped package, and leaves it on a little silk stalk. His hungry girlfriend could pick it up later, once he'd got the hell out of being dinner. It was like giving a girl a box of candy, thought Mike snidely, and with much the same reasoning, too, but without all that expensive intermediate stuff.

For the first time in several years, Mike thought both hard and fast. His brain was pretty rusty, but it did have a mine of normally useless zoological information. So: This was a species who, by their own claim, had destroyed twenty-seven other intelligent species. A species that could wipe the floor with the human race without even noticing. His racing brain brought him no further rewards, except to decide that he needed a stiff drink badly. He looked down at his postbag with vague regret. Even in a little country where postmen still got issued red bicycles, life wasn't that bad. And then, like a tequila sunrise, the idea exploded into him.

"I think, lovely legs, that I've got a nice *indecent* proposition to make to you . . ."

The lieutenant colonel was doing a fine impersonation of the Duke of Plaza-Toro, sitting in his command tank at the very, very back of the armored column. He could barely see the silver ships from here. It was still too close, as far as he was concerned. He hadn't worked so hard at achieving promotion to be a target.

"Message from one of the forward sniper squads, sir," said the radio operator. "There's someone with a white flag coming away from the ships."

The alien vessels had casually destroyed four armored units and sixty-two men. And now someone with a white flag was coming out from them...

"The snipers want to know what action to take, sir?"

So far, his soldiers had not even been able to fire a rifle without being obliterated, and even the Air Force had yet to score the most insignificant of hits on the gleaming hulls of any of the alien ships. There'd been no response to the many attempts at communication. And now... his snipers wanted to know what they should do?

"Hold their fire. Let them approach. Deploy a suitable escort."

"It's just one man, Sir."

"One *man*?"

"One man... and a bug."

The lieutenant colonel ordered the driver to take the command tank forward, then set about making contact with his commander-in-chief. This was definitely above his paygrade.

Walking down the road, seemingly unaware of the smoking remains of the armored cars and the dead soldiers, was a bug. A bloody giant centipede! It was only the figure beside the horrible creature that stopped the lieutenant colonel's instinctive order to open fire. There was a postman, wheeling his bike, apparently unconcerned by the company he was keeping.

Then the two of them stopped, and the bug turned back, and skittered away with amazing speed. The postman gave a cheery wave, and continued to walk forward calmly, even when joined by a nervous escort of men with automatic weapons at the ready. His calmness seemed to infect them, so that, by the time that they came to the lieutenant colonel's tank, they all looked relatively relaxed. The postman was in the act of finishing off telling a very filthy joke, and looked, to the colonel's jaundiced eye, both scruffy and a little drunk.

The commanding officer had to wait for the faintly hysterical laughter of his men to subside before he could get a word in. "Well!" he barked. "What are their terms?" He knew that communication channels from the vehicle were open to the President, and to the heads of state of several other countries who were rushing in firepower as fast as it could be flown.

"Top o' the morning to you, mate." The postman waved cheerily, circuits in his brain registering irritation at the fat old fart having several million dollars of pretty new tank to sit in, while his troops lacked body-armor, and the postman had to make do with a three year old bicycle with rusty spokes. Still, he was riding on too much of a high to let it peeve him as much as it would have normally. He gestured vaguely behind him. "I've told them to piss off, so I wouldn't waste any more effort on them."

The lieutenant colonel's rise in the army had been attributed by many to the volumes of hot air he could produce. This time the best he could manage was a strangled parrot noise. "Awrkk! Wh . . . wha . . . *what!?*"

The postman looked up at him innocently, still smiling as if he'd just won the grand lottery. "They're leaving. I struck us a deal. Listen, do you mind moving out of the road? I got to finish my round, and then I need to talk to the Boss."

"Th-th-the President?" stuttered the lieutenant colonel. "I have him . . ."

The postman frowned slightly. "I hadn't thought of ol' puffguts." Then he plucked at his grey uniform. "Nah. The postmaster-general is the one I really need to speak to."

Power. That was the best way to describe the people in that room. Presidents, premiers, prime ministers. The *de facto* rulers of most of the world. Oh yes, and the postmaster-general of a tiny island nation. A nice bloke. Plump, balding, with glasses, a photograph of his wife and three kids in his wallet, too many problems, and too small a budget. The rest of this august group was listening to Mike Smith's words with great care. Mike, on the other hand, was only speaking to the balding man with glasses. He was just hoping his vodka courage didn't make his breath smell too obviously.

"So you see, sir, their species has been in space for about forty thousand years. They're way, way ahead of us in weaponry, and some aspects of engineering. They've overrun twenty-seven other intelligent species, and they occupy at least a hundred planets.

They've arrived to settle here. They could wipe us out totally in a couple of months."

The president, a florid gentleman (despite his makeup team) had been getting redder and redder as he listened to this. He was renowned for his fiery patriotic bombast, and one got the awful feeling he wasn't very bright. In fact, he was a politician to fear: Dispassionate observers had a terrible suspicion that he actually *believed* in what he said. However, he looked nice and paternal on TV, and that was all it had needed to ensure his re-election.

When told humanity stood no chance, his face had reached the sunspot league. He could restrain himself no longer. "They're lying to you, boy," he burst out, spraying his audience, "and we'll resist them . . . to the last *man*!"

One of the beribboned dictators, with half of his country's gold reserves on his uniform, began to moan loudly, and call on the saints in Spanish, while various other people called "Hear, hear!" Some of them were agreeing with the president. Others, perhaps the more sensible ones, were appealing to the saints to listen.

The postman looked up at the president with some annoyance, and then registered who the maroon face belonged to. He managed to resist the urge to say, "Last man? I guess that rules you out, bumtrinket." Instead the postman sighed and tried reason, even if he suspected it was wasted on someone whose two brain cells didn't connect. Okay, maybe there was geniune courage there, but right now they needed courage, brains, balls the size of watermelons, and absolutely no pride. "They aren't lying, Mr. President. We haven't even scratched the paint on one of the ships, have we?"

As might be expected with this crowd, reason had little effect. However, the Secretary-General of the UN had the sort of voice to slice through the hubbub. She was a tall, patrician lady with a delicately carved nose, who had been avoiding Mike's breath in the happy delusion that what she was smelling was cheap aftershave.

"Can ve not negotiate?" she asked loudly, trying not to breathe in after saying it.

Jeers came from various sources, possibly from those who had lied their way through UN negotiations before, but the postman gave her a serious hearing.

"Well . . . I have cut us a kind of deal, ma'am, but they've never negotiated with anyone else before. May I continue?"

She nodded. Then an angry premier leapt onto a chair and began an impassioned speech full of angry gestures and loud references to the filthy capitalist sellout.

"Shut your stupid mouth, you fucking moron!" snapped the Secretary-General. There was a stunned silence. And no wonder: Her bellow would have quelled a barroom riot. Glazed wide eyes looked at her. This was the woman once known as the queen of international diplomacy, who had smiled benignly on the ramblings of mass-murderers, as long as they too were UN members. Rumor had it that she'd never had any children, because participating in sex might cause her to utter an indelicate expression. The postman, blissfully ignorant of all this, continued.

"Thanks, ma'am. I'll try and be quick, but I've got to give you some background first." He paused, organizing his thoughts. The memory of his close encounter of the third kind came flooding back. Huh! This bunch of unpleasant windbags that had crawled out from under wet stones weren't even in the same league as the Chilopodii! Courage, and his sense of humor, returned. He grinned impudently.

"After all, I'm only a bloody postman, not a zoologist. All the biological research funding's gone into social spending, which means I might just be the best postman in the world when it comes to identifying the plants, animals, and bugs that try to bite, scratch, and pester me every day. But I suppose we should all be thankful for that social spending. Without it, I wouldn't have been in the right place at the right time."

An impatient chorus of murmurs and a few cries of "Get on with it!" urged him on.

"The Chilopodii are predators, just like our own centipedes, and normally they don't form social units above the family of a single eggbrood. They spend their adult lives being solitary. To any post-adolescent, another member of his own species is just his favorite dinner. Being really tactful to another Chilopod is saying, 'You don't look tasty.' Even on their ships, each individual's section is totally physically isolated from the rest. They'd never get *anything* cooperatively built if they didn't have a long, peaceful, cooperative adolescence. Look, all this means the history of their species development has been very, *very* different from ours. All their machinery is evolved around combat and speed. You can't really say they have a society at all. Their whole adult life is spent attacking each other, or watching each other in case they're attacked. If one group of them settles on a new planet, the others follow. Partly for the chance to have one of their favorite dinners, and partly to see if the others have found something better than them." The room was silent now, and the silence hung like a waiting vulture.

Mike cleared his throat. "But they've got to get together at least once as adults . . . for sex." There were scattered snorts, muffled chuckles, and schoolboy-privy comments. He shook his head impatiently, "It's not *funny* to them. It's the most dangerous time in a Chilopodian's life."

"So, what about zem is so fery different to us?" called out a plump prime minister, with a broad smile. With shock, Mike recognized him. He was the fat guy he'd seen being slapped down by the waitress in Broad Suzie's topless bar half an hour ago. Mike smiled at the man.

"In about one case out of seven, both partners survive a mating. Okay, it's rough for humans out there, but our sex lives are really not *that* bad." Mike grinned at his spiritual fellow, and continued, without waiting for a reply, "Look, I mean, it's so dangerous for the Chilopodii, they don't actually touch. The male scents the female, sees her recognition dance. He secretes a little silk stalk, and pops a spermatophore—that's a parcel of semen—on it, and then backs off and watches to make sure his female gets it. Sometimes, she comes too close too soon, and he attacks her. Sometimes, she forgets what she's come for, and attacks him. Respect in Chilopodian circles is based on just how many matings you've survived."

He looked directly at the postmaster-general. That worthy wasn't looking at him. He'd fished his out wallet instead, and was looking at the photograph of his wife and his three kids, with an expression of vague horror. Mike had to clear his throat to get the postmaster's attention. "That's where we come in, Sir. Our postal district just got extended by a hundred planets."

The postmaster-general looked at him with alarm. "My *budget!*" he said, in an anguished voice full of quiet desperation. He put his face in his hands and began to sob helplessly.

The president put an arm around his shoulder. "There, there, Fred. Even if it pushes the deficit through the roof, and we have to cut defense spending a little, we'll increase the Post Office budget somehow. You might have to downsize on bicycles . . ."

"Actually, sir, the aliens will be delivering the first FTL postalships next week. I explained that this was what we humans did. That we were evolved for the job. So, no bicycles needed, sir. But the ships will be red. With our logo." Mike, in a rare dose of tact, didn't mention it was a pornographic symbol to the Chilopods.

"Zo they're going to give us spaceships?" The Secretary-General stared incredulously at him.

Mike nodded. "Yeah. We'll have to train new staff, I guess. Experts in committing sexual harrassment and non-PC speaking. I dunno. Maybe frat boys. And we have to supply the video equipment for filming the mating dance, and packaging for all the little bottles of mating pheromone they're posting. And then we bring back the male spermatophores by return post."

"Will they be paying for postage?" asked the postmaster. "What do we charge for these parcels?"

"Um. I don't think we charge. But for fang-to-fang delivery the human race gets as many spaceships as we need, so long as they're red with a Post Office logo. And Earth becomes a non-combat zone—I told them we can't breed elsewhere. And of course we humans come off the chow-list. Er. Provided we do things properly, or, rather, improperly. That's why they didn't really want to eat me; I was just rude and offensive enough, without being threatening. I got lucky and now we'll have to learn to do it on purpose."

There was a long silence, finally broken by the Secretary-General, who was eyeing him speculatively. Her cultured voice was tinged with deep suspicion. Her normally polished English vanished with it.

"Zat's all fery vell, young man, but vhy von't your postal run chust end up vith ze postmen being eaten instead? And chust how did you get avay vithout being eaten up in ze first place?"

Mike had the grace to look embarrassed.

"I said the right thing by accident. What we consider sexual harrassment, they think of as basic etiquette and good manners. And then there was the *garlic*. Maybe half an inch thick on my steak." Then, when she looked puzzled, he added. "And two-thirds of a bottle of dark rum... the night before a long, hot bicycle ride." She stared at him, as first comprehension, and then horror dawned on her. It showed in the spreading a white pallor beneath her exquisite makeup.

"And we don't look very appealing to them either," Mike admitted, pulling a wry face. "Too few legs and *far, far* too squishy. You see, Ma'am, it'd be a bit like you being offered a really over-ripe, Limburger-scented, giant cockroach for dinner. We stink and look gross to them."

The silence in the room of powerful people was long and deep.

The Secretary-General was a strong woman, able to surmount any challenge. Even her husband would testify to that. But her pride ran deep, and this one took some swallowing. When she finally spoke, her voice was pure liquid nitrogen.

"Zo," she said at last, looking at him as the bride might at steak being served at a Hindu wedding feast. "Ze human race, Homo Stinky, chust got ze postman's chob for ze interstellar porn ring of a race of fery nasty creepy-crawlies. Tell me: Is zere any uzzer good news you vant for me to give ze vorld, Mr. Zoologist?"

He knew that look. And his response was the same as the ones that had lost him a dozen jobs in as many interviews.

He could have said, "We get FTL craft that we can pull apart and learn to make, or even make better." Or, "We get to explore under safe conduct their defenses." Or, "We make them reliant on us to reproduce, and then pull the rug out from under them."

But instead, his chin lifted. He looked her straight in the eye, and his eyes said, "Stuff you, you old bag," in three-inch-high letters. Then he shrugged.

"Yeah. They've got no jobs for zoologists either. They said all they need to know about zoology is: Either you eat it, or it eats you. Don't think they need Secretary-Generals either. So: You want be the first course, or in the postal service?"

Light

KACEY GRANNIS

In my dream a great mountain fell,
Pinned me to the ground, trapped my feet beneath it.
A great glare of light overwhelmed me.
A man like any other—
Such a man as we have never seen—
Stepped forth from the light.
His grace and beauty were more,
More than any on this earth.
He freed me from the mountain,
Gave me water to drink,
Quieted my heart.
He put my feet back on the earth.
—from Tablet V of *The Epic of Gilgamesh*

It started with noise. My Iraqi copilot and flight engineer were joking about the cool night air over the Cauldron of Shamash, the ancient name for the barren stretch of desert we were flying over. Suddenly, the helicopter lurched, and they began screaming in Arabic.

I grabbed the controls of the Iraqi Air Force Mi-17 and slammed the collective to the floor as I pulled back hard on the cyclic in an attempt to convert our airspeed to rotor energy. The sultry-electronic voice of "Nagging Natasha" informed me that the left and right turbine engines were failing.

I fought the controls as I watched the ground come closer and closer. I inhaled as I leveled the bird just before we impacted with the desert floor. There was an enormous crunch and a sideways lurch, then something hit the back of my head.

"Captain . . . Captain . . ." The words were soft and insistent, whispered in my ear. I started to groan, but a hand came down, hard, over my mouth.

"They aren't far," he said, barely speaking at all. I could feel his breath against my cheek as he spoke close to the earcup of my helmet. "Can you move? Quietly?"

"Where's the crew?" I asked, my own lips barely moving.

"We're it," he said, and that was all he needed to say for a moment. I opened my eyes, but there wasn't much to see. The night was moonless, and the desert stars stretched high above us in the black. He was a darker shadow above me. I shifted, and he leaned back, then took my hand and helped me to stand. I pulled off the helmet that had probably saved my life and looked around.

I didn't know where we were. To my right, an ugly orange smear marred the satin black of the sky. I couldn't see it from here, but my gut told me that that smear came from my aircraft, burning. We were down in a gully of some kind, shielded from the light and flames.

But not the sounds. I could hear them, shouting, celebrating, firing their AK-47s into the air.

"Chris?" I said, softly.

"Come on, Captain," he said. "Let's go."

We didn't go very far at first. Just down the gully, until it met a larger cut through the desert floor. Then we turned and doubled back up that terrain feature until we found the ruins of a building. By this time, we were well away from the crash site, and we both needed to rest.

Neither of us said much at first. We got inside, found a place with the most level-looking floor, and sat down, slumping against the crumbling wall. Somehow, I still had my camel-bak strapped to my back, and I took the drinking hose in my teeth. The water was stale, and tasted of the dust that coated the bite-valve, but it was wet, and that was good enough for the moment. I looked up and offered the hose to him.

"Thanks," he said as he took it and bit down to drink.

"What happened?" I asked. To my surprise, my voice sounded eerily calm. I didn't feel calm. I felt... I don't know what I felt. But it wasn't calm.

"I don't know. I saw the ground fire, but I didn't see what took out the engines," he said. He'd been on comm, with a helmet, so he'd heard Natasha's warnings as well. Like me, Chris was an Air Advisor. We were serving as USAF personnel trained to advise and assist the fledgling Iraqi Air Force in our respective jobs. He'd been a non-volunteer for this assignment, but had surprised everyone, including himself, by really taking to the Arabic language and culture. Though his primary duty was dealing with ordnance and munitions, he often flew along with us as a back-up interpreter. "We crashed... I think you auto'ed?"

I nodded. Autorotation. What helicopter pilots do when there's no other option. It's supposed to keep you alive. I still wasn't sure it had worked entirely as advertised.

He nodded back. "We hit, and then we rolled to the side. I was in a seatbelt, but I saw the right gunner get thrown..." He stopped for a moment. "I think I passed out for a second. When I came to, I could see that both gunners were dead. Fuel was leaking out of the internal tank. I got up and looked up front. The copilot's skull was bashed in. The flight engineer had been thrown through the windscreen. I couldn't tell if you were dead or not, so I cut your straps and hauled you out with me."

"Thanks," I said, dryly. The sudden urge to giggle came over me. I supressed it by taking another drink of water. My whole crew was dead, with the exception of Chris, my passenger. And we were stuck out in the desert, not far from the people who'd shot us down.

The wind picked up sometime before dawn. We weren't planning on staying in the little building for too long, but the wind brought dust with it, and visibility dropped to nearly nothing. Dirt poured in through the open roof and the square-cut windows of our dubious shelter.

Chris hadn't managed to grab much in the way of gear when he egressed the wreck, so we sat huddled together in a corner, eyes closed, faces covered by the cut-off bottoms of our T-shirts. The wind howled, and the dust was like poison in the air.

"At least they can't come to get us in this," Chris said at one point. He reached up and brushed his hand across the top of my hair. Dirt rained down onto my shoulders. I laughed, a short, almost choked sound.

As it turns out, he was wrong.

Just before noon, I heard them.

"Chris," I whispered. My lips felt coated in powdery dust. I elbowed him in the ribs softly, trying not to make any sounds. He grunted softly and opened his eyes.

"I hear trucks," I said. His eyes went first wide, then narrow, and he nodded. Outside, the wind still roared, and dust still filled the room, but the unmistakable sound of vehicle engines approached. We had to leave.

We got up as quietly as we could. Out near the front of the house, tires crunched on the gravel road. So the front door was out. That left the window, behind which was a drop of maybe seven feet, a small ledge, and then another ravine down to the desert floor. The major highway was down there, a few miles away. Not that we could see that far, in the unearthly orange dust of this storm.

"You first," Chris breathed in my ear. He cupped his hands together to make a step and boosted me up onto the window ledge. I tried not to let my boots scrabble at the stone wall, but the dust made everything slick. Eventually, though, I got up on the ledge. Chris handed me his backpack and his M-4 rifle, and then levered himself up beside me.

I turned and dropped down outside the building. My boots hit the gravel and slid a bit, and I pressed tightly to the stone wall for a moment. I could feel my pulse thudding in my ears as I squinted against the dust and tried not to breathe too loudly. Then I looked up and motioned for Chris to pass me the rifle and pack.

A few moments later, he joined me outside the building and we took off for the slope, running as quietly and as carefully as we could, hoping to get lost in the dust and the wind.

"The GPS says we're still on course," I said, shielding my eyes and squinting down at the display screen. The small device was the size of my palm, which meant that it fit in my body armor. It also meant that it was hard as hell to see. When we'd taken off the night before, I'd obviously not been wearing my sunglasses. If I'd thought that I might be trekking through the desert the next day, I would have stuck them in my pocket. Lesson learned. The noon sun was punishing, even through the orange haze of the dust that hung in the air. The wind had died down, and the world seemed suspended in dirt and agonizing light.

"How far is that highway?" Chris asked me. I lifted the hose of my camel-bak in inquiry, but he shook his head. We didn't want to drink all of the water right away.

"It's not on here, but I know it's down in this valley," I said. "It can't be far. We just can't see it, due to the dust. But we're on a straight line course for Archuleta Base." I reached up and wiped my forehead. The dust and sweat was combining to make mud on my skin. Fantastic.

Chris grinned at me. "That's hot," he said, his voice almost tentative. We hadn't joked since the crash, though we were close friends back at the base. I was startled by the sudden humor, but it made me smile.

"Isn't it, though?" I asked. "I always knew sweaty, muddy, scared shitless chicks were your thing," I said as I started walking again.

"Hells yeah," he replied as he fell in step beside me.

An hour later, we had to stop. The light was blinding, and it diffused through the dust into a haze of omnidirectional pain. My eyes burned, my nose burned, my throat felt blistered from the heat and the dust. We drank sparingly, but we still finished my camel-bak way too early. And we still hadn't found the God-damned highway.

"Take a break," Chris said, indicating a mound of crumbling wall that jutted up out of the desert scrub. There was a small patch of shade at the base, maybe big enough for both of us. "Come on, we won't survive by pushing it."

I nodded, too tired and hurt to speak. I could barely see him, my eyes streamed continuously with tears brought on by the brightness and the irritation. He was just a blur, a slightly darker spot in the punishing light.

I followed him to the dubious shelter of the wall and watched as he sat back against it. Something caught my eye, and I paused to look at the capstone on top of the wall. I heard someone chuckle, and was surprised to find it was me.

"What's so funny?" Chris asked, his voice rasping.

"Shamash," I said. I barely got the word out of my dry throat, and I could feel my lips crack as I smiled in spite of myself.

"Who the fuck is Shamash?" Chris asked, gesturing impatiently for me to join him in the meager shade. I turned and settled beside him, feeling his solid body against my hip and shoulder.

"Shamash was the ancient Bablylonian god of the sun," I said after a moment. "You know Lieutenant Colonel Layth, the Iraqi maintenance chief? He told me the legend. Apparently Shamash helped those who suffered unjustly. This must've been a small roadside shrine to him. I think we must be by the ancient Road to Damascus."

He grunted sardonically in reply, which made me grin a little bit more. Leave it to me to be geeking out about a crumbling pile of brick and rock when we're running for our lives.

The heat of the day made the ancient brick burn, even in the shade, but I was too worn to care. My smile faded as I pulled my knees up and put my head down, trying to breathe air that was just a degree or two cooler for being in the shade.

"You okay?" he asked, a while later.

"Yeah, I just can't see," I said. "The light..."

"Yeah," he said. "It's brutal."

And that was all we said for a while.

Unforgivable, perhaps, given the circumstances, but those exact circumstances made us both so exhausted that we soon drifted off.

Through the haze, I dreamt of dust and light.

I felt the dust begin to swirl and a great shadow pass over us. I looked up and saw a giant eagle with the head of a lion. With every wingbeat, more and more dust rose into the air, until we were enveloped in a great storm. I tried calling out to Chris, but the dust overwhelmed me, filling my mouth and eyes and ears, smothering me as I choked and gasped. I huddled closer to the warm reassurance of the wall, shielding my face as best I could, as I tried to spit out all the dust.

As the dust storm began to abate, I could feel the brick's heat growing where my shoulder touched it, to an intensity that would've scorched my flesh if it had been bare. Again I felt the sun upon my back. I could feel its light grow stronger as I huddled in a ball, the heat and the light becoming so intense I thought my uniform would burst into flames. I rolled onto my back to spare it being burned. Though I shielded my face with my arms against the intense heat, I sensed a shadow passing over the sun. I peered skyward through slitted eyes and there, in the center of the blazing sun, I saw a man wearing strange robes, with a long braided beard. As he reached toward me, the sun blazed even brighter, and I screamed as the beautiful, deadly brilliance of the sun consumed me.

Even as I lay stunned, I could feel the light and the dust leaching away my skin and tissues, leaving me a white, perfect sculpture of bone on the desert floor.

From the deep, soothing darkness of the desert night, a sudden halogen flash pinned me to the crumbling brick behind me. I barely opened my mouth to scream when hands clamped down on my throat and somebody's fist impacted my cheek. I felt Chris struggling next to me. I swung out with my feet, wildly, fighting to get to the pistol tucked under my arm. Somebody struck me with their fist again, and despite my best efforts, I went limp as the taste of my own blood filled my mouth.

I heard voices shouting in Arabic. Someone jerked my hands in front of me and bound them tightly with some kind of wire. I felt someone take the gun from under my arm. I rolled to my side and saw Chris on his back with someone on his chest, hitting him repeatedly in the face.

"Stop," I croaked, blood spitting everywhere. "Stop!" I cried a bit louder, utilizing the tiny bit of Arabic that I knew. "Please," I added, reasoning that it never hurt to be polite. The man beating Chris paused at the sound of a female voice and turned to look at me, his interest growing.

Sudden fear shot through me as Chris's head rolled to the side. I licked my lips instinctively, my eyes meeting his. He shook his head, as if to tell me, "No, don't." I took a deep breath and spoke again. "Please stop hurting my friend," I said, or tried to say, in Arabic. I tried to tell myself that most people in this country respected women in their own way... that everyone I'd met had been kind and generous and law-abiding...

The only problem was that these guys were already not law-abiding. They were insurgents who shot down a helicopter marked with the flag of their own country. They'd already beaten us up, and there was a good chance that we wouldn't survive to see the dawn.

But I couldn't not try.

"Please," I said again. "Please stop hurting my friend." I licked my lips again, and this time it was a bit more deliberate. My stomach churned with fear and loathing at the look in the eyes of the men that surrounded us, but I forced myself to keep my head high and focus only on Chris and the man who held him down.

That man licked his own lips and got to his feet. Chris rolled to his side. "Captain..." he croaked. The man kicked him in the ribs, almost absently, and took a step toward me. I shook my head sharply, telling Chris to shut the hell up, and lifted my gaze to meet the man's. My chin inched higher in defiance of the fear that shivered through me, threatening to make my knees buckle.

The man smiled widely and slapped me hard, backhanded. My already bruised jaw popped out of alignment, and for a moment, I doubled over in agony, my bound hands flying to my face. I pushed on my chin and forced my mouth to close, but the taste of blood filled my mouth again. I spat it out on the desert sand just as hands grabbed my shoulders roughly.

"Stop!" a voice commanded. The sudden scuffling noise that had broken out ceased, and another man wearing clothing that vaguely resembled a unform stepped forward. A barrage of rapid-fire Arabic ensued. The man who had hit me looked sullen. The uniformed one repeated his command and the sullen one turned abruptly and stalked away, as if he'd been reprimanded. Uniform issued another command, in a less angry tone, and two men stepped forward to take my bound hands. Next to me, I could see another pair holding Chris by the arms as they made him stand. I risked a glance up at him. His nose looked like raw hamburger, but his eyes burned with anger that made my throat close up. I blinked and looked down, just in time for the insurgents to start prodding us roughly forward with the butts of their AKs.

I stumbled, my foot twisting awkwardly on the gravel, and stumbled into Chris. He probably would have caught me, if his hands hadn't been bound. "I'm sorry," I managed to whisper.

"Me, too," he said, before one of his guards cuffed him and shouted in Arabic that we weren't to talk.

They loaded us in the back of a truck and covered us with blankets that smelled of animals and unwashed humans. We lay there, jostling against the metal bed of the truck as it jounced over the ungraded goat paths that served as roads to these guys. Before long, the scent of engine exhaust combined with my fatigue, injuries, lack of food and real sleep to produce nausea. As if that wasn't bad enough, the metal of the truck bed began to heat up. The sun had risen. We were in for another hellish day.

I don't know how long they drove before we stopped. The bouncing had eased, which made me think that we'd left the goat path and were travelling on an actual paved road. I'd fallen into a kind of doze against Chris's shoulder. I felt, rather than heard, the tone of the engine's hum change, and then the truck started to slow. I could feel Chris become instantly alert next to me, because I felt that same terrifying tension in my own body. We were stopping.

Footsteps, accompanied by muffled voices, approached. The metal latch on the back of the truck door thunked as someone unlocked the doors. Light flooded in, turning the darkness under the blankets to something merely dim. There was an agonizing pause, and then I felt a hand grip the blanket over my face and flip it back. I was left staring, blinking up into light that burned my eyes.

"What?" a voice yelled in Arabic. More rapid fire language followed, and the dim figure standing in the rectangle of light whirled away. Confused and scared, I turned to look at Chris.

And saw nothing.

Well, not nothing, exactly. I saw the truck bed, and the lump of blankets that may or may not have looked like they were bunched over a human body. But though my eyes burned, and I squinted in the blinding light, I didn't see my friend.

Even though my shoulder was still touching his. A shoulder that also wasn't visible. I looked down at my body, but it wasn't there.

"Captain?" I heard him whisper.

"Oh God, Chris, I can't see you," I breathed. "I can't see me."

"I can't see you either, and I don't think they can see us..." He trailed off, because a door slammed at the front of the truck and running footsteps pattered down the gravel beside us. I felt him go still next to me, and I held my breath. The shadow reappeared in the truck door, and was soon joined by another. This second shadow turned to the other and started shouting in an accusatory tone. I tilted my head back as far as it would go and rolled my eyes upward, so I could see what was going on.

The man who'd hit Chris repeatedly, the one who'd nearly assaulted me was standing there, yelling into the face of another, shorter man. The short one yelled back, waving his arms around wildly. I drew in a breath as I saw my 9mm tucked into the taller man's waistband. Beside me, I felt Chris move.

I sat up and scooted slowly to the opposite side of the truck, near the wheel well. I know I wasn't silent, but the two insurgents were too involved in their argument to notice. I saw the butt of my 9mm move, and the taller insurgent paused and looked around.

I felt my chest heaving as I fought for breath through the light and the fear and the adrenaline. My mouth felt dry. I couldn't see him, but I could almost *feel* Chris not far away, his fingers outstretched, reaching for the gun.

I pulled in a deep breath, filling my lungs, expanding my diaphragm. "Hey!" I shouted, belting it out, using every trick I'd ever learned from being a high school cheerleader. Both insurgents jumped, but more importantly, so did my 9mm. It jumped right out of the tall man's waistband and up level with his ear, where it fired.

His head exploded all over the other insurgent. He turned shocked, wild eyes to face the specter of a gun floating in midair. Broken, gibbering Arabic fell from his lips as the gun swung to point directly at him. The man feebly reached behind his back for the AK-47 slung there, almost by instinct, though he didn't know where to point it.

The gun fired again, and the second, shorter insurgent slumped against the open door of the truck and fell to the ground. I realized my hands were at my mouth, and they were shaking. The truck door swung closed, followed quickly by its mate. I heard the 9mm clatter to the bed of the truck.

Hands were on my wrists, lowering my hands, unwinding the wire that bound them. In the sudden dimness of the back of the truck, I could once again make out Chris's shadowy profile, just before he pulled me into a hug.

"Oh my God," I said, and again, "Oh my God."

"I think that's all of them," he whispered. I could feel his accelerated breathing, it matched my own. "I think the others left."

I forced myself to slow down, calm down, and think. "I think you're right," I said. "Otherwise the gunfire would have drawn more attention."

He froze against me. "I had to..."

"Yes," I said, as firmly as I could manage. "You did." I could feel my body trembling, as if I were cold, but I forced my voice to be as steady as possible. "Now we have to figure out what to do next." I paused for a moment, and then drew back away from him. I lifted my hands between us.

"Can you see me?" I asked.

"Yes," he answered. "A little, you're a darker shadow."

"That's how I see you," I said. "But with the door open..."

"Nothing," he agreed. "I think... I think it's the sunlight. I had this strange dream..."

The dream. The Light of Shamash.

I hardly recognized my own trembling voice when I asked, "Was there a bird? And a man with a braided beard?"

I could barely make out his nod.

I gulped. My voice sounded wooden as I spoke. "In ancient Babylon, the Zu bird symbolized the summer sandstorms, and the man in the sun must've been Shamash. But it was just a dream, right? Are we awake now?"

I held my hand up in front of my face... it looked like my hand, just indistinct because of the darkness. I reached out and opened one of the doors to the truck, letting the late afternoon light flood in again. I heard Chris curse and turn away from the light just before he disappeared altogether. I blinked through the tears and pain and forced myself to look at my hand again.

Nothing.

Oh my God.

"Wait," Chris's voice came from deep inside the truck. "Look," he said. I'm sure he was pointing at something, but since I couldn't see him, I didn't see what... at first.

But then I began to see, just barely, a blur there, not far from me. It was his hand, held outstretched toward the doors, but not directly in the sunlight. I stared at it, willing it to become more and more distinct... but I couldn't see any change.

"What time is it?" he asked. I blinked. Then I turned wildly and looked outside. Sure enough, the sunlight slanted in through the open doors because the sun was setting directly behind us. We'd been travelling eastward. The light burned so badly that I couldn't look directly at it, but the sun sat on the horizon, slipping slowly out of sight. And as it set, he became clearer and clearer.

After a minute or so, I shook myself to clear my head.

"We need to get out of here," I said, trying to force my mind to practicalities. If I thought too much about the dream and the light and what it had apparently done to us, I'd lose my mind. Even more.

He nodded. "What about them?" he asked me, gesturing out the open door to the two fallen bodies.

"Bring them," I said. "They'll need to be identified and if... if there are consequences, I'll say you shot on my order."

"The hell you will," he muttered, but he slid out of the truck and started picking up the remains of the two insurgents. I followed him, and together we got the bodies stacked in the back of the truck, wrapped in the same blankets that had hid us earlier.

As we drove down the road, we sat in silence, accompanied only by the two bodies, as the rising night made us materialize slowly before each other's eyes. When it seemed fully dark, I looked over at him, surprised at how well I could see.

"There you are," I said, in a weak attempt at humor. He smiled raggedly.

"I can see you really well," he said, voicing my own thoughts on the matter. "I wonder if that's why the light hurt so bad earlier."

"I don't know."

"We probably never will."

It took us most of the night to drive back down the highway to Archuleta Base. When we showed up at the gate, Chris and I presented our IDs and informed the gate guards that there were two dead insurgents in the back of the truck. That got us inside quick.

It also got us a private interview with the base commander.

He didn't believe us. At least not the part about turning invisible in daylight. Hell, if I were in his shoes, I would've assumed it was PTSD too.

But we laid out the story for him, step by step, and offered to demonstrate our... condition, as soon as the sun came up. He agreed, as long as we agreed to submit to a psychologist's care immediately afterward.

I didn't even need to look at Chris, I just agreed. Because either the colonel was right, or we were. Either way, we were safe. And either way, our lives had changed irrevocably.

While we were debriefing, the sun had officially risen. I found it interesting that the artificial lighting of the colonel's office seemed to have no effect on us. We looked a little gray, but that was fatigue and dust more than anything else. The Old Man didn't even seem to care that we'd made a mess of his chairs.

"All right, Captain, Sergeant," the colonel said, as he stood up. "Let's go outside."

Chris and I stood and saluted.

When we reached the door to the outside, I wrapped my hand around the colonel's wrist.

"Captain?" the colonel said as he pulled away.

"Trust me, sir," I said, and the weariness in my tone convinced him, if nothing else did. He nodded, and instead took my elbow in one hand, and held my hand reassuringly with the other. We must've looked like hell. Or he just wanted to have a good hold on me in case we freaked out.

With my other hand, I reached for Chris's, mostly because I didn't want to lose him in the light. We'd come through a lot together, and I wouldn't let us get separated now.

Chris took my hand and pushed open the door with his free one. Aching, painful light streamed in.

And we vanished.

The Question

PATRICK A. VANNER

I've always had what my mother called a selective memory. I could not, and to this day, still can't remember her birthday.

Hearing, "Augustus Adrian Andropov, you forgot our anniversary?!" once, and fourteen subsequent times with the caveat *"Again?!"* followed by a week on the couch each and every time, got that particular item ingrained into my memory. But, then again, finally remembering to use the appointment function on my data pad may have helped with "remembering" that important little tidbit.

Yet, to this day I can still remember the characteristics of the XR-30 heavy assault rifle. "Light-weight, magazine-fed, electrically operated, air-cooled, shoulder-fired weapon; firing three-millimeter, explosive-tipped, caseless rounds in single shot, five-round burst, or fully automatic, by use of a selector switch." I heard that the first day I was issued my rifle in training, and I swear I can still feel the spittle from the sergeant screaming it ten centimeters from my face.

I personally think there is a link between fear and memory. I love my mother, but she is a nonentity; never once has she ever even raised her voice, let alone been remotely imposing. My wife scares me, I'll admit it, but she loves me anyway, despite my questionable memory, so I've never stressed over it. The training sergeant terrified me, but, then again, his job was to train men and women in the art of warfare, and how to survive that violent endeavor. Fear and intimidation are great teaching techniques, and, as I remember his screaming lecture to this day, I would say he did his job rather well.

Finally, there was the abject panic and absolute, bowel-loosening horror that encompassed my first, last, and only interaction with the Decarsi. I can still remember every subtle nuance of that fateful mission, from the day I was *honored* with being selected to head the bodyguard detail of the first diplomatic mission to the Decarsi Empire, right up to the moment the verdict was read at my court martial. If I had known then what I know now, I would've told the colonel to strap his *"mission of vital Imperial importance"* to a star-drive and shoot it into the star of his choice. But I'm getting ahead of myself.

"Captain Andropov, the colonel wants to see you in his office," a loud voice yelled across the training bay. I was in the middle of hand-to-hand combat training with my team—something to keep in mind when you turn towards someone calling your name and forget tell your sparring partner to take a break.

After taking the proffered hand from my sergeant, I dragged myself off the deck. "Take a break, Simms, while I go see what the old man wants," I told him as I massaged my sore jaw back into a semblance of working order.

"Yes, sir." Simms was a tall, powerful, and intimidating man. When someone brings up the subject of the Imperial Commandos, he's the picture that comes to my mind. On the other hand, I'm what anyone would call average. Across the board: average height, average looks, average build. Not that I never wished that I had rugged good looks, the thousand-meter stare, and sleepy eyes of a killer that many of the men and women in our profession possess; I'm just happy to deal with people without the first thought entering their mind being "psychopath."

Peeling off my training gloves, I trotted across the bay towards the passageway leading to the colonel's office, trying to guess what my boys and girls had done *this* time. Imperial Commandos, an orbital station full of regular troopies and civilians, and two months since our last mission had lead to several requests for my presence before the colonel's desk over the past several weeks. My people didn't handle down time very well.

Knocking on the colonel's hatch, I waited for his standard bark of "Enter!" counting the seconds off on my chrono. I'd determined there was a direct correlation between the amount of time he left me standing in the passageway and the amount of trouble my people had caused; the longer I waited, the more damage they had caused. So I was pleasantly surprised by the almost immediate order to enter, assuming I wasn't about to have a large piece of my ass chewed off. Looking back on it, I would've rather had the ass chewing.

I had one foot on the deck in his office and the other still in the passageway when Colonel Franklin spoke quietly, and got immediately to the point. "Captain Andropov, good. Hit the showers, get into your class As, and meet me in the admiral's conference room in thirty minutes; you've got a mission of vital Imperial importance." Not one for idle chitchat myself, I finished entering his office, snapped to attention, said, "Yes, sir," turned around, and headed off to my quarters.

Twenty-eight minutes later, I entered the conference room and took a seat in the middle of the table between Colonel Franklin and some major I didn't know, helping myself to a glass of water from the carafe in front of me. Several officers I didn't recognize were already there, along with other men and women in civilian dress. My gaze swept across a couple of majors, Colonel Franklin, and finally stopped at the man seated at the head of the table. I almost spit the water I'd just taken a sip of all over the major sitting next to me. Senior plenipotentiary for the Imperium and chief counselor to the Regent, one of the most powerful men alive, Chancellor Jonathan Nguyen, was speaking quietly into the ear of one of his aides. The picts and vids I had seen of the man did not do him justice in person. Even seated, I could tell he was tall, with a head full of immaculately styled silver hair and bright blue eyes that radiated intelligence. I knew the man was nearing a century old, yet even with the wrinkles, he exuded a power and confidence that gave him the appearance of someone half his age. He leaned back into his chair, waved a hand at his aide, sending him scurrying out of the room, and cleared his throat, calling the meeting to order. Every voice speaking stopped in mid-syllable; the silence was so profound, I imagined that every soul in the room could hear me swallow the mouthful of water I had. I can't speak for everyone there, but I know he had my full attention.

"I'd like to start off by thanking Admiral Cryer for being so kind as to let me commandeer her conference room." A consummate politician, his voice was smooth and cultured as he indicated the small blonde woman seated to his right. Granted, there was no way in Hades that anyone on the station was going to deny Chancellor Jonathan Nguyen anything, let alone the use of a conference room, but, then again, he didn't get to the position he was in by not being polite and playing to the crowd.

Chancellor Nguyen continued, "Now, as some of you may not be aware, the Imperium has recently made contact with a new species. They call themselves the Decarsi Empire, and His Royal Highness and the Regency Council have decided to begin diplomatic relations with them." That had a few people looking surprised, myself included, as it had been almost one hundred years since humanity had come across another alien race. We had made contact with a dozen different species and sub-species of aliens since humanity crawled its way out of the cradle of Terra, and between treaties, annexation, and all-out warfare, we were the undisputed (most of the time, but that's what Imperial Troops are for) rulers of the known sentient galaxy, so a new race was important news.

Imperial Commando training included bodyguard missions for high-level dignitaries, and since mine was the only Commando team on the station, and a high-level diplomatic mission was now in the works, it became clear why I was included in this high-level meeting. My team just became the lucky winner of the bullet soak and human shield award. The various officers and civilians discussed at length how important this mission was, and how much of an honor it was to be involved. Since this was not the actual mission brief, I tuned out. The sad part of the whole thing was that, at the time, I actually did consider it an honor, and a way to run my name up the chain of command for some recognition. Just goes to show you, irony is a bitch.

Less than twenty-four hours later, my team and I were on board Chancellor Nguyen's private yacht, though whoever thought to call it a yacht obviously didn't know what a true yacht was. Picture, if you will, a destroyer class warship, fitted out with the most luxurious of amenities, and packed full of the most sophisticated equipment and weapons that humankind had to offer. The fact that such a thing existed was the most surreal thing I had ever experienced, a feeling that lasted for about thirty seconds after our shuttle landed in the bay; even more surreal was the fact that waiting at the bottom of the exit ramp was Chancellor Nguyen himself.

He waited patiently, chatting with Admiral Cryer, this mission's military attaché, while my team exited the shuttle and formed up. I, on the other hand, was trying to will my people to move faster, which, short of performing a combat deployment, wasn't going to happen, as they could see Chancellor Nguyen waiting on us just as well as I could, and were moving as damn fast as they could.

Standing at attention in front of my team, I gave the admiral a curt nod, to let her know we were ready to go. So, I am sure you can imagine my shock when Chancellor Nguyen, trailed by the admiral, came striding over to me, extending his hand.

"Captain Andropov, nice to finally meet you. I've heard good things about you and your team." I had started to snap off a salute to the man before I caught myself and took his hand, shaking it once before letting it go and coming back to attention.

"Sir, the pleasure is all mine, I can assure you," I managed to say without too much difficulty. Seriously, what else would you say to a man who could disappear you and an entire team of Imperial Commandos with just the snap of his fingers? I continued to stand there as he ran a critical eye over me, a warm comforting smile on his face, before stepping around me to head for my team. I must say, I was impressed by the way he took a few moments to greet and speak to each of the ten members of my team. Then again, we were the bodyguard unit, so looking back on it, I suppose it was in his own best interest to make sure we liked him well enough to take a bullet for him.

I was leading my team though the ship's passageways and Chancellor Nguyen and Admiral Cryer walked beside me, picking up their conversation where it left off when we disembarked. I was stunned at the opulence and sheer decadence of the ship, so you can understand my lack of response to the Chancellor's statement: "I would like to invite you to dine with me and my staff this evening."

It took the admiral clearing her throat and giving me a death glare as she tilted her head in the direction of the Chancellor to catch my attention. After a moment, my mind caught up to the question, and this time I was actually speechless, not inattentive.

The admiral's glare intensified as I stood there staring at the Chancellor before stammering out an answer.

"Yes, sir. I would be honored, sir." I hastily did a mental inventory of my luggage, hoping that I'd packed an appropriate uniform for dining with such esteemed persons. Thankfully, I remembered the mad scramble to pack my gear in the rush to get the mission started; I'd simply tossed the dress uniform I had worn to the meeting in my kit as opposed to taking the time to store it my closet. Now all I needed to do was hope I could find the laundry on the ship so I could at least press out the wrinkles in time for dinner.

I managed to get my uniform squared away in time and dinner turned out to be a pleasant affair. Admiral Cryer and I were the only two military persons in attendance; the rest were the aides and various diplomatic functionaries along for the mission. The conversation was intelligent and varied, and my opinion on the current military situations of the Imperium was solicited many times during the meal. I didn't need the admiral's warning glance to alert me to the potential political mine field I was entering. I had come up with the perfect way to address each of these enquiries: "As an Imperial Commando, I am a tool of the Imperium, and am proud to serve in any capacity that the Emperor wishes."

Chancellor Nguyen sat at the head of the table, like a king holding court. He didn't contribute much to the conversation, but I could see that he was paying very close attention to the ebb and flow of the questions, and, more importantly, the answers. The admiral, unfortunately, was much higher up in the political food chain than a mere infantry captain, and had to actually respond to the enquiries directed at her. Rank has its privileges, but also its pitfalls.

Following dinner, I was included in what was supposed to be a "friendly little game of cards," but turned out to be more like a mugging. Granted, I was nervous and intimidated by the company in which I found myself—Chancellor Nguyen, three of his senior aides, and Admiral Cryer—but it was the Chancellor who was responsible for taking a month's worth of my pay. I came to find out over the length of our voyage and many subsequent games, that nerves and intimidation or not, Nguyen was an expert at reading people, almost as much as he was at misleading them. He was a professional politician, after all. A fact my wife was kind enough to point out at a later date when I had to explain to her where almost a year's worth of pay went.

The morning following my somewhat taxing dinner and very expensive card game, I assembled my team for our first real brief on the Decarsi and what was expected of us during the mission.

"Good morning, ladies and gentlemen," the overeager, minor diplomatic functionary greeted us as he walked into the compartment and up to the podium at the front of the conference room. There was a quiet chuckling from the audience. Imperial Commandos are called many things—however, ladies and gentlemen has never been on any list I've ever seen. "Today, I will be discussing what we know about the Decarsi, which is not much, to tell you the truth."

I shifted nervously in my seat, and I wasn't the only one. No one in the compartment, with the possible exception of the flunky at the podium who seemed totally oblivious to what he was saying, liked the idea of going into any kind of situation without any solid intelligence on a possible foe. It's not like it would be the first time, but you never get used to it.

Mr. Junior Diplomat pointed a remote at the holoprojector next to the podium and the image of what can only be described as a large, upright house cat sprang into existence. As the information scrolled down the side of the image, I could see that most of the entries were labeled as "unknown." What little information there was, I paid close attention to. One and a half meters tall on average, slight of build, vocal cords incapable of human speech, and from the few interactions the diplomatic corps had with them, very intelligent. As the presentation droned on, I found it harder and harder to keep my focus, though I did try. I could see why our tour guide into the vast unknown of the Decarsi Empire went into diplomacy. I've never heard someone explain they didn't know anything is as many different ways as he did for as long as he did. I was obviously not the only one having problems with the near total lack of information being imparted to us, or the utter boredom that had set in after the first one and a half hours of the briefing.

"Here kitty, kitty, kitty," a voice muttered from the back row of seats, eliciting a round of laughter. My head snapped around and tried to identify the speaker. Ten innocent looking faces stared back at me, but I was fairly certain it had been Corporal Murdock. I stood up and walked to stand directly in front of the speaker, my eyes raking over my entire team—but I focused on Murdock, and she had the decency to give me a slight chastened look.

"Now listen up, all of you," I growled out. "You will secure that shit right now and get your game faces on. This is not a weekend visit to a zoo, this is a high-priority diplomatic mission." I paused to make sure I had everyone's complete attention; I couldn't tell them I was as bored as they were at the useless waste of time we were experiencing, but I could make sure that they had everything that was available to us. They might drive me to distraction from time to time, but this was my team and I wanted to keep every one of them alive. When I was sure I had their attention, I continued. "While it is obvious we don't have much intelligence on the Decarsi . . ." I turned and pointedly looked at our briefer, indicating that we'd heard enough of what we didn't know, and it was time to move onto the next part of the briefing; the jerking nod of his head indicated he got the message loud and clear. I never said I couldn't be intimidating; after all, as an Imperial Commando, it was all part of the package. I just hadn't had the opportunity to put it into effect the last few days and was quite enjoying being the big fish in the little pond at the moment. "What we are going to move on to is how to behave in a diplomatic fashion. While this is a bodyguard detail, it is a *diplomatic* bodyguard detail, and I have no doubt that you all have no clue how to move and act on a high-level diplomatic mission. The smallest little action or lack thereof can lead to anything from a pissed off alien to an interstellar war. And I swear to Apollo that if anyone on this mission causes so much as the smallest wave, you will be in front of a military tribunal so fast you'll think you warped there." Everyone paid rapt attention to me, even the diplomat at the podium, so it was no surprise when I asked, "Does everyone understand that?" that I got a chorus of loud "Yes, sir," including his.

"I second what Captain Andropov said," came the cultured voice of Chancellor Nguyen from the hatch.

"Attention on deck!" I barked, turning the briefing room into a statuary of eleven Imperial Commandos, and one slightly shuffling junior diplomat.

"At ease," Chancellor Nguyen said, with a friendly smile on his face. "Please, everyone, take your seats and we'll get what I am sure you will find to be the most boring part of the day over with." There was a soft chuckling from the team as I returned to my seat. Once again, I was surprised by how well the Chancellor could handle a group of people, though I probably shouldn't have been. He waved the still-shuffling diplomat away from the podium and took his place.

"Why don't we do this a bit differently than your regular sort of briefing," he said. "Let's start off with any questions you might have, then I'll go back and fill you in on everything else." I watched as everyone in the compartment looked at everyone else, waiting for someone to be the sacrificial lamb and ask the first question. It didn't take long for ten sets of eyes to turn my way, clearly letting me know, that as team leader, they expected me to lead the way, even here. Bastards. Someone could've stepped up, but no, I had to be an officer, and this time, letting an admiral take the heat while I spouted off a rote answer wasn't going to work. Even the Chancellor was looking at me expectantly, so I clearly had to come up with some kind of question to get this ball rolling.

I stood up and taking a deep breath, I asked the first question that popped into my head. "Sir, from what we heard earlier, you will be meeting directly with the Decarsi monarch. Won't it be considered a slight to have someone other than the Emperor handling these negotiations?" I knew as soon as I finished the question how wrongly it could be taken. I had basically just insulted the Chancellor by insinuating that he wasn't good enough to treat with the Decarsi monarch. Granted, I was just curious, but the collective gasps from the rest of the team let me know curiosity could still kill the cat. No pun intended. Thankfully, Chancellor Nguyen did not choose to interpret my question as an insult as I dropped back into my seat to listen to his answer.

"Good question, Captain," he started, though if he thought so, I am sure he was the only one in the compartment who did. "The Emperor is still a child, but don't tell him I said that—you all know how fifteen year old boys can be." He gave a short snort of laughter at his own joke before continuing. "As I was saying, the Emperor is still young, and the Regent is overseeing the day-to-day running of the Imperium, which as far as we have been able to determine, is roughly twice the size of the Decarsi Empire. Also, it appears that the Decarsi Empire is composed of just their race, as opposed to the Imperium, which is a union of a multitude of different races, leading to a very fluid and dynamic political climate that requires constant leadership. I have been assured by our diplomats who have been interacting with the Decarsi that this situation has been explained to them, and they have agreed to accept my presence as a representative of the Emperor with the full authority of the Imperium behind me." I nodded my understanding and waited to see if anyone else would have a question for the Chancellor. Corporal Murdock stood up and waited for the Chancellor to give her leave to ask her question.

"Sir, with almost no history of interaction with the Decarsi, will we have full or even partial translation programs uploaded to our suits?" Corporal Murdock was an outstanding soldier, and minus her propensity to cause havoc when bored, she would have been a sergeant years ago—but every time she came close to promotion eligibility, she invariably did something to bump her name to the bottom of the list, so I was a bit surprised by the astuteness of her question. Being unable to understand what a potential enemy or ally was saying is a liability in any instance, especially in one as sensitive as the upcoming situation. Even if we had translation programs, they wouldn't be fully reliable. It takes quite a while to build up a full linguistic database that would be able to handle all the subtle nuances inherent in any language.

"Another excellent question," Chancellor Nguyen said. "Yes, you will have the most up to date translation program uploaded to your suit. However, I would ask that you not engage them during negotiations, as a wrong word or phrase can be more damaging than you might imagine." His tone of voice clearly indicted it was an order, not a suggestion, no matter how he phrased it. "Also, keep in mind the Decarsi will have their own translation programs, and we have no intelligence on their signal collection capability, so assume that anything you say, even over your suit's encrypted comms, may be intercepted and possibly misunderstood." No one felt the need to inform the Chancellor that Imperial Commandos operated under strict communication protocols, and even when we did utilize our comms, we spoke almost entirely in coded battle language.

There were several more questions from the team before the Chancellor began his crash course on the dos and don'ts of the diplomatic arena that the heads of states regularly operated in; while my team had performed bodyguard details for politicians in the past, nothing was as important, or as unpredictable, as the detail my team and I were about to undertake. However, most of what the Chancellor said could be distilled down to either "keep your eyes and ears open and your mouth shut" or "don't do or touch anything without permission." Both points I planned on drilling into my team over the course of the three week voyage to the border between the Imperium and the Decarsi Empire.

As the Chancellor was finishing up his lecture, he made one final point. "Before we wrap this up, I want to go on record and reiterate what Captain Andropov said earlier. Anything that causes even the slightest incident during these negotiations will result in the most severe of consequences." With that, I called the compartment to attention as the Chancellor departed.

If I had any kind of foresight, I would've kept my mouth shut and not planted the idea of heavy repercussions for infractions in his mind. But, hindsight is always twenty-twenty, especially when it's your own words that are coming around to bite you in the ass.

In the three weeks it took to get to the Decarsi border, I drilled my team mercilessly in every scenario I could think up, from total boredom to running firefights down passageways, attempting to keep our principals "alive." Each team member took turns being "Chancellor Nguyen," myself included, and, thankfully, by the end of the first week, "Nguyen" didn't look like a child's kaleidoscopic painting, after suffering numerous marker round hits. Don't ask about what the rest of team looked like by the end of each day. Let's just say that bodyguards are expected to take a bullet for the principal, and my people were good at their jobs.

I had stressed to my team that while there were several people who would be involved in the initial meeting with the Decarsi monarch, each with his own bodyguard, Chancellor Nguyen was the primary principal on this mission, and, if necessary, our other principals would be left to their own devices should things truly start circling the drain. We were going to try out best not to let that particular situation develop, but, as the saying goes, life is what happens when you are making other plans.

Between worst-case scenario training, regular briefings from the Chancellor and his senior aides, politically-charged dinners, and rounds of "steal Captain Andropov's money" (otherwise known as cards), I was in a constant state of flux between apprehension and intimidation—sprinkled liberally with terror each time my team finished a practice run only to find Nguyen standing there seeing "himself" covered in marker round paint, disappointment and displeasure clear on his face. No matter how much time I spent with the man, I never quite got over my intimidation by him. Not to say I didn't actually like him—he was a very charming fellow, and he kept our card games lively with stories of his past exploits—but in the back of my mind was a little voice reminding me of his reputation for both ruthlessness and an inability to accept failure. I'm amazed that I managed to get any sleep at all during my time on his yacht.

It was almost a relief when we boarded the shuttle to begin the short flight to the Decarsi ship where negotiations were going to take place. But what little relief I had managed to gain was short-lived, as I entered the flight deck to pass my final instructions to the crew and got my first glance at the Decarsi ship. It was sleek and deadly-looking, a deep-space predator. Easily half again as big as the largest warship in the Imperial Fleet, it dwarfed Chancellor Nguyen's yacht and compared to that, our assault shuttle was practically nonexistent.

Eleven Imperial Commandos, five shuttle crew members, two senior aides, one admiral, and one senior plenipotentiary for the Imperium and chief counselor to the Regent, were about to be surrounded by Gods knew how many potentially hostile aliens. Every worst-case scenario began to play back in my mind, and I began to feel overwhelmed, though looking back on it, panicked would've probably been a more apt description. Tearing my eyes away from the view in front of me, I gave the pilot his final instructions, the same instructions I had been giving him for the past three weeks during our training. Stay sharp, keep the engines on standby, and be prepared for immediate dust off. He absently nodded his understanding as I left him to focus on his controls.

I re-entered the troop bay, which thankfully looked like a troop bay, giving me a comforting sense of familiarity. The Chancellor's yacht might've been a well-disguised destroyer, but the assault shuttle looked like nothing other than an assault shuttle. Granted, it was the nicest assault shuttle I've ever seen; it had a perfect paint job, the latest upgrades, and a maintenance record that any pilot in the Imperial Navy would be envious of. I was almost afraid of scuffing the deck with my armored boots.

Pushing everything extraneous out of my mind, I slipped effortlessly into "Captain Andropov, commanding officer of the best team of Imperial Commandos in the Imperium" mode and began my final mission brief. "Okay, everyone, listen up." All conversation in the troop bay stopped, and I had all eyes on me, the Chancellor's included.

"We are about to land on the Decarsi vessel and I want to go over our game plan one last time." My team was used to this last minute overview, and took it in stride, and surprisingly, so did Admiral Cryer and Chancellor Nguyen. The Chancellor's aides looked bored, but at that moment I really didn't care about them. They were going to take their orders from the Chancellor, and if the shit hit the fan, they were going to be nothing more than squirming luggage to my people as they were dragged back to the shuttle anyway.

"Watson, Jean-Luc, you two are on shuttle detail." I wasn't happy about leaving behind my two heavy weapons troopers, but even though our shuttle might not be much compared to the other ships in the neighborhood, it was the only one we had, and I didn't relish the idea of having to ask the Decarsi for a ride home, no matter what the situation was. "Sergeant Simms, you are the Chancellor's shadow—where he goes, you go, and I won't accept anything less than your cooling corpse if he gets so much as a scratch on him." The sergeant nodded, and I could see he knew I was putting on a bit of a show for the Chancellor and the admiral.

"Corporal Murdock, the same goes for you," I said, as I turned my attention to her. "Once we're on the deck, you and Admiral Cryer are joined at the hip." I continued to go over the team assignments, giving each of the Chancellor's aides their very own Imperial Commando; the rest of the team would be taking up various positions around the group diplomats and the Admiral. "I'll be sticking close to the Chancellor along with Sergeant Simms." I remember how uncomfortable I felt about having to broach the topic with the Chancellor that I would not be his primary bodyguard, as I was going to be in overall command of the whole detail. Thankfully, the Chancellor had dealt with this kind of situation in the past, and reassured me that he hadn't even considered that I would be taking the position as his primary protector. "Keep in mind, from the moment we land, the

Chancellor is in command. What he says goes, got it?" A chorus of assent followed my question as the shuttle begin to decelerate. Everyone in the troop bay knew that if things did go south, it would be my orders they were following, not the Chancellor's, but this time I had the wisdom to keep my mouth shut and not undermine the Chancellor's authority by actually mentioning it.

As I felt the shuttle settle onto the hangar deck, I gave my final order before it became the diplomatic corps's show. "Booted and suited people, let's get our game faces on." With that, I snapped the visor on my helmet closed and watched as the rest of my team follow suit. The admiral had decided to forgo a helmet, as she was officially a member of the diplomatic mission and would be expected to deal directly with the Decarsi.

The Chancellor and his aides were wearing suits, not full-powered armor like the rest of us, but I had been assured by the Chancellor that while their clothing wasn't up to combat armor standards, they were made from armor-weave material, and would stand up to some punishment should the need arise. I couldn't help but feel that they were all terribly exposed in those outfits, but I guess you can't have a friendly diplomatic chat with the potentate of another empire while wearing sealed combat armor.

The first thing that struck me as odd, other than being greeted at the shuttle ramp by oversized house cats carrying very large weapons, was how small and confining the ship's passageways were. Equilateral triangles with two meter sides, the passageways forced our party to walk in a nearly single file line. Even more disconcerting was that the passageways themselves were very smooth and bare. Outside of the occasional hatch, there was nothing to break up the surface—or, more to the point, nothing to take cover behind should the need arise.

We walked for nearly twenty minutes, taking innumerable turns and passing though multiple hatches and compartments of varying sizes. Thankfully, the internal navigational unit in our armor let us map our progress though the ship, or even the most astute scout would've been lost in a matter of minutes.

Finally arriving in what appeared to be, for lack of better words, an ornate throne room, we came face-to-face with what I assumed was the Monarch of the Decarsi Empire. I was far from impressed. Actually, I think "pillow room" would work better at describing it, as opposed to throne room. Against the far bulkhead was a raised dais, covered in what looked to be purple and yellow velvet pillows, and amidst those pillows was a curled up Decarsi, tail and whiskers twitching, clearly asleep. There we were, an official diplomatic mission from a neighboring empire, there to hopefully establish a mutually beneficial dialogue, and the feline we were there to treat with was dead to the world. And snoring. I guess it's true: it *is* good to be the king.

Apparently the Decarsi monarch was a bit of a slow riser. Followed by what I presume was a trip to the royal litter box, and the tripling of the guards in the compartment, upping the number to a little over forty armed and armored Decarsi, it was finally time to actually get the meeting started.

The Decarsi monarch's fur was grey with black stripes; he was dressed in a simple white robe, with a jade pendant on a leather thong around his neck, and gold leaves on his head. Standing beside him in rather more ornate robes, holding a wooden staff with some kind of gold device on the top, was an orange and white Decarsi, who I assumed was an advisor to the monarch. Just behind the monarch was a solid black-furred Decarsi wearing armor and cradling a heavy looking rifle, clearly the monarch's bodyguard.

The other Decarsi in the room were a variety of colors and appeared to be guards of some sort, as each was wearing armor and bristling with weapons. Their armor, while looking archaic, like an ancient knight's plate mail, was a burnished gray, and obviously functional, not ceremonial. It reminded me of our own combat armor, immaculately turned out and clean, but fully operational. I wasn't fooled by the old-fashioned appearance of the armor; any race capable of creating a ship of this size and complexity could build a suitable set of body armor. And, of course, they had weapons that were most likely comparable to our own.

"I am Grand Vizier of the Decarsi Empire, and I welcome you on behalf of His Royal Fuzziness, may his whiskers never droop." There were several snorts of suppressed laughs over the comm line as the small speaker around the Chancellor's neck translated the ornately-dressed Decarsi's words. The same translation was simultaneously broadcast over the comm system in my armor. It looked like the Chancellor was as good as his word—we had current translation software installed, though it was obvious that

it could use some more tweaking. The Chancellor ignored the slight *faux pas* by my team as he began to offer his hand to His Royal Fuzziness.

As the Chancellor's hand extended towards the monarch, several things happened in quick succession. The armored Decarsi grabbed the Chancellor's wrist, stopping his hand. The Decarsi holding the Chancellor's arm suddenly sprouted the barrel of an assault rifle from his left ear as Sergeant Simms snapped his rifle up to a firing position. Immediately, both Imperial Commandos and Decarsi guards brought their weapons up and found targets. The Grand Vizier began to hiss, spit, and growl, which was immediately translated. *"His Royal Fuzziness, may his claws never dull, is not to be touched."*

"My apologies, Your Royal Fuzziness," Chancellor Nguyen said in a calm, soft voice, while slightly bowing at the waist. "It was merely a human custom and I ask your forgiveness."

"His Fuzziness, may his fangs always be sharp, says you are forgiven." The monarch continued speaking into the vizier's ear. *"He also considers it an insult that he cannot see the eyes of your protectors, yet you can see the eyes of the royal guard. He asks that you have your protectors reveal themselves."*

"Of course, Your Fuzziness, I will have them do so," the Chancellor replied before turning his head towards me. "Captain Andropov." The order was clear, and I did the only thing that I could do in that situation.

"Visors," I said as I pressed the button on the inside of my face plate with my tongue, causing my visor to swing up. I watched as the rest of my team's visors did the same.

Even before my visor had locked into the open position, my eyes began to water, and my nose began to run. While I was surreptitiously blinking my eyes to try and clear them, His Royal Fuzziness, followed closely by his bodyguard, walked up to Sergeant Simms and leaned forward slightly to stare into his eyes. Simms simply stood there and stared back unblinkingly. Several heartbeats later, the Decarsi monarch moved on to Corporal Murdock, repeating the procedure while I tried to suppress a cough and keep myself from sniffling. Then it was my turn to be sized up by the fuzzball. That was when everything went horribly, horribly wrong.

I sneezed. A simple biological function that was to have consequences that I could not even imagine at the time. The abruptness and cacophony of my sneeze caused everyone within the compartment to jump, before they froze in shock, each and every being staring at me and His Fuzziness. Or, more likely, to stare at the large glob of mucus that was splattered across the Monarch's nose and whiskers.

"Oh shit." The cultured and refined voice of Chancellor Nguyen echoed throughout the compartment, proving that even the most seasoned diplomat can be caught unawares. The silence following the Chancellor's quiet exclamation seemed to be interminable, but that was broken by the Monarch's bodyguard screaming.

"Blasphemy!" It was clear he wanted to bring his rifle to bear on me, but with the monarch between the two of us, he didn't dare. Chancellor Nguyen's attempt to diffuse was a mistake, as all he managed to do was draw the attention of the bodyguard. I was still sneezing as I slammed the visor of my helmet back into position and croaked out over the comm net. "Black Swan!"

With that simple code phrase, I had transferred responsibility for this mission squarely onto my shoulders, and transformed Chancellor Nguyen from the Imperium's highest-level diplomat into a package that needed to be delivered back to the shuttle. Sergeant Simms acted with the calm, smooth confidence of a consummate professional, grabbing the Chancellor and pulling him into his chest as he spun around to place his armored back to the bodyguard seconds before the bodyguard opened fire. Fully automatic weapons fire impacted on the sergeant's back and dozens of small explosions erupted from his neck to his kidneys, tearing open his armor and spraying viscera across the deck. As Simms's cooling corpse hit the deck with a metallic clang, I reached out and grabbed the completely unscathed Chancellor and threw him to the deck as I attempted to cover his body with my own while not crushing him under the weight of my armored form.

The entire compartment had exploded into a furious firefight before Simms's body had even completely settled on the deck.

The Decarsi monarch's bodyguard's body followed Sergeant Simms to the deck, his body chopped to pieces by Corporal Murdock's murderous return fire, one hand holding her rifle while using her other to push Admiral Cryer behind her.

For her part, Admiral Cryer didn't protest, but instead let herself be pushed towards the hatch we had entered as she drew her sidearm. Sprinting to the hatch, the Admiral paused and took up a perfect firing stance, placing precise return fire on the Decarsi royal guard. I was impressed with her calm demeanor and level head under fire. Unfortunately, she literally had a level head in the next exchange of gunfire, as explosive rounds blew shrapnel from the bulkhead directly into her unarmored head.

Corporal Murdock turned towards where she thought the admiral would be, directly behind her, but I watched as she continued turning, clearly scanning the compartment for the admiral. Obviously seeing that the admiral was no longer in need of bodyguard services, Murdock continued her spin, bringing her rifle up to engage more Decarsi. She had just gotten a burst of fire off before a small explosion blossomed in the center of her chest, catapulting her backward to land on the deck, flat on her back.

While this was going on, I was busy trying to get my respiratory system under control. I continued to hack and sneeze while I balanced myself on one arm over the Chancellor's body, my other bringing up my rifle. I aimed at the largest cluster of Decarsi I could see though my watering eyes and pulled the trigger.

The Decarsi may have had exploding rounds, but the Imperial military had no need of them, as hyper velocity rounds make explosives redundant. The kinetic energy imparted by the impact of my rounds blew bodies to pieces and huge chunks out of the bulkhead, and not caring one whit about fire discipline at that moment, I simply held the trigger down and sprayed rounds across the compartment.

After my rifle's magazine ran dry, I took a moment to assess the situation. The firing had stopped, and since I was still alive, I took that to mean that we had won the brief battle. Standing up while dragging the Chancellor with me, I saw that I had four of my team still alive, all of them sporting divots in their armor where a Decarsi round had impacted. Corporal Murdock was among the survivors, the shot to her chest having only knocked her over, though it looked like it had come dangerously close to breaching her armor.

"Murdock, package," I snapped, while exchanging the spent magazine in my rifle for fresh one. As she walked over and grabbed the Chancellor by the arm, I was surprised to see two more persons in civilian clothing being grabbed in the same way. Both of the Chancellor's aides had survived the firefight, and I had to wonder how many of my team were dead on the deck to have kept them that way. That thought was pushed out of my mind as I was wracked by a series of sneezes that resulted in the inside of my helmet being liberally covered in mucus, rendering a sizeable portion of my heads-up display unreadable. Not that I could do much reading with my eyes watering as they were. Before I could do anything else, a horrible ululating screeching sound erupted, and I interpreted that as the signal indicating that we were no longer welcome on the Decarsi ship, a sentiment I was more than willing to share.

I scanned the compartment with my helmet cam, capturing the carnage for the record, and saw the remains of the Decarsi monarch. "Damn," I muttered. Not that I cared if the monarch lived or died, but with him being dead, I had no bargaining chip to use to buy our way off the ship, leaving us with the only one option: shooting our way out. I pointed to one of my team, then at the hatch, indicating I wanted him on point and that we were leaving.

"Doorman, this is Actual," I sent over the comm line to the guards I'd left at the shuttle, my voice sounding raw and scratchy. "Party's over, and we're coming in hot."

"Understood, Actual, reception will be ready."

I acknowledged the response from Watson as I ran down the passageway, trailing after the man on point. As he rounded a corner, he was blown back into the bulkhead, his entire body seeming to disappear in a series of miniature explosions. I grabbed an incendiary grenade from my belt, thumbing the activation switch as I did, and hurled it around the corner. A loud crump, a gout of flame, and loud screaming that quickly ended told me that the passageway was clear. With the point man down, and the rest of the team handling a package, I was now on point. Lucky me.

We proceeded to head to the hangar bay with all due haste. In an attempt to avoid becoming a smear on the bulkhead like the last point man, I cleared each passageway the way I had the first one. Unfortunately, there were dozens of compartments filled with armed Decarsi hiding in wait that we had to go through, and a screaming horde of Decarsi chasing us. To make matters worse, I was still suffering from respiratory distress. I would highly recommend not participating in a running firefight while sneezing, being half-blind due to watering eyes and a mucus-splattered heads-up display, and suffering from congestion so bad it feels like you're suffocating. It sucks. I've no doubt it was more luck than skill that kept me alive.

By the time we were in the passageway leading directly to the hangar bay, we'd exhausted our supply of grenades, lost one of the Chancellor's aides, and, most importantly, two more of my team.

"Murdock, go," I said, watching as she dragged the Chancellor through the hatch in into the hangar bay. I had just grabbed the remaining aide and began dragging him towards the hangar, spraying suppressive fire down the passageway in the hope of keeping the Decarsi discouraged long enough to make it into the hangar. Not that it had worked so far, but every Decarsi dead was one less shooting at us.

As the aide and I ran into the hangar bay, I could see Corporal Murdock on her hands and knees, clearly trying to get back onto her feet, and Chancellor Nguyen lying on the deck, thrashing around, laughing.

"Gas!" Murdock croaked out as she finally regained her feet. I shoved the aide towards her and bent down to check on the Chancellor. I looked up and saw that Murdock had reached the shuttle with the nearly catatonic aide in tow.

Chancellor Nguyen was still laughing, yet I could see the fear in his eyes and the pain on his face as he didn't stop. I picked him up and slung him over my shoulder as I sprayed the last of my ammunition at the Decarsi beginning to pour out of the hatch and into the hangar bay. I watched in satisfaction as several of them were blown apart before turning towards the shuttle and sprinting for all I was worth.

I passed the shredded remains of Jean-Luc as I pounded up the ramp and into the troop bay, Watson quickly following. As he slapped the button to close the ramp, I yelled over the comm net, "Get us out of here now!"

Looking back, I have to give that shuttle pilot credit. He was, without a doubt, the best pilot I've ever seen. He managed to get us back to the Chancellor's yacht without so much as a scratch on the paint. Considering the volume of fire the Decarsi ship was putting out, it was a minor miracle. Unfortunately, senior plenipotentiary for the Imperium and chief counselor to the Regent, Chancellor Jonathan Nguyen, died before we made it back to the yacht. Whatever that gas he was exposed to was, according to the medical examiner aboard the yacht, it caused him to go into complete organ failure in a matter of minutes, laughing the whole time.

I had Corporal Murdock contact the yacht to apprise them of our situation, though I am sure they had figured it out, what with the amount of fire they were taking from the Decarsi ship. I was still finding it hard to breathe, but fortunately my sneezing had subsided to only one or two every couple of minutes.

The shuttle had barely touched down in the yacht's hangar when I felt the familiar sinking sensation in the pit of my stomach that indicated we'd activated our star-drive. I could only hope that we were on our way back to the Imperium, and, as it turned out, we were. There is an old saying: "Be careful what you wish for, you just might get it." I never really paid it any mind, truth be told. Unfortunately, I know better now.

It took us just under two weeks to get back to Terra. Apparently, the captain had redlined the engines to get us home and get the news about the Chancellor and our mission's status reported as soon as possible. I'd spent a vast majority of the return trip writing letters for the surviving family of my fallen team members, reviewing everything we had on the actual "incident" that precipitated the current status of events (which was quite a large volume of information, thanks to our helmet cams), and preparing my after action report for Colonel Franklin upon our return. Seeing as how my report became exhibit A at my military tribunal, I probably shouldn't have been so diligent and meticulous in my writing, or at least tried to show myself in a better light, if that was at all possible.

As the Chancellor's yacht had a fully-staffed medical team, composed of some of the best doctors in the Imperium, I also took the opportunity to have myself checked out, concerned I had been exposed to some kind of chemical or biological weapon due to my reactions at the negotiations. Two days before we reached Terran orbit, the doctor called me down to sick bay to deliver my test results. The short version: I was and do suffer from severe, debilitating, allergic rhinitis to *Felis catus*. Translation; I'm highly allergic to house cat dander. That particular piece of information was exhibit B at the tribunal, though I must say, the prosecutor made it sound much more damning. "Captain Andropov's failure to disclose his full medical history, as required by Imperial Military regulations, directly resulted in the death of ten Imperial citizens, and ignited an interstellar war that will cost hundreds of thousands more."

My defense—growing up on an orbital station and never seeing a cat before I came face to face with the Decarsi, thus not being even remotely aware of any allergies—fell on deaf ears. As I watched my defense attorney try to explain this to the jurors, I realized that the verdict was determined before I'd even made it into the courtroom. The Imperium needed a scapegoat, and I was it. I may as well have spent my time hammering a square peg through a round hole with my forehead; I probably would've had less of a headache than I did by the end of the very short hearing if I had.

"Guilty. On all counts." The verdict was read by the judge after the jury's five minute deliberation. Once I understood that I was on the sacrificial altar, I didn't even bother to point out that the foreman of the jury had handed his verdict to the judge on the way *out* of the courtroom for deliberations. The sentencing, which I assumed was going to find me on the wrong end of either a rope or a firing squad, was as unexpected as it was surprising. "Captain Andropov is hereby stripped of his rank, dishonorably discharged from the Imperial Military, and further he is forever banned from Imperial civil service," the judge said, right before banging his gavel. "Court dismissed." At which point, my mind stopped tracking.

It was about two months after my trial that I began to function in a somewhat coherent fashion, and I realized why the court had spared my life. A dead man doesn't stay in the media long, but a live one can be a scandal for months. I'm sure I would've bounced back faster, if it wasn't for the media tracking my every move and action, splashing my face and story across every single monitor in the Imperium. It's difficult to take your mind off of a topic when you're bombarded with it night and day, and it's even harder when you're the center of attention, but I finally managed to do it.

That made things worse, because by then, reports from the front lines were coming in and I felt a constriction in my chest each time I saw one. Men and women I knew, friends and comrades, were dying out there at the end of Decarsi guns and it was my fault. It was a combination of morbid curiosity and what I felt was penance that had me paying close attention to each and every one of those news reports. That was when the puzzle, one I didn't even know needed to be solved, began to come together.

The Decarsi were being pushed back on all fronts, almost as if there were fleets prepositioned to strike all along the border. In fact, the first conflict of the war, not counting my little escapade, was fully engaged even before the verdict was read. If history has taught me anything, it is that empires need to expand, and the Decarsi Empire was in the way of the Imperium's expansion. It was, and still is, my opinion that the Decarsi war was planned, long before Chancellor Nguyen stepped foot onto their ship. Of course, I'm sure that the grand machinations of the Imperium didn't count on me blowing snot all over the face of an alien monarch, and I'm sure the plan included Chancellor Nguyen being alive at the conclusion of negations, but they ran with it anyway. The war was sold to the citizens of the Imperium as aggression on the part of the Decarsi Empire. Considering how masterfully the Imperial propaganda machine pieced together the imagery from my team's helmet cams to portray Chancellor Nguyen as a hero of the Imperium, viciously cut down by an unscrupulous alien menace, and me as a bumbling idiot that caused an interstellar war due to my apparent inability to tie my own boots, I wasn't in the least bit surprised that the citizens of the Imperium swallowed the entire thing.

I take comfort in the knowledge that no matter how it started, the war was not my fault, no matter what the history books say. Though what still eats at me to this day is the fact that even though I now know the war was inevitable, were it not for a previously unknown allergy to the Decarsi, I would not be vilified as one of the Imperium's worst criminals.

I looked down into the wide brown eyes of my thirteen year old daughter as I finished speaking. I had never told her why people shunned me in public, or when they were not ignoring me, hurled insults at me, and, by association, why she was picked on in school. Her lower lip stuck out, a mixture of a sad pout and confusion marring her freckled face. "Oh," she said in a soft, sad voice that suddenly changed to bright and chipper. "But, Daddy, that doesn't answer my question."

"I'm sorry, sweetie," I said, putting my arm around her shoulder and giving her a one-armed hug. "What was your question?"

"Can we get a cat?"

The Price

MICHAEL Z. WILLIAMSON

Four Jemma Two Three, Freehold of Grainne Military Forces (J Frame Craft, Reconnaissance, Stealth), was a tired boat with a tired crew.

After two local years—three Earth years—of war with the United Nations of Earth and Space, that was no small accomplishment. Most of her sister vessels had been destroyed. That 4J23 was intact, functional, and only slightly ragged with a few "character traits" spoke well of her remarkable crew.

"I have a message, and I can't decode it with my comm," Warrant Leader Derek Costlow announced.

The crew turned to him. This could be a welcome break from the monotony of maintenance. Jan Marsich and his sister Meka, both from Special Warfare and passengers stuck aboard since the war started, paid particular attention. Any chance of finding a real mission or transport back to Grainne proper was of interest to them.

"Want me to have a whack at it, Warrant?" asked Sergeant Melanie Sarendy, head of the intelligence mission crew.

"If you would, Mel." He nodded. "I'll forward the data to your system."

Sarendy dropped her game control, which was hardwired and shielded rather than wireless. Intel boats radiated almost no signature. The handheld floated where it was until disturbed by the eddies of her passage.

Jan asked, "Why do we have a message when we're tethered to the Rock? From who?" Meka wrinkled her brow.

"That's an interesting series of questions," she commented.

"The Rock" was a field-expedient facility with no official name other than a catalog number of use only for communication logs. The engineers who carved and blasted it from a planetoid, the boat crews who used it, the worn and chronically short-handed maintenance personnel aboard had had too little time to waste on trivialities such as names. There were other such facilities throughout the system, but few of the surviving vessels strayed far enough from their own bases to consort with other stations. "The Rock" sufficed.

They were both attentive again as Sarendy returned. She looked around at the eyes on her, and said, "Sorry. Whatever it is, I don't have a key for it."

Meka quivered alert. "Mind if I try?" she asked.

"Sure," Costlow replied.

She grabbed her comm and plugged it into a port as everyone waited silently. She identified herself through several layers of security and the machine conceded that perhaps it might have heard of that code. A few more jumped hoops and it flashed a translation on her screen.

The silence grew even more palpable when she looked up with her eyes blurring with tears. "Warrant," she said, voice cracking, and locked eyes with him.

Costlow glanced around the cabin, and in seconds everyone departed for their duty stations or favorite hideyholes, leaving the two of them and Jan in relative privacy. Jan was family, and Costlow let him stay. In response to the worried looks from the two of them, Meka turned her screen to face them.

The message was brief and said simply, "YOU ARE ORDERED TO DESTROY AS MANY OF THE FOLLOWING PRIORITIZED TARGETS AS POSSIBLE. ANY AND ALL ASSETS AND RESOURCES ARE TO BE UTILIZED TO ACCOMPLISH THIS MISSION. SIGNED, NAUMANN, COLONEL COMMANDING, PROVISIONAL FREEHOLD MILITARY FORCES. VERIFICATION X247." Attached was a list of targets and a timeframe. All the targets were in a radius around Jump Point Three, within about a day of their current location.

"I don't understand," Jan said. "Intel boats don't carry heavy weapons. How do they expect us to do this?"

"It was addressed to me, not the boat," Meka replied. "He wants me to take out these targets, using any means necessary."

That didn't need translating. There was a silence, broken by Costlow asking, "Are you sure that's a legit order? It looks pointless. Why would they have you attack stuff way out here in the Halo?"

Meka replied, "We know what the enemy has insystem. We know where most of their infrastructure is. If Naumann wants it taken out, it means he's preparing an offensive."

"But this is insane!" Jan protested. "The Aardvarks will have any target replaced in days!"

"No," Meka replied, shaking her head. "It's a legit order. All those targets are intel or command and control."

Costlow said, "So he wants the command infrastructure taken out to prevent them responding quickly. Then he hits them with physical force."

"Okay, but why not just bomb them or use rocks in fast trajectories?" Jan asked.

Costlow said, "It would take too long to set that many rocks in orbit. Nor could we get them moving fast enough. Maneuvering thrusters and standard meteor watch would take care of them. As to bombing them, they all have defensive grids, and we're a recon boat."

Jan paused and nodded. "Yeah, I know. And there aren't many real gunboats left. I'd just like a safer method." He asked Meka, "So how could you get in?"

"UN stations have sensor holes to ignore vacsuits and toolkits. Ships can't get in, but a single person can."

Costlow looked confused. "Why'd they leave a hole like that?" he asked.

"Partly to prevent accidents with EVA and rescue, partly laziness. They lost a couple of people, and that's just not socially acceptable on Earth," she said. "It's the Blazer's greatest asset to penetrating security. Systems only work if they are used. Backdoors and human stupidity are some of our best tools."

"Didn't they think anyone would do what you're discussing?" Jan asked. That was dangerous. It would push EVA gear to the edge.

"No," she said, shaking her head. "They would never give such an order. The political bureaucracy of the UNPF requires all missions be planned with no loss of life. Not minimal, but zero. Yes, it's ridiculous, but that's how they do things."

"And they don't think we'd do it?" Costlow asked.

"Why should they assume we'd do it if they wouldn't? You're having a hard enough time with the concept."

Jan asked, "So you EVA in, and then back out?"

"How would I find a stealthed boat from a suit? How would you find me? It's not as if there's enough power to just loiter, and doing so would show on any scan." Her expression was flushed, nauseous, and half-grinning. It was creepy.

"But even if you get through, they can still get new forces here in short order," Jan said. He didn't want his sister to die, because that's what this was—a literal suicide mission. His own guts churned.

"No," Meka replied. "Or, not fast enough to matter, I should say." She tapped tactical calculus algorithms into her comm while mumbling, "Minimum twenty hours to get a message relayed to Sol . . . flight time through Jump Point Two . . ."

Jan had forgotten that. Jump Point One came straight from Sol, but it no longer existed. Professor Meacham and his wife had taken their hyperdrive research ship into it, then activated phase drive. The result of two intersecting stardrive fields was hard to describe mathematically, but the practical, strategic result was that the point collapsed. No jump drive vessel could transit directly from Sol to Grainne anymore, and the UN didn't yet have any phase drive vessels that they knew of.

Meka finished mumbling, looked up, and said, "Median estimate of forty-three days to get sufficient force here. They could have command and control back theoretically in forty hours, median two-eighty-six, but that doesn't help them if they are overrun. It's risky, but we don't have any other option."

Costlow said, "That may be true, but they *can* send more force. It's a short term tactical gain, but not a strategic win."

"I know Naumann," Meka replied firmly. "He has something planned."

"Unless it's desperation," Costlow said.

Shaking her head, her body unconsciously twisting to compensate, she said, "No. He never throws his people away, and he has very low casualty counts. If he wants me to do this, then he has a valid plan."

"Trusting him with your life is dangerous, especially since you don't even know that's him," Jan said. They'd almost died three times now. She'd almost died a couple more. This one was for real.

"We're trusting him with more than that," she said. "And that's definitely him. Security protocols aside, no one else would have the balls to give an order like that and just assume it would be followed. Besides, it authenticates."

"Okay," Costlow reluctantly agreed. "Which target are you taking?"

She pointed as she spoke, "Well, the command ship *London* is the first choice, but I don't think I can get near a ship. This crewed platform is second, but I'd have to blast or fight my way in. If I fail, I still die, and accomplish nothing. I suppose I have to chicken out and take the automatic commo station."

"Odd way to chicken out," Jan commented in a murmur.

"Are you sure of these priorities?" Costlow asked. His teeth were grinding and he looked very bothered.

"Yes," she replied. "If I had more resources, I'd take *London*, too. We don't have any offensive missiles, though."

"We have one," the older man softly replied. They looked at him silently. "If you're sure that's a good order," he said. His face turned from tan to ashen as he spoke.

"I am," she said.

"Then I'll drop you on the way. Just think of this as an intelligent stealth missile," he said, and tried to smile. It looked like a rictus.

"Are you sure?" she asked.

"No," he admitted. "But if it's what we have to do to win..."

There was silence for a few moments. Hating himself for not speaking already, hating the others even though it wasn't their fault, Jan said, "I'll take the automatic station." Saying it was more concrete than thinking it. His guts began twisting and roiling, and cold sweat burst from his body. He felt shock and adrenaline course through him. "That takes it out of the equation, and you can fight your way into the crewed one."

Costlow said, "It's appreciated, Jan, but you're tech branch. I think you'd be of more help here."

It was a perfect escape, and Meka's expression said she wasn't going to tell his secret if he wanted to stop there. He was a Special Projects technician, who built custom gear for others, usually in close support, but too valuable to be directly combatant save in emergencies. The act of volunteering was more than enough for most people, and he could gracefully bow out. He felt himself talking, brain whirling as he did. "I do EVA as a hobby. I'm not as good as Meka, but I can manage, given the gear." There. *Now* he was committed.

"You don't have to, Jan," Meka said. "There are other Blazers. We'll get enough targets."

"Meka, I'm not doing this out of inadequacy or false bravery." Actually, he was. There was another factor, too. When she looked at him, he continued, "I *can't* face Mom and Dad and tell them you did this. No way. I'm doing this so I don't have to face them. And because I guess it has to be done."

After a long wait, staring at each other, conversation resumed. The three made a basic schedule, hid all data, and undogged the cabin. They each sought their own private spaces to think and come to grips, and the rest of the crew were left to speculate. The normal schedule resumed, and would remain in force until the planned zero time, five days away.

The three were reserved during the PT sparring match that evening. The crew each picked a corner or a hatch to watch from in the day cabin, a five-meter cylinder ten meters long, and cheered and critiqued as they took turns tying each other in knots. Sarendy was small but vicious, her lithe and slender limbs striking like those of a praying mantis. Jan and Meka were tall and rangy. Costlow was older and stubborn. Each one had his or her own method of fighting. They were all about as effective.

Jan was strong, determined, and made a point of staying current on unarmed combat, partly due to a lack of demand for his services. He and Costlow twirled and kicked and grappled for several minutes, sweating and gasping from exertion, until Jan finally pinned the older man in a corner with a forearm wedged against his throat. "Yours," Costlow acknowledged.

Jan and Meka faced off from opposite ends, both lean and pantherlike. They studied each other carefully for seconds, then flew at each other, twisting and reaching, and met in a flurry of long limbs. Meka slapped him into a spin, twisted his ankles around, locked a foot under his jaw, and let her momentum carry them against the aft hatch, where her other knee settled in the small of his back, pinning him helplessly as she grabbed the edge. Her kinesthetic sense and coordination never ceased to amaze the rest of them.

Passive Sensor Specialist Riechard gamely threw himself into the bout. He advanced and made a feint with one hand, orienting to keep a foot where he could get leverage off the bulkhead. He moved in fast and hard and scored a strike against Meka's shoulder, gripped her arm, and began to apply leverage. She countered by pivoting and kicking for his head.

Riechard spun and flinched. "Shoot, Meka, watch it!" he snapped.

"Sorry," she replied. Nerves had her frazzled, and she'd overreacted, her kick almost tearing his ear off. "I better take a break. Default yours."

The crew knew something was up. Costlow and the Marsichs were on edge, irritable, and terse. The session broke down without comment, and everyone drifted in separate directions.

Jan signed out and headed into the Rock the next morning. The scenery was no more exciting, being carved stone walls with sealed hatches, but it wasn't the boat. The air seemed somehow fresher, and it was good not to see the same faces. It wasn't his choice for a last liberty, but there wasn't any alternative. It was either the ship or the Rock.

Throughout the station, soldiers and spacers moved around in sullen quiet. The reserved faces made it obvious that other boats and ships had similar instructions. Jan had to smile at the irony that everyone had the same orders, and no one could talk about it. Then he remembered what was to happen, and became rather sullen himself.

He'd wanted Mel Sarendy for two years, but crew were off-limits, and it grew more frustrating as time went on. Their society had no taboos against casual nudity, and the spartan supplies and close quarters aboard the boat encouraged it. He'd spent hours staring at her toned body, surreally shaped in microgravity. Her ancestry, like her name, was Earth Cambodian, diluted perhaps with a trace of Russian. That he occasionally caught what he thought was a hint of reciprocation in her speech and actions made it almost torture.

He didn't want to drink, in case he crawled into the bottle. He settled for a small cubicle where he could just sit in silence and be alone, a luxury unavailable aboard the boat.

Costlow was excited when he returned. Jan recognized cheerfulness when he saw it, and was impatient to find out what had changed.

Some time later, the three gathered on the command deck and sealed it off. "Talk to me, Warrant," Meka demanded.

"There's enough guidance systems to set a dozen charges. We can do this by remote," he said.

"No, we can't," Meka stated flatly.

"Shut up and wait," he snapped. "We program them to loiter outside sensor range, then do a high-velocity approach on schedule."

"Thereby running into sensor range and right into a defensive battery. I suppose you could hide a charge in a suit, but I doubt it would maneuver properly, and you couldn't program it to steer itself. We aren't using us to deliver from lack of resources—it's because we can get through and a drone can't. If you want to try to program them for a fourth target, do so. It can't hurt, unless of course you need them as decoys later."

Jan breathed deeply and slowly, feeling sick to his stomach. Crap, this was the worst experience of his life. Were they going to do this or not?

Costlow looked sheepish. "I thought I had it there. Sorry," he said.

"Don't apologize, sir," she replied. "The fact that you missed that means the Earthies think they are solid and can't be taken. This will work."

A depressed silence settled over them, but then Jan had a different thought. He cleared his throat.

"There's another factor," he said. "The crewed station might have viable oxy or escape pods. After Meka takes it out, she can hunker down and await rescue... there's a chance you could survive, sis."

"Well, good!" Costlow said.

Meka flushed red. "Yes, but that's hardly fair to you two."

He shrugged. "What's fair? We do what we have to. After that, who can say?"

She looked at Jan. He smiled, of course, because he was glad of the possibility. He was also furious, nauseous, frightened, and there was nothing to say, except, "Good luck, then."

It was wholly inadequate. They were all lying, they all knew it, and it was just one more cold lump in the guts.

Two tediously painful days later, the two soldiers and the pilot gathered in the crew cabin once more. They checked off lists of essentials that had been requisitioned or borrowed, finalized the schedule, and prepared to start. The equipment made it fairly obvious what they planned.

"First order of business, clear the ship," Costlow said. He sounded the intercom for all hands, and everyone boiled in. When they were clumped around him, he said, "We have a mission for which we must reduce mass and resources, so the rest of you are being temporarily put on the Rock. Grab what you need, but you need to be off by morning."

The crew and techs looked around at each other, at the three who would remain, and it was seconds only before Pilot Sereno said, "How much mass are you stripping?"

Costlow replied, "None yet. We'll be doing that later in the mission."

More looks crossed the cabin, thoughts being telegraphed. After an interminable time, Sereno said, "Yes, Warrant," and headed away. The others silently followed his lead.

Yeah, he knows, Jan thought.

Over the rest of the day, they returned one by one to make their cases. Every single member of the crew was determined to accompany the boat on its last mission. Death was to be feared, but staying behind was unbearable.

Sereno spent some time arguing with his superior that he was more expendable. While true, Costlow was the better pilot. He left dejected and angry.

Boat Engineer Jacqueline Jemayel had more success. She simply handed over a comm with her checklist, and said, "No one else has the years of training and familiarity to handle your hardware in combat. If you think you can handle that while flying, I'll leave." Costlow twitched and stalled, but relented to her logic and determination. They'd been friends and crew a long time, and he was glad to have her along.

Engine Specialist Kurashima and Analyst Corporal Jackson got nowhere. Neither were needed for this. They might be needed on another vessel. Costlow wasn't taking anyone except Jemayel, and only because she did have a valid case. A good boat engineer was essential generally, and for this especially. He listened briefly to each of the others, wished them well and sent them packing. He was proud that his crew were so dedicated and determined, and he left recommendations for decorations in his final log file.

It was mere hours before departure time when the hatch beeped an authorized entry. They looked over as Melanie Sarendy swam in, followed by Sergeant Frank Otte, the equipment technician for the intelligence crew.

Costlow was annoyed, and snapped, "Sarendy, Otte, I ordered you to—"

She interrupted with a stern face, "Warrant, the *London* has Mod Six upgrades to its sensor suite. If you want to get close, then you need offensive systems as well as sensors. This is a recon boat, not a gunboat. I'm the best tech you're going to get, I can get you in there, and I'm coming along. Sergeant Otte is here to build a station for me on the flight deck, and modifications for offensive transmissions, then he's leaving." She moved to swim past them toward her station. How she'd found out the details was a mystery. No one had told her. Costlow blocked her. She looked determined and exasperated, until he held a hand out. "Welcome aboard, Sergeant," he acknowledged.

It took Otte, Jemayel, and Jan to build the devices necessary. Sarendy's requested station wasn't a standard item for a recon boat, and there were few spare parts aboard the Rock. Judicious cannibalization and improvisation yielded an effective, albeit ugly, setup. Additional gear was used to build an offensive electronic suite, and some of it had obviously been stolen from other ships. As promised, Otte left, but not before trying desperately to convince them he was as necessary as Jemayel. He failed, but not for lack of determination.

4J23 departed immediately. The time left was useful for rehearsal and training, and those were best done without distractions. The short crew strapped in as Costlow cleared with Station Control, detached the umbilical, thereby cutting them off from communication, the boat being under transmission silence, and powered away.

It would avoid awkward goodbyes, also.

Meka began laying out gear for herself and Jan. They each would take their duty weapons. Jan had a demolition charge large enough for the structure in question. She took extra explosives and ammo. Both would carry their short swords—not so much from need, but because it was traditional. They both needed oxy bottles. He'd wear her maneuvering harness; she had a sled designed for clandestine missions. They had enough oxy mix, barely, to last them two days. That was tantalizingly close to enough for a pickup, but still short. A boat might conceivably get into the vicinity in time, but rescue operations took time. If they could run this mission in the open . . . but of course, they couldn't.

Costlow spent the time getting trajectories from the navigation system. He needed to pass by two stations whose locations were approximate, get near the *London*, which was in a powered station orbit around the jump point, observe, plan an approach, execute the approach while staying unseen, and arrive at a precise point at an exact time with sufficient fuel for terminal maneuvers. Very terminal. He consulted with Sarendy as to detection equipment ranges and apertures to help plot his path. Jemayel tended the engines, life support, and astronautics. None of them spoke much.

Jan had little to do until his departure. He spent it moping, getting angry, and finally beating on the combat practice dummy for hours, twisting in microgravity. When Meka called him over to explain the gear, he was more than eager to just get things over with.

She showed him the mass of gear and began to go through it. He checked everything off with her. Weapons and gear needed little explanation. He was familiar with the technical details of her maneuvering harness and the munitions fuses even though he'd never used them. The briefing would be far too short a distraction.

"We'll synch our chronos," Meka said.

"Goddess, don't give me a clock," Jan begged, shaking his head. "If I have to watch it count down, I'll be a basket case. Just put me there with some stuff to read and let me go." He spoke loudly, eyes wide, because the stress was getting to him.

"You need one in case the auto system fails," Meka said. "You're getting a triple load of ammo. It seems unlikely, but if anyone shows up to stop you—"

"Then I hold them off as long as I can."

"Right," Meka agreed.

Costlow showed the plotted course in a 3D, and asked, "We let you off here. Are you sure you can maneuver well enough for that distance?"

Shrugging, Jan replied, "End result is the same for me either way, but I'm sure. I do a lot of EVA. Unlike some people, I like it."

"Bite me, bro," Meka replied and laughed, too loud from stress. She had always *hated* long EVA, and that's what this was. She was assembling a pile of gear including her powered sled, two oxy bottles, the basic demolition blocks from everyone's standard gear plus her own larger pack, weapons, and stuff the others wouldn't recognize. Her actions were trained, expert, and only a little shaky from tension. She'd done long trips in the dark before, and survived, but that didn't make it fun. She had her sled for this one—Jan was making a far shorter infiltration—and the boat wasn't her concern. She prepped everything, had Jan and Jemayel double check, and went through exercises to calm herself. Those didn't work for Jan.

With less than four hours until his departure, Jan sat staring at the bulkhead of the day cabin. His bunk was folded, and his few effects sealed in a locker. He'd recorded a message and written instructions, all of which made things rather final. He didn't feel thoroughly terrified yet, but did feel rather numb. Rest was impossible. He nodded briefly to Sarendy as she swam in, and tried not to dwell on her. It was all too easy to think of justifications to break the fraternization ban. He didn't need rejection or complications now, and the sympathy ploy was the only approach he could think of. It wouldn't work, as she was in the same boat as he, quite literally.

"Come back here," she said, gesturing with a hand. She turned and swam for her intel bay.

As he followed her in, she closed the hatch and dogged it. It was dimly lit by one emergency lamp, there being no need for its use at this time, and there was just enough room for the two of them inside the radius of couches and terminals set against the shell. While his brain tried to shift gears, she grabbed him by the shoulders and mashed her mouth against his while reaching to open her shipsuit. Both their hands fumbled for a few seconds, then his stopped and drew back while hers continued questing.

"Mehlnee," he muttered around her kiss. She drew her full lips back a bare few millimeters, and he continued, "I appreciate this . . . but it won't help me deal with . . . this."

"It helps me," she replied, voice breathy, and wrapped herself more tightly around him. Her lips danced over his throat and he decided not to argue with her logic. His hands were on the sinuous curves of her golden-skinned hips, and long-held fantasies solidified into reality. Frantic, unrequited lust made thought impossible, and that was a good thing right then.

Jan was first out. He doffed his shipsuit and donned his hard vacsuit, intended for short duration EVA maintenance and not the best for this mission. It was what he had, though. Meka's assault harness fit snugly over it and would provide thrust. Three bottles rode his back, two oxy-helium, one nitrogen for the harness. His rifle and clips were along the right bottle, and his comm on his wrist, programmed with everything he needed. Strapped to his chest was a large, bulky pack with over twenty kilos of modern military hyperexplosive. It would be more than enough for the station in question.

Melanie and Meka checked him over and helped him into the bay. The other two were busy on the flight deck. Ignoring his sister's presence, Melanie kissed him hard and deeply. He kissed back, shaking, wanting to leave before the whole situation caused him to go insane. Meka waited until Sarendy was done, then clutched him briefly. "Good luck," she said.

"Good hunting," he replied.

Behind him he heard, "Oh, I will," as the hatch closed.

Jan stared out the open bay into cold black space with cold, bright pinpoints of light. "God and Goddess, I don't want to do this," he muttered. His stomach boiled and churned, and he wished he'd filled his water bottle with straight alcohol. Even the double dose of tranquilizers was not enough to keep him calm.

A light winked once, twice, then a third time, and he jumped out briskly, feeling the harness shove him in a braking maneuver. He was immediately thankful for the suit's plumbing, and his brain went numb. *I'm dead now,* was all he could think.

The station Jan was attacking would note the passage of the anomaly that was the boat as well as it could, and report later. Meka's target was more complicated. It was crewed, and they would react if they saw her. She'd have to ride her sled for some distance and most of a day, and try to time it for a covert approach. That might be the hardest part of this mission.

In the maintenance bay, she strapped herself to her sled and had Jemayel check her over. With a final thumbs up and a lingering hug, she turned to her controls and counted seconds down to her launch.

The boat passed through the volume as stealthed as possible, oriented so the bay opened away from the station's sensors. There were no emissions, only the operating radiation and a bare hint of the powerplant. Her braking thrust was hidden by the mass of the boat, and should be almost invisible at this distance. That should put her right on top of the station at Earth clock 1130 the next day, when the crew would hopefully be at lunch.

Once the vibration and heavy gees tapered off, she checked her instruments and took a tranq. It would be a long wait, and very eerie in complete silence and blackness.

And now I'm dead, she thought.

Sarendy reported when they were outside the known range of the station, and Costlow waited a planned extra hour before bringing up the plant and engines. He wanted to be lost in background noise.

The thrust built steadily in a rumbling hiss through the frame. Most of the impulse would be used now, with only enough left for margin and maneuvers. That would simplify the approach by minimizing emissions then. The velocity increased to a level the boat had rarely used, and he nodded to his remaining crew as they completed the maneuver. Now they had to wait.

"Anyone for a game of chess?" he asked.

Jan watched for the station. It was a black mass against black space, and he was glad to see it occult stars. He'd been afraid the intel was wrong and he was sailing off into space for nothing. Odd to feel relieved to see the approaching cause of one's death, he thought. It had been a three-hour trip, and he was hungry. He would stay that way for the next day and a half, because his suit was intended for maintenance EVAs only, not infiltration, and had no way to supply food. So much for the condemned's last meal. Then, there was the irony that his boat had IDed this particular piece of equipment, which is why it was on the list, and why he was here.

The occultation grew, and he got ready to maneuver for docking, landing, whatever it was called in this case. He switched on the astrogation controls, adjusted his flight toward it, then braked relative. He was tense, lest the reports be inaccurate and the station blast him with a defense array, but nothing happened. He didn't overshoot, but did approach obliquely and had to correct for touchdown.

There was no one and nothing nearby, which was as expected. He snapped a contact patch out, slapped it to the surface, and attached his line. There were no regular padeyes on the unit.

A short orientation revealed where the power cell was. He planted the standoff over it and slapped it down with another contact patch. When it triggered, the blast would turn a plate of metal beneath it into plasma and punch it through the shell into the power cell. He armed it, and all he had left to do was defend it against what appeared to be nothing, wait until it detonated and die with it. Simple on file. Doing it didn't seem quite that by the numbers.

At first, he was terrified of being near the charge. He realized it was silly, as it would kill him anyway, and if it didn't, suffocation would. He compromised between fear and practicality by hiding over the horizon of the small, angled object. It was a bare three meters across, five meters long, and almost featureless except for a docking clamp inset at one end. Its signals were all burst through a translucent one-way window. He longed to tear into it for the sheer joy of discovering if the intel briefs were correct about this model, but that might give him away. He'd sit and wait.

He did have emgee, and a suit, and a tether. He decided to rest floating free. The technique had helped him before when stressed. He stared out at the stars and the distant pointy glare of Iota Persei, their star, and fell into a deep sleep, disturbed by odd dreams.

Meka approached the station gradually. She'd have to leave her sled behind and finish the trip in just her suit to avoid detection. While a bedecked suit would register as maintenance or a refugee with the sensors, the sled would trigger alarms as an approaching threat even if the enemy didn't have knowledge of the precise design. She made one last correction to her orbit, set the autopilot, pulled the releases, and drifted loose from the frame. Her minuscule lateral velocity should be of negligible effect.

The sled burped gently away on gas jets rather than engines, and would hopefully never be detectable to the station. It was near 0800 by Earth clock, and another three hours should bring her quite close. That's when it would become tricky.

First, she'd have to maneuver with an improvised thruster. Jan had her harness; she had only a nitrogen bottle and a momentary valve. He'd—hopefully—made his approach with power but no navigation. She had the navigation gear in her helmet, but improvised power. The risks they were taking would cause a safety officer to run gibbering in insanity. On the other hand, they were dead either way.

There was also the substantial risk of the station noting her approach to its crew. They might await her, or send someone to investigate, or shoot her outright. She was betting against the last, but it was just that—a bet. If they met her, it meant a fight. She would win one-on-one against anybody she faced, but the station might have up to twenty crew. It was effectively a large recon boat with maneuvering engines, and she didn't relish a fight within.

Unlike her previous long EVAs, she was relaxed and calm. Perhaps it was experience. Maybe it was the complexity of the task and the associated thought that kept her too busy to worry. Perhaps it was fatalism. As she neared her target, more issues interfered and she dropped all those thoughts.

There were no obvious signs of disturbance as she approached. That meant that if they did see her for what she was, they were at least holding their fire. She checked her weapon again by touch, and began readying her muscles for a fight. If someone met her, she'd go along peacefully to the airlock, then start smashing things and killing on her way inside.

Nothing happened. Either the station's sensors didn't see her, or they assumed she was performing maintenance and ignored her. It was good to see the intel was accurate, but it still felt odd that her presence wasn't even reported. Perhaps it was and they were waiting for her. Dammit, no second guessing.

She was close enough to think about maneuvering now, and there were still no signs of enemy notice. The nitrogen bottle beside her breathing bottle was plumbed into a veritable snakepit of piping Jan had built for her, that ended front and back at shoulders and hips, much like a proper emgee harness. She hoped the improvised controls worked so she wouldn't have to attempt it by hand. Her record on manual approaches was less than perfect.

She vented a pulse of gas and the harness worked as planned. Two more short ones brought her to a bare drift. She sent more thoughts of thanks after her brother, who had turned out to be essential to almost every mission she'd fought in this war. His technical skill in every field was just genius.

She managed a gentle touchdown on the station hull, letting her legs bend and soak up momentum. She caught her breath, got her bearings, and went straight to work. She had no idea how long she could go unnoticed.

She placed the prebuilt charges with a rapidity born of years of practice. Each charge was designed to punch a hole into a compartment, hopefully voiding them all and killing the occupants instantly. She danced softly across the hull to avoid noise inside that might give her away, swapping tethers as she went, and planted them precisely with the aid of thoughtfully provided frame numbers. Magnetic boots would have made it easier . . . if the shell had been an iron alloy and if clanking noises didn't matter.

She caught movement out of the corner of her eye. She pivoted to see a UN spacer in gear, staring at her in surprise.

Her combat reflexes took over. He was unarmed, meaning he was conducting routine maintenance or inspections. It was possible he wore a camera that was observable inside on a monitor, and he would definitely report her as soon as he recovered from the oddity of the situation. She twisted her right arm to unsling, then pointed her rifle and shot him through the faceplate.

The eruption of atmosphere and vaporized blood indicated he was dead. She put two more bullets through him to make sure, the effect eerie in the silence. The recoil of the weapon was mild, but with no gravity or atmosphere it started her tumbling. She steadied out with a grasp of her tether, and brought herself back the half-meter to the shell. Now what?

Her pulse hammered and her breath rasped. Despite the massive damage and casualties she'd caused in her career, it was only the second time she'd killed someone directly and up close. She forced her emotions into quiescence and considered the situation. If he'd reported her, she had seconds to deal with it. If not, she had a little longer before he was missed. If she killed the crew early, they might miss a scheduled report and the secrecy of her mission would be compromised. If she waited, they could report her presence. She didn't see much of a choice.

Her fingers activated the system through her comm, she paused a second to confirm the readings, and then detonated the charges.

If the atmosphere gushing from her enemy's helmet had been impressive, this was awe-inspiring. Brilliant bursts of white were swallowed by fountains of spewing air and debris. The station shook beneath her feet as the hull adjusted to lost pressure. Anyone not in a suit should be dead. Now to hope no report was expected before her mission zero time. It was a long shot, but all she had. And it was unlikely that the omission would be considered more than a minor problem at first.

Costlow was a first class pilot, but this would strain even his capabilities. The astronautics would take over for evasive maneuvers only. The approach would be manual.

While there was a timed window for attacks, the closer together they were the better. Any hint of action would alert the enemy and reduce the odds of success for others. He wanted to time this to the second, as much as possible. To avoid detection, he had to rely on passive sensors operated by Sarendy across from him. Passive sensors didn't give as accurate a picture as active ones, which meant he'd have to correct the timing in flight. As he would approach at a velocity near the maximum physics and Jemayel's bypassed safeties would allow, that left little time for corrections. He wanted to get inside their weapons' envelope and right against the skin before they deduced what he was. That also increased the risk of their particle watch picking him up, assuming him to be an incoming passive threat, and shooting preemptively.

They were only a few hours from target, and he'd already brought them around in a long loop behind the *London*'s engines. The emissions from them would mask their approach in ionized scatter. He wondered again just how hard this would have been without Sarendy, Jan and Otte. Sarendy was pulling all her intel from the sensors up to the flight deck and using it to assist in astrogation, was preparing a counterintel system for use when they were detected, and would utilize the active sensor antennas as offensive transmitters. He hadn't realized that was even possible, but Sarendy was a witch with sensors, Jan an expert on improvising hardware, and Otte had kept up with both of their orders and put the system together. Amazing. If a crew had ever earned its decorations, this one had.

"Your turn, Warrant," Sarendy reminded him.

Right. Chess. "Um . . ." He moved his queen, looked at the board with satisfaction, and leaned back. Her rook's capture of his queen and declaration of checkmate stunned him.

"Perhaps we should stop now," he suggested. "I didn't see that coming and I have no idea what you did. And both my bishops are on white."

"They are?" she asked. "So they are. Let's call it a game."

Meka swam through the main corridor, counting bodies with faces reminiscent of dead fish, and checked that every compartment was open to vacuum. Nodding to herself, ignoring the grisly scenes, she made her way to the power plant and unlimbered the large charge on her chest. In seconds it was armed, placed, and she swam back out to face the outer hatch. Little to do now but wait.

She wondered how other troops and units had done. Was anyone trying to recapture the captured Freehold facilities? Or just destroy them outright? Would the attacks be successful, and allow the presumed counter to work? Would they win?

She'd never know. She could only wish them luck.

Jan awoke with a start. Guilt flooded over the adrenaline, as he realized he'd slept past when he was supposed to be on guard. He shrugged and decided it didn't matter, as the chance of anyone interfering was incredibly remote. It still bothered him.

It was close to deadline, and he realized he didn't even know what this operation was called, only that it probably involved the entire system, aimed for infrastructure, and was suicidal. That was probably enough.

He still had a couple of hours of oxy.

Hypoxia/anoxia would be pretty painless. A little struggle for breath . . . he could take those two hours. It wasn't impossible a rescue vessel might show up. It just took a hell of a lot of zeros to make the odds. Two extra hours of life, though.

He decided he didn't have whatever it took to let himself die slowly. He was already shivering in shock; the tranqs were wearing off.

He snagged the tether and dragged himself hand over hand to the station. He hooked to the contact patch near the charge. The only thing worse than being blown to dust, he thought, would be to be injured by it and linger for hours in pain.

He wished Meka luck, aching to know if she'd make it. That hurt as much as anything else. There were a few less zeros on her odds, but they were still ludicrously remote. Their mission was to smash enemy infrastructure, not occupy and set up housekeeping.

There was nothing left. He settled down to read, gave up because he couldn't focus, and turned on music to break the eerie silence. If he had to die, he wanted it to be painless and instantaneous.

When the charge underneath him detonated, he got his final wish.

Costlow sweated, with aching joints and gritty eyeballs from sitting far too long at the controls. He watched the display in his helmet, trying to ignore the way the helmet abraded behind his left ear, and made another minute flight correction. He had minutes left to live.

4J23 was close behind the *London*, and undiscovered as far as they knew. Sarendy screwed with their emissions, inverted incoming scans, sent out bursts low enough in energy to pass as typical, powerful enough to keep them hidden and the gods only knew what else. He wished there were some way to record her competence. She was a twenty year old kid, and likely knew more about her job than all her instructors combined. Add in her bravery, and she deserved ten medals.

No, he thought, she deserved to live. Rage filled him again.

He forced the thoughts back to his mission. He was hungry and thirsty, but he daren't pause to do either. This could all come down to a fractional second's attention. Especially now that they were so close.

He brought 4J23 in on a tight, twisting curve from the blind spot behind the drives, and aimed along the approaching superstructure. *London*'s defenses found him, and a launch warning flashed in his visor. It missed because Sarendy switched to active jamming and burned its sensors out with a beam that should have been impossible from a recon boat, and would almost fry an asteroid to vapor. The brute force approach was an indication that all her tricks were exhausted, and it was doubtful they could avoid another attack. He flinched as the missile flashed past, even though it was detectable only as an icon in his visor, and heard a cry of sheer terror start quietly and build. He realized it was his voice. He'd wet himself, and was embarrassed, even though he understood the process. He could hear Sarendy panting for breath, hyperventilating behind him, and wondered what Jemayel was doing in the stern. His eyes flicked to the count in his visor—

Now.

Alongside the *London*, within meters of her hull and at closest approach to her command center, a small power plant overloaded and detonated. It was enough to overwhelm her forcescreens, vaporize her forward half, and shatter the rest in a moment so brief as to be incomprehensible. One hundred UN spacers were turned into incandescent plasma by the blast, along with the three Freeholders.

Meka watched the seconds tick away in her visor. She dropped her left hand and grasped the manual trigger, set it, and held on. It would blow if she let go, or on schedule, and her work was almost done. The count worked down, and she closed her eyes, faced "up" and took a deep breath to steady herself. She opened them again to see it count 3 . . . 2 . . . 1.

Whether her thumb released or the timer acted first was irrelevant. The blast damaged the station's fusion plant, which shut down automatically, even as it vented to space. She felt the cracking and rumbling of the structure through her body, fading away to nothing. It would take a dockyard to repair that, and they'd have to remove the wreckage first. She moved back toward the power plant, navigating by touch in the dust, and dragged herself around several supports twisted by the blast. She entered the engineering module and waited. The particles cleared very slowly, as there was neither airflow nor gravity. It all depended on static charges and surface tension to draw things out of vacuum, and Meka stayed stock still until she could get a good look through her faceplate, cycling through visible, enhanced and IR to build a good picture. She nodded in approval of the damage. The blast and fusion bottle failure had slagged half the module.

Her task was now done, but she had no desire to die immediately. She could have embraced the charge on the reactor and gone with it. Her rationale had been that she should be certain, although the charge had been three times larger than she'd calculated as necessary. The truth was, she couldn't bring herself to do it. Death might be inevitable, but she still feared it.

She studied the life support system whimsically. Without a

proper deckplan, she'd just vented every compartment from outside to be sure. Her charge over this one had punched into the makeup tank. There was a functional air recycling plant, but no oxygen. A meter in any direction...

There were no escape bubbles. This was a station, not a ship. If damaged, the crew would seal as needed and call for help. She'd fixed that when she vented atmosphere. There were extra suit oxy bottles, but the fittings didn't match. Even if they did, there was no heat, and her suit powerpack was nearing depletion. Jan would easily have cobbled something together, or tacked a patch over the hole in life support and used the suit bottles, but even if she could do so before her own gas ran out, it still meant waiting and hoping for a rescue that would likely never come. There was no commo capability, of course. That had been her prime target. No one knew to look for her. Once the main attack began, even if the UN forces noticed this station had gone silent, it would be quite some time before anyone came to check, if ever. The remote possibility of rescue they'd discussed had been for Jan's benefit, to let him hope she might survive. He'd probably figured out the lie by now.

With time and nothing better to do, she planted charges on every hatch, every port, every system. She fired bullets liberally to smash controls and equipment; wedged the airlocks with grenades to shatter the seals and render them useless. Even the spare parts inventory was either destroyed or blown into space.

Finally, she sat outside on the ruined shell, watching her oxy gauge trickle toward empty. Her weapons were scattered around her, some lazily drifting free in the emgee, each rendered inoperable and unsalvageable, all save one. She really had harbored an unrealistic hope that there'd be some way out of this, and cried in loneliness. There was no one to see her, and it wasn't the first time she'd cried on a mission. Blazers didn't look down on tears and fear, only on failure. She had not failed.

The stillness and silence was palpable and eerie. She brought up her system and cycled through her music choices. Yes, that would do nicely. *La Villa Strangiato*. The coordination and sheer skill impressed her, and the energy in the performance was powerful and moving. It filled the last five hundred seconds and faded out. Silence returned.

A warning flashed in her visor and sounded in her ears,

becoming more and more tinny as oxygen was depleted. She'd black out in about a hundred seconds.

One thing she'd always wondered was how far her courage went. People died all the time. Soldiers died when ordered to fight and the odds ran out. Sick people died because life was not worth living.

But could she die by choice? Her courage had been tested throughout her career, and this last year to an extreme. But did she have the strength to pull that switch herself?

After prolonging the inevitable this long, it was rather moot, but her life wouldn't be complete without the experiment. She armed the grenade, stared at it as her body burned from hypoxia, and tried to force her hand to open. Lungs empty now, she gritted her teeth, pursed her lips, and threw every nerve into the effort. Her wrist shook, thumb moving bit by bit. Willpower or self-preservation?

She was still conscious, though groggy, as her thumb came free and the fuse caught. Three seconds. Hypoxia segued to anoxia and her thoughts began to fade. The last one caused a triumphant smile to cross her face, even as tears pooled in her eyes.

Willpower.

On slabs of green and black marble in Freedom Park are the names of two hundred sixteen soldiers who accepted orders they could not understand and knew meant their deaths. Words were said, prayers offered, and torches and guards of honor stand eternal watch over them. Their families received pensions, salutes, and bright metal decorations on plain green ribbons, presented in inlaid wooden boxes.

One family received two.

Earth's First Improved Chimp Gets a Job as a Janitor

JOHN RINGO

"No, Mark. You can't." Mark Second had heard those words too many times in his life. The student's dark face did not flicker but the coach still had a wary look in his eye. "It's not my rule, Mark. It's the rule of the High School Sport Board. Anyone with 'excessive enhancement' cannot participate in intramural sports. Period."

"Why not?" asked the exasperated teenager. He knew the true answer but he wanted the coach to admit it. His features were as still as granite despite his fury. "Or rather, 'why me?' Half the kids in school have one modification or another. What? You don't think Patty Rice naturally has that curly, platinum blond hair? Do you?"

"They're not built from the ground up, Mark," said the heavy-set football coach with a cautious shrug. "They're just... fixed. They're not specifically designed for... physical activity the way you are. They're not—"

"Monsters," said Mark, bitterly.

"That's not it," said the adult, watching the still, flat, square face across from him carefully. Mark never showed what he was thinking, which was one of the things that frightened people. It was currently frightening the burly former football player. Teachers had learned to worry about the quiet ones, the outcasts. Regular troublemakers were bad enough, but the education system had slowly learned that it was the ones who just took it and never fought back that exploded. And if this one ever went mokker nobody would be able to stop him. "Their changes didn't come from illegal genics. Kids like Patty and Tom have the normal, limited enhancements. The sort of thing that anybody can get done through body surgery. Yours are—"

"Evil," Mark finished for him, snarling. He flexed a thigh-thick forearm. "Frightening."

"You keep *saying* things like that," snapped the coach, becoming exasperated. He gestured at Mark as if to take in the whole picture; the armored forehead, the flat, masklike face with eyes set deep in ripples of bone, the tree-trunk legs, the expanded, armored and massively muscled chest. "The rule was practically designed for you, Mark. Putting you on the field with regular kids would be like them playing a Pop Warner team! You're different; face it!"

"So I have to stay the school outcast, huh?" asked the teenager, his face finally starting to show his anger. "Is that the bottom line?"

"Sports won't change that, Mark," said the adult with a sigh, losing his anger as fast as it had developed. "Only you can."

"Get real," snarled the student. "You don't live this life, I do." He stood up, nodded at the coach and stalked out.

The coach waited until the door cycled closed and sighed in relief. As the designated enforcement officer for the Delta Wing of the school he had had to take down more than one mokking student. But he was afraid if that one ever cracked it would require a bazooka.

Mark walked up to his locker and took a long, cleansing breath. Then another. Stress management exercises were his earliest conscious lessons, even before reading. How to confront and manage the anger, the easy descent into berserk rage, that was his heritage. He took another breath, feeling the trickle of ultraline he had been unable to contain fritter away against the wall of his control. Breathe in, breathe out. Let the rage subside. All in the mind.

He looked hard at the poor inanimate locker but finally resisted punching it. Not only would he probably break a knuckle, the punch would undoubtedly shatter the security plastic. And he didn't need the resulting whispers added to the current around him. Breathe in, breathe out. He leaned his head against cool plastic, hoping that some lightning bolt would just strike him dead on the spot. Maybe if he just stayed here until the end of school. Or, at least, until the next PE class came in.

As it was, he stayed there, leaning on the plastic, until his shoes became wet.

"Some super-soldier," opined a gravelly voice. "You've got lousy situational awareness."

Mark leaned back and cracked an eyelid. The Imp janitor peered back at him with soft brown eyes as the kid examined the mop resting on his shoes. "I'm not a super-soldier," said Mark, tiredly. "I'm not any kind of soldier. I've never held a gun. I don't want to hold a gun. But I would like you to take your mop off my shoes; you're getting my feet wet."

"Okay," said the improved chimpanzee, pulling the mop back. "But I need to mop the floor."

"Could you maybe give me a minute," said Mark in a low, growling tone. He rarely let himself sound like that because most people found it intimidating. And that didn't help his reputation either. However, he really didn't have any interest in moving. And the damn chimpanzee was getting on his nerves.

"Kid, I'm not in the mood for adolescent angst right now," said the unintimidated Imp. "I'd like to finish this floor. See, if I finish the floor, I can go prop my feet up for a few minutes and have a coffee and a banana. But, until I finish it, I gotta stay on my dogs. So, I'd really like you to move. Okay? Just, stand on the bench or something."

Mark bemusedly climbed up on the locker room bench as the janitor swept the mop efficiently back and forth. "Aren't there robots to do that?" the student asked. He had sort of noticed janitors around the school, but he'd never really thought about them. However, this was the first person in a long time who recognized him for what he was and didn't act scared.

"Yeah," answered the Imp, expertly flicking the butt of a joint out from under the bench and into the mop bucket. The janitor must have been an earlier model; he seemed both quicker and more intelligent than the current norm. *Pan sapiens* was a diverse species. There had been a variety of early experiments before the current "normal" form was settled on, and then, in the wave of revulsion after the Oligen Incident, locked in by legislation. "But robots are lousy at getting under benches. It's easier to just mop the hard stuff myself and leave the robots for the hallways at night."

"Was mine the last gym class?" asked Mark, stripping off his shirt. The sweat-soaked jersey was the result of a few warm-ups and a solid forty minutes in the weight room fast-pumping four times his body weight; nobody was going to ask him to join the scheduled basketball game.

"Yep. Then I go get a banana until you brats get out of the buildings. Turn on the robots, turn off the lights and go home."

"Seems like an easy enough job," said Mark, pulling on a baggy, button-down shirt. The loose cotton concealed his Herculean physique, but nothing could conceal his face.

"Sure, sure, kid," snorted the janitor. "Every day's a holiday and every meal's a banquet."

Mark slowed in buttoning the top button of his shirt and treated the chimpanzee to a quizzical look. "I've heard that somewhere before."

"Well, I didn't say I made it up," said the chimp, dumping the mop in his bucket and regarding the kid mildly. "Tell you what, kid, wanna banana?"

"I should be getting back to class," said Mark with a sigh.

"Screw it," laughed the chimp. "It's algebra. You can afford to skip a day."

"How did you know what class I'd be taking?" asked the genie, interested.

"I got eyes, kid," said the chimp, pointing to his deep-set orbs. "Just like yours. You want that banana or not?"

"Sure," said Mark, with a nod. "Thanks."

"*De nada*," answered the chimp with a gesture. "Us test-tube types gotta stick together."

"Yeah," said Mark with a rare smile. "I guess. What's your name, chimp?"

"Charlie," answered the janitor. "Charlie Algernon."

"Well, my name's Mark," said the genie. He took the proffered paw and squeezed it gently, but was surprised at the strength of the returning grip.

"Don't worry, Mark," said the chimp with a broad grin. "One of the reasons I ain't worried about you is chimps is pretty strong, too."

✧ ✧ ✧

Able Tyburn looked up from his reader. "Good morning, Mark," he said calmly. Able and his wife Shari did everything calmly. Which was why they had been chosen as Mark Two foster parents.

When the remnants of the Cyberpunk entry team had finally broken through the Mark One defenders of Oligen and taken the nursery, the Terrestrial Union had faced a dilemma. There were forty-eight Mark Twos completed, but they were, to all appearances, human babies. Unlike the chimp derivative Mark One offspring, all of which had been put down, the Mark Twos fell under the rules regarding human genetic modification. They were, despite universal revulsion, held by the Supreme Court to be humans. Therefore, they could not be killed out of hand.

But the Mark Two was designed as a high-intensity combat model. They had no purpose beyond entering heavy firefights and winning. They were, effectively, genie tanks. As such their ultraline glands were tweaked to produce at the slightest provocation. The testosterone-adrenaline-nicotine neural enhancer gave them the ability to go into "hyper-state" at a moment's notice. The downside was that they were extremely aggressive.

The Terrestrial Union had dealt with this by finding, among its four million residents, forty-eight couples with almost preternatural calm. Couples who could raise and train pseudo-human hand-grenades in a loving and nurturing environment.

"Good morning, Father," said Mark, with a smile. He opened the cold-door and pulled out a jug of milk and a bunch of bananas then headed for the door of the apartment.

"Where are you going, Mark?" asked his father. The question had no negative overtones; it was a perfectly formed query. Able Tyburn never used a negative tone.

"I'm going to go have breakfast with Charlie," Mark answered, grabbing his reader and coat.

"I had been meaning to discuss that with you, Mark," said Able, setting down his own reader. The morning news had been mildly distressing, with another outbreak of the Thuggee Cult in California. Unlike the traditionalists in India and Europe, the American branch of the nihilistic religion believed that shedding blood in their executions was the best way to worship their goddess. The slaying in the downtown LA-San school had been particularly bloody.

"You understand that we do not want to slow your societal

development," said the foster parent, calmly. As he did the house chimp emerged from the kitchen and silently began laying out his breakfast. "However, it would be a preferred condition if you could spend socially enhancing time with a human as opposed to a chimp."

"Unfortunately, Father," said Mark, almost automatically suppressing the stab of irritation he felt at the comment, "I have found it difficult to make human friends. As you know."

"Yes, Mark. I am, sadly, aware of that," said the foster parent. He was, in fact, very aware of that fact. Mark was on the low end of sociability among the fifteen surviving Mark Twos. As the most recent e-mail from The Program had pointed out in no uncertain terms. "However, I am sure that when you begin attending college, and have a larger population to draw from, you will find more companions."

"Until then, Father," said the young man, as calmly as a Buddha, "my sole socializing outlet is this chimp janitor you seem to disapprove of."

"Mark, there is a difference between humans and chimps," said the control. He gestured at the servant who was serving him his cholesterol-free egg substitute. "I would suggest that you could actually hurt your socialization process by developing skills that are inadequate. The social reactions you develop from interacting with this 'Charlie' are going to be different than those you should be acquiring. This will delay your development. I cannot find this to be a positive outcome."

"So," said the student taking a calming breath and suppressing the stab of ultraline that threatened to send him into a berserk rage, "you are recommending that I stop socializing with 'this chimp.' "

"Yes," said the father, picking up his fork. "That is my recommendation."

"I shall take it under advisement, Father," said the student. "But not this morning." He knew that the next step up from advice was orders.

"Very well," said the parent. "Have a good day at school, Mark. Remember . . ."

"Calmness is next to oneness," said Mark.

"Be one with the universe and nothing can anger you," said his father with a smile.

✧ ✧ ✧

Mark opened the door to the boiler room and tossed Charlie the bunch of bananas. "Mornin', monkey."

"Mornin', freak," said the chimp with a grin. He looked up from the reader he was repairing to catch the bundle. "Whassa word?" he asked, pulling off a piece of fruit and pouring the kid a cup of coffee.

"My dad wants me to stop seeing so much of you," Mark grumped. He took the coffee and sipped it appreciatively. "How in the hell do you make such a good cup of coffee?" he asked.

"Old secret," winked the chimp, taking his own sip and a bite of banana. "Pinch of salt. It's called 'goat-locker' coffee."

"Whatever," said the kid. "It's good."

"I told you Abe would kick up a fuss," said the chimp. "And he's got a point, you *do* need friends your own age."

"But I can't make them," said Mark. "And besides, they're not my own age!"

"Well, there's that too," said the chimp with a grin. "Not many twelve-year-olds in their senior year. But you're basically eighteen in every way but actual years, kid. Don't bitch about that."

"I won't," said Mark, sadly. "It's not like I'm gonna live to seventy."

"Oh, I don't know," said the chimp. "All that 'ongenic increase' stuff might be bullshit. They told me I'd be long dead by now when I got uncanned. And here I am."

"Yeah, but I'm sort of programmed to die in my thirties," said the teenager. "I don't think I can avoid it."

"Worry about that when the time comes, kid. Geneticists fuck up more than they get it right, trust me," the chimp chuckled. "Me? I was originally designed for intensive loyalty."

"Really?" asked Mark, looking at him askance. "What happened?"

"I got over it," said the chimp, with a smile. "The coding was... sort of open. So I convinced myself that my 'employer' was... not my original one."

"What did your employer think of that?" asked Mark with fascination.

"Well, it was a little company that had just gone out of business," said the chimp. "So I had to find my own way. And I did. And so will you, kid. You just have to figure out what comes natural to you."

✧ ✧ ✧

Mark looked up as Tom Fallon sat down on the seat across from him. The lunchroom was crowded; obviously Fallon felt it was better to sit by "Dr. Demento" than anywhere else.

Fallon wasn't a bad guy. Unlike most of the other kids in school he didn't actively reject the big genie. However, he also didn't spend more time in his presence than he had to.

"Mark," said the teenager with a nod. "How'cha?"

"'Kay," said the genie, taking a big bite of his peanut-butter-and-banana sandwich. Charlie had turned him on to the mix and he found it fulfilled a craving he hadn't even realized was there.

"You missed algebra the other day," said the other teen, carefully.

"I was trying to get the coach to take me in football," answered Mark, equably.

"Did it... work?" asked Tom, picking at his food. Just because sitting by a human time-bomb was better than the other choices available didn't mean he had to like it.

"No," said Mark with a shrug. Charlie had, rightly, pointed out that football wouldn't have been a challenge and that was what he really craved. It was surprising the insights the chimp had.

"Oh," said the other teen, as the doors to the cafeteria opened, "okay."

Mark never answered, as his ultraline gland opened up full-bore and he dove out of his seat. The first 9mm round cracked just behind his moving body but he was already accelerating too fast for the masked gunman in the doorway to track.

His movements were too fast for the human eye to follow as he dove across the serving counter, submachinegun rounds smashing the sneeze-guards and splashing red blood from the servers across the food. He popped back up halfway down the counter as the gunman turned his attention to the mob of shrieking teenagers.

"*Hey!*" shouted the genie, attracting the gunman's attention. As the masked and body-armored gunman turned to see who the impudent youth was, his larynx intercepted a spinning metal pie-pan.

Mark darted through the doors to the kitchen and snatched up a serving knife, still running on ultraline. It was the longest he had ever been under the drug's effect and he was unsure how long the neural enhancer would hold out. For as long as it did, he was four times as fast as an unenhanced human and nearly twice as "smart." Although, at the moment, he didn't feel that way.

He had not heard an emergency announcement, though. As long as the kids in the school were trapped in their classes they were dead meat. He looked around and spotted the fire alarm. Good enough for now.

Once the alarm was shrieking he headed for the principal's office. If he could get on the announcement system he could warn the school. He had seen the red hand on the terrorist's vest; the Thuggees had hit and they would keep killing until a TAC team arrived to stop them.

Mark looked both ways and darted across the hallway as distant shots and screaming broke out in D Wing. He tore open the door to the office and threw himself through low, hoping there wasn't a Thuggee on the other side. When no gunfire erupted he sniffed then stood up. He could smell somebody in the room, but it smelled like . . . "Patty?" he called.

The blond cheerleader poked her head up from behind the receptionist's desk. "Yes?" she called warily. She ducked back down as another burst of fire broke out. "Who is it?"

"It's me, Mark Second. It's Thuggees, Patty, make an announcement."

"But then they'll know there's somebody here!" she said shakily.

Mark had to admit it was a valid argument, but the students and teachers needed to have some warning. He started to walk over to the desk then caught a faint whiff of cordite.

Dara Kidwai was not the name the gunman had been born with. But he had had it legally changed the year before when he became a full member of the House of Kali. Participation in the religion was not a crime, despite the horrors being perpetuated in its name. Like Islam in the previous century, the Kali Cult and other religions were simply places for like-minded individuals to meet and gather. And use the mantle of the religion for their own ends.

Dara Kidwai was about to do just that. He could see the stupid teen, probably a Kali-be-damned football player from his physique, just beyond the metal door to the office. After he had killed this one he would send everyone else in the office to his goddess. And all the other bastards and bitches in the school. Sacrifice them all to the greater glory of Kali.

✧ ✧ ✧

Mark spun in place as the door opened, catching the barrel of the MP-12 in his left hand and carrying it up and away as he grabbed the back of the cultist's head. The sound of the genie's armored forehead hitting the forehead of the cultist was wet and sodden as blood spurted out of the gunman's nose and ears.

"Patty," he snapped, wiping the blood off of his face, "make the damned announcement. Now." He bent down and tried to figure out how to detach the machine-gun from the terrorist's harness. He'd never seen a firearm in his life; The Program had made sure of that.

"What happened?" asked the fluff-head, peeking over the top of the desk. "Oh, *gross*!" she continued, turning to throw up.

Mark had to admit it was pretty gross with the blood pooling under the terrorist, but as pumped as he was on ultraline he was pretty much immune to any feeling but anger. He finally figured out how to take off the whole harness and walked over to the desk with the sopping gear draped across one shoulder. He picked up the microphone and keyed it. "Warning, all students and faculty. Kali Cultists in the building. One terminated in office and one terminated in cafeteria. Anyone with a cell phone, please call for Tac Teams. I am on my way to Delta Wing in support. Mark-Two Gen-One Combat System out." Let the bastards chew on that announcement.

He wiped some blood off his front—apparently one of the bullets had hit his sternum plate and bounced—then pulled the gun around to his front. Holding it in one hand, as he had seen on TV, he pulled on the trigger. It put bullets all over the wall. Oh, well. He'd just have to figure it out as he went along.

Mark stalked down the empty corridors of D Wing leaving bloody footprints behind him. He had to admit that inviting the cultists to kill him was stupid. But if they concentrated on trying to take him out, they wouldn't be killing the other kids. What the hell, it wasn't like he was designed for a long life.

He had just stalked past Mr. Patterson's classroom when he sensed a movement behind him and smelled blood and cordite.

He didn't know where the damn Kali had come from but the red-hand bastard had him dead to rights. Mark spun and turned with supernatural speed as the cultist opened fire, but this terrorist was good. Nine-millimeter rounds impacted into the youth's unarmored back and sides as he slammed into the wall, the gun in his hand spraying everywhere but the cultist.

The only thing that saved the genie was that both of them were just about out of rounds. Mark's MP-12 and the terrorist's clicked back at almost the same moment. Forgetting that his best bet was hand-to-hand, the badly wounded teen scrabbled for a new magazine as he tried to figure out how to reload the gun.

The Kali had no such problems. The cultist expertly dropped the thirty-round magazine and slipped in another. He chuckled as he pulled back the slide. "Some gene unit," he said, as a loop of wire dropped out of the ceiling. "Pun... urk."

The loop of 12-gauge insulated wire snapped up and to the side, expertly breaking the terrorist's neck, and Charlie dropped down on the body. He bent over and started slipping off the terrorist's gear as he shook his head at Mark.

"Stupid, stupid, stupid. I thought Oligen made you smart?"

"I was trying to get them off the other kids," said the teen, weakly. The ultraline was fading and the bullets peppered throughout his body were starting to hurt.

"I was talking about not looking up, kid," said the chimp. "You need to learn to look up."

"I thought I'd smell him," said Mark, doubtfully.

"Yeah, so he put himself by an intake, just like me," said Charlie. The chimp threw the body-armor over his head and looked down with a laugh; the Kevlar-titanium vest dangled to the ground. "Oh, well. Shit happens." He walked over to the teen and reloaded the youth's MP-12 then took all but one spare magazine.

"I think I'm going to need these more than you," the chimp commented as he dragged the bleeding genie into Mr. Patterson's classroom. There was a kid huddled in one corner but otherwise the room was empty.

"Charlie?" asked the combat-unit. He coughed up a drop or two of blood. "I don't think I'm gonna make it, Charlie."

"Bullshit," said the chimp with a grin. "You're a Mark Two, you lucky bastard. Most of that shit will be healed in a couple of days; you're probably already clotting like mad. Just sit there and do your calmness exercises until the medics find you. Oh. And kill any terrorist that comes through the door. Your left hand goes on the *stock*, you idiot."

With that the janitor was gone. As Mark faded in and out he dreamed of a distant one-man war. But the screams were all torn from the throats of adult males.

Mark had never seen anyone who looked like him before. The SWAT team commander was a Normal but broad and flat as a human tank.

"So, you have no other information about this 'Charlie Algernon'?" the officer asked calmly.

Mark had never realized that the calmness of his parents was a positive trait in a tactics team member. But all the SWAT guys that he had been talking with since the incident were like that. Calm, controlled, focussed. These guys did not believe in rage as a character trait. "No. I'd barely gotten to know him."

" 'Goat-locker coffee,' hmm," said the police lieutenant. "I think that says it all."

"Why?" asked Mark. "Where did Charlie learn that stuff?"

"Well, son, you know you're a Mark Two, right," said the lieutenant with a grim smile. "You know what Mark Ones were."

"Oh," said Mark, his chin dropping.

"Yeah. The whole Oligen thing was originally an outgrowth of the Cyberpunk-SEAL program. Their instructors in close combat were all SEALs and Cybers; thus Navy-brewed coffee. Their training was one reason it was so hard for the Cyber team to take the Oligen facility when the Council found out about the Mark Twos and Oligen's plans for a coup. The SEALs thought that they had tracked down and killed all the Mark Ones but at least one apparently escaped."

"He told me that he had been designed for loyalty to his 'original owners,' " said Mark. "But he had figured out a way around the conditioning."

"Maybe by broadening it," said the commander with a sad smile. "I was aware of the conditioning. But I think maybe he decided that since the government paid for the program, his owner was actually the government. And since it is a representative democracy..."

"The whole world was his owner?" asked Mark.

"Maybe," said the lieutenant. "Sort of like any good soldier; he gave his loyalty to the 'bigger picture.' Anyway, I'm glad in a way that he was killed in that explosion. The termination orders are still active on all Mark Ones. We would have had to put him down."

"I understand," said Mark, somewhat bitterly. "But I don't have to like it."

"Neither do I," said the lieutenant. "But it's better this way. We have a toe and some other scraps for a positive genetic ID, but that satchel charge didn't leave much."

The officer saw the kid's face harden and thought about the talk he had had with the teen's guidance counselor. Especially with the media play on this attack, the kid was going to be even more ostracized than before. Which was, frankly, stupid.

"Hey," said the officer with a faint grin. "After you get out of the body and fender shop, gimme a call." He proffered a card to the genie. "There may be a rule against a Modified in football, but there ain't one against them in SWAT."

"Okay," said Mark with a returning smile. "I will."

It might not make up for bananas and coffee in the morning but it would be something to do while he waited to die.

The door was marked "Arthur Commons, Assistant Principal." A heavily-furred hand knocked on it, softly.

"Come in," said a voice from the interior.

"I understand you need a janitor?"

The Long Watch

ROBERT A. HEINLEIN

"Nine ships blasted off from Moon Base. Once in space, eight of them formed a globe around the smallest. They held this formation all the way to Earth.

"The small ship displayed the insignia of an admiral—yet there was no living thing of any sort in her. She was not even a passenger ship, but a drone, a robot ship intended for radioactive cargo. This trip she carried nothing but a lead coffin and a Geiger counter that was never quiet."

—from the editorial *After Ten Years,* film 38, 17 June 2009, Archives of the *N. Y. Times*

I

Johnny Dahlquist blew smoke at the Geiger counter. He grinned wryly and tried it again. His whole body was radioactive by now. Even his breath, the smoke from his cigarette, could make the Geiger counter scream.

How long had he been here? Time doesn't mean much on the Moon. Two days? Three? A week? He let his mind run back: the last clearly marked time in his mind was when the Executive Officer had sent for him, right after breakfast—

✧ ✧ ✧

"Lieutenant Dahlquist, reporting to the Executive Officer."

Colonel Towers looked up. "Ah, John Ezra. Sit down, Johnny. Cigarette?"

Johnny sat down, mystified but flattered. He admired Colonel Towers, for his brilliance, his ability to dominate, and for his battle record. Johnny had no battle record; he had been commissioned on completing his doctor's degree in nuclear physics and was now junior bomb officer of Moon Base.

The Colonel wanted to talk politics; Johnny was puzzled. Finally Towers had come to the point; it was not safe (so he said) to leave control of the world in political hands; power must be held by a scientifically selected group. In short—the Patrol.

Johnny was startled rather than shocked. As an abstract idea, Towers' notion sounded plausible. The League of Nations had folded up; what would keep the United Nations from breaking up, too, and thus lead to another World War? "And you know how bad such a war would be, Johnny."

Johnny agreed. Towers said he was glad that Johnny got the point. The senior bomb officer could handle the work, but it was better to have both specialists.

Johnny sat up with a jerk. "You are going to *do* something about it?" He had thought the Exec was just talking.

Towers smiled. "We're not politicians; we don't just talk. We act."

Johnny whistled. "When does this start?"

Towers flipped a switch. Johnny was startled to hear his own voice, then identified the recorded conversation as having taken place in the junior officers' messroom. A political argument he remembered, which he had walked out on . . . a good thing, too! But being spied on annoyed him.

Towers switched it off. "We *have* acted," he said. "We know who is safe and who isn't. Take Kelly—" He waved at the loudspeaker. "Kelly is politically unreliable. You noticed he wasn't at breakfast?"

"Huh? I thought he was on watch."

"Kelly's watch-standing days are over. Oh, relax; he isn't hurt."

Johnny thought this over. "Which list am I on?" he asked. "Safe or unsafe?"

"Your name has a question mark after it. But I have said all along that you could be depended on." He grinned engagingly. "You won't make a liar of me, Johnny?"

Dahlquist didn't answer; Towers said sharply, "Come now—what do you think of it? Speak up."

"Well, if you ask me, you've bitten off more than you can chew. While it's true that Moon Base controls the Earth, Moon Base itself is a sitting duck for a ship. One bomb—*blooie!*"

Towers picked up a message form and handed it over; it read: I HAVE YOUR CLEAN LAUNDRY—ZACK. "That means every bomb in the *Trygve Lie* has been put out of commission. I have reports from every ship we need worry about." He stood up. "Think it over and see me after lunch. Major Morgan needs your help right away to change control frequencies on the bombs."

"The control frequencies?"

"Naturally. We don't want the bombs jammed before they reach their targets."

"What? You said the idea was to *prevent* war."

Towers brushed it aside. "There won't be a war—just a psychological demonstration, an unimportant town or two. A little bloodletting to save an all-out war. Simple arithmetic."

He put a hand on Johnny's shoulder. "You aren't squeamish, or you wouldn't be a bomb officer. Think of it as a surgical operation. And think of your family."

Johnny Dahlquist had been thinking of his family. "Please, sir, I want to see the Commanding Officer."

Towers frowned. "The Commodore is not available. As you know, I speak for him. See me again—after lunch."

The Commodore was decidedly not available; the Commodore was dead. But Johnny did not know that.

Dahlquist walked back to the messroom, bought cigarettes, sat down and had a smoke. He got up, crushed out the butt, and headed for the Base's west airlock. There he got into his space suit and went to the lockmaster. "Open her up, Smitty."

The marine looked surprised. "Can't let anyone out on the surface without word from Colonel Towers, sir. Hadn't you heard?"

"Oh, yes! Give me your order book." Dahlquist took it, wrote a pass for himself, and signed it "by direction of Colonel Towers." He added, "Better call the Executive Officer and check it."

The lockmaster read it and stuck the book in his pocket. "Oh, no, Lieutenant. Your word's good."

"Hate to disturb the Executive Officer, eh? Don't blame you."

He stepped in, closed the inner door, and waited for the air to be sucked out.

Out on the Moon's surface he blinked at the light and hurried to the track-rocket terminus; a car was waiting. He squeezed in, pulled down the hood, and punched the starting button. The rocket car flung itself at the hills, dived through and came out on a plain studded with projectile rockets, like candles on a cake. Quickly it dived into a second tunnel through more hills. There was a stomach-wrenching deceleration and the car stopped at the underground atom-bomb armory.

As Dahlquist climbed out he switched on his walkie-talkie. The space-suited guard at the entrance came to port-arms. Dahlquist said, "Morning, Lopez," and walked by him to the airlock. He pulled it open.

The guard motioned him back. "Hey! Nobody goes in without the Executive Officer's say-so." He shifted his gun, fumbled in his pouch and got out a paper. "Read it, Lieutenant."

Dahlquist waved it away. "I drafted that order myself. *You* read it; you've misinterpreted it."

"I don't see how, Lieutenant."

Dahlquist snatched the paper, glanced at it, then pointed to a line. "See? '—except persons specifically designated by the Executive Officer.' That's the bomb officers, Major Morgan and me."

The guard looked worried. Dahlquist said, "Damn it, look up 'specifically designated'—it's under *'Bomb Room, Security, Procedure for,'* in your standing orders. Don't tell me you left them in the barracks!"

"Oh, no, sir! I've got 'em." The guard reached into his pouch. Dahlquist gave him back the sheet; the guard took it, hesitated, then leaned his weapon against his hip, shifted the paper to his left hand, and dug into his pouch with his right.

Dahlquist grabbed the gun, shoved it between the guard's legs, and jerked. He threw the weapon away and ducked into the airlock. As he slammed the door he saw the guard struggling to his feet and reaching for his side arm. He dogged the outer door shut and felt a tingle in his fingers as a slug struck the door.

He flung himself at the inner door, jerked the spill lever, rushed back to the outer door and hung his weight on the handle. At once he could feel it stir. The guard was lifting up;

the lieutenant was pulling down, with only his low Moon weight to anchor him. Slowly the handle raised before his eyes.

Air from the bomb room rushed into the lock through the spill valve. Dahlquist felt his space suit settle on his body as the pressure in the lock began to equal the pressure in the suit. He quit straining and let the guard raise the handle. It did not matter; thirteen tons of air pressure now held the door closed.

He latched open the inner door to the bomb room, so that it could not swing shut. As long as it was open, the airlock could not operate; no one could enter.

Before him in the room, one for each projectile rocket, were the atom bombs, spaced in rows far enough apart to defeat any faint possibility of spontaneous chain reaction. They were the deadliest things in the known universe, but they were his babies. He had placed himself between them and anyone who would misuse them.

But, now that he was here, he had no plan to use his temporary advantage.

The speaker on the wall sputtered into life. "Hey! Lieutenant! What goes on here? You gone crazy?" Dahlquist did not answer. Let Lopez stay confused—it would take him that much longer to make up his mind what to do. And Johnny Dahlquist needed as many minutes as he could squeeze. Lopez went on protesting. Finally he shut up.

Johnny had followed a blind urge not to let the bombs—his bombs!—be used for "demonstrations on unimportant towns." But what to do next? Well, Towers couldn't get through the lock. Johnny would sit tight until hell froze over.

Don't kid yourself, John Ezra! Towers could get in. Some high explosive against the outer door—then the air would whoosh out, our boy Johnny would drown in blood from his burst lungs—and the bombs would be sitting there, unhurt. They were built to stand the jump from Moon to Earth; vacuum would not hurt them at all.

He decided to stay in his space suit; explosive decompression didn't appeal to him. Come to think about it, death from old age was his choice.

Or they could drill a hole, let out the air, and open the door without wrecking the lock. Or Towers might even have a new airlock built outside the old. Not likely, Johnny thought; a *coup d'etat* depended on speed. Towers was almost sure to take the quickest way—blasting. And Lopez was probably calling the Base right now. Fifteen minutes for Towers to suit up and get here, maybe a short dicker—then *whoosh!* the party is over.

Fifteen minutes?

In fifteen minutes the bombs might fall back into the hands of the conspirators; in fifteen minutes he must make the bombs unusable.

An atom bomb is just two or more pieces of fissionable metal, such as plutonium. Separated, they are no more explosive than a pound of butter; slapped together, they explode. The complications lie in the gadgets and circuits and gun used to slap them together in the exact way and at the exact time and place required.

These circuits, the bomb's "brain," are easily destroyed—but the bomb itself is hard to destroy because of its very simplicity. Johnny decided to smash the "brains"—and quickly!

The only tools at hand were simple ones used in handling the bombs. Aside from a Geiger counter, the speaker on the walkie-talkie circuit, a television rig to the base, and the bombs themselves, the room was bare. A bomb to be worked on was taken elsewhere—not through fear of explosion, but to reduce radiation exposure for personnel. The radioactive material in a bomb is buried in a "tamper"—in these bombs, gold. Gold stops alpha, beta, and much of the deadly gamma radiation but not neutrons.

The slippery, poisonous neutrons which plutonium gives off had to escape, or a chain reaction—explosion!—would result. The room was bathed in an invisible, almost undetectable rain of neutrons. The place was unhealthy; regulations called for staying in it as short a time as possible.

The Geiger counter clicked off the "background" radiation, cosmic rays, the trace of radioactivity in the Moon's crust, and secondary radioactivity set up all through the room by neutrons. Free neutrons have the nasty trait of infecting what they strike, making it radioactive, whether it be concrete wall or human body. In time the room would have to be abandoned.

Dahlquist twisted a knob on the Geiger counter; the instrument stopped clicking. He had used a suppressor circuit to cut out noise of "background" radiation at the level then present. It reminded him uncomfortably of the danger of staying here. He took out the radiation exposure film all radiation personnel carry; it was a direct-response type and had been fresh when he arrived. The most sensitive end was faintly darkened already. Half way down the film a red line crossed it. Theoretically, if the wearer was exposed to enough radioactivity in a week to darken the film to that line, he was, as Johnny reminded himself, a "dead duck."

Off came the cumbersome space suit; what he needed was speed. Do the job and surrender—better to be a prisoner than to linger in a place as "hot" as this.

He grabbed a ball hammer from the tool rack and got busy, pausing only to switch off the television pick-up. The first bomb bothered him. He started to smash the cover plate of the "brain," then stopped, filled with reluctance. All his life he had prized fine apparatus.

He nerved himself and swung; glass tinkled, metal creaked. His mood changed; he began to feel a shameful pleasure in destruction. He pushed on with enthusiasm, swinging, smashing, destroying!

So intent was he that he did not at first hear his name called.

"Dahlquist! Answer me! Are you there?"

He wiped sweat and looked at the TV screen. Towers' perturbed features stared out.

Johnny was shocked to find that he had wrecked only six bombs. Was he going to be caught before he could finish? Oh, no! He *had* to finish. Stall, son, stall! "Yes, Colonel? You called me?"

"I certainly did! What's the meaning of this?"

"I'm sorry, Colonel."

Towers' expression relaxed a little. "Turn on your pick-up, Johnny, I can't see you. What was that noise?"

"The pick-up is on," Johnny lied. "It must be out of order. That noise—uh, to tell the truth, Colonel, I was fixing things so that nobody could get in here."

Towers hesitated, then said firmly, "I'm going to assume that you are sick and send you to the Medical Officer. But I want you to come out of there, right away. That's an order, Johnny."

Johnny answered slowly. "I can't just yet, Colonel. I came here to make up my mind and I haven't quite made it up. You said to see you after lunch."

"I meant you to stay in your quarters."

"Yes, sir. But I thought I ought to stand watch on the bombs, in case I decided you were wrong."

"It's not for you to decide, Johnny. I'm your superior officer. You are sworn to obey me."

"Yes, sir." This was wasting time; the old fox might have a squad on the way now. "But I swore to keep the peace, too. Could you come out here and talk it over with me? I don't want to do the wrong thing."

Towers smiled. "A good idea, Johnny. You wait there. I'm sure you'll see the light." He switched off.

"There," said Johnny. "I hope you're convinced that I'm a half-wit—you slimy mistake!" He picked up the hammer, ready to use the minutes gained.

He stopped almost at once; it dawned on him that wrecking the "brains" was not enough. There were no spare "brains," but there was a well-stocked electronics shop. Morgan could jury-rig control circuits for bombs. Why, he could himself—not a neat job, but one that would work. Damnation! He would have to wreck the bombs themselves—and in the next ten minutes.

But a bomb was solid chunks of metal, encased in a heavy tamper, all tied in with a big steel gun. It couldn't be done—not in ten minutes.

Damn!

Of course, there was one way. He knew the control circuits; he also knew how to beat them. Take this bomb: if he took out the safety bar, unhooked the proximity circuit, shorted the delay circuit, and cut in the arming circuit by hand—then unscrewed *that* and reached in *there,* he could, with just a long, stiff wire, set the bomb off.

Blowing the other bombs and the valley itself to Kingdom Come.

Also Johnny Dahlquist. That was the rub.

All this time he was doing what he had thought out, up to the step of actually setting off the bomb. Ready to go, the bomb seemed to threaten, as if crouching to spring. He stood up, sweating.

He wondered if he had the courage. He did not want to funk—and hoped that he would. He dug into his jacket and took out a picture of Edith and the baby. "Honeychile," he said, "if I get out of this, I'll never even try to beat a red light." He kissed the picture and put it back. There was nothing to do but wait.

What was keeping Towers? Johnny wanted to make sure that Towers was in blast range. What a joke on the jerk! Me—sitting here, ready to throw the switch on him. The idea tickled him; it led to a better: why blow himself up—alive?

There was another way to rig it—a "dead man" control. Jigger up some way so that the last step, the one that set off the bomb, would not happen as long as he kept his hand on a switch or a lever or something. Then, if they blew open the door, or shot him, or anything—up goes the balloon!

Better still, if he could hold them off with the threat of it, sooner or later help would come—Johnny was sure that most of the Patrol was not in this stinking conspiracy—and then: Johnny comes marching home! What a reunion! He'd resign and get a teaching job; he'd stood his watch.

All the while, he was working. Electrical? No, too little time. Make it a simple mechanical linkage. He had it doped out but had hardly begun to build it when the loudspeaker called him. "Johnny?"

"That you, Colonel?" His hands kept busy.

"Let me in."

"Well, now, Colonel, that wasn't in the agreement." Where in blue blazes was something to use as a long lever?

"I'll come in alone, Johnny, I give you my word. We'll talk face to face."

His word! "We can talk over the speaker, Colonel." Hey, that was it—a yardstick, hanging on the tool rack.

"Johnny, I'm warning you. Let me in, or I'll blow the door off."

A wire—he needed a wire, fairly long and stiff. He tore the antenna from his suit. "You wouldn't do that, Colonel. It would ruin the bombs."

"Vacuum won't hurt the bombs. Quit stalling."

"Better check with Major Morgan. Vacuum won't hurt them; explosive decompression would wreck every circuit." The Colonel was not a bomb specialist; he shut up for several minutes. Johnny went on working.

"Dahlquist," Towers resumed, "that was a clumsy lie. I checked with Morgan. You have sixty seconds to get into your suit, if you aren't already. I'm going to blast the door."

"No, you won't," said Johnny. "Ever hear of a 'dead man' switch?" Now for a counterweight—and a sling.

"Eh? What do you mean?"

"I've rigged number seventeen to set off by hand. But I put in a gimmick. It won't blow while I hang on to a strap I've got in my hand. But if anything happens to *me—up she goes!* You are about fifty feet from the blast center. Think it over."

There was a short silence. "I don't believe you."

"No? Ask Morgan. He'll believe me. He can inspect it, over

the TV pick-up." Johnny lashed the belt of his space suit to the end of the yardstick.

"You said the pick-up was out of order."

"So I lied. This time I'll prove it. Have Morgan call me."

Presently Major Morgan's face appeared. "Lieutenant Dahlquist?"

"Hi, Stinky. Wait a sec." With great care Dahlquist made one last connection while holding down the end of the yardstick. Still careful, he shifted his grip to the belt, sat down on the floor, stretched an arm and switched on the TV pick-up. "Can you see me, Stinky?"

"I can see you," Morgan answered stiffly. "What is this nonsense?"

"A little surprise I whipped up." He explained it—what circuits he had cut out, what ones had been shorted, just how the jury-rigged mechanical sequence fitted in.

Morgan nodded. "But you're bluffing, Dahlquist, I feel sure that you haven't disconnected the 'K' circuit. You don't have the guts to blow yourself up."

Johnny chuckled. "I sure haven't. But that's the beauty of it. It can't go off, *so long as I am alive.* If your greasy boss, ex-Colonel Towers, blasts the door, then I'm dead and the bomb goes off. It won't matter to me, but it will to him. Better tell him." He switched off.

Towers came on over the speaker shortly. "Dahlquist?"

"I hear you."

"There's no need to throw away your life. Come out and you will be retired on full pay. You can go home to your family. That's a promise."

Johnny got mad. "You keep my family out of this!"

"Think of them, man."

"Shut up. Get back to your hole. I feel a need to scratch and this whole shebang might just explode in your lap."

II

Johnny sat up with a start. He had dozed, his hand hadn't let go the sling, but he had the shakes when he thought about it.

Maybe he should disarm the bomb and depend on their not daring to dig him out? But Towers' neck was already in hock for treason; Towers might risk it. If he did and the bomb were disarmed, Johnny would be dead and Towers would have the bombs. No, he had gone this far; he wouldn't let his baby girl grow up in a dictatorship just to catch some sleep.

He heard the Geiger counter clicking and remembered having used the suppressor circuit. The radioactivity in the room must be increasing, perhaps from scattering the "brain" circuits—the circuits were sure to be infected; they had lived too long too close to plutonium. He dug out his film.

The dark area was spreading toward the red line.

He put it back and said, "Pal, better break this deadlock or you are going to shine like a watch dial." It was a figure of speech; infected animal tissue does not glow—it simply dies, slowly.

The TV screen lit up; Towers' face appeared. "Dahlquist? I want to talk to you."

"Go fly a kite."

"Let's admit you have us inconvenienced."

"Inconvenienced, hell—I've got you stopped."

"For the moment. I'm arranging to get more bombs—"

"Liar."

"—but you are slowing us up. I have a proposition."

"Not interested."

"Wait. When this is over I will be chief of the world government. If you cooperate, even now, I will make you my administrative head."

Johnny told him what to do with it. Towers said, "Don't be stupid. What do you gain by dying?"

Johnny grunted. "Towers, what a prime stinker you are. You spoke of my family. I'd rather see them dead than living under a two-bit Napoleon like you. Now go away—I've got some thinking to do."

Towers switched off.

Johnny got out his film again. It seemed no darker but it reminded him forcibly that time was running out. He was hungry and thirsty—and he could not stay awake forever. It took four days to get a ship up from Earth; he could not expect rescue any sooner. And he wouldn't last four days—once the darkening spread past the red line he was a goner.

His only chance was to wreck the bombs beyond repair, and get out—before that film got much darker.

He thought about ways, then got busy. He hung a weight on the sling, tied a line to it. If Towers blasted the door, he hoped to jerk the rig loose before he died.

There was a simple, though arduous, way to wreck the bombs beyond any capacity of Moon Base to repair them. The heart of each was two hemispheres of plutonium, their flat surface polished smooth to permit perfect contact when slapped together. Anything less would prevent the chain reaction on which atomic explosion depended.

Johnny started taking apart one of the bombs.

He had to bash off four lugs, then break the glass envelope around the inner assembly. Aside from that the bomb came apart easily. At last he had in front of him two gleaming, mirror-perfect half globes.

A blow with the hammer—and one was no longer perfect. Another blow and the second cracked like glass; he had trapped its crystalline structure just right.

Hours later, dead tired, he went back to the armed bomb. Forcing himself to steady down, with extreme care he disarmed it. Shortly its silvery hemispheres too were useless. There was no longer a usable bomb in the room—but huge fortunes in the most valuable, most poisonous, and most deadly metal in the known world were spread around the floor.

Johnny looked at the deadly stuff. "Into your suit and out of here, son," he said aloud. "I wonder what Towers will say?"

He walked toward the rack, intending to hang up the hammer. As he passed, the Geiger counter chattered wildly.

Plutonium hardly affects a Geiger counter; secondary infection from plutonium does. Johnny looked at the hammer, then held it closer to the Geiger counter. The counter screamed.

Johnny tossed it hastily away and started back toward his suit.

As he passed the counter it chattered again. He stopped short.

He pushed one hand close to the counter. Its clicking picked up to a steady roar. Without moving he reached into his pocket and took out his exposure film.

It was dead black from end to end.

III

Plutonium taken into the body moves quickly to bone marrow. Nothing can be done; the victim is finished. Neutrons from it smash through the body, ionizing tissue, transmuting atoms into radioactive isotopes, destroying and killing. The fatal dose is unbelievably small; a mass a tenth the size of a grain of table salt is more than enough—a dose small enough to enter through the tiniest scratch. During the historic "Manhattan Project" immediate high amputation was considered the only possible first-aid measure.

Johnny knew all this but it no longer disturbed him. He sat on the floor, smoking a hoarded cigarette and thinking. The events of his long watch were running through his mind.

He blew a puff of smoke at the Geiger counter and smiled without humor to hear it chatter more loudly. By now even his breath was "hot"—carbon-14, he supposed, exhaled from his blood stream as carbon dioxide. It did not matter.

There was no longer any point in surrendering, nor would he give Towers the satisfaction—he would finish out this watch right here. Besides, by keeping up the bluff that one bomb was ready to blow, he could stop them from capturing the raw material from which bombs were made. That might be important in the long run.

He accepted, without surprise, the fact that he was not unhappy. There was a sweetness about having no further worries of any sort. He did not hurt, he was not uncomfortable, he was no longer even hungry. Physically he still felt fine and his mind was at peace. He was dead—he knew that he was dead; yet for a time he was able to walk and breathe and see and feel.

He was not even lonesome. He was not alone; there were comrades with him—the boy with his finger in the dike, Colonel Bowie, too ill to move but insisting that he be carried across the line, the dying Captain of the *Chesapeake* still with deathless challenge on his lips, Rodger Young peering into the gloom. They gathered about him in the dusky bomb room.

And of course there was Edith. She was the only one he was aware of. Johnny wished that he could see her face more clearly. Was she angry? Or proud and happy?

Proud though unhappy—he could see her better now and even feel her hand. He held very still.

Presently his cigarette burned down to his fingers. He took a final puff, blew it at the Geiger counter, and put it out. It was his last. He gathered several butts and fashioned a roll-your-own with a bit of paper found in a pocket. He lit it carefully and settled back to wait for Edith to show up again. He was very happy.

✧ ✧ ✧

He was still propped against the bomb case, the last of his salvaged cigarettes cold at his side, when the speaker called out again. "Johnny? Hey, Johnny! Can you hear me? This is Kelly. It's all over. The *Lafayette* landed and Towers blew his brains out. Johnny? *Answer me.*"

When they opened the outer door, the first man in carried a Geiger counter in front of him on the end of a long pole. He stopped at the threshold and backed out hastily. "Hey, chief!" he called. "Better get some handling equipment—uh, and a lead coffin, too."

"Four days it took the little ship and her escort to reach Earth. Four days while all of Earth's people awaited her arrival. For ninety-eight hours all commercial programs were off television; instead there was an endless dirge—the Dead March *from* Saul, *the* Valhalla *theme,* Going Home, *the Patrol's own* Landing Orbit.

"The nine ships landed at Chicago Port. A drone tractor removed the casket from the small ship; the ship was then refueled and blasted off in an escape trajectory, thrown away into outer space, never again to be used for a lesser purpose.

"The tractor progressed to the Illinois town where Lieutenant Dahlquist had been born, while the dirge continued. There it placed the casket on a pedestal, inside a barrier marking the distance of safe approach. Space marines, arms reversed and heads bowed, stood guard around it; the crowds stayed outside this circle. And still the dirge continued.

"When enough time had passed, long, long after the heaped flowers had withered, the lead casket was enclosed in marble, just as you see it today."

About the Authors

JOHN KEITH LAUMER (June 9, 1925–January 23, 1993) is best known for his Bolo stories and his satirical Retief series. He served in the US Army in World War II in Europe, and then did two hitches in the US Air Force, 1953–56 and 1960–65, attaining the rank of Captain in the latter tour. In between the two USAF hitches, Laumer was a member of the US Foreign Service in Rangoon, Burma, during which time he had his first stories published. After completing his military service in 1965, Laumer turned his attention to writing full time.

ERIC FRANK RUSSELL (January 6, 1905–February 28, 1978) was a British author best known for his science fiction novels and short stories. Much of his work was first published in John W. Campbell's *Astounding Science Fiction* and other pulp magazines in the US. A few of his stories were published under pseudonyms, of which Duncan H. Munro was used most often. After serving with the Royal Air Force during World War II and working briefly as an engineer, Russell took up writing full-time in the late 1940s. "Allamagoosa" garnered him his first Hugo Award. In 2000, he was inducted into the Science Fiction and Fantasy Hall of Fame.

MURRAY LEINSTER (June 16, 1896–June 8, 1975) was a nom de plume of William Fitzgerald Jenkins, an award-winning American writer of science fiction and alternate history. He wrote over 1,500 short stories and articles, 14 movie scripts, and hundreds of radio scripts and television plays. During World War I, Leinster served with the Committee of Public Information and the United States Army (1917–1918). In 1921, he married Mary Mandola, and the two had four daughters. During World War II, he served in the Office of War Information.

SIR ARTHUR CHARLES CLARKE, CBE, FRAS (16 December 1917–19 March 2008) was a British science fiction author, inventor, and futurist, most famous for the novel *2001: A Space Odyssey*. For many years, Robert A. Heinlein, Isaac Asimov, and Arthur C. Clarke were known as the "Big Three" of science fiction. Clarke served in the Royal Air Force as a radar instructor and technician from 1941–1946. Clarke initially served in the ranks, and was a Corporal instructor on radar at No 9 Radio School, RAF Yatesbury. He was commissioned as a Pilot Officer (Technical Branch) on May 27, 1943. He was promoted Flying Officer on November 27, 1943. He was appointed chief training instructor at RAF Honiley and was demobilised with the rank of Flight Lieutenant.

GENE WOLFE (born May 7, 1931) is an American science fiction and fantasy writer best known for his three linked series, The Book of the New Sun, The Book of the Long Sun, and The Book of the Short Sun. He is a prolific short story writer and a novelist, and has won many awards in the field. Wolfe was drafted by the US Army during the Korean War, where he saw some limited combat duty. He served in the 17th Infantry Regiment of the 7th Infantry Division from 1952 to 1954, attaining the rank of Corporal.

HARRY CLEMENT STUBBS (May 30, 1922–October 29, 2003) better known by the pen name HAL CLEMENT, was an American science fiction writer, an SFWA Grand Master, and a leader of the hard science fiction subgenre, credited by many to have created the subgenre with his novel *Mission of Gravity*. During World War II Clement was a pilot and copilot of a B-24 Liberator and flew 35 combat missions over Europe with the 8th Air Force. After the war, he served in the United States Air Force Reserve, and retired with the rank of Colonel. He taught chemistry and astronomy for many years at Milton Academy in Milton, Massachusetts.

JERRY POURNELLE (born 1933) is an American science fiction writer, essayist and journalist who contributed for many years to the computer magazine *Byte,* and has been maintaining his own website/blog since 1998. Some of Pournelle's best known fiction, including "Peace with Honor," centers on the fictional mercenary infantry force known as Falkenberg's Legion. Pournelle, along with Stefan T. Possony, wrote numerous nonfiction publications, including *The Strategy of Technology*, onetime textbook at the United States Military Academy (West Point) and the United States Air Force Academy (Colorado Springs).

DAVID DRAKE (born 1945) is an author of science fiction and fantasy literature. A Vietnam War veteran who has worked as a lawyer, he is now one of the premier authors of the military science fiction subgenre. Drake graduated Phi Beta Kappa from the University of Iowa, majoring in history (with honors) and Latin. His studies at Duke University School of Law were interrupted for two years when he was drafted into the U.S. Army, where he served as an enlisted interrogator with the 11th Armored Cavalry in Vietnam and Cambodia. His best-known work is the Hammer's Slammers series of military science fiction. His ongoing Republic of Cinnabar Navy (RCN) series are space operas inspired by the Aubrey–Maturin novels.

In 1967, **JOE W. HALDEMAN** was drafted into the US Army and served as a combat engineer in Vietnam. He was wounded in combat and his wartime experience was the inspiration for *War Year*, his first novel. Haldeman's most famous novel *The Forever War* (1975) was also inspired by his Vietnam experiences; it won both the Hugo and Nebula Awards. He later turned it into a series.

DAVE FREER is a South African-born science fiction author writing mostly humorous or alternate history novels. He was conscripted into the South African Defence Force and sent to the Angolan Border as a medic. Upon completion of his military obligation, he attended university and then became an ichthyologist, working as research officer for the Western Cape commercial fishery. He managed a fish farm for a time but the farm was forced to close (through no fault of his own...) and he started to write. Six years later, his first book (*The Forlorn*) was published by

Baen Books. An ardent rock-climber, he is also an accomplished chef and winetaster who also enjoys fly-fishing and diving. He currently resides in Australia.

CAPT. KACEY GRANNIS is a graduate of the United States Air Force Academy, class of 1999. Thanks to childhood dreams of being a dragonrider, she got it into her head to go to pilot training, and got her wings from Fort Rucker, AL in 2001. After eight years flying stateside, Capt. Grannis deployed to Iraq for a year as a Combat Air Advisor. "Light" was written during her deployment there. She is a senior rated pilot with over 1600 hours in the Bell UH-1N Huey and the Mi-17 Hip helicopters. As of this writing, Capt. Grannis has logged 100 combat hours in Iraqi airspace. When not in the desert, Capt. Grannis lives in Alexandria, VA with her father and her daughter.

PATRICK A. VANNER was born into a Marine family, and, after attending Penn State University, majoring in aerospace and electrical engineering, he enlisted in the Marine Corps like his parents before him. He served from 1995 to 1999, attaining the rank of Sergeant. After his successful military tour, he earned a degree in network administration and began a career in telecommunications and information technology. He divides his time between working, reading, writing, gaming and spending an exorbitant amount of money on anime, giving truth to the saying, "Anime, it's more addictive than crack." Patrick currently lives with the love of his life, Heather, and four insane cats that make their lives interesting in every sense of the ancient Chinese curse.

MICHAEL Z. WILLIAMSON (born 1967) is a science fiction and military-fiction author. Born in Birkenhead, England, he and his family emigrated to Canada, then the United States in 1978. He is best known for his military sf novels set in the Freehold universe, as well as his "Target: Terror" series of military thrillers. "Mad Mike," as he is often known, served 25 years in US military, with five years active duty in the USAF, seven years Army National Guard and thirteen years Air National Guard. He was deployed twice, for Operation Desert Fox and Operation Iraqi Freedom. He was medically retired in 2010 in the rank of Technical Sergeant (E6).

JOHN RINGO joined the US Army after graduating high school, and rose to the rank of Specialist Four as a member of the 82nd Airborne Division. During his four years of active duty, he was assigned to the 1st Battalion 508th Parachute Infantry Regiment which was reflagged into 3rd Battalion, 505th Parachute Infantry Regiment when the 82nd regimentally organized its 3rd Brigade on 3 October 1986, plus he served two years of reserve duty with the Florida National Guard. Among his awards are the Combat Infantryman Badge, Parachutist Badge, Army Commendation Medal, Good Conduct Medal, Armed Forces Expeditionary Medal (Grenada), Cold War Victory Medal and the National Defense Service Medal.

ROBERT ANSON HEINLEIN (July 7, 1907–May 8, 1988), known as "the dean of science fiction writers," was one of the most influential and popular science fiction writers of all time. He was one of the first writers to have science fiction stories published in mainstream magazines such as *The Saturday Evening Post*, and for many years, Heinlein, Isaac Asimov, and Arthur C. Clarke were known as the "Big Three" of science fiction. Heinlein graduated from the United States Naval Academy in Annapolis in 1929, and served as an officer in the United States Navy. He served on the new aircraft carrier USS *Lexington* (CV-2) in 1931. He also served aboard the destroyer USS *Roper* (DD-147) in 1933–1934, reaching the rank of Lieutenant. In 1934, Heinlein was discharged from the Navy due to pulmonary tuberculosis.

About the Editors

JOHN RINGO is a *New York Times* bestselling author of science fiction and thriller novels. He had visited 23 countries and attended 14 schools by the time he graduated high school. This left him with a wonderful appreciation of the oneness of humanity and a permanent aversion to foreign food. After serving in the military, he chose to study marine biology and really liked it. Unfortunately the pay is for beans. So he turned to database management where the pay was much better. His highest hopes were to someday upgrade to SQL Server at which point, he thought, his life would be complete. But then Fate took a hand: John became a professional science fiction writer. Since that day, he has published numerous science fiction novels at a rate that amazed and offended his publisher. He also has done stints as an op-ed writer for the *New York Post* and a guest commentator for Fox News, thus ensuring the loss of what little soul was left.

BRIAN M. THOMSEN was the editor of seventeen anthologies and collections, including the highly acclaimed *The American Fantasy Tradition.* He was also the author of several books, including the fantasy novels *Once Around the Realms* and *The Mage in the Iron Mask.* A noted scholar, he authored numerous articles, ranging in topic from history to media tie-ins to religion. He began his career in publishing at Warner Books, and was for many years the executive editor/publisher of TSR Books. Brian M. Thomsen passed away September 21, 2008, less than a month after delivering the proposal for *Citizens.*